Ruth Hamilton is the bestselling author of *A Whisper to the Living, With Love From Ma Maguire, Nest of Sorrows, Billy London's Girls, Spinning Jenny, The September Starlings, A Crooked Mile, Paradise Lane, The Bells of Scotland Road, The Dream Sellers, The Corner House, Miss Honoria West, Mulligan's Yard* and *Saturday's Child*. She has become one of the north-west of England's most popular writers. Ruth Hamilton was born in Bolton, which is the setting for many of her novels, and has spent most of her life in Lancashire. She now lives in Liverpool.

For more information on Ruth Hamilton and her books, see her website at:
www.ruthhamilton.co.uk

MATTHEW & SON

Ruth Hamilton

CORGI BOOKS

MATTHEW & SON
A CORGI BOOK : 0 552 14906 3

Originally published in Great Britain by Bantam Press,
a division of Transworld Publishers

PRINTING HISTORY
Bantam Press edition published 2002
Corgi edition published 2003

1 3 5 7 9 10 8 6 4 2

Set in 11/12pt Baskerville by
Falcon Oast Graphic Art Ltd.

Corgi Books are published by Transworld Publishers,
61–63 Uxbridge Road, London W5 5SA,
a division of The Random House Group Ltd,
in Australia by Random House Australia (Pty) Ltd,
20 Alfred Street, Milsons Point, Sydney, NSW 2061, Australia,
in New Zealand by Random House New Zealand Ltd,
18 Poland Road, Glenfield, Auckland 10, New Zealand
and in South Africa by Random House (Pty) Ltd,
Endulini, 5a Jubilee Road, Parktown 2193, South Africa.

Printed and bound in Germany by
Elsnerdruck, Berlin.

I dedicate this book to the memory of Lillian Helm
who died February 2001

May she rest in peace.

Acknowledgements

My thanks to

My family.
My publishers, Transworld.
Joanna Frank, my agent at AP Watt.
Dorothy Ramsden for secretarial support.
Avril Cain for strawberry tarts, carrot cake and many
other forbidden treats, but mostly for the laughs.
My wonderful animals, Samson, Fudge, Geri,
Dumb and Dumber (really Jack and Vera).
Helen Fielding for writing Bridget Jones and making
me laugh until I cried.
All my friends on the world wide web for making life
more . . . interesting.
Tess Scott, for her invaluable friendship and for help
with research.
Her daughters, Polly and Harriet, for the pleasure
they give, for their exceptional talent, for dancing
during my Evening with Ruth Hamilton.
Her son, Jack, for tech advice on the phone.
This brilliant Northampton family has done a lot for
me and I value their company greatly.
Loyal readers – thank you from the bottom
of my heart.

One

The dog was the only one who seemed to understand.

The rest of them made the right noises, said the words, wore suitable expressions and black clothes. Yet there stood Bess, brown velvet eyes, fur dark as midnight, patina glinting in a pale and watery September sun. The Labrador-cross pointed her snout skywards and she howled, poured out her anger, her fear and bewilderment. She was honest; the rest went through the motions.

The vicar paused, meaningless incantations frozen, drowned by the noise of this sad beast. It was plain that the man did not know what to do, young face reddened by embarrassment, prayer-book tilting forwards, tongue flicking nervously over thin lips. Whatever was a dog doing at a funeral, anyway? It was unseemly, disruptive and very annoying.

Matthew stepped forward and placed a hand on the dog's head. She whimpered, turned and pushed herself against his legs. This was Molly's dog; Molly's dog had every right to be here. How many hours had the animal spent in her company? Ten, twelve each day? Yes, this faithful retainer had kept a vigil, had been watchful and loving right to the end.

He nodded curtly at the vicar. 'She'll be all right now, because she's had her say. She was close to Molly, very close.' His voice cracked and, seeking to conceal his frailty, Matthew Richards squatted down and comforted his late wife's dear canine friend. Dear God, what was he going to do with the rest of his life? There were years ahead – he was only forty, but he did not wish to live another single day without Molly. Nothing mattered, not the house, not the business. There was Mark, of course, but he seemed to take care of himself. At sixteen, what did a boy need?

He closed his eyes and rested his forehead against the animal's neck, so warm, so smooth, like Molly had been. He saw her in his mind's eye, black hair flowing down to her waist like a sheet of silk, those bright, violet eyes, skin as soft as peaches, so lovely, so alive. There was no future, no hope, no reason to continue without her—

'Dad?'

There was Mark. 'Yes, son?'

'Stand up, they're all waiting for you.'

Waiting? For what? For the world to end?

He heard her. 'Well, you are Matthew, so we shall call this one Mark. Two more, a Luke and a John, we'll have all the gospels.' But there had been no more children. Molly had become thinner, older, sicker. At the age of thirty-five years, three months and seventeen days, Molly Richards had slipped beyond the reach of earthly beings. It was wrong, so wrong. There was no comfort now, no easing the pain.

He stood up and cast an eye over the small gathering. How could they linger here and pretend to mourn? His own father, God damn him, for whom Molly had never been good enough. Her father, bitter, twisted, here for what he could get out of the situation, no doubt. Friends. Friends? He almost laughed, was forced to swallow a bubble of hysteria that threatened to escape from deep within his chest. Where had they been?

'Dad?'

Where had they been when she had developed all those filthy illnesses, the tumours in her womb, her liver, her brain? Oh, yes, Molly had been acceptable – just – when at her best. From a poor family, she had scrubbed up well, had rounded her vowels, had carried the clothes well. But the creature she had become, blind, crooked, jack-knifed in the bed until her body had been rendered weightless, that sight had been too unpleasant for these sensitive souls.

What had they said? They hadn't wanted to intrude, had stayed away to give the family peace. Was this peace, then? Was peace a box, a hole in the ground, piles of earth, grave-diggers secreted behind an oak, cigarette smoke advertising their discretion? Oh, God, he wanted to strangle the vicar. Ashes to ashes, dust to dust? This was all a charade, invented for the living, nothing at all to do with the dead. And if this vicar thought for one moment that he was helping, then he needed a rethink on a grand scale.

'Dad?'

Matthew stepped forward, gloved fists curled into balls, head lifting so that everyone would hear the words he was about to deliver. 'Shut up,' he ordered, the words encompassing the whole gathering. He closed his eyes for a second, swayed on the spot and seemed in danger of losing his balance. 'God, please take me, too,' he mouthed silently.

The vicar dropped his black-jacketed book. It landed on the coffin, bounced, landed again face down, pages spread across the lid of Molly's container.

'Leave it,' snapped the widower, 'and bugger off, the lot of you. None of you gave two hoots when she was alive, so why are you here now, when it's too late, when she's been scraped up and tidied away? Why are you here?' he asked again. 'She isn't with us and she was worth ten of any of you.'

Mark grabbed Matthew's sleeve, although he knew that his action would have little or no effect. Thrust away by his father, the boy took the dog's lead and guided the sad animal out of Heaton cemetery. A fury simmered in his chest. Even now, with his mother dead, he felt as if Dad did not need him.

The mourners cast sideways glances at each other, weight shifting from foot to foot, many stepping backwards as the dreaded situation continued to deteriorate. People simply did not let themselves go at funerals; this behaviour was not acceptable, especially from a respected businessman with a reputation to maintain. Embarrassment lit many cheeks, while some faces were downturned in an attempt to avoid the gaze of others.

But Matthew was too far gone to care. 'Where were you when she was in pain, when the bedsores cut so deep that her spine was on show? And in the night when she screamed until the morphine silenced her? Go on, get home. Molly needed you then, but she needs none of you now. You are surplus to requirements.' As he spoke the final five words, he glared at his own father.

The vicar took a step forward. 'I just thought we might . . .' The words died when Matthew's eyes fixed themselves on him. Something in the widower's stance served as warning to this man of God. Some people, it seemed, were beyond the help of the Almighty's mediator.

'You can go, too,' ordered Matthew. 'Don't worry about your book, just send me the bill. All that stuff about ashes and dust – it doesn't mean a bloody thing, never has and never will. It's a farce, that's all, a bloody play put on to take weak minds off the truth. Damn and blast you all, she is dead and I wish it could be any or all of you in her place.' He had said the unsayable, had spoken his truth, his grief. He sagged against a gravestone and waited for the unwanted congregation to leave.

Silence reigned. After a few seconds had

elapsed, a bird rattled the upper branches of a tree, rose out of it, fluttered away, seemed to break the mood. Temporarily distracted, Matthew watched the starling as it soared freely towards emptiness, wished with all his heart that he could join it, up and away, not landlocked, not planted here with all these fakes, these pretenders.

And it happened, swelled inside him, months and years, aeons of grief too huge now to be held back. Like the dog, he howled, raged at heaven, shook his fists at a God who had never been visible. Yes, God – where had He been? On holiday, a quick trip to the Costa bloody Brava, white rum and Coke, bring your own cornflakes?

'I told you lot to bugger off.' Sobs fractured the words, but did not render them completely incomprehensible.

Bewildered, they crept away, just as they had when Molly had been ill. Her parents, his, the people from the neighbourhood, colleagues, customers, business acquaintances, all gone, all disappeared.

There was just Matthew now. Matthew and two thin streams of cigarette smoke. He dried his eyes, walked to the broad oak, grabbed a shovel. 'Carry on smoking,' he snapped at the surprised men. 'I looked after her myself, I shall bury her myself.'

So Matthew Richards, who had loved his wife more than life itself, buried her. It was the right thing to do. Apart from nurses and some domestic helps, he alone had cared for the sweet woman, had tended her ravaged body, had remembered and respected the unbreakable spirit of this fine human being. He no longer believed in heaven, but he knew hell, embraced it, almost, because the pain was right, it was just.

On the road outside, a boy with a dog watched the proceedings. Excluded, as always, he saw his father shovelling earth on to his mother. Mark's eyes were wet and his hollow heart ached to be a part of what was happening. So lonely, so ignored and insignificant.

But Mark Richards had never been a part of his parents' lives. Molly and Matthew Richards had belonged to a private club, membership of two, no visitors allowed. Mother had been kind and loving, but she had died long before the death certificate had been issued. Now, there was a new club, just himself and the dog. So he brought Bess to heel and walked her towards that cold and empty home.

Tilly Povey was famous for two things: her whiplash tongue and her ironing. The former rendered her unapproachable when she had the mood on her; the latter brought forth grunts of begrudged admiration from all who witnessed the fruits of her labour. Tilly had ironed for all the best people, for great houses on the moors, for the slightly less grand in Heaton and Rivington, and was currently employed as housekeeper at Coniston, the Chorley New Road home of the Richards family.

She stood now in the doorway between her own scullery and kitchen, thin arms akimbo as she addressed her husband. 'What do you mean, you're only going fishing? There'll be no going nowhere, not in that shirt. I've got me reputation to think about.' She eyed him balefully. He looked like a bag of rags ready for the cart, shirtsleeves frayed, jacket bunched up, buttons missing, cap all greasy and battered. 'Take my word for it, Seth Povey, you'll not set foot out yon while I've got breath in my body. Go and change yourself.'

Seth wished he could change himself, would have liked to change into somebody else, anybody else, preferably with a wife who didn't carry on like it was still 1930, step-stoning, bleaching, starching his collars till they felt like something out of a medieval torture chamber. It was 1962 and the world was changing. Slums were being pulled down, folk were moving into nice corporation houses up Lever Edge Lane, there was no war on, no rationing, fewer bloody rules. Until it came to Tilly Povey.

'Did you hear me?'

Did he hear her? Half of bloody Tonge Moor Road must have heard her. She could have been useful down in Liverpool, might have been a good substitute for a foghorn at a push. 'Yes, I heard you.' Or a referee at Burnden Park . . .

Tilly folded her arms. She always folded her arms when she meant business. 'And what's this about fishing? You've never done it before.'

He had never strangled his wife before, but there was always a first time. 'Ted Moss thought I might like it for a change. I were going to give it a try, see how I get on with it. It's supposed to be relaxing.'

Tilly Povey did not believe in relaxation, had never seen the need for it. Eight hours' sleep a night was rest enough for anybody. This philosophy had seen her through three births, one stillbirth, several miscarriages and piles of ironing which, if laid end to end around the equator, would probably encircle the earth at least twice. 'Relaxing?' she yelled. 'Relaxing? Get yourself up yon ladder and relax while you mend that bloody guttering. When you've done that, there's the loft wants sorting and me window-frames could do with a lick of paint. Relaxing.' She spat the last three syllables as if ridding herself of a very bad taste. 'Time enough to relax when you're six feet under with a nice headstone and a bunch of flowers.'

'I can't wait,' he mumbled softly.

But not softly enough. Tilly advanced on him. 'How can you say that, eh? Do you want to tempt fate and faith? 'Cos He hears you, I can guarantee that without filling in any forms. Look at poor Mrs Richards. She were nobbut twenty-five when that cancer got a grip. Ten bloody year she had, in and out of hospital like a shuttle on a loom. And you know what?'

He didn't know what and he said so.

'He buried her himself, sent us all packing. So don't be wishing death on yourself, not till I've borrowed a shovel, any road.'

Seth Povey let out a deep breath. Tilly was on one of her horses and she likely wouldn't climb off till tea-time. He glanced at the clock on the mantel. It had a black and green face and a tendency to stop unless laid on its side. Tilting his head to align with the clock, he calculated the hour. Ted would get fed up in a minute. He would be standing outside the Starkie after a nice, peaceful pint, would have his basket, his bait and his rods, an afternoon of solitude before him, some butties made by his wife . . .

'Put a different coat and hat on, then get gone, you're getting on me nerves,' snapped Tilly. 'Yon face is enough to turn milk sour. And make sure you catch summat, then you can clean it and gut it and we'll have it for our tea.'

Seth frowned in amazement, then shot off at speed, anxious to escape before Tilly changed her mind. Tilly's mind-changes were swift and could affect the weather for days, so he got going while the going was good.

Tilly sat on a dining chair, head in her hands. She had never been as upset as this in a month of Sundays, and it wasn't Seth's fault. Four years she had been with Mr and Mrs Richards, four years during which he hadn't let her help, not with the personal side. Oh, she'd done the washing and ironing, the cleaning, some cooking, but he hadn't let her into his pain, hadn't allowed anyone near. Even the nurses who had sat with Mrs Richards had been treated with courtesy, no more.

Then there was his business going to pot, everything left to one side while poor Mrs Richards had struggled to breathe for these last few weeks. Richards Antiques was a big place on Deansgate. It sold all sorts. Mrs Richards, God rest her, had been in charge of all the small stuff, ornaments, thimbles, dolls, dolls' houses, bric-à-brac. He dealt with furniture and bigger stuff like paintings. He emptied houses. Tilly sighed. Aye, he emptied houses and so did his son, though Mark Richards didn't wait to be invited. He acquired his stuff while folk were away on holiday or out at work. It was a shame about Mark, it really was, because all he needed was a bit of attention. And a good hiding, perhaps, just to set him on the right path.

Sooner or later, some daft bugger would walk down Deansgate and see his own stuff for sale in Richards' window. Then Mark, son of an honourable man, would get a prison record. What must she do? And why was she asking herself what she must do? She knew what to do.

Tilly, who had never known fear since her breeding days had ended, took herself off into the scullery for a bit of a swill. She might have used her new bathroom, but she couldn't be bothered. After drying herself, she pulled on a sensible brown coat and some sensible brown shoes.

The mirror displayed a woman in her fifties, a bit drawn about the mouth, rather tired around the eyes. The brown outfit topped off with a sensible hat, she picked up a shopping-bag, purse, keys and a handkerchief, made sure she had her bus fares, then stepped outside.

Seth, on the opposite side of the road, was quickening his step, disappearing fast in the direction of the Starkie. Tilly smiled to herself. She had done a good job on the wild boy, had brought him up properly, had managed to push a bit of sense into material encased in a skull as thick as a plank. Aye, he was all right.

But Mark Richards was not . . .

It was a lovely big house, symmetrical, nice pointed porch over the main entrance, deep windows, huge front door with a lion's head brass knocker. Tilly didn't need to knock, because she had a back-door key, a great long thing that looked as if it should have been used to lock criminals in their cells. Aye, well, there was a criminal here and she was going to sort him out, by God, she was. If she could find him . . .

She went round to the back and let herself in, soaking up the special silence that visits a truly empty house. The funeral had been at eleven o'clock this morning, so the boss and his son should have been home, but there was no sight or sound of either of them. The dog basket was empty, as was the kennel in the rear yard, so the dog, too, was missing. A great believer in industry, Tilly looked for something to do.

Things wanted seeing to. The last few months had been terrible, Mr Richards at work for brief periods, the lad at school – well, supposedly at school – silent nurses flitting about with covered bedpans, covered kidney bowls, faces neutral as they coped with what needed doing. It all wanted shifting, yet she dared not move any of it, but she could tidy up, aye, she could. Mrs Richards' stuff would have to stay where it was until Himself decided what to do with it – moving any of that would surely cause trouble.

The dining room at the front of the house was

no longer a dining room. Meals were taken now in the kitchen at a great big table, white deal, plain, large enough for a family of ten. Food was consumed in silence, Himself at one end of the table, the lad at the other, acres of space between them in more ways than one. Mrs Richards, reduced to eating in liquid form only, had been ensconced in the dining room, bed, wardrobe, chest of drawers, a little bedside table with what seemed like a thousand bottles on its surface, pills, lotions for her sores, liquid medicines, hypodermics, bags of clear stuff for the drip stand.

Yes, somebody would need to get this place back in order, and that someone would have to be Tilly Povey. She walked into the hall, listened to the antique grandfather as it ticked away everyone's life. Aye, even now, with the mistress cooling underground, Father Time, unimpressed, continued to do his job, no pause for thought.

It was sad, yes, but life had to go on. Tilly perched for a moment on the lid of a monks' bench, remembered Molly Richards as she had been three or four years ago, already frail, already suffering, but as full of life as any twenty-year-old. So tied up in each other, the Richardses had been. They did everything together, work, play, reading, entertaining – if you found one of them, the other would be close by. But the lad had been different. Already solitary due to lack of siblings, Mark Richards was a sullen boy, one who existed on the fringe of his parents' marriage, a truly lonely creature who sought to please his father at all costs.

'Aye, that's why he keeps coming in with silver vases – "Hey, Dad, look what I bought with my pocket money," face lit up like a Christmas tree, licking up crumbs of praise like a puppy at a table.' Where was he? Out with the dog, with Bess. Bess had received more love than Mark had . . . 'I wish I didn't care,' she told the clock. 'It'd be a lot easier if I could just walk away and say to hell with the lot of 'em. But I can't, because I'm daft and I want me head seeing to.'

Aye, well, talking to a clock would get her nowhere. Tilly rose and walked into Mrs Richards' room. She paused in the doorway, a hand to her throat. Matthew Richards was here, spread out on the bed. For a split second, she thought that the man was dead, then she saw a small movement, realized that he was breathing, thank God.

All the pills had gone, disposed of days ago by one of the nurses who had tended the dead woman. Well, that was a relief, because Tilly could not have coped with his suicide. Bad enough that he should lose a beloved wife; had he killed himself, Tilly would have gone mad. She backed out, closed the door softly. Even had he been awake, she couldn't have told him about Mark's carryings-on, because he wasn't fit for it, hadn't been fit for years. As for today, well . . . no. And she couldn't imagine him recovering in a hurry, either.

Tilly sat down at the deal table. She pictured him as she had seen him just before lunchtime, shovel attacking the earth, his face twisted with emotions too powerful to be kept inside. All the fury of an injured animal had been in his movements, quick, frustrated, almost mad. And, outside the cemetery, a boy and a dog had stood for a while, the animal's tail drooping in that age-old stance of abject misery, the boy's shoulders rounded, hopeless, unbearably sad.

But it had to be tackled. No use sitting here with a head full of nonsense, because it all wanted sorting out. No matter what, Molly Richards was dead and she wouldn't be coming back this side of Judgement Day. Her grieving husband was asleep on her deathbed; their sad and lonely son was out somewhere with a dog that was as miserable as he was.

Tilly got up, opened a tall cupboard and began to remove its contents. As always in times of stress, she set to, piling up dishes, scrubbing shelves, creating order where she could, ignoring the chaos over which she had no power. Shelves she could manage, folk she could not – well, not always.

The back door opened and Bess wandered in. Behind her, his face inscrutable, Mark Richards ambled slowly into the kitchen.

Tilly, half-way through cleaning a colander, dropped the object into the sink and addressed the young master of the household. 'Are you hungry?' There had been no wake after the funeral, no gathering of friends and relatives. From the way Mr Richards had carried on, he likely had no friends left. As for relatives, they, too, had probably headed for the hills.

'No,' he replied, a reluctant 'thanks' following the word after a split second.

Tilly thought about what needed doing, decided to wade in straight away. 'You've been pinching stuff, haven't you? Look at me while I'm talking to you.'

He blanched. 'No.' God, she was always ordering people to look at her while she talked to them. Also, she seemed to stare straight through him, and she wasn't exactly an oil painting—

'Oh, yes, you have. Remember, I'm the one who cleans your bedroom and I've seen your bag of tricks, lad, screwdrivers and a jemmy and bits of silver, ornaments, too. It all goes in the paper, you know, every burglary gets written down. There were that house up Heaton, were it Greenmount Lane – old couple, she'd been in hospital with a broken leg? Remember? In the *Bolton Evening News* a few weeks back?'

He stepped back, collided with the cooker.

'Solid silver teapot, coffee pot, sugar and cream, tray, the lot. They're in your wardrobe, Mark. I suppose they'll stop there till the fuss dies down, then you'll go along to your dad's shop in a few months, pretend you'd saved up to buy them on the cheap.'

Mark swallowed audibly, his throat suddenly as dry as blotting paper. This had been a terrible day, and it was showing no signs of improvement.

Tilly stared hard at him. 'I know what's gone on, son. I know you've wanted attention and got none. But your mam were dying and your dad's heartbroken – they were very close. Mark, listen to me.' She stepped nearer to him. 'You've exams coming up. Your dad wants you to do well. He does care, I know he does. Come on. Sit down here with me and we'll have a butty and a cup of tea. Let's work it out, shall we?'

The miserable boy threw himself on to a chair. Bess, sensing his distress, sat beside him. While she buttered bread and made tea, Tilly tried not to look at the two of them, because the vision cut her to the quick. That dog had taken over, was supervising Molly's son just as she had supervised Molly's last two years. Tilly gulped, turned away and layered boiled ham and slices of tomato on the bread. Sometimes life was so terrible that she could not even think about it. But she had to, had to think. Now.

Mark waited. He felt as if he had been waiting all his life for someone to notice him, question him, even to tell him off. And now, when he had finally achieved some attention, it came not from a parent, but from a servant. 'I don't know why I did those things,' he said. 'I don't want to steal. I just had to do something.'

Tilly knew why. He had wanted recognition, affection, even anger. Oh, they had got him into Bolton School, a place that was on a par with most southern public establishments, but they hadn't bothered to get to know him. She wondered how they had treated him when he was small, during those going-to-the-park years, the time when parents showed their little ones how to play ball, how to feed the ducks, how to build with wooden blocks.

She brought the makeshift meal to the table, was not surprised when he pounced on the food like someone who had been starving in Africa for a decade. Because Mark *was* starving. He wanted to belong, to matter. He wanted what every kid wanted, never mind public schools and a posh uniform and a new bike with fancy gears.

He swallowed the last mouthful. 'I didn't know I was so hungry,' he said, his tone apologetic. 'Sorry, I left none for you.'

Tilly smiled. 'Seth's gone fishing. I told him to fetch our tea back, but I bet he'll catch nowt. I reckon he'll call in at the Jubilee shop on his way home and buy a couple of steaks of silver hake. And he'll expect me to believe he's caught them, all cut up nice and ready for a bit of seasoned flour and a hot pan. Still, I shall get my tea, so don't you fret. Now, let's think on and decide what we're going to do with all yon stuff. Because you can't carry on, not without being caught. And, more to the point, them folk you're robbing don't deserve it, do they?'

He shook his head.

'Give it to me,' she said, 'I'll get shut of it.'

'But . . . but how?' he asked. 'And if you get caught—'

'Eeh, they'll not catch me, son. See, hang on while I tell you summat, a thing I've never told nobody in all me life. I married a bad lad, the best shoplifter in Lancashire. He could pick a pocket and his nose at the same time, could Seth – and I'm not joking. But I straightened him, no danger.'

'How?'

Tilly stretched her spine and looked him right

in the eye. He was a good-looking boy, dark like his mother and with the same bright eyes, so blue that they looked almost purple at times. He was ready, she judged. Young, but ready. 'I put a bolster down the middle of the bed, Mark. If he went wrong, he got no time with me, no private time. So he soon learned. Men are like children. You have to teach them to behave.'

He struggled not to laugh. It was strange that he had never noticed how funny Mrs Povey was. She looked so fierce, plain and businesslike, a no-nonsense style of person, wrap-around aprons, hairnets and scrubbed face. Yet here she sat, humour on show, the usually savage lines of her face relaxed as she said her piece.

'Now, you've got to learn,' she told him, 'because if you carry on bad ways, you'll end up worth nowt a pound, not even fit for weighing in with all the scrap down the rag-and-bone yards. That's not what you want.' She paused, thought for a moment. 'What do you want?'

No one had asked him that question before. He could see that she was genuinely interested, that she wanted to hear the answer. 'I want to go into the business,' he replied. 'I'm not one for books and I shan't be queuing up to get into university. No, I'd be quite happy learning about antiques. Mother used to—' He stopped short, gulped back a lump of emotion. 'She used to talk to me about china, porcelain, what she called small collect-ables. That was before she got the cancer on her brain. After that . . .'

'After that, she was well on her way to heaven,

love. And your dad, well, he were too tied up in what he could see happening to her. Nobody neglected you on purpose, Mark. I mean, there's been times when my kids didn't see much of me or their dad. We had to get on with earning money. He still works shifts, so we never know when we'll see him, but that's the way life is. It's cruel, Mark. And you've had to learn that while you're still very young.'

Mark bowed his head. He didn't want Tilly Povey getting into trouble, yet he needed a way out, a lifeline. 'I wanted them to notice me,' he said quietly. How many times had he knocked on the door of his mother's ground-floor bedroom only to find them in there together, Mother flat and white against her pillows, Father with a hand to his lips? 'Go away or you will wake her,' the unspoken message had read. So Mark had slipped away, unremarkable, unnecessary, an intruder.

'I know,' answered Tilly.

'The things for the shop, I thought they'd—'

'You thought your dad would be grateful.'

'Yes.'

Tilly inhaled deeply. 'See, it's this road, pet. No use getting yourself noticed for the wrong reasons. My Seth used to do that. Lucky not to get caught, because it's the getting caught that changes your life, sends you down a different road. Once you've been to prison, it's all over and done with, no life any more, no chances. Now, get all the stuff in your bedroom and pack it up. Wipe it all and wear gloves, then you leave no marks. I'll put it back where it belongs.'

His face whitened. 'But I can't remember all of the addresses—'

'No need. I shall dump it outside the main police station in town.'

'But—'

'Let me do the butting.' She took his hand. 'This day is like a bookmark in your life, son, something you're slipping between pages so as you'll know where you're up to. Your mam went under, so you'll not forget the date. But your mam would want you to do this other thing. Do it for her, for her memory.'

He cried then, noisy sobs that fractured the air and caused Bess to stiffen. Tilly Povey held her master's son to a bosom that had never been much of a cushion, yet the heart that beat beneath that thin chest sent out all the comfort it could muster. She blinked back her own scalding tears and sent a prayer to Mrs Richards. 'I think I've saved him, lass,' she said silently. 'Go with God, Mrs Richards.'

Outside the door, between kitchen and hall, a widower stood. He heard his son's grief, could not walk towards it. Like one in a dream, he moved to the staircase and raised his head, looked at the obstacles before him. Each step was a mountain to be climbed, each minute a lifetime. He no longer wanted to see, hear, touch, smell, talk, exist, function, remember. Yes, it had been time for Molly to go; no, she should not have suffered for a single moment longer. And yet . . .

Why her? Why not some of the evil people,

those who deserved to suffer? Had his thinking mechanism been in order, Matthew could have nominated a legion of people who should have taken Molly's place on the list of the damned. But no. He had to put one foot in front of the other, was forced to climb. And it mattered not what was at the top of the stairs, because Molly would never breathe again.

Stella Dyson brushed a tear from her face, pretended to tidy the curtains, her eyes fixed on the house across the road. But Coniston, named after her dead sister's favourite lake, was as impassive as ever. Not for over two years had Molly been visible. Before the cancer had removed all bodily control, Molly had been good company, but the brain had deteriorated and poor Molly had floated away on a sea of morphine, clawlike hands finally relaxing, some semblance of beauty returning briefly to a face that had become no more than a parchment-covered skull.

Molly Richards' younger sister sat at her desk and waded through some notes. Surgery would open in half an hour, life must go on. At the age of thirty-three, Stella was new to general practice, had qualified late, because the whole process of becoming trained had been funded by herself and a small pittance from the government. Mam had made encouraging noises from time to time. Dad had not wanted to know; Dad had required his children to work from the age of fifteen, get the money in and to hell with the future, because Joe Dyson needed his drink.

So Molly had married a future, while Stella, determined to succeed off her own bat, had worked endless hours in cafés, pubs, shops and nursing-homes. Now, with her apprenticeship well and truly served, she had borrowed enough to enter this practice as a junior and was in possession of a flat upstairs, no rent to pay, but longer than average periods on call evened out the score. She was content with her lot, lived opposite her sister . . . lived opposite the house in which her sister had died.

She stopped writing, lifted her head, thought about that ghastly funeral. Mam and Dad, the former trying not to weep, the latter hopping from foot to foot, his body screaming for the alcohol on which it now depended. Matthew's parents, tight-lipped, controlled, no emotion visible on their features even when their son had screamed his fury into the pale September morning. Mark, poor Mark, only the dog to comfort him, his father careering about the place like a psychotic, his mother cold, his companions colder than poor Molly had been. 'I am cold,' she said aloud. Yes, she could think 'poor Mark', but had difficulty in feeling it.

The pencil snapped. Stella, unaware until now of the tension in her body, jumped when wood and graphite cracked. God, she was a mess. Unmarried, unloved, her brief contact with her fellows achieved through medicine, she felt only guilt when she thought about her dead sister. Yes, she had loved Molly, of course she had. The guilt remained all the same.

Because Stella Dyson, General Practitioner, respected member of a respectable profession, was not normal, was not like ordinary, decent people. While cut to the quick by her sister's death, a small flame of hope drew oxygen from a forbidden source.

He was free now. There would be a period of mourning, a year or so during which a new liaison would not be appropriate, but after a decent interval Matthew Richards would return to life. And he might well look to a familiar face, one he had always known, a comforter, an established friend. And Stella Dyson would be there.

She rose from the desk, played with the curtains again. That Povey woman was in there, as was Mark, as was the dog. The car had been there all the time, because Matthew and his son had travelled in the undertaker's vehicle. Where was he? Yes, he had loved Molly desperately, but surely he would not damage himself? No, he would be safe, would be inside Coniston with his son and his housekeeper.

For a few moments, she stood by the window, wondered whether she should go across after surgery, wondered when, if ever, he would notice her. She looked very like Molly, dark hair, blue eyes that were a little less bright, good skin, a slender figure, similar facial features. But she was not Molly. Matthew had adored Molly's vulnerability, her childlike innocence, the joy she had derived from everyday pleasures. Whereas Stella, the fighter, had toughened up while travelling the long, solitary road towards medicine. She remained a virgin, her heart, such as it was, claimed many years ago by her own sister's husband; she had been unwilling to experiment with sex, was certain in her soul that only the very deepest love would induce her to make intimate contact with a man.

So. He was there and she was here, and there was a surgery to run. Sighing, she picked up Mr Arthur Bowles' notes and read about his hernia. The secret was to be busy, to engage her mind in something positive, something achievable.

Tonight, she would visit her brother-in-law.

Emily and Joseph Dyson lived in Eldon Street. Their house was a potentially comfortable one, set in the middle of a council-owned terrace, three bedrooms and a bathroom upstairs, a decent living room and kitchen on the ground floor. Here they had been placed when their names had risen to the top of the list, which happy incident had released them from the slums at the bottom end of Deane Road, a more industrialized sector of Bolton.

There had been five children, three boys who had gone straight into manual jobs, followed by Margaret, who was commonly known as Molly, then Stella, who had become a doctor. Both girls had thought a lot of themselves, too much, in the opinion of their father. One had married above and beyond her natural reach, while the other had educated herself into money. Now alone, the Dysons lived back-to-back with Tilly Povey, their rear garden abutting the alley behind Tonge Moor Road.

Joe Dyson, retired on health grounds from a Westhoughton coal mine, had acquired for himself a little window-cleaning round, which job enabled him to come and go as he pleased. What pleased him most was best draught, so he made enough to put some meat and bread on the table, then sufficient extra to buy himself a pint when he needed one. As he needed one most of the time, the food money was barely enough to keep the two bodies and souls together, so Emily worked part-time at the Co-op stores on Tonge Moor Road.

She returned alone from her daughter's funeral, leaving Joe to drown his sorrows at the Starkie. Once inside, he would weep crocodile tears, thus encouraging other customers to buy his ale until the pub closed; after that event, he would pick up his ladders and work, drunk or sober.

Emily took off her navy coat and hung it from a peg on the kitchen door. She didn't know how to feel. Lonely, she supposed. The rearing of five children had not been easy, especially when their father had drunk most of the housekeeping money. It was as if there had been no time for love, no time for anything, as Emily had been forced to work, children deposited wherever she could find a niche, body too tired at the end of a day, too weary for games and for demonstrations of affection.

Poor Molly. The girl had certainly suffered,

though Emily had seen very little of her in recent months. It wasn't fair; none of it had ever been fair. Married to a man who was married to his ale, Emily Dyson had led a sad, lonely life, money worries plastered in front of her brain, money on her mind morning, noon and night, money, bloody money.

She sat at the kitchen table, a wonky affair with a bad leg, an item that had been on Joe's list for at least two years. He never did anything properly, never did anything at all. He was useless. Something rose in Emily's gorge and she rushed to deposit it in the sink, heaving for breath once her stomach was evacuated. She stood there, hands gripping porcelain, a terrible anger rising in her chest, rising just as her stomach had risen. 'I hate him,' she told a surprised face in a small mirror pinned to the window-frame. 'Aye, that's it, I bloody hate him.'

Dragging herself back to the table, Emily mopped her face with a tea-towel. 'Why didn't you visit her?' she asked herself. Why? Because . . . because none of these were her children. She had given birth to them, but Joe had turned her into a husband, a provider. So busy had she been catering for the family's needs that she had not noticed her own flesh and blood.

Her skin crawled. He had stolen her children away from her, had dedicated himself to drink. And now, with Molly dead, everything was suddenly meaningless. 'You do love them,' she reminded herself, 'you do, but they grew away, especially the girls. Aye, girls are quicker than lads, cleverer, more sense. So they buggered off and made a life for themselves. I lost them. Then I lost the guts to go back and find them. I should have told her I was sorry. He lost me my children.' She threw back her head and called to the ceiling, 'I'm sorry, Molly. I did it wrong. He made me do it wrong and, in the end, I didn't know you.' She didn't know Stella, either.

It was as if all the damped-down fury had reached boiling point and she could find no valve, no release point. Wild-eyed, she gazed around this kitchen with its meat safe, its cracked lino, the cheap pots piled on shelves, pans hanging from hooks next to the window. It was time, time to stand up and – and get rid of it all. She jumped up, grabbed plates and cups, smashed them into a thousand pieces. From the pulley line, she ripped clothes and towels, rending them apart with a strength of which she had never been aware.

He had destroyed her. Now, she destroyed all that she remembered of him, every cheap ornament, every chair, every item of clothing. She went through the bedroom, the bathroom, the living room, larger items dragged out into the garden where she applied paraffin before throwing a match into the pile. There. All up in smoke, all gone.

The neighbours were suddenly out in force, heads peering sideways out of windows and doors. 'Got your eyeful?' she screamed. 'They buried my girl today and – and it should have been him.' She tossed one of Joe's shirts into the inferno. 'Send your kids round,' she yelled, 'tell 'em bonfire's early this year, give 'em a slice of parkin and a baked potato.' She wasn't herself, didn't know herself, didn't care, either. There was a job to do here and she was going to finish it good and proper.

Tilly Povey, on her way back from her visit to Chorley New Road, was just about to lift the latch on her back gate when she noticed the commotion. So absorbed had she been in her own thoughts, she hadn't noticed that Emily Dyson was doing a fair imitation of the Great Fire of London. Quickly, she stashed Mark Richards' ill-gotten gains in her own yard before crossing the street to Emily Dyson's back garden.

As she approached the little green gate, she noticed the state of Emily, eyes as wild as a trapped tiger's, face covered in smudges, hair sticking up all over the place. Tilly had never had much time for Emily, because the woman had ignored that lovely dying daughter but, oh, she looked to be in a bad way. 'Emily?'

Emily swung round, the remains of a plaster Alsatian dog in her hands. 'What?'

'What are you doing?'

'What does it look as if I'm doing? I'm frying bloody pancakes.'

'Eeh, well, that's a fair blaze for a Pancake Tuesday in September,' commented Tilly drily.

Emily lifted her tone. 'I'm only doing what I should have done years ago, that's all. Cleaning up, Mrs Povey.' She picked up two bottles of brown ale and smashed them, together with the

37

Alsatian, on the path. 'I'm doing what my son-in-law did this morning, Mrs Povey, I'm sorting out the dead, burying him, getting bloody shut, wiping him out, cleaning the slate, trying to remember who I was before I got tied up with that useless, drunken bastard.' The usually quiet woman paused for breath; she was beginning to frighten herself.

Tilly opened the gate and stepped on to Emily Dyson's property. Although Tilly had worked for this woman's daughter, there had been little or no contact over the years. Emily Dyson was somebody who lived back to back with Tilly; she wasn't even a neighbour in the true sense, was certainly not a friend. 'You're making a right mess,' she said quietly.

'And what's that got to do with you? Are you in charge or summat? Just because you go cleaning up the posh end, that doesn't mean you can throw your weight about round here. Just leave me alone.'

'Where will you sleep?'

Emily blinked slowly. She hadn't thought, hadn't got that far. She would go to her son's house, she supposed, because she didn't know Stella, hadn't known Molly. She fixed her gaze on Tilly. 'I were ashamed,' she said, ' I couldn't face me daughters, because they've got . . . they had . . . Stella's still got a decent life.'

'All right, all right,' soothed Tilly.

'They got out and I never tried to stop them. I didn't know them, you see, because I had all to do and he never pulled his weight, so my kids were strangers, then it got too late and I didn't want him traipsing after me up Chorley New Road begging for beer money.' She stopped for breath. 'And today, when our Molly went under, it all boiled up. What have I done? Oh, God, look at all this – there's nowt left.'

Tilly clicked her tongue encouragingly.

Emily stopped, stood dead still, then folded slowly on to the grass. Her mouth opened in a perfect O and she cried, ranted, used language that seldom emerged from the throat of a woman. She screamed at the Almighty, berating Him for the hand she had been dealt in life, a load of deuces, not a single ace, just a knave where the king should have sat. She mourned her children, those long-ago tiny humans, white-faced and ill-clad as they queued for free milk, free dinners, for the nurse to find unwelcome visitors about their little persons. Most of all, Emily Dyson shouted at herself.

Tilly's eyes pricked. She rushed to the grieving woman, squatted down beside her, drew the head into her own bony bosom. Well, her Seth might have started out a right pie-can, might still enjoy the odd pint, but he was a saint when compared to Joe Dyson. 'Come on, lass. See, let me look after you, eh? I've a nice bottle of sherry indoors, still sat there since last Christmas. Ooh, and I think I've a couple of teacakes – we can toast them. Please, Emily, please.'

Emily dried her face. 'I kept me own stuff,' she said, suddenly calmer. 'Me clothes and that. But I can't stop here now, can I?'

39

Tilly thought about that. 'No, I reckon you've burnt your boats and most of his shirts as well. I think it might be a good idea if you weren't here when he comes back. Let's get your things and go across to my house, then we can put some thinking caps on. Unless you've set fire to them and all.'

Emily stared at Tilly as if seeing her for the first time. 'You're all right, you are,' she declared, the words wearing the edge of truth that arrives with deep emotion. 'Aye, I reckon I could put meself in worse hands.' She stood up, steadied herself by placing a hand on Tilly's shoulder, then went inside to retrieve her few paltry possessions.

Tilly checked the fire, made sure that it was not about to spread, then stepped back to address the neighbours. 'Show's over, girls. And if Joe Dyson comes across to my house looking for his missus, I'll know who sent him, won't I? Well, won't I?' She stood, hands on hips, until all the heads had shot back inside their shells of bricks and mortar. 'Load of flaming tortoises,' she muttered to herself, 'just the head out, no bloody belly to them.' Yes, they would have left Emily Dyson to her fate, would have taken the usual policy of non-interference to its limits. Bloody cowards.

Emily staggered out of her kitchen, her possessions tied in a sheet.

'Shall I shut the door?' Tilly asked.

The burdened woman allowed a grim smile to visit her lips. 'Please yourself,' came the reply, 'there's nowt in yon worth pinching.'

Tilly led her shaking companion across the

narrow alley to the back gate of 301 Tonge Moor Road. Bolting the gate firmly, she picked up her own parcel and ushered Emily into the scullery.

'What's in that?' Emily asked.

'Somebody else's sins,' answered Tilly. She wasn't going to tell Emily about her grandson's bad habits, so she hid the evidence under the sink. Yes, there was that to deal with, too. But for now, Tilly concentrated on the mending of Emily Dyson. Emily would sleep in the attic while Tilly thought on.

One way and another, there was a lot of thinking on to do . . .

Two

Jack Richards did not approve of public displays of emotion.

His son's behaviour at this morning's funeral had left him embarrassed, ashamed and thoroughly annoyed with him. If a person insisted on becoming hysterical, then such self-indulgence should be allowed only in privacy, in a bedroom or a bathroom, door firmly closed, curtains pulled across the window, handkerchief employed as a muffler against unseemly sounds.

Jack poured a double Scotch from a crystal decanter, then a gin and vermouth for his wife. He wondered where they had gone wrong, how they had managed to produce a son so demonstrative, so uncontrolled. What would his friends have made of such behaviour? Would it get out? Would Matthew's collapse become general knowledge, an item to be discussed at the Conservative Club, the golf club, at church?

Irene took the proffered drink and sipped elegantly. 'Well, it is my belief that poor Matthew went wrong from the very beginning. She was clever, my dear, far too clever.' Irene Richards wanted to defend her son at all costs, so it was easier to blame the dead wife. Unfair, perhaps, but certainly more convenient. Though Irene nursed a secret suspicion that Molly had been quite good for Matthew, she dared not express that thought to her angry husband.

'She was brainless.' Jack hitched up his trousers from just above the knees before sitting. 'Empty-headed, stupid sort of a woman, wrong calibre, wrong type altogether.'

Irene agreed, yet differed. 'In the academic sense, yes, she was rather barren. But her brains came from the power of great beauty, Jack. Women like that know how to comport them-selves. Also, she did become useful in the business and she was always pleasant with customers.'

Jack Richards acknowledged the comment with a grunt. An ex-major in the Coldstreams, he was a man of few words, was apt to speak staccato, like a man barking orders. 'Sometimes wish we hadn't wandered into antiques.'

Irene glanced round her beautiful drawing room and disagreed, though she did not air her views. The pieces had all come together so delight-fully in Eagley Farmhouse, each article a gem, the setting subtle and well considered. No, Irene nursed no regrets about her history in antiques; the furniture here was probably worth more than the building. Yes, it had all turned out terribly well, she with her perfect home, Jack with his horses. And yet, there was so much missing from her life . . .

'Hard to know what to do about the boy,' said Jack. 'Damned shop did it. The minute he gave Molly Dyson the job, she had him hooked and netted like a salmon. Far too easily led.'

'Hardly a boy, my dear – he is forty now. But I understand you perfectly. Matthew is not a man for the single life.' She placed her glass on a coaster on the surface of an inlaid side-table. 'I wondered about Caroline Hunter-Jones.'

The major shook his head. 'Rides well, but looks like a horse. No, can't see him taking to Carrie, not for one moment. To be fair, she probably smells like a horse, never away from the stables. Matthew wants something . . . feminine.'

'Lucy Pemberton? We might give her a try, get Matthew to come up here for a weekend – he could bring young Mark. We might chivvy him up at the same time, find him a mount.' Yes, then she would see them again, would be able to reassure herself that Matthew would be fine. Of course he would. His behaviour today had been born of grief and that would pass in time.

The major grunted his approval and they settled back to await dinner. Scotch and gin would smooth their feathers, then a good chunk of rare beef would fill the gap nicely, bridge four this evening, drinks with the Pembertons, cosy, predictable, the organized life.

Irene Richards thought about her poor son for several minutes, such a sad day, such a dreadful display of emotion. A part of her wanted to rush to his side but, as the dutiful wife, she knew that her place was here, with Major Jack. Wasn't it? Oh

44

dear, she felt so ruffled. How furious Matthew had been this morning, how uncivilized. Yet she managed to curb her feelings so that they stopped short of actual shame. It had happened, it was over and she hoped that Matthew felt better for it.

Then she distracted herself with a copy of *Vogue*, immersed herself in fashion and dismissed all unpleasantness from her mind. This was how she had been reared by her husband, to make the right noises, to show just the correct amount of interest, to be feminine, available for bridge, good with horses. She dropped the magazine. Something was tugging at her chest and she felt . . . lonely. But time was a great healer of wounds . . .

Stella Dyson looked at herself in the mirror, studied the understated makeup, the dove-grey suit, pale blue blouse, black leather shoes. Yes, she would do, not too overdressed, not too funereal. She had taken her hair back into a French pleat, sensible, tidy and very unlike Molly. Molly's hair had hung free for much of the time, though illness had dictated a change in style, shorter, easier for staff to wash, manageable.

It was not yet time to look like Molly. That would come later, when she could coax him out of the house, a ride on the moors, visits to little country pubs, a concert, a play. Subtlety for now, she reminded herself. Concern for her nephew, for her brother-in-law, meals to be served, shopping lists to create. The mistress of Coniston was dead and Matthew would soon be in need of help and companionship.

She picked up bag and keys, emerged from her top-floor flat, skipped down the stairs. Calls were to be redirected by the post office to the home of another junior doctor, because Stella was in mourning. She stopped in the hallway, guilt colouring her view yet again. At the old coat-stand, she steadied herself, spoke to herself. 'You love him, so stop this now. You didn't ask to love him, never wanted to hurt Molly. She is dead and that is terrible. Look after him, look after them both.'

Thus fortified, she left the house and walked down the short path. Chorley New Road was a wide thoroughfare with aspirations. At the lower end, where it neared the township, it was ordinary enough, as were some of the streets of large terraced houses that ran down to the road. But after a mile or two's travel out of town, the place gave itself airs – a sweep of lawn in front of the very grand Bolton School, houses set back, old trees preserved, long driveways reaching out towards large houses, each of unique design.

Stella and Matthew lived somewhere around the half-way mark, Middlesville, as Stella termed this stretch. The houses on her side of the road were huge, but in terraces, while those opposite, of which Coniston was one, served as a precursor of things to come, detached, medium-to-large gardens, individual styles. Matthew did not aspire to grandeur, so anything higher up Chorley New Road would have been too precocious, too *nouveau riche* for his taste. Was he an inverted snob? she asked herself. No. He liked decent furniture and plain rooms, wanted the pieces rather than their container to stand out. And Molly had agreed with him. But Molly had always agreed with him. Completely.

She crossed the road, walked up the path and round to the back door. Bess greeted her, tail waving madly, the short, sharp barks friendly. Well, the dog seemed to have bucked up, at least. She opened the back door, walked into the kitchen. It was empty. 'Mark?' she called. 'Mark?' There was no reply.

Cautiously, she ventured into the hall, admired for the thousandth time the ancient grandfather clock, crept into the room in which her sister had died. No one. The drawing room was empty, as was Matthew's small ground-floor study. Perhaps he was upstairs, then, in the larger office? Mark often went out in the evenings, though Matthew had tended to stay put since Molly's ability to go out had been curtailed.

Upstairs, then. His car was outside, so surely he was in? She climbed quietly, ears alert for the slightest sound. From the kitchen, Bess whined. Stella froze, wished that she could shush the dog. Yes, there was a small sound, a rustling that came from Matthew's room. On tiptoe, she approached the door, opening it an inch at a time.

He looked up. 'We all begin with M,' he said, 'Matthew, Molly and Mark.'

Like a statue, she stood in the doorway, unable to move or speak. She was a doctor, for goodness' sake, she could cope. Couldn't she?

He sat on the floor in the centre of the room,

Molly's belongings scattered around him. On his face he wore an expression of confusion, staring at her as if she were a stranger. Scarves were entwined about his fingers, bottles of perfume had spilled their contents on to the carpet, sweet scents mingling to produce an odour that was sickly and unpleasant. 'Ten green bottles,' he said.

Stella coughed nervously. 'Matthew?'

He nodded. 'And Molly. Molly is asleep.'

'Asleep?' She felt stupid, knew that her question was insane. Molly was dead, while Matthew . . . Matthew was in shock. 'Would you like a drink?' she asked.

'On the wall,' he replied, 'ten green bottles, hanging.'

Stella swallowed a huge lump of anxiety, riffled through the textbooks in her mind, photographic memory, 'Dealing with Emotional Trauma', chapter seven. Shock. Questions. 'What's your name?' she managed.

'Matthew.' He frowned like a five-year-old whose teacher did not value him. 'Matthew Richards.'

'And . . . er . . . where is Molly?'

'At the shop,' came the immediate response, 'doing the books. She has a very good head for figures. Nine green bottles.' So the Molly he had recently believed to be asleep was now doing books at Richards Antiques.

Oh, God, oh, God. One of Molly's lipsticks had rolled off under the dressing-table and he advanced like a crawling infant, jaw hanging as he concentrated on the gilded cylinder that was

48

his prey. She did not know where to start. Who was his GP? Yes, of course, it was Simon MacRae, Mornington Road. Should she run down there and fetch him? No, no, Matthew was spreading face cream on his hands . . . 'Matthew?'

He looked at her quizzically.

'What are you doing?'

A deep frown knitted his brows and he made no effort to reply.

Galvanized by panic, Stella fled from the room, down the stairs and into Matthew's smaller office. She grabbed the phone, dropped it, retrieved it, searched her remarkable memory for numbers, remembered nothing. Handbag. Diary. She retraced her steps, fled across the landing, heedless of pins as they clattered from too-clean hair on to polished floorboards at the edge of the carpet runner. Handbag, diary.

'Molly!' The moment she entered the room, he leaped up and embraced her. 'Darling, you're back.'

'No, no, I'm Stella. Matthew, please—'

His mouth silenced her, lips pressing urgently against hers, arms holding her tightly, clamping her against his body. She was suddenly two people – no, she was three. Or was it four? She was Stella the sensible woman, Stella the doctor, Stella the woman who wanted this man. For him, she was Molly, the beloved wife whose attentions he had missed for many years.

The sensible woman struggled, the doctor tried to break free in order to seek help. The woman who desired Matthew responded, her mouth opening beneath his, senses stupefied by his nearness and by the cloying smell of confused perfumes. And Molly? Molly was dead.

He was running his fingers through her hair and it occurred to Stella that the hair had been the cause of this behaviour, that his mental state, which helped him deny his wife's death, was sufficiently disturbed for him to 'recognize' Molly simply because Stella's French pleat had lost its pins; but now she was the lost one, reason abandoned, just the woman who needed this man, no longer sensible, no longer the doctor and never, ever Molly. Knowing his insanity, aware of his condition, she wished that the chemistry could be different, that she might change the formula, eliminate the elements that turned her into a wild and grasping animal, yet she could not.

Afterwards, on the bed where their joining had been completed, he slept, features relaxed, torture exorcized. She rose softly to avoid disturbing him, collected her scattered garments, left her sister's belongings exactly where Matthew had abandoned them. Her hands trembled as she dressed, shook while she found hairgrips on the landing, continued clumsy as she reconstructed the French pleat at the bathroom mirror.

'Hello, Aunt Stella.'

She felt as if her heart would explode, so wildly did it beat. 'Oh, Mark.' Her voice was high, wrong, too surprised. 'You made me jump. Where did you come from?' She noticed that he looked rather strange, that he was blinking slowly, rather like someone who was emerging from a dream.

Yes, the poor lad had endured a terrible day.

'Just went for a walk,' he replied. 'How's Dad?' He had the distinct impression that he had forgotten something important, a recent event, as if a chapter from the book of his life had gone missing. His eyes would not focus properly. Where had he been? What had happened? Bess was home, yes. 'I feel unwell,' he said. 'How's Dad?'

Stella inhaled sharply. 'I . . . er . . . I looked in on him a moment ago. He seems to be sleeping.'

'Good.'

God, if she had stayed with Matthew for one more minute— It did not bear consideration. 'Shall we go down and make some cocoa and toast?' she asked. 'If you eat, you will soon feel better. A cup of tea?'

'If you like.' He walked away from the open bathroom door.

She had managed to tidy up her hair just in time. There had been no chance to consider what she had done, to wonder about Matthew's state of mind; her behaviour had been, at best, rather less than professional. As for the passionate embraces she had so recently relished, she had no opportunity to savour them, to relive the wonder of that man, to remember those kisses, the touch of his hands . . . Now, she was blushing.

The sensible Stella returned, bringing Dr Stella with her. She would remain with her nephew, nominally to keep him company at the end of this grim day, really so that she would be here for Matthew when he woke. Determinedly, she closed her mind against the picture of him sitting there on the floor, Molly all around him, scarves, gloves, jewellery, cosmetics.

In the kitchen, she managed a semblance of normality, putting bread under the grill, feeding the dog, washing her hands, chattering about inanities. This poor boy had just lost his mother, so she had to try to buck him up. Her breasts ached. She discussed the changeable weather, talked about Bess, remembered Matthew's words, felt the caresses.

'Are you all right, Aunt Stella?' He felt calmer now. He had been for a walk, had returned and had forgotten nothing. Probably . . .

'Of course I am.' She busied herself with butter and marmalade. 'It's just been rather a wretched day for all of us. People act atypically after funerals, I read about it. Trust me, I know these things.'

He accepted a plate of toast. 'Aunt Stella?'

She sat in the chair opposite his, toyed with her food. 'Yes?'

'Do you love your parents?'

The cup in her hand trembled. Did she love her parents? Goodness, what a question. 'Why do you ask?'

'Just something Mother said a few months ago. About Grandad being selfish and about Grandmother not being able to manage him. Didn't he make all your brothers leave school early so that they could make money?'

'Yes. Yes, he did.'

Mark waited.

'I think there may be an excuse for my mother.

52

She worked every hour God sent, farmed us out to various aunts and neighbours. Yes, she was always exhausted. I think his drinking destroyed her, turned her into an earning machine. So . . .' She pondered. 'I think the answer is that I probably love my mother, but I despise my father.'

Mark thought about that. 'So, when you were young, you got no attention? Did you not feel angry about that?'

Stella smiled, tried to appear collected. 'Angry, no. I was too busy reading, spent all my free time in Tonge Moor library. Molly was the same. She used to bring home books about ballet dancers. Dad tore one up when he was in his cups, so Molly and I did hundreds of errands for old people, swept floors, cut grass, just so that we could pay for the book. Afterwards, we didn't bring books home. We read them in the library or kept them at friends' houses.'

'So my grandfather is a bad man?'

'He is an alcoholic. He also has lung problems after working in the mines, but he carries on smoking and drinking.'

Mark drank some cocoa. 'You won't miss him when he dies.' This was not a question.

'No,' she replied, 'I won't.'

Mark missed his mother, but couldn't understand why. For years she had been confined to the dining room, often drugged against pain, seldom making sense as she made her slow exit from life. As for Father – well, he was not a bad man, was generous and reasonable. 'They didn't need me,' he said quietly, 'they needed just each other.

Sometimes, I felt as if I didn't really exist – as if I imagined myself.' He looked straight at her. 'Does that sound crazy?'

It didn't sound half as crazy as Matthew had appeared only three-quarters of an hour earlier, but Stella shut that memory out of her mind. Perhaps, after a sleep, Matthew would be well again. 'No, it does not sound crazy at all. They were very close, Mark. The illness was always going to be fatal – even after Molly's first surgery, they both knew that there was a strong chance of the cancer returning. When it did come back, they made the most of those final years. It is a miracle that she survived as long as she did.'

Mark chewed on his toast. There was a huge void inside him, a hopelessness that startled him. 'I wonder what will happen now?' he asked.

'In what way?'

He raised a shoulder. 'Aunt Stella, my father's reason for living was my mother. Even the business has been left to slide. How will he go on?'

'I don't know.' There was no point in lying to this young man, no reason to pretend that life would change, would remain the same, would improve—

The door opened and Matthew stepped into the kitchen. He was stark naked and his eyes were glazed almost to the point of lifelessness. He looked around the room, his attention settling on neither occupant. Mark jumped up.

'Don't touch him.' Stella spoke in a whisper. The man was not sleepwalking, yet he seemed unaware of his condition, unconcerned by his lack of clothing. 'We're going to need some help,' she told her nephew, 'so stay with him while I go across the road.'

Dr Stella was in charge now, telephone calls to make, assessments to be done. But if Matthew had to go away, there was Mark to be cared for . . . That woman . . . Mrs Povey, yes, perhaps she would help.

'Find your father's dressing-gown,' she said.

The boy walked upstairs, picked up his father's robe, looked at his own reflection in the mirror. The glass clouded and he stared through the fog, dredging up memories, sounds, her face, Mother's beautiful face. '*Look, Mummy, I found a frog.' She peered into the bucket and laughed at her son's discovery. They named him Fred, then Father came. Fred stayed in his bucket, Mark stayed in the garden, Mother and Father hugged and kissed, then walked into the house.* 'They scarcely knew I was there,' he said softly, before walking back downstairs to cover Matthew Richards' nakedness.

Stella left by the rear door, unwilling to walk past Matthew, anxious to get away from a scene that served only to illustrate her worst fears. He was insane. She had made love to a crazed man; she had betrayed her sister, the only person in the world for whom she had ever felt real love. Except for Matthew, of course. Except for him . . .

Tilly knocked on the door of the attic bedroom. 'Emily?'

'Come in, I'm decent.'

The hostess placed a mug of cocoa on the

bedside chest. 'Get yourself outside of that,' she advised. 'This room's a bit dampish, so you'll need central heating in your stomach. Nothing like a mug of Rowntree's best to line your innards, as my mam used to say.'

Emily lifted the cup and took a sip. She leaned back on the pillows and sighed. 'I went a bit too far, didn't I?'

Tilly shrugged. 'Depends what you were aiming for. I mean, if you wanted a bit of a row with your husband, yes, you did go too far. But if you were aiming to start a world war, you got it right, just about. Now, are you ready to talk, or shall I go back down and help that daft article with his jigsaw?'

Emily was shocked to hear herself laughing. 'Does he know I'm here?'

'Course he does. I had to tell him in case he falls over you in the morning. He's on earlies, so he needs the bathroom first. Don't worry, he doesn't mind you being here, lass. And he won't say nothing. Mind, that daft lot across the back might not keep their gobs shut. Eeh, love, whatever possessed you to go that far? It were a right mess.'

What had possessed her? After all these years of abuse and deprivation, why had she suddenly snapped? Molly, of course. Molly and the fact that Emily had felt forced to stay away from her because of him. Molly and Stella, two daughters she had never known because of him. It was all mixed up in her head, yet it would come clear once she had made her way through it an inch at

56

a time. 'I'd had enough,' was all she managed by way of a reply.

'Molly brought it to a head, didn't she?'

Emily nodded.

'Well, I'll say me piece, then I'll leave you to sleep. Now, you're very welcome here, stay as long as you like. But think on. For a start, we're back to back with him. For another thing, he knows where to find you, because you work at the Co-op. So like I say, think on. I've seen him at his worst, three sheets in the bloody wind, hanging on to walls on his way back from the pub. If you stop round here, he'll find you, same as he always finds his way home. I think you'd be best off in another part of town.'

'I'd be best off emigrating to China,' said Emily. 'Even then, I'd be watching for him behind every blinking pagoda.'

Tilly chuckled. 'What's a pagoda?'

The guest shrugged. 'I don't know, but it sounds Chinese.'

They looked at each other and wondered why they had never become friends before, because the camaraderie had been immediate. It was as if they had been close for years rather than for just a few hours.

'Is he home?' asked Emily.

'Your Joe? Oh, aye, he's home, all right. Me and Seth stood in the yard and listened to him coming home. He's having you sued by the corporation for damaging civic property, but then he's going to give you the hiding of your life – we couldn't work out whether he was going to do that before or after you got sent to prison. His daughter has died, so he's in mourning and you've poured water all over his bed – nowhere to sleep. He hasn't a rag to his back, and would somebody please lend him some clothes. Last and worst of all, there's nowt for him to eat.'

'What a bloody shame,' commented Emily. 'Me piles bleed for him.'

'Have you got piles, love?' Tilly asked.

'No, I haven't.'

For some inexplicable reason, this admission sent the women into acute paroxysms of laughter. Emily couldn't work herself out at all. Here she was, laughing her head off, carrying on as if there was a Laurel and Hardy film on, when she had just lost a daughter. Tilly heard the hysterical edge and waited for the storm. It arrived, but was no tornado, just quiet weeping. 'I think you'd best try and catch some sleep,' advised Tilly. 'Whatever happens, you're going to need all your strength. Or do you want me to stay?'

Emily shook her head. The clearing out of the Eldon Street house had been just the beginning, the top taken off the egg. Now, she had to spoon her way through the rest, had to ask herself a lot of questions. Could she go and live with one of her sons? If no one would have her, where would a woman of fifty-nine find the means of keeping body and soul together? Did she want to keep her body and soul together?

Tilly left the attic, abandoning Emily to her thoughts. This was a rum do and no mistake, neither rhyme nor reason to any of it. The man across the back had raged for the best part of an hour, but at least he hadn't come round here, so they could all feel grateful for that. She descended the second staircase, found Seth struggling with a bit of sky. She joined him, picked up the right piece and set it into the puzzle. 'Seth?'

'What?'

She touched his arm in a rare moment of tenderness. 'Thanks.'

'What for?'

'I'm not sure,' she replied. But she was sure. She was thanking Seth and the Almighty because she had managed to marry a decent man, because she had three adult offspring who seemed safe and well, because she wasn't like the poor woman upstairs, devastated and crying her eyes out in a strange bed.

Seth looked hard at his wife. 'You're upset, aren't you? Is it the funeral, or is it Emily Dyson?'

'It's everything,' she said, after a pause. 'It's like the world's all wrong, Seth. I mean, that lovely girl dead, Emily Dyson trying to set the world on fire, Mr Richards lying there on the bed where his wife died. Everybody I know's in a mess. Even the drunken bugger over yon's suffering.'

'Aye, and so he should,' answered Seth. He placed an arm around his wife's shoulders. 'He's been heard bragging in the Starkie, love, carrying on about how he's sorted her out in the past. You know what, Tilly? I never could put up with a man who belts his missus and his kids.

Thieves and bloody vagabonds is one thing, but a man who hits a woman is no man.'

Tilly nodded. 'There's been times when I've looked at you and thought, Eeh, that lad wants sorting. But that's just my way. It's not that I don't love you, it's just me carrying on, have to be in charge, have to be the bossy-boots, always the last word.'

He drew her in to his chest. 'Tilly, there's moments I feel like filling your gob with concrete, but I'd not swap you for all the tea plants in China and Ceylon, plus every coffee bean in Brazil. There's a kind of comfort in the shouting. Like today, when you went on about fishing, I knew you were really fretting about Molly Dyson-as-was. And when you do all that mithering, I think daft thoughts about shutting you up and running away from home.'

She raised her head. 'Who'd bloody have you, daft beggar that you are?'

Seth swallowed. 'You would, love.'

'Aye, I would.' It was true. Were she to be given her time over again, Tilly Povey would have taken on the same man, lock, stock and miscarriages. He had worked damned hard for his kids, hadn't moaned when his plate hadn't been over-full, had fought for king and country, had made sure in every sense possible that his family was safe.

'My life would have been so different if you hadn't took me on, Till. You brought up the kids all decent, you did your best. Now find the rest of this bloody sky, because it's getting on me nerves. Why do they make all that flipping sky, eh? There must be over three hundred blue bits.'

But Tilly clung to him for a few more seconds. Then she pushed him away and set to with his jigsaw, separating sky from flowers, houses from trees. She wished life could be this easy: separate the bits, build them all together again. But it wasn't, and her heart remained troubled.

Philip Dyson wasn't much to look at, and he was acutely aware of that fact.

At the age of thirty-nine, he had never married, was not experienced with women and, for the most part, he kept himself to himself. He lived above a lock-up shop at the Folds Road end of Tonge Moor, a little place with a shoe-box bed-living room, a tiny bathroom and a kitchen that held just a cooker, a cupboard, one chair and a small table. But when compared to home, this place was paradise.

A man of predictable habits, he might well have been described as a recluse, yet solitude was not really his preferred mode of existence. Philip wanted a wife, a child, a proper home, something to work towards. Earlier today, he had watched while the casket containing his sister's remains had been lowered into a gaping hole in Heaton cemetery. He had seen the carryings-on of his brother-in-law and had approved unreservedly of Matthew Richards' behaviour. To hell with vicars and priests, damn and blast all that rigmarole – death was death, no need for the trimmings.

He gazed into his gas fire, wondered how much longer the shilling would last. But he had come up in the world, that was a fact. A dedicated saver, Phil had opened a bank account in his mid-teens, had saved every spare penny, was now in possession of enough money to make a sizeable deposit on a little house. Working for the Prudential, he collected insurance money, picked his own hours and, best of all, he knew that his employers would help when he wanted a mortgage. Yes, his life plan had worked out very well indeed.

It had been a rocky road. Plunged by his father into a cotton mill at the age of fifteen, Phil had toiled for twenty years in that filthy, damp atmosphere, had suffered ear damage from the noise, had spent two full decades trying to get out of the damned place. And now he had arrived, sit-up-and-beg bike, people to visit, every week different, every chance of promotion. As a trustworthy man with a good brain, he had opportunities that would have been no more than pipe dreams just a few years ago.

Poor Molly. He scarcely remembered her. As children, she and Stella had clung together, two girls with only twenty months' difference in age, both readers, both verging on the academic turn of mind. Each had rounded on Dad, defying him to the limit, clearing out of Eldon Street at the earliest opportunity, one into marriage with a good man, the other almost breaking her back to attain that medical degree. He, Tony and Eddie, worn down by their unscrupulous and demanding father, had taken the line of least resistance, straight into manual labour. The other two were married; Phil remained unfulfilled in that area, yet a chance had arisen . . .

Annie. A childless widow, she had paid insurance and Phil, her agent, had taken her through the rigmarole, helping her to fill in the forms that would release funeral money and a small life policy to tide her over for a year or so. She liked him. He knew she liked him, because he had an open invitation to call in for a cuppa whenever he was collecting in the Thicketford Road area. She had even baked for him on one occasion, an Eccles cake for now, another to take home, a little meat and potato pie for tomorrow's dinner, a chunk of parkin for the weekend.

Phil was not given to excitement, yet his heart always picked up speed when he neared her house. But he must not read too much into this. Annie was lonely and he was lonely; perhaps she was just filling a gap in her life. After all, who would want to marry a short, plain man with short, plain reddish-brownish hair that was receding? Yet the hope refused to be squashed.

He closed his eyes and thought about Matthew Richards, wondered how he was getting on. That business at this morning's funeral had spoken volumes about the poor man's state of mind. Phil had visited the house on Chorley New Road just a few times, always after an invitation. His sisters were different from the rest of the family. They lived well, spoke well, dressed well. He supposed that he had always been in awe of them, but how could he remain in awe of a poor dead girl? And she had been so pretty, much prettier than Stella.

While their appearances were similar, Molly had owned the gentler face, the sweeter personality. She had been—

What was that? Who the heck would be banging at the shop door at this time of night? Responsible for security, Phil paid rent that had been reduced accordingly, and he took the job seriously. Mrs Burton, the elderly widow who owned the ladies' outfitter's, depended on Phil to keep the place guarded at night. And some daft beggar was banging on the front door like a lunatic, was threatening to break the glass.

He picked up his weapon, a rounders bat he had found on Castle Hill School playing-field, crept down the stairs, negotiated the stock room and walked into the shop. 'Who's there?' he called.

'Me. Your bloody father.'

Phil's blood froze. Apart from this morning, he had not seen his father in months. He visited Mam whenever he was working in her area, but he avoided Joseph Dyson like the plague. Aye, he was a flaming plague, a disease that had pervaded the childhood of five kids, an evil being who had beaten his wife and children at every opportunity.

'Open this bloody door.'

Why should he? Why should he allow the old sot into Mrs Burton's shop? He was likely drunk enough to make a right mess of things, pretty things, stockings and dresses—

'Open this door before I kick it in.'

Phil opened the door. 'What do you want?' he asked.

'What do I want? I'm your bloody father, now let me in.'

Phil stood his ground. 'I can't. You're drunk and there's stuff in here that could get broken.'

'Am I hell as like drunk! Bloody homeless, that's what I am. Your mother destroyed the house today, every flaming stick of furniture bar the bed, and she saturated that with water.'

A shocked smile tugged at the corners of Phil Dyson's mouth, but he managed to swallow it. Good for Mam. It had taken long enough, but the worm had finally done a full turn. 'So what do you want from me, then?'

Joe tried to push his way into the shop, but his son raised the rounders bat and widened his stance. 'No,' Phil said softly.

'No? What do you mean, "no"? I've nowhere to go, have I? I need food and a bed. I looked after you for long enough, so you can give me a bed for one night. That's the least you owe me.'

Phil shook his head. 'I owe you nothing. Long enough you made our lives a misery, so go and lie in your wet bed – I hope you drown in it. What's the matter? You stand there – well, sway there – telling me what you did for us. You did nowt. You sat drinking in pubs, spent all the money killing yourself, kept us starved. If it hadn't been for Mam, we'd all have been put in orphanages.'

'Don't you talk to me like that.'

Phil smiled grimly. 'Right, you've two choices. You can bugger off out of here, or I can call the police. Pick your favourite out of them two and be quick. I want my supper and my bed.'

Joe Dyson's chin dropped. His mind addled by drink, he simply failed to remember how life had been. 'She's burnt all me clothes,' he said piteously. 'I've not a rag to me back.'

'We were the same. Except for Mam working and picking things up at rummage sales, we would all have gone barefoot and bare-arsed to school. Time you got a taste of your own medicine. Right, what's it to be? Are you going to bugger off, or do I make a phone call?'

Joe Dyson raised his huge fist, focused drink-blurred vision on the rounders bat, dropped his arm immediately. Their Phil might be a runt, but the bat made a difference. 'Have you a few bob?' he wheedled. 'Get meself a bag of chips on the way home?'

'No, I haven't. And if I did have any spare money, it'd go to me mam. Where is she, any road?'

'I don't know and I don't bloody care.'

Phil stepped back into the shop and slammed the door so hard that the glass rattled. He took a deep breath and hoped for strength, because he had just come very close to battering his own father to death. Where was his mam? He couldn't imagine her doing that, wrecking the house and then taking off on her own. Would she have gone to their Stella's? No. Mam had always taken care to keep her troubles away from the girls, because she didn't want her husband going knocking on doors down Chorley New Road, cap in hand, long face, tale of woe, could they give him a couple of bob till the weekend.

'Bastard!' yelled the creature outside.

'I wish I were a bastard,' mumbled Phil. 'Then, at least, I'd know that thing weren't me dad.' He counted to ten very slowly, tried to hang on to fraying patience. He knew that if he opened that door again, he would likely take Joe Dyson limb from limb, and the man wasn't worth it.

Mam, though. She had no real friends, had never had time for a social life. The poor woman was thrilled to bits if she scraped enough together for a cheap seat at the Crompton cinema, ninepence to get in, twopence for an ice lolly in the interval – if she was lucky. Aye, long enough she'd worked there, too, usheretting after a full day in the mill – her idea of luxury now was watching a film without having to show people to their seats. Where could she be? Had she met someone at the Co-op, a fellow worker who had given her shelter? Or had she gone to one of her brothers or to another son's house?

'Right, I'm going now,' shouted the leader of the Dyson tribe. 'You'll live to regret this, I can promise you that much.' He lurched off into the night, leaving Phil relieved, yet still concerned about his mother. Was she alive? Had that bad bugger killed her, then messed up the house himself to cover his tracks? It was not exactly summer and the nights were drawing in . . . What if she was sleeping rough? What if she got too cold? She could get that hypothermia.

Phil went back upstairs, his heart leaden with worry. He toyed with the idea of calling the police, but if Mam had destroyed the house, she might get into trouble. Well, there was nothing he could do until tomorrow, and he wasn't sure what his course of action would be once daylight arrived. Mam's life had been so small, so contained, that he could not begin to imagine where she might have gone. He wondered whether she had managed to save a few bob, enough for a couple of nights in a bed-and-breakfast place. Or she might have made a new pal lately, somebody who would give her a bite, a hot drink and a sofa where she could lay her head.

So he sat and worried for a while, then made his supper, went to bed and slept fitfully. All his dreams contained Mam and Molly and he woke several times, his heart filled with dread. He couldn't remember what had happened in the dreams, but he recalled the characters, all right. Oh, God. Their Molly was gone, and he hoped that his mother had not followed her.

Three

Simon MacRae sat at the kitchen table, sleeves rolled, stethoscope dangling, chest heaving with breathlessness. Opposite him, his friend and occasional colleague, Stella Dyson, seemed almost dazed.

'Well,' he said, 'that's knocked him out for tonight, but there's no guarantee that he'll be any better tomorrow. He seems to have taken his wife's death very badly. Oh, I am sorry, Stella, she was your sister, of course. So what on earth happened here?'

Stella hoped that the heat in her cheeks did not advertise her guilt. Although she and Simon were not close friends, they worked together, sometimes stepping in when needed to cover one another's patients. 'We buried Molly today. Matthew lost his patience with everyone – he was clearly distressed. Anyway, he made us all leave the graveside, then he picked up a spade and buried her himself. We couldn't stop him, he was like a man possessed, but he was still talking sensibly. I went back to the practice, did a surgery, then came across to see how he and Mark were getting along.'

'I see.'

And I made love to him, she said inwardly. I have always loved him. He was gentle and tender, as wonderful as I knew he would be. I gave him my virginity, which I have guarded jealously for many years. But he was making love to my sister. Had my hair not fallen down—

'Stella?'

'I'm sorry, but this has been a dreadful day. I shall have to stay here, of course, because I can't abandon Mark. If Matthew becomes difficult again, the poor boy would not be able to cope.'

Simon reached across and touched her hand. 'Don't hesitate to call me, I'm very close by. But if his present state persists, you may well have to hand him over to the specialists. Mental health is such an extensive area – most of us wouldn't know where to begin.' He stood up. 'I must go, in case someone else needs me. But I must insist that you do not attempt to deal with Matthew yourself. He is extraordinarily strong.'

Stella nodded her agreement. Oh, she could deal with Matthew. All she needed was loose hair and the rest would follow – but, no, she could not take that route again. It was false pretences, was cruel and unethical. She watched Simon MacRae as he left the room, found herself thinking how attractive he was. Dear God, had she opened the floodgates? Was she a nymphomaniac in embryo?

Mark returned as the doctor left. 'What did he say?' His eyes were full of questions.

'Your father is unwell, but you didn't need a

doctor to tell you that. It may be shortlived, but he is certainly very disturbed.'

The boy dropped into a chair and stared into space. The sight of his father's nakedness had been more traumatic than the funeral. He felt that as long as he lived he would carry in his mind a picture of the man's vulnerability. Without clothes, the human form was so fragile, thinner than one might have expected, pale, forked, unprotected. 'I never expected Dad to behave like that. And I'm scared,' he admitted.

'So am I.' Stella, too, was being honest. All general practitioners came into contact with mental and emotional disturbances, but the true depth of that area of medicine lay way beyond the capacity of a family doctor. She knew enough, though, to be aware that Matthew would need to walk to the same drummer as everyone else if he were to keep his freedom. His behaviour was well outside the category commonly called eccentric: Matthew had lost his mind, and she hoped that it had fallen not too far out of reach.

'They might lock him up,' said Mark.

'And they might not.'

He swallowed. 'Is he crazy?'

'I don't know. Your mother's funeral may just have been the last straw. You see, Mark, we all have a container in which we keep our emotions. Some of us can cope with huge amounts of stress, while others collapse after events which might have been taken in their stride by the rest of us. Once the bucket overflows, we bow under the weight of it, no matter what its size. The trouble is, we don't know what is too much for us until we get there. By then, it is often too late to throw ourselves into reverse.'

Mark sniffed. 'What will happen to me?'

Stella attempted an encouraging smile. 'We'll manage. If the worst happens – and I'm sure it won't – you and I will look after each other. I'm not too far away, remember that, just across the road and up the stairs.'

'Thank you.'

'I am your aunt, Mark.'

Yes, she was his aunt. Mother and Father had always clothed and fed him, because they, too, had been attached to him by words that denoted relationship. That was all this was, a group of words, meaningless in the true sense, completely without value when it came to love. This woman was his mother's sister, so that very position dictated that she, too, must fulfil a certain function should the need arise. 'Aunt Stella?'

'Yes?'

'If Dad goes into hospital, might it be possible for Mrs Povey to stay here? Or perhaps there would be room for me in her house.' Yes, there was one person he trusted, a new and valuable friend.

Stella frowned. 'That fierce-looking woman? The one who was a professional ironer before she came here?'

He nodded.

'But why?'

Too injured and afraid to employ niceties, Mark told the truth. 'She likes me and she helps me. And that's not just because she has to like me, you see. My parents always did the right things, but that was because they were my parents. You are my aunt, my mother's sister, so you have to be here. But Mrs Povey chose me. I want to be with someone who likes me for myself, not with people who are stuck with me just because I'm a relation.'

The silence that followed was acutely uncomfortable. Stella knew what he meant because she had come from a difficult family, a home where there had been tension, fear and little space for love. But she felt hurt, too. Was she injured because she had always planned to woo Mark in order to gain the attention and affection of his father? Or did she truly feel something for her nephew? She forced herself to reply. 'Whatever you wish, Mark. But I do hope that none of this will be necessary, that your father will be well within a short space of time. Try not to worry too much – easy to say, I know, but stay as strong as you possibly can.'

They shifted uncomfortably, each aware that Matthew Richards was far from well. He had fought the doctor, had almost thrown the poor man down the stairs, so strong had he been until the sedative had taken hold. The onset of his illness had been sudden, but would it clear up as quickly?

Stella, riddled with guilt, wondered why she did not mourn her sister more acutely, why she had made love to Matthew even though she knew he had been unwell. Was her lack of shock at Molly's death the result of all those years of knowing that her sister was doomed? Or was she slightly relieved now that Matthew was a widower? Was Stella capable of love? Did she really care about this boy, or was he about to become a pawn in her plan to capture Matthew? Could she love a man who was insane? What sort of a person was she?

'It's all right,' said Mark quietly. 'If you don't want to have Mrs Povey here, I shall manage.'

'No, no,' answered Stella. 'Whatever you want, whatever can be done.'

Mark wandered off to bed, leaving Stella to spend the night downstairs. She thought of sleeping in Molly's room, decided against it. The sofa in the drawing room was comfortable, so she brought a blanket from the airing cupboard and settled down fully dressed to wait for morning. The whole day had been a nightmare, and she was not prepared for the dreams that plagued her.

She woke at seven, glanced at her watch, sat up and looked straight into the eyes of her brother-in-law. Still reeling from nightmares whose content eluded her, she rubbed her eyes. 'Hello, Matthew.'

He continued to stare at her.

Immediately, she knew that her worst fears had been realized. The man was clothed, at least, was still half wearing the pyjamas into which he had been forced, while drugged, by Simon MacRae, buttons undone, feet bare, hair tousled like that of a two-year-old.

'Matthew?'

He blinked just once. His eyes reminded her of an empty house, a place that had been occupied

74

until just recently, a home newly abandoned by its tenants, vacant, unwanted, lacking care. Her eyes pricked. She knew right away that he could not stay here, that he was incapable of caring for himself. Knowing that she must summon his doctor, she rose and pulled a hand through her hair. It was loose, had lost its pins during the night, but he did not notice.

Stella left the room and went into Matthew's little ground-floor study. A terrible weariness hit her like a sledgehammer and she sank into his leather chair. Simon's number. She picked up the phone to dial, then noticed an open notebook, hard-backed, narrow-lined and filled with writing she recognized as her brother-in-law's. This had not been here last night. The lamp was switched on. So the sedative had worn off: Matthew had been here, had been scribbling through the hours of darkness.

She read,

My Darling, the blackness is in my soul. You were here, then you were gone, but I felt you, heard you. I am descending into hell and you will not be there. So quiet, I can hear the flowers growing. In hell, there will be no flowers. I went to the door and you were not there. Words going. With you soon.

There were some drawings, scribbles consisting of jumbled letters and numbers, then a few more disjointed phrases, a description of an inlaid table, a list of things to do.

Uniform ready tell her. Dog cry. Woman in there.
Must go. Love you love you love y . . .

And it stopped.

Stella read it again. During the first paragraph, sedation had calmed him, so the script was clear. Agitation had arrived, had caused him to scribble. She guessed that the woman in there was herself, that he had wondered about Mark's school uniform, but the rest was just ravings.

She closed the book, dialled Simon's number. With sobs fracturing her words, Stella Dyson ordered the ambulance that would take away this sad, disordered man, that would carry him into real madness. Because in the opinion of many doctors, Stella among their number, the way to true insanity lay behind doors that were locked and bolted against reality. The chances of recovery lay not within those walls but in the patient's desire to escape. And that desire came only when sanity began to rear its head once more.

Yet there was no alternative. She could not leave him here, could not abandon him, could not remove him to a place that was not secure. Drying her tears, she went upstairs to inform Mark of the latest development. First Molly, now Matthew. The house called Coniston was falling down.

When he woke Joe Dyson was not in the best of moods. He had slept in all his clothes, both indoor and outdoor, including his best suit, a navy-striped two-piece bought for a few bob a week. Its first outing had been yesterday at his daughter's funeral, and it looked as if it might never be fit to wear again unless he got it to the cleaner's soon.

He staggered up from the hearthrug, his memory temporarily impeded by sleep and drink. Then the full picture raced into his mind, cutting across his consciousness like a hot knife through butter. There was nothing left, just a few piles of old rags, a couple of cushions and the base of a sofa, unpadded, its covers cremated yesterday in the back garden. It was unreal: she was not the type, had always been cowed and afraid.

If he could only get his hands on her he would break her scrawny neck, would snap it in two like a stick of Blackpool rock. She wanted showing up, she did, should be dragged across the town hall steps in sackcloth and ashes; hanging, drawing and quartering would be too good for her.

He wandered into the kitchen, what was left of it. There was no kettle, but he found an old pan and set it to boil on the stove, then opened the cupboard to find tea. There was none. In fact, there was none of anything, bread, butter, jam, all gone, cupboards as bare as a newborn baby's backside. Under the sink yielded nothing, just an old pan-scrub, some carbolic soap, not a sniff of the brown ales he had stashed in there a few days ago. Had he drunk them all? No, he hadn't. And she hardly touched the stuff, wouldn't have dared to shift it. Until now. Until yesterday.

Right, this was a bloody pickle and no mistake. He hadn't a penny to his name, couldn't go out and earn, not in this suit. Had she really got rid of all his clothes? What about his ladders? Dear God, they were wooden – aye, they would have gone up a treat on that fire of hers. He dashed outside, found his ladders chained to the downspout, bucket, chamois and cloths nearby. Well, that was something, he supposed.

Now, what about his breakfast? He cast a bleary eye up and down the back-street, wondered who to ask. He was bloody starving, needed a fry-up to settle his stomach, fancied a couple of rashers, some eggs, a nice bit of black pudding. No flaming chance. The bitch had ruined his reputation round here, had turned them all against him.

He'd tried their Philip last night, hadn't he? Aye, he seemed to remember going to that shop and being told to bugger off. He'd have no better luck with their Tony and their Eddie, both wed with kids, both on shifts down the mines, both with wives who wouldn't even open their bloody doors to their father-in-law.

Which left Stella. A deep unease crept into his stomach and kept very poor company with raging hunger. No, he wasn't frightened of their Stella. He remembered her when she'd had a snotty nose, just another kid from round here, no airs and graces at the start. Why should he be afraid to visit his own daughter? Em had always insisted on staying away, as if she was ashamed of herself, but he was a man, so he could face anything. Couldn't he? He coughed. Their Stella would probably tell him to bugger off, too, especially if he arrived up Chorley New Road in this suit.

Flora Crompton's back door opened and he

seized his chance. 'Have you seen the state of this lot?'

She stood still, eyes rounded, looked like a hare caught in headlights, terrified, frozen. Then her mouth opened and closed a few times, though no sounds escaped from between her lips.

'Look what she's done,' he shouted. 'Nowt to eat, no tea for a brew, no milk, no bread. I'm supposed to go to work in this best suit, and I've had to sleep in it.'

Flora opened her mouth just once more, slammed it shut, followed suit with her door.

Joe Dyson shook his head. All he wanted was a hot drink, a bit of food and something to wear while he did his window round. An honest worker, he was, worn out with it all, sorry for himself, a wronged man. Nobody gave a damn; he might as well just lie down and die.

'Mr Dyson?'

He looked towards the gate. That miserable-looking woman from across the back had arrived, chest as flat as a board, hair scraped into a net like something out of an old photo of munitions workers. 'What do you want?' he asked.

Tilly's words almost stuck in her craw, but she wanted to put him right off the scent. 'I've brought you this.' She thrust a greaseproof-wrapped package in his direction. 'I knew she'd gone and I saw what she did, so I made you a couple of bacon butties.'

His mouth watered as he accepted the gift. Without a word of thanks, he tore off the paper, threw it to the ground and sank his teeth into manna. After a couple of noisy mouthfuls, he went for the kill. 'I can't work,' he whined. 'She's got rid of all me clothes – this funeral suit's all I've got. Do you think you could see if you've any old cast-offs? It's just so I can work.'

Tilly contained herself. Instinct told her to give him a good talking-to, but she nodded and walked back to her house. As she leaned against her closed gate, she comforted herself with the certainty that, one day, someone would kill Emily Dyson's husband.

When she re-entered the scullery, she placed a hand on Emily's arm. 'Don't say a word,' she said, 'I'm just throwing him off the scent. Yes, I'd sooner be chucking him in the cut with a bag of bricks round his neck, but I can only do me best.'

She put together a few of her son Stuart's old clothes, stuffed them into a brown-paper carrier, then took them across the back-street. 'Here,' she said, 'that's all I could find. Our Stuart left these here years ago when he moved out.'

He peered inside the bag, sighed, muttered something about supposing they would have to do.

Tilly, her temper simmering, dashed back to her home before she boiled over. It was a good job she lived in the town, because if she had been a farmer's wife with a gun for shooting vermin, she would surely have rid the world of one of its most obnoxious rats. She slammed her back door, turned the key. 'I shall have to lock meself in,' she told Emily, 'because I can't trust meself within a mile of yon bloke. How did you put up with it, eh?'

But Emily had got past worrying about that: the full weight of yesterday's actions had hit her in the face, and she gazed into a future whose only certainty was its uncertainty. She had four kids left, each with his or her own way to make, no room for surplus baggage. Stella was educated, would not want to be dragged down by a gutless mother; Phil, coming up in the world, had met a nice woman and Emily wished him all the best; the other two, Tony and Eddie, were married with children, houses scarcely big enough now, certainly not fit to take in yet another dependent relative. And she was too old for a fresh start, new job, different address.

'I didn't say it would be easy,' said Tilly, 'but there's no use letting it all drive round in your mind like a ride at the fair.'

'Rides stop,' said Emily, 'when the man in the middle puts the brakes on, but I haven't got any brakes.' And there was certainly no music to this flaming ride, unless she imagined a funeral dirge. Poor Molly. Bright as a button, eyes shining because she'd found a new book about dancing, a photo of some woman called Markova up on her toes, arms outstretched, dying swan. How had she managed to remember that? Their childhoods had slipped by unnoticed while she had spun cotton in the daytime, quick bite to eat, then off to the cinema, pick up the torch, show people to their seats, try to stay awake for the same film five nights on the trot.

'We'll think of something,' Tilly promised.

'Will we? What's there to think about? Me family's a shiftless lot. Only Mam was ever any use and she's long dead, God love her. I've no friends—'

'You've got me now.'

'Aye, and how long will that last when he starts putting housebricks through your windows?'

Tilly drew herself up. 'Nobody says who stops here, nobody except me and Seth, and even he usually does as he's told. See, people think I'm hard on him, but he needed a mother as well as a wife, so he's not been put in his place as much as folk think. He's secure and it's what he wants. He was short on framework, so I gave him Blackpool Tower and he stood up once he had that bit of scaffolding. Emily, we'll look after you.'

'You know I daren't stop here, Tilly.'

'Aye, well, that's as may be. For now, Joe Dyson thinks I'm his friend, what with bacon butties and them clothes for work. Back gate's bolted in case he comes begging for more. Let him go off on his rounds and—'

'Heck,' interrupted Emily, 'what about the Co-op? I should be there for three hours this afternoon.'

'You're not going – he'd find you.'

'I know that. But who's going to tell the boss?'

'Everybody,' answered Tilly. 'Including me. By dinner-time, they'll have found somebody else to talk about. And, no, I shall tell nobody you're here. I've to go up in a minute for some spuds and a cabbage, then I'll be able to tell you what's being said. In fact, I shall go now. Pass me that shopping-basket, then get the kettle on. There'll be that much chatter going on in yon shop, we'll be ready for a cuppa when I get back.'

Tilly queued at the top end, where Mr Simpson was serving. The manager, when he served, always stayed furthest from the door, often with a STATION CLOSED sign in front of him, as he had all the paperwork to do. He tallied dividend sheets, ordered goods and supervised his staff, all the time wearing a friendly smile, unvaryingly polite and gentle.

Once she reached the front of the queue, Tilly placed her basket on the mahogany counter. 'Can you weigh me five of King Edwards, please?' she asked.

'Certainly. Chilly for September, Mrs Povey?'

'Yes. I bet it's chilly for Joe Dyson now as that fire's died down. Emily seems to have destroyed everything in yon house. I'm surprised she didn't set fire to the back door and all.'

Mr Simpson weighed the potatoes, shovelling them into the scales. 'Did you say cabbage, Mrs Povey?'

'I did.'

'One moment, please. I have some fresher ones in the yard.' He waddled off, his brown overall seeming to flap even more than usual as it billowed behind a wearer too plump to allow for fastened buttons. Contrary to Tilly's forecast, the shop, though moderately full, was as quiet as an undertaker's parlour. It was plain to Tilly that everyone here knew the story, right down to the fact that Emily was at 301 Tonge Moor Road. She waited, fingers tapping on the counter. What was he doing? Growing the bloody cabbage?

He returned, face pinker than ever, his eyes glued to Tilly's face. 'There's the recipe I promised you, Mrs Povey. My mother swore by it.' His expression was deadpan. Tilly got the message. She palmed the note, smiled as sweetly as her face allowed, paid for her goods and left the shop.

At home, Emily had brewed and was cleaning the grate. She had to work for her keep and Tilly understood that. 'Sit down a minute,' she said. 'Mr Simpson's sent you a note. Oh, and thanks for all the groceries, love. There was no need—'

'Oh, yes, there was. I wasn't leaving him anything, I'd rather you had the bits and pieces. Throwing them away would have been a sin.' She sat, took the note and read aloud, ' "Dear Mrs Dyson, I heard about your troubles and I am glad that you are with Mrs Povey, who is a good and honest person. I know that you will not be able to come to work, but please do not worry. If he comes into the shop, he will be dealt with. Also, if you need a reference or any kind of help, do not hesitate to ask. I remain your good friend, Archibald Simpson." '

'What a lovely man,' declared Tilly. 'Now, come on, dry your eyes and we'll have a gingernut to dip in our tea. Aye, he's a good one, that Simpson, damned sight nicer than that po-faced bugger we had during the war. Hey, Emily, do you remember him?'

Emily dashed a tear from her cheek. 'Oh, God, yes. I think he slept there, you know, guarded that place like a quartermaster on the front lines. He could shave cheese that thin you could see through it. And ugly – I swear he could send butter rancid just looking at it.'

'He had a hammock in the store room.'

'Aw, Tilly, you're joking.'

'I'm not. Three bloody years he lived there, shaving tackle on a shelf near a great big sink, clothes behind a curtain in the corner. I think he knew every rat by name, because he'd tell me he'd caught Reginald and Bertie – took me a while to work out what he meant. Slept in an ARP tin hat, too, gas mask next to his hammock.'

'Give over.'

'It's true – I did his washing and ironing. They took him away at the finish in a big blue van, kicking and screaming, he was. That was because he started shouting, "Halt, who goes there?" to every poor bugger who walked past the back gate after closing time, thought he were guarding Buckingham Palace. Aye, that were a rum do.'

Someone rattled the front door and both women stopped laughing immediately. 'Get upstairs,' ordered Tilly. 'Take your cup with you. Go on, hurry up.'

Emily gulped, grabbed her tea and shot off up the stairs. Tilly waited until her new friend had negotiated the second flight up to the attic, then she sauntered nonchalantly to her front door. 'Hello.' She could not keep the surprise from her tone. 'I don't pay till Thursday, Phil.'

He nodded nervously. 'I know. I've not come collecting, Mrs Povey. Mrs Crompton says she thinks my mam's here and she says to tell you that all the neighbours are together and they won't say anything to him. Oh, and she told Mr Simpson, so Mam hasn't to worry over her job.'

'Get that bike in here,' muttered Tilly. 'We don't want to advertise.'

Phil parked his bike in the hall, then followed her into the kitchen. Tilly doubled back and shouted Emily's name up the stairs. 'Come down, it's only your Phil.'

Emily descended the stairs very slowly. Listening to the faltering steps, Tilly whispered to her newest guest, 'She's scared to death, so go easy on her.'

'Don't worry, I will,' he promised.

Emily came in, a hand to her mouth. She stood two or three feet away from the table, looking as if she expected trouble. When Phil smiled at her, she joined them, perching nervously on the edge of her chair.

'Mam,' he began, 'don't worry, I think you did the right thing. The fire's out now, by the way, I had a quick shufti before. He's out and all, ladders have gone, so he'll be earning his beer money.'

Emily nodded mutely.

'You forget I'm the oldest,' he continued, 'so I remember more than the rest of them. You did your best.'

'I were never there, Phil.'

'No, you were never there because you were out doing what he should have done, putting food on the table and clothes on our backs. Nobody can be father and mother, nobody. Aye, you were like a stranger at times, but what else could you do?'

'I don't know, love.'

'Well, neither do I, so stop looking backwards and start looking at where we are now.'

Emily bit her lip. 'Where you are is here when you should be working. And where I am is called homeless.'

'Not while I draw breath,' insisted Tilly. 'Even if my Seth has to build a drawbridge and a moat, that swine'll not get near you while you're in my house. Now, I'll leave you to talk to your lad, I've got some salty gammon wants boiling and skimming.' She went off into the scullery.

Phil reached across the green gingham cloth and took his mother's hand. 'I want you to listen to me. Don't say anything until I've finished, or I shall forget me drift. All right?'

She smiled encouragingly at him.

'Mam. I've been saving up and I'm nearly ready for a deposit on a house. It won't be much, two up and two down, bathroom if we're lucky—'

'But that's for you,' interrupted Emily.

'Mam, shush and listen, right?'

'I just thought I'd—'

But Phil drove on. 'Now, our lads and our Stella will be thrilled to bits when I tell them what you've done. They'll chip in with a few bob a week if needs be, especially our Stella. You're fifty-nine and you can't work for ever, so we'll see to you. I'm not fixed right to have you at my flat just now, because me bed's in the living room and the kitchen's about the size of a stamp, but just give me a bit of time. Will that do you?'

She dabbed at eyes that had been excessively leaky of late. 'What about Annie?'

'What do you mean, what about Annie? What's Annie got to do with it?'

'Well, I just thought—'

'Mam, just because I've had a few cups of tea with somebody, that doesn't mean we're having the banns read. Nay, we'd have to be eating chips out of the same newspaper before we could be called wed. So, Mam.'

'So what?'

'Exactly, so what?'

In the scullery, Tilly Povey rubbed at an eye. She wasn't crying, oh, no. It was just a speck of dust, wasn't it?

The silence was deafening. Stella Dyson sat in the dead house of her dead sister, her mind still filled by the noises Matthew had made while they had taken him away. Oh, God, that term, 'taking him away', it was a joke from her childhood, a comment made in fun between friends, neighbours, members of a family – 'Put your face straight, else the men with white coats'll come and take you away.' Well, when that happened in reality, it was not in the slightest way amusing.

Mark, who had refused point-blank to go to school, had disappeared with the dog just minutes after his father had left. The lad had lost both parents, one committed to the earth yesterday, the other committed to the mental hospital today.

Well, that was one thing she could tackle. Matthew would certainly not stay in that hospital. He was reasonably wealthy and could afford to go somewhere rather more salubrious – it was just a matter of finding out where. Stella knew little enough about general hospitals, let alone psychiatric facilities, and she knew even less about what was available in the private domain.

The back door opened and she went to greet Mark, surprised to find Simon MacRae entering the kitchen, 'Simon—' she began.

But he cut right through whatever she was about to say. 'Stella, he can't stay there.'

'I was thinking the same thing myself.'

He continued. 'A perfectly normal and evenly balanced person would become insane in one of those places. Have you any idea how many psychiatrists go crackers?'

She shook her head.

'More than a few, Stella. And when they do fall apart, they never go to where they dole out their own medicine, oh, no, not them, not a public psychiatric hospital. They go elsewhere.'

'Where?'

'That's what I'm going to find out. Stella, if I could have hung on to him, I would have done just that. But we could not have ensured his safety. He will be fed and cared for where he is and that will give us the chance to find a more suitable placement. Also, as I am sure you will agree, Mark has seen quite enough.'

'Thank you.' She burst into tears.

Simon MacRae hesitated. He had kept an eye

on this woman for some time and even admitted to himself that his interest in her was strong, was not just a passing fancy. Pulling her into his arms, he stroked her hair and made soothing noises. She would make a wonderful partner in more than one sense, but he should not be thinking about such things at the moment.

'I'm sorry,' she wept.

'So am I, Stella. He's a good man who has simply had enough. You have all had enough, including Mark. He, too, must be watched. While mental illness is not, *per se*, contagious or infectious, it can unseat members of a patient's family to the point where they, too, become excessively depressed or anxious.' Determined not to obey the instincts of his body, he drew away from her. 'I have spoken to the seniors in your practice and they do not expect to see you for several days.'

'Thank you,' she repeated.

'I shall find somewhere, Stella.'

'Somewhere close by?'

He nodded. 'Scout's honour. Now, make yourself something to eat, try to relax and leave all the donkey work to me.' He left as quickly as he had arrived.

For want of something to do, Stella wandered upstairs to begin tidying the devastation left by Matthew. She looked at the bed where he and Molly had made love countless times, where she, Molly's sister, had allowed herself to succumb, just a matter of hours earlier, to the advances of a seriously ill man. Oh, for some peace from these feelings of guilt.

She picked up scarves, gloves, handkerchiefs, underclothing, pushed them back into drawers that still hung open. Then, as she placed jewellery in a huge antique case, she touched a tiny knob and a secret compartment revealed itself. And there she saw dozens of letters, notes that had been passed between Molly and her lover, one set tied in blue ribbon, another in yellow, some in red. She hesitated, closed the mechanism, opened it again. Here on paper was Matthew as she had never known him, as she intended to know him. Or would she know him? Would he ever be completely well again?

Determined to act honourably at this point, Stella closed the case firmly. But she knew now where to find the letters. Should she need or desire to do so, she had only to press a button and there he would be, spread out and unprotected, hers to learn. He would get better, he had to. The alternative was unthinkable.

She stripped the bed, could smell him on the sheets, soap, warmth, Matthew. That Povey woman would be here at some stage, so she could wash the sheets and pillow-cases. Now, Stella must go to the shops for food and other essential supplies, would need to produce meals for herself and for Matthew's son. Molly's son, too, she reminded herself.

Where was Mark? At what point did one begin to worry about a missing boy? Was he missing? What did he like to eat? Questions, questions, while exhaustion seemed to eat into her very bones, draining her not only of strength, but also of thinking power. She lay on the bedroom sofa, intending to rest for just a few moments.

'Aunt Stella?'

She sat up.

'I brought you a cup of tea. You were asleep for a while and I didn't want to disturb you.'

'Thank you.' She had meant to shop, cook, keep house for her nephew, but she had been useless. 'Have you eaten?'

'Eggs and bacon,' he replied. 'Do we know how Dad is?'

Stella sipped her tea. Matthew would be sedated, forcibly put to sleep, because disturbances were not allowed on wards for the mentally ill. From the little she had heard and seen during her training, it seemed that psychiatric units were run for the convenience of staff rather than for the improvement of patients. No one was allowed to rage, especially at night. He would be in a bed with neat corners, a bed that matched all the others, regimented, perfect, silent.

'Aunt Stella?'

'No, there's no news yet, Mark.'

Symptoms, masked by the application of heavy drugs, would be left untreated. Really, the places were unofficial prisons into which society placed members who did not conform, who made life difficult for family, neighbours, community. Placed together like sheep in a pen, the poor souls drifted along on a sea of medicines, glassy-eyed, uninterested and without hope.

Mark saw her pain and crept out of the room.

Stella remembered learning about cases

concerning people who had been trapped for ever, lost within mental hospitals, no help, no hope, no real attempts to return them to relatives who no longer wanted them. No one wanted them; they lived in a twilight world, souls confined for ever to the valley of the damned.

Where was Mark? She rose and walked to the door. Matthew would not become one of the damned, she would make sure of that. At Mark's door, she stopped and knocked. 'Hello?'

'Come in.'

Stella entered. 'I'm so sorry – I was half asleep when you spoke to me.'

'It's all right,' he said. 'I've got used to being ignored.'

'It's not all right.' He looked so young, so vulnerable, lying on his bed. 'Things will get better, I promise,' she said.

'No,' he answered, 'they won't, Aunt Stella. Before Mother died, they were together all the time and I wasn't needed. Now, I'm all he has left, but I'm still not enough. He should be with me. He should care too much about me to get ill. But, no matter what I do or say, I'm not really here – I don't matter. A lot of people die – every day people die. And mothers who are widows look after their children. Fathers whose wives die look after their children. They all do, they all stay with their children. When one parent dies, the other takes over. But not my dad, oh, no – he has to go to pieces. He never spoke a single word to me after my mother died.'

'Mark, I—'

'He wouldn't notice if I disappeared. I tried everything, getting antiques, reading about them, learning hallmarks, trying to tell him what I knew. But he used to look straight through me – I might have been a window for all the attention he gave me. So why am I here?'

Stella, taken aback by this tirade, could not think of a single sensible word that might help to form an answer. The boy was hurt, terribly damaged. She should have noticed – no, they should all have noticed.

'I don't know what to do,' he said now. 'I feel as if I shouldn't be here, that I should be living with people who care, who will help me, talk to me, teach me things we don't learn in school.' He sat up and leaned forward. 'I'm not stupid, you see. But I don't want university, don't want to stare at books for the next five years, yet my father doesn't know that. He doesn't know anything about me, because he's too worried about himself. I don't know how he felt about my last report, don't even know whether he read it, because he never mentioned it to me. Now, he's gone. And I feel like going, too.'

Stella had no idea how to cope with this. It was too big, too much for her. 'You mustn't go anywhere,' she told him. 'You're only sixteen—'

'Old enough to leave school and get a job,' he said.

'But, Mark—'

'What?' His voice was louder now, higher in pitch. 'I'll tell you what, Aunt Stella. From now on, I'm alone. I have no family and no duty to anyone.

Alone is how I have been for as long as I can remember, so alone is my choice from now on. My choice, my own. Matthew Richards is no longer my father. Please close the door as you leave.'

She staggered away from the bed, a hand to her forehead, her mind reeling. Her mouth opened of its own accord, yet no sound emerged, because there really was nothing she could say. The boy was right. Matthew had devoted all his time to Molly, then Molly had died. The rest was such recent history that she had no need to think about it.

Mark turned to the wall and drew his knees up to his chest. His parents' love for each other had been special, almost all-consuming. But would it have stayed like that? Would he have felt left out for ever, or might they have changed? He would never know. Six years old when his mother had contracted her first cancer, Mark Richards had watched while Matthew had pulled up the draw-bridge, while he had fought ceaselessly to find a cure for Molly's illnesses. The tears pricked. He should have looked after me, too. Was he being unfair? Was he?

On the landing, Stella realized that her hands were shaking. Nevertheless, she pressed on, determined to do the ordinary things. People needed a pattern in life, some form and predictability to which they might cling in their darker hours. And this hour was very black indeed.

She found clean sheets and blankets, made up Matthew's bed, went downstairs to check on the dog. When Bess had been out and come in again,

Stella made a piece of toast, another cup of tea, stared unseeing at the newspaper. What if Mark ran away? Had he sounded as if he might do that? Perhaps the answer was that woman, the one who helped in the house several times a week. Povey, that was the name. She would be here soon . . .

She put her head in her hands. Dear God, she had asked for none of this. 'Oh, Molly,' she muttered, 'tell me what to do. Please help me.'

And it arrived then, the grief and sadness that she had skirted during these past two days. Molly, so beautiful, so kind and gentle. Molly with that thick sheet of hair down her back, Molly playing marbles in the gutter, Molly singing at a school concert: Mam hadn't been there, because she would have been working right through both houses at the cinema; Dad hadn't been there because he hadn't cared enough to stay sober.

So that was it. Joe Dyson had not cared enough to stay off the drink; Matthew Richards, in his son's opinion, did not care enough now to stay out of the mental hospital. The same history, the same film, please, God, let the ending be different.

She went upstairs, sat in Matthew's room, wept softly. Her daydreams were of Molly and Matthew, of Mam and Dad, of schooldays and games. As she slipped into a fitful siesta, she saw a lost little boy in a roomful of strangers. No matter what she did, that child remained alone and abandoned by the fates. This was a cruel, vicious world, best not thought of, best not worried about. It was time to stop her own pain, time to start being sensible.

Four

Annie Hurst lived in a neat terraced house on Thicketford Road, a pleasant thoroughfare that owned a few little shops, a church and many houses like Annie's. She was the sort of woman whose looks were unremarkable – average height, mid-brown hair, no flaws, no areas of outstanding merit. Only when a person got close to Annie did those soft brown eyes become beautiful; only when a person sat for some time with Annie did her soul shine through to advertise a woman of good humour and great kindness.

In recent months, her humdrum life had picked up in pace, because she had finally met a man as gentle and as sweet as George had been. George, now laid to rest in Tonge cemetery, had been a steeplejack who had gone to his work one morning and never returned. His fall had been from a height that had left his remains unrecognizable, so Annie had never been able to bid him goodbye. Closed coffin, closed chapter, heartbreak locked away in a part of her mind that she seldom visited.

She spent her days knitting and listening to the radio. The former activity brought her a small income via a wool shop just three doors away from her house, while the latter filled her mind with music and chatter, thereby allowing little space for fretting. Annie accepted her lot, bore it, lived in the quiet hope that things would improve with time.

Then the insurance man had arrived to carry her through the small print of her policies. Philip Dyson was the best man she had ever known – except for George. He even reminded her of him, not too tall, sandy-brown hair with a tendency to recede, blue eyes, soft voice, a man who genuinely cared about other people and their fate. It was an easy friendship, no need to dress up, no fuss about how her hair looked, no necessity to impress him with home-made pies and cakes. She cooked for him only when she cooked for herself, no need to lay out a red carpet for Phil Dyson.

She waited for him, knew that he would arrive exactly on time, found herself worrying when he did not come. What had happened to him? Had a car hit his bicycle, was he lying by the roadside, would there be another closed coffin? Thus it was that Annie Hurst fell in love with a man who wasn't even there; it was his absence, not his presence, that proved her feelings.

She put down the baby's shawl she was making for the shop, got up, walked to the window. It was a small bay, so she could stand right in the corner and see all the way up to the junction with Tonge Moor Road where the Starkie public house sat.

There was no sign of him and he was now over half an hour late.

Perhaps some other widow had been created; perhaps he was going through another devastated person's policy. No. He would have come here first, would have warned her about the delay. Although the situation had never been discussed, Phil understood her nervousness, was sensitive enough to realize that she worried about him. This knowledge served only to make her more edgy, and she found herself pacing back and forth in the small living room, head filled with all kinds of pictures, none of them pleasant.

By the time the door knocker rattled, Annie was close to tears. She dashed through the hall and tore open the door. 'Where have you been?' were her first words. 'I've been out of my mind with worry.'

He knew then that she was the right one, that she cared a great deal about him. 'I'm sorry, so sorry. It was my mother – I had to go to see her.'

She led him into her sitting room. 'It's just with George dying like he did, so suddenly, I worry that the same thing might happen to you. People get nervous, you know.'

'I won't get killed.'

'You're on that bike with all those cars and lorries, you could be knocked down and flattened. Stop smiling at me – it's not funny.'

'No, I'm sorry,' he said again. He was grinning because she cared. After the morning with Mam, it was a wonderful surprise. Annie was not a demonstrative woman, was not given to declarations of emotion, so he knew that she must be serious. 'I'll make sure it doesn't happen again,' he promised. 'If I get held up, I'll let you know. As long as I'm not held up at gunpoint, because I wouldn't be able to come and tell you so—'

She hit him with a tea-towel, thereby putting an end to his hypothesizing.

Annie made tea and they sat in the habitual comfortable silence. Then Phil told her about Mam. He had not mentioned his family before, not because he had avoided the subject, but it had simply not arisen. 'So she's stuck with Mrs Povey, running to the attic every five minutes, scared to death of the old man turning up. She's a good sort, is Mrs Povey, but you can see she's worried underneath it all. My dad's dangerous sober. Drunk, he could start a revolution before tea-time.'

Annie heard the full story, finished her tea, pondered for a few moments. 'Bring her here,' she suggested. 'If you think he's going to find her at Mrs Povey's, let her stop with me. There's room and she knows round here, the shops and all that – she'd be at home, like. We'd be company for each other and all.'

'Aye,' said Phil. 'Only so does he – my dad. He knows round here, too, cleans windows up and down this stretch when he feels like it. He drinks at the Starkie – and another thing, Seth Povey may not be up to much, Annie, but he's a bloke. You'd be here on your own, two women, and he's as mad as a box of snakes when he's got himself outside of a few pints. And you're not that far from the Starkie. Imagine the damage he could do.' He shivered. 'He even put the wind up me last night when he came to Mrs Burton's shop, and I was ready for him with a rounders bat. No, love, she can't come here, else I'd be round the bend with worry about both of you. It wants thinking about, does this, Annie.'

She hadn't thought, but she was thinking now, all right. This was the wrong way round, but it wanted doing. He was going to sit there like last week's cabbage, nothing to say, too timid to get to the point. Annie knew her place. She was only a woman, but she had an idea about what needed sorting out. There was no point in hanging about: time moved on, skipped by, life changed and people disappeared. 'Phil?'

'What?'

She took in a huge draught of oxygen. 'You're on your own, I'm on my own, and your mam needs somewhere to live, right?'

'That's about the size of it, yes.'

'You've got money saved, I've got a house. So I sell this house, add the money to the money you've got – after I've paid off the mortgage.'

He scratched his head.

'Then we get married,' she said, chin raised, a determined edge to her soft voice. 'I could sit here till the cows come home and you'd say nothing, Phil.'

'Erm—'

'Never mind "erm". You need looking after, I need looking after, your mam needs looking after.

Bring her round for her tea as soon as you like.'
She paused. 'All right? For goodness' sake, Phil,
say something,'

Phil coughed. He seemed to be engaged. 'Yes,'
he said.

Annie laughed at him. 'Well, I reckon that's the
most romantic proposal I've ever had, Phil.
Thanks for going down on one knee, ta for this
lovely ring and I'm really enjoying my
champagne.' She drained her teacup.

'It's funny,' he said, 'because I was just telling
my mam that people aren't tied to one another till
they've eaten chips out of the same newspaper.'
He stood up, walked to her chair, knelt. 'Annie?'
he said.

'Yes?'

'Do you fancy fish and chips tonight?'

She pretended to consider the prospect. 'That
depends. Can I have salt and vinegar?'

He nodded.

'Peas?'

'Eeh, well, that might be taking things a bit too
far. If we have peas, we could finish up with a shot-
gun wedding. We don't want the neighbours
talking, do we? Tell you what, though. I've only a
few calls today, so how about a trip to town later
on? Have a look for a nice ring.'

'Instead of peas?'

'Aye.'

She spat on her palm, waited for him to do the
same, then she shook his hand, her face a picture
of solemnity. 'All right, then, but I want a bottle of
Tizer with me chips. And a kiss now – as a down

payment. You can pay the rest off in instalments.'

So Philip Dyson and Anne Hurst were betrothed almost by accident just before lunch-time on a September morning. They made their plans for a second-hand ring and an engagement supper from the chip shop. For both, it was a red-letter day.

Tilly let herself in at the back door of Coniston. It had already been a rum day, bacon butties for Joe Dyson, note from Archie Simpson in the Co-op for Emily Dyson, Emily's son coming to see how she was. Now this. 'What do you mean by that? He's gone? Gone where? People don't just disappear off the face of the earth without a good reason. What have you been and gone and done now, eh?'

Mark Richards dragged a weary hand over his face. 'They've put him away in a mental hospital near Manchester. He went strange. Dr MacRae said he wouldn't be safe here, that he needed putting away for his own good. That's all I know.'

Tilly Povey placed herself in the chair opposite Mark's, watched him as he doodled senselessly on a pad. This was terrible. In the last few days, the lad had been through more than most people experienced in a lifetime. 'Who's looking after you?'

Mark shrugged. 'That depends on what you mean by looking after. I've looked after myself for a long time – you know that. My mother was too ill and my dad didn't seem to notice I was there. If you want to know who's in charge of me, that'll be Aunt Stella.'

'And where is she?'

He finished drawing an aeroplane, smoke coming out of its engines, outlined a few clouds. 'She has a lot to do. She's trying to get my father out of the hospital, because the hospital isn't good enough. Then she has to tell another doctor about one of her patients who needs an operation – oh, then there's shopping to do. She'll come back when she finds time for me, no doubt, in a month or so.'

Tilly swallowed. 'So you've been left on your own?'

'There's Bess.' He pointed to the dog in her basket. 'There's always Bess. She never walks out on me unless she really has to. Dogs are like that, you see. Faithful. You can depend on a dog, but not on a person.'

Tilly didn't know what to say. He was hurting so badly that he looked in danger of going over the edge himself, his face white, mouth tense, a twitch at the corner of an eye. If anybody in this house needed help, it was Mark. Mrs Richards was gone and buried, Mr Richards was a grown man, but Mark was still a child. Oh, he was the age when he could leave school and get a job, but he should not have to face it all by himself.

He screwed up his drawing into a ball and looked straight at Tilly. Like Bess, she was interested in him, watched him, seemed to care about him. 'Did you know that my father never spoke a word to me after my mother died? And that for a long time before that we didn't have a real conversation?'

104

She shook her head. She had known, but she did not want to make the boy any more sad.

'Now, I don't know what will happen. Aunt Stella has a job and she'll have to go back to work soon. There's no one else who can stay with me. I suppose I'm old enough to live alone—'

'She's only across the way. She can live here and work there. Come on, Mark, your dad will get better. He won't be in that hospital for ever, you know.'

He didn't want to upset Tilly by telling her that he no longer considered Matthew Richards to be his father. He could not describe the emptiness inside himself, the space where there should have been love and security. There were no words that could colour in the pictures, the memories, the loneliness he had endured after his mother had stopped speaking. 'I wish you lived here,' he said. 'I'd like that.'

Tilly cleared a throat that was suddenly dry. 'What about your grandparents?' she asked.

Again, he raised his shoulders in a gesture of listlessness. 'My father's parents aren't interested in anyone. They care about horses and golf, but not about people. I don't know my mother's parents. They were at the funeral. I think I've seen my mother's mother before, a long time ago, but I didn't know him. Aunt Stella says he drinks a lot and isn't nice.'

'Your grandma's nice,' she told him.

'Is she? How do you know?'

'She lives near me.' She decided that he wasn't ready for the whole truth. 'I've seen quite a lot of her just lately. She's been sad since Molly died, but she's a nice person, Mark.'

'She never visited when Mother was ill.'

Oh dear, thought Tilly. 'There were good reasons for that. Don't judge folk too quickly. Sometimes things get done or left undone for very good reasons. Emily Dyson is a fine woman who has had a very hard life, Mark. Now, it's not up to me to tell you about what's gone on in that family, but you've got to understand that you can't go jumping to conclusions till you know the full story. It's the same with your dad. We're all different and he's ill because of your mam's death. That's not his fault, it's just how he's made. Things might have been very different if your mam hadn't been ill on and off all those years.'

In Mark's opinion, his father was made of very poor stuff. He knew other people whose parents had died, but they had continued part of a family, the single parent doing his or her best, all grieving together, living together. But he did not have the energy for argument. 'I think there's some washing,' he said now, 'and I made a mess on the cooker, spilled fat on it while I was frying some eggs. Sorry about that, I had a bit of an accident.'

Tilly got up and started her job. She could feel his eyes on her back as she scrubbed the hob, as she washed and dried dishes, as she set up the ironing board. Something was going on in Mark Richards' head, something deep. He was airing anger and disappointment, yet there was little obvious emotion behind his words. The boy was up to something and Tilly Povey's bones ached with anxiety.

Stella returned, Dr Dyson, the aunt who should have been dealing with the situation. She piled shopping on the table, asked Tilly to put it away, then dashed off to see about the patient who needed an operation. As Tilly sorted out the groceries, she could feel Mark's eyes continuing to follow her every move. In the end, at the fridge, she stopped and turned to him. 'Don't do it,' she said, her tone very quiet, especially for her.

'Don't do what?'

'Whatever's in your head, the plan you're working on.'

Some people were psychic, it seemed. 'I haven't made any definite plans – yet.'

'No, but you're working your way up to it. I wasn't born yesterday, Mark Richards, and I didn't come down in last week's showers. I've kids of my own and I know when they're up to something – aye, even now when they're all grown-up and gone.'

'Tell me about them,' he said.

She closed her eyes for a second and begged for patience. 'Alan's thirty-one, married to Tricia. They live up Breightmet, and my other son, Stuart, lodges with them. Both my boys are postmen. Then there's our Alice, she's a nurse at the infirmary, lives in a flat at the bottom of Chorley New Road, not far from here. They like porridge for their breakfast, all of them, and they've got brown hair. Will that do?'

'Yes.'

'Right. Shall I get on with what I'm doing or do you want me to draw pictures of them? Or I could bring some photos next time I come.'

'No, thank you.'

Tilly was rapidly reaching the conclusion that Mark could well be in need of the same treatment as his father. On a whim, she grabbed her coat and walked to the door.

'Where are you going?' he asked.

She put a finger to the side of her nose. 'That's for me to know and for you to wonder about. Just carry on drawing aeroplanes and feeling sorry for yourself. Some of us have things to do.' She left the kitchen and closed the door firmly in her wake.

Once certain that he was not following her, she walked round the side of Coniston on to the main road. Oh, he might be watching from a front window, but Tilly was well past caring. It was a case of desperate measures to suit a desperate situation. She crossed Chorley New Road and walked into the surgery. An extremely ugly woman was at the desk. 'Yes?' she asked, the single syllable managing to contain an element that was no stranger to contempt.

'I want to see Dr Dyson.'

'Are you a patient?'

'No.'

'Then what is the nature of your business?'

Tilly sniffed. 'Personal.'

'Well, I'm sorry, but—'

'Are you sorry? Why? What have you done?' Tilly took great pleasure in putting this sort of person in her place. 'I suppose you know that Dr Dyson's sister was buried recently? Well, my business is pursuant to that matter.' She'd read 'pursuant' in a newspaper somewhere and thought it sounded good. 'So, if you would kindly show me where to find her?'

'Bell at the bottom of the stairs,' snapped the receptionist.

'Thank you so much for your kind assistance.'

Tilly rang the bell and a flustered Stella Dyson put in an appearance. 'Come up,' she said breathlessly, turning to run back the way she had come.

When she reached the top of the stairs, Tilly was surprised to find that Stella had company in the form of Simon MacRae, a doctor from another practice, one who had attended poor Mrs Richards. He looked quite at home, was parked in an armchair, legs outspread, coat off, shirtsleeves rolled.

'What is it, Mrs Povey?' Stella asked.

Oh, yes, Tilly could see which way the wind was blowing here, all right. Young fellow-me-lad Dr Simon looked at Stella Dyson as if he owned her, like a man with a new car – lovely lines, ooh, what a nice colour and how many miles to the gallon? She turned her back on him and addressed Stella. 'He's not right,' she began, 'that nephew of yours. I know he's old enough to keep body and soul together, won't starve to death, but he's fretting. He's lost his mam, his dad's in hospital, and he's up to something.'

'He's upset,' said Stella. 'That's only natural.'

Tilly got the distinct feeling that Stella Dyson

was talking down to her and she didn't like it. Some folk were not as well settled as they pretended to be, and this was one of those folk. Dr Dyson might have had her head filled with textbooks and photos of people's innards, but she knew nowt when it came down to the nuts and bolts. 'Now, listen to me,' she said, then stopped dead. 'Can I talk to you on your own, like?'

Simon MacRae jumped up, grabbed his jacket and made for the door. 'I'll contact those people, then, Stella, see about getting Matthew moved as soon as possible.' He closed the door behind himself.

Tilly waited until his footfalls on the stairs had died away, then she turned her attention to the matter in hand. 'That boy is your nephew,' she said, 'and he is suffering. Something else you should know – your mother wrecked the house yesterday and moved in with me.'

Stella lowered herself into an armchair. 'What?'

'Emily's sleeping in my attic because she burned the contents of her own house yesterday. I think it was her way of telling your dad that she's had enough.'

'My God.'

'God had nothing to do with it,' replied Tilly. 'Your mam saw your Molly going under and she just snapped. She couldn't take any more. We've talked a lot, me and Emily. All them years she worked and never got chance to be a proper mother, well, she's blamed it all on him and she's bloody right. He wants stringing up.'

Stella closed her eyes for a few moments. What

next? Molly dead, Matthew locked away and . . . and yes, she had been to bed with him. Now Mam had gone haywire, Dad was living in a shell, Mark was out of sorts. What next, indeed? 'And how do you suggest I cope with all these problems, Mrs Povey? I cannot take my mother in, would not take my father in. As for Mark, there's not a great deal I can do.'

Tilly was suddenly at a loss. How could she train people to love one another, to care for each other? If feelings weren't there, how could she create them? It was a maze, an endless series of passages with no maps, no arrows pointing in any direction, let alone the right one. This woman did not know how to love; this woman had probably never felt love, so how could she pass it on? 'I know you're a doctor,' she said eventually, 'but the answer isn't always on a shelf at the chemist's.'

'I'm not stupid,' said Stella.

'And neither am I. Yes, you've a lot on your plate with Mr Richards ill and a surgery to run, but your mam needs you and your nephew needs you. Now, if they both need somebody, why don't you put them together? Bring Emily down here and put her in yon house. She can have my job if she wants it.' Tilly knew full well that she could go back to her ironing – there were folk all over town who wanted her services.

There was some sense in that suggestion, Stella realized, yet she felt uncomfortable with the thought of having her mother so close by. Yes, she knew that Emily had endured a lot, that Joe Dyson was the real reason why the family had been such a mess, but . . .

'Think about it, then,' said Tilly.

Stella had a lot on her mind, so she decided to offload this burden immediately. 'Don't leave, Mrs Povey.' She paused. 'I would rather you carried on working at Coniston. My mother and I did not really know each other and—'

'No need to tell me,' Tilly reassured her, 'because I've heard it all from your mam. And don't forget, I've known you for most of your life. We might have been out of touch for a while, Stella, but I do know you.'

'Sorry.'

'No bother. All I thought was, with her being stuck in my attic, you being fastened to your job, Mr Richards away in hospital and young Mark coming over all maudlin, you might want to get things organized, make it a bit easier on yourself. And you won't need to be hopping backwards and forwards across Chorley New Road all the while, because the lad won't be on his own if Emily's there.'

'Keep the job for now, please,' pleaded Stella, 'in case my mother and Mark don't hit it off.'

'They will,' promised Tilly. They would. Because Tilly would make damned sure of that.

That woman was here again. Every time he opened his eyes, she was here, great big hairy wart on her chin, teeth that were decidedly yellow and a voice like a foghorn, too much to say for herself and—

'Mr Richards? Are we not going to eat our dinner?'

She never stopped. He had waited all this time for Molly to come, but there was no sign of her. Flowers. Lots of flowers everywhere, a hole in the ground, dog howling, no! Pale, pale sun, almost white, the boy walking away with the dog, smoke behind a tree—

'We're getting upset again, aren't we?'

That hole in the woman's face kept opening and closing, noises coming out, no sense to it. She wanted him to eat. She always wanted him to eat. All he needed was sleep, sleep and peace until Molly came. A blue dress, floating, dancing around her, daisies, summer rain just yesterday—

'Mr Richards. Open your mouth.'

The spoon came nearer, but he was half-way there, just at the bottom of Rivington, long grass, the smell of green, the smell of fear . . . He dashed the spoon away and roared, causing the wart-faced woman to back away. She stank of terror and he was not here, refused to be here. 'I am not here,' he roared. 'I am there, with Molly. Go away. You are ugly, do you hear me? This is hell and you can stay here, but I am going back to Molly.'

Sighing resignedly, the nurse pressed the bell that would summon help.

The others came, big men, white coats, sharp pain, needle, bliss, floating away up to the Pike, top of the hill, Easter Day, Molly laughing, no more pain.

* * *

113

Running away was all very well, but away was the easy part. Any fool could walk off, never a backward glance, hey-ho, here we go – but how to choose a destination? And how to choose a place in which to settle when one was attached to a medium-sized dog? Now, there was the question. Bess was his best friend in the world and he could not abandon her.

At sixteen, Mark was big enough to fend for himself, had access to a bank account into which money had been paid for at least ten years; he had his health, his strength and enough determination to make a life away from Bolton, if necessary. But there was Bess. Dogs got pushed around, dragged about by tides created by humanity, their trust betrayed time after time. Mark knew how that felt.

He continued to doodle idly, creating a row of hills, some trees, a house on a slope, wished that he could find that very house, imagined a big log fire, himself and Bess stretched out before it, toast on a long fork, butter dripping from the knife, peace, perfect tranquillity. 'I'm like a dog,' he told his canine companion. 'They needed just each other, you see, so I was like an animal, something from a different species. Did you know, Bess, that they even wrote letters to each other if they were apart for a few minutes?'

He tried to remember being small, managed to recall attention, a lively mother, days at the fair, holidays by the sea. Then Mother had gone away into hospital and life had never been the same after that. She had quietened, had needed rest, while Dad, always devoted to Mother, had concentrated solely on her. 'Surplus to requirements, Bess,' he said. 'You and I, we're optional extras, so we wouldn't be missed, not at all.'

Mark leaned on his elbows, dug deep in his memory. So close, Mother and Father had been, so inseparable. There had been secrets, little whisperings, looks that travelled across rooms, across time and space. 'They were always kind to me,' he said aloud. 'Perhaps they didn't know that I felt left out. Perhaps I wasn't supposed to feel left out.' He swallowed. 'Both gone now, Bess, and I shall never know how it would have been, how it should have been.' So sick, Mother had become, too sick to be close to a son who had needed her as much as he had needed oxygen . . .

Grandparents. Oh, what a nightmare. The Richardses had always disapproved of Mother, so Dad disapproved of them. They visited two or three times a year, sat stiff and starchy in good clothes, remarked on Mark's appearance, gave him a few pounds, then disappeared quickly to comfort themselves with horses, golf, bridge and the county set. They were not true gentry, as their background had been in the army, then trade, but they rubbed shoulders with tweeds, cashmere and some of the best horseflesh in east Lancashire.

Mother's parents lived somewhere in the Tonge Moor area. Grandmother Dyson had made the odd appearance from time to time, had always been apologetic, quick to leave and seemed to look over her shoulder all the time. Dad's opinion was that Grandmother Dyson was always on the look-out for Grandfather Dyson, a fearsome bully with a fondness for alcohol and no affection at all for work. Mark had a name for Grandmother Dyson: he called her Rabbit, because she always looked ready to run.

So that was that. There was Eagley Farm and a small council house at the other end of Bolton where a wife-beating man drank himself into a stupor several times a week. Aunt Stella was cold; she seemed fond enough of Dad, but Mark was a creature she tolerated, just as she bore with the dog. He was there, he needed to be fed, but he didn't count.

Which left Mrs Povey. She had turned out to be a surprise, a person he could trust, gentler than she appeared, commonsensical, amusing, warm, for such a thin, grim-faced person. But Mrs Povey knew him. It didn't matter that she had learned about his past foolishness, his stupid attempts to impress his father by 'finding' items for the shop. No. Mrs Povey's knowledge of Mark went deeper than that – she knew that he was 'up to some-thing', that he was concentrating hard on . . . On what?

On a dog. He smiled at his faithful friend. She was holding him back, was impeding his progress, yet he was not prepared to imagine life without her. 'Mrs Povey's across the road,' he told Bess. 'She's with Aunt Stella and they'll be discussing Dad. Or they may be discussing me. Oh, Bess, if only we could go to live with Mrs Povey.'

Bess panted her agreement.

The back door opened and Tilly Povey walked

in. 'It's getting like November out there,' she complained, 'freeze your toes off right up to your earholes.'

That was another thing – Mark enjoyed her turn of phrase. Like an antique item, she had her special individualities, those little flaws and foibles that arrived with the truly unique, as if her Maker had left his mark somewhere on that reed-thin skeleton.

'Well, I've got you sorted,' she announced, 'so you can do summat for me. Get your backside out of that chair and fetch some coal in. It's time you fettled, lad. And you can go back to school tomorrow, 'cos you're not that clever, still plenty to learn.'

'How am I sorted?' he asked.

'Fetch yon coal and happen I'll tell you.'

Hindered by Bess, he filled the scuttle from the coal store behind the house and carried it back into the kitchen.

'How am I sorted?' he enquired again.

She glared at him with pretended annoyance. 'Well, for a kick-off, your ill-gotten gains are with the police. They might be a bit bent, because I threw 'em over the back gate of the bobby shop, but it's the thought that counts. I always think a few dents gives silver a bit of character, any road.'

'Thank you,' he said – and he meant it. This was the one adult who could make a joke out of so serious an issue. He imagined her heaving the loot over that back gate, tried not to smile at a mind-picture of her running hell-for-leather away from the police station.

'And your grandma might be coming to stop with you.' She watched his face, tried not to laugh. 'Good God, shut your mouth, there's a double-decker bus coming. I don't mean your posh gran – she'll be too busy polishing her horse-brasses and counting her rosettes. I mean the other one. Emily Dyson, your mam's mam.'

He swallowed audibly. 'The Rabbit,' he said quietly.

Tilly's ears were legendary and she caught all three syllables. 'I've warned you, Mark, don't be so quick to judge. You've got to make room for people.' She sniffed dramatically. 'Same as I've made room for a lad daft enough to go piking about with other folks' solid silver tea-sets. Now, just you give her a chance. She's nice. Now, what is she?'

'Nice,' he said, without enthusiasm. 'Our English master says nice is an insipid adjective.'

Tilly squashed a smile. 'Aye, well, you can tell him from me that if he wasn't . . . what was the word?'

'Insipid.'

'Tell him if he wasn't insipid, he'd have a gradely job. I bet he wouldn't know a pick from a shovel. English teacher.' She produced a loud hissing sound through her teeth. 'Send him down the pit for half an hour on a Monday, that'll straighten him. Now.' She sat down and invited him to do the same. When they were eye to eye, she leaned forward, adopting the air of a conspirator in some revolutionary plot. 'Now. Look at me properly. Never mind that bloody dog, I'm talking to you.'

He obeyed, wishing with all his heart that this little woman could be his grandmother. That was another of her sayings, 'Look at me while I'm talking to you.'

'She needs looking after. Your gran, I mean. She's run away.'

'Run away?'

Tilly nodded. 'Aye, same as you're planning on doing. Am I right?'

He offered no reply.

'The difference is,' said Tilly, her words separated very carefully, 'that she has good reason. You are upset. She is heartbroken.'

Mark would have quite enjoyed being heartbroken, would have loved to own a heart, but all he had in his chest was emptiness, a void where all human emotion should have lived. He was a shell, no more, just a vessel stripped bare of all its contents. Yet no, because he liked this woman, would have been happy to continue indefinitely in her company. That was a feeling rather than a thought . . .

'Mark?'

'Yes?'

'What's going on inside that head of yours? It's like looking at machinery through glass, but glass with a pattern on it. I can see the wheels turning, but I can't tell which direction you're going.'

Well, thank goodness for that, he told himself. He was a book that was almost open for Tilly Povey to read, index and illustrations included.

'I bet you're only here because of yon daft dog.'

Mark allowed himself a tight smile. Life was all

extremes, he thought. There were those who managed to ignore him completely; there was one who seemed to know him like the back of her own hand. How did Tilly Povey manage to be so sensible, so plain-spoken, yet almost as clairvoyant as a gypsy might purport to be? It was because she really cared, he guessed. Tilly was probably no great reader, yet she managed to have insight into most of her immediate world's ills. 'Your family is very lucky,' he told her.

Tilly laughed like a hyena. 'Try telling my Seth that.' She hooted. 'There's times when he'd swap me for a bag of marbles – in fact, he'd likely give you a quid to have me shifted with last week's rubbish. Did I tell you about after the fishing?'

Mark shook his head.

She inhaled deeply and prepared for launch. 'See, with my Seth, you have to keep a straight face. No good laughing at him, 'cos that just makes him worse. He came back wet through and with somebody's false teeth. Just the top set, mind. He's never been what you might call thorough.'

Mark Richards was surprised to find himself doubled over in pain, glee trying to escape from every inch of his skin.

'So I asked him what had happened. God, he stank like a midden in August, Mark, bloody slime all over him, cap missing. You could hear his feet squelching in his boots every time he breathed. No flaming fish, of course, just these teeth and half the bloody river all over my kitchen floor.'

'Stop it,' begged Mark.

'Aye, that's what I said at the time. I had to stick

120

him in the backyard, there were nowt else for it. I stopped short of pegging him to the line, mind. So you know all these folk who put their trophies on the wall? Big fish stuffed? Well, all I got was some poor beggar's National Health choppers and a cartload of ruined clothes.' She wiped her eyes.

'How did he get so wet?' Mark asked.

'Oh, that was the pram. He thought he'd hooked Moby Dick, didn't he? It was the other way round, 'cos he got dragged in by a Silver Cross, said it wouldn't let him go. Ted Moss weren't best pleased – it cost him a good fishing rod. See, I shouldn't really let him out, should I?'

'You can't keep him in, though.'

Tilly's face rearranged itself into severe mode. 'No such word as "can't", Mark. Just think about that these next few days. Whatever you're brewing needs chucking in the swill bin. Remember how I told you about marking days in your life?'

He nodded just once.

'Well, chew on that. No matter how clever you are, on any given day, there's always somebody a stride or two in front.'

'And you are that someone.'

'Yes, son, I am. And don't you ever forget it.'

The argument with the lamp-post began just after throwing-out time.

Joe Dyson, whose credit at the Starkie on Tonge Moor Road had overreached its due date, had come into town to meet some old mates from his pit days. He had replayed his daughter's funeral *ad nauseam*, had cried many tears of pure Magee's ale and was feeling his way home in the general direction of Tonge Moor.

Nobody cared. He had been a victim all his life, had married an old bag who no longer gave two straws for him, was undervalued, undermined and almost under a bus before he had staggered fifty yards. Misery oozed from every wide-open pore on his body. He fell out of the path of the bus and gripped the lamp-post with each ounce of energy he could muster. Home. He was going home – wasn't he?

There was no home. He lived from pie shop to chip shop to pub, had not enjoyed a proper cooked meal since . . . ? Oh, he couldn't remember. And she'd made a lovely steak and kidney pie, had whatsername. Em. Em, aye, that was her name. A blonde, she'd been, but she was fading to salt-and-pepper. And so was he, because salt, pepper and vinegar were all he had left in his cupboard. Except for a bottle of Camp coffee that wasn't fit for a dog.

The lamp-post would not keep still, so he thumped it, recoiling immediately when red-hot knives of pain shot through his fist. There was no comfort to be had, no place for a decent, honest man to lay his weary head. 'Keep bloody still,' he ordered his inanimate support. The earth was turning in an endless circle, arcs of light from shop windows, from the King Billy pub whose landlord had recently ejected him, from inside his own head. He was not a well man. From a pocket, he drew a quarter-bottle of Johnnie Walker and tried to remove the cap. But the container of this precious nectar slipped from his fingers and smashed into a thousand pieces in the gutter.

Infuriated beyond measure, he slithered to the floor and tried to mop up valuable drops of Scotch. Glass pierced his skin, but he was beyond pain now, seeking only to save what he had lost. 'Buggeration,' he cursed, though the word was born with some deformities. Nothing ever went right. The world was a sea of misery and all life-rafts were disappearing fast.

A pair of improbable feet arrived next to Joe Dyson's nose. He stopped licking up the Scotch and raised his head. 'Biggest feet I ever saw,' he said.

The policeman was not amused. 'Stand up, if you can,' he ordered.

Joe dragged himself up with the questionable aid of the lamp-post, which continued to sway like a flag in the wind. He tried to focus on the constable, slid down again, was dragged to his feet by the collar of his one remaining shirt. 'She took everything,' he slurred, 'even the bread and milk.'

'Did she?'

'Not a chair to sit on. Bed wet through. I'll bloody kill her when I find her.'

'Not a good idea, sir. Now, where do you live?'

'Nowhere. It's gone. Set fire to it all, she did. I've got emphy-emph – summat wrong with me tubes. From the pit. Do windows now. D'you need a window-cleaner?'

'No. But you need a good wash. I think we'd best get you indoors, though, before the rain starts, because your skin would get a shock if it felt water.' He manhandled Joe across the road and into the central police station, depositing him at the front desk. 'Look what I found,' he told the sergeant. 'Three sheets in the wind and homeless. Any ideas about what to do with this article, Sarge?'

There were two of them now. Joe struggled to remain upright, eyes sliding from one man to the other, skin crawling with sweat, bladder ready to burst at any second.

'I suppose we could always put him in a jar. God knows, he's pickled enough to keep for a long while. Name?' he asked.

'Joseph Dyson,' managed the swaying drunk. 'She left me.'

'Somebody's got a bit of sense, then,' commented the constable, 'which is a lot more than can be said for this beggar. Found him in the gutter trying to lick his Scotch up. Bloody dog piss and all sorts, more than likely. And he stinks like the fish market before it's had a swill. I'm sorry I had to fetch him in, Sarge, but the Doffcocker bus missed him by about an inch, if that. He doesn't know whether it's Tuesday or breakfast time.'

'It's Thursday,' announced Joe proudly.

'He's right,' said the sergeant. 'It must be, 'cos I know it's Friday all day tomorrow. Shove him in number two, Eric, leave him to sober up.' He pushed his face closer to Joe's. 'Right, you miserable devil, you wet that mattress and I'll do you for abuse of municipal property. Oh, get him out of my sight, will you? And out of reach of my nose and all.'

Joe found himself abandoned in a small cell, just a bed of sorts, thin mattress, one blanket, bucket in a corner. He relieved himself, fell on to the bed and passed out immediately.

He woke with a start, bright light cutting through his skull, throat as dry as a Methodist's, skin trying to crawl off his body, each eye with a raging hot needle in its centre. Bloody hell, there were thousands of them, red, they were, bigger than saucers, crawling up the walls, disappearing under the door, which was impossible, as the door was a very tight fit. They chattered like crickets, but they were spiders, Joe's least favourite among the earth's creatures.

There was one big bugger right next to his face. It had eyes on stalks, a bit like a lobster's, but bright scarlet and evil. He knew then that they were coming for him and he screamed. They stopped moving, every one of them frozen stiff, watching, waiting.

He blacked out again, grateful for the blanket of darkness as it slid over him, warm, protective, opaque. But they got him. He felt them pinning his arms, tying him up, lifting him from the bed. His arms were crossed over his chest, fastened so tightly that he could scarcely feel them. They carried him outside and he came to for a while, saw a vehicle with its back door open, then darkness encompassed him once more.

He woke up in a white place, some big daft so-and-so slapping his face.

'Come on, Mr Dyson, let's be having that stomach washed out.'

Joe tried to warn the man about the big red things. There was one slap bang in the middle of the bloke's head, but no one seemed to be able to shake the creatures off. Neither could Joe Dyson, because, after a short while, the same arachnid started to shove a snake down Joe's throat. He gagged, swallowed painfully, felt his stomach emptying. So they were inside him now, those monsters from some other planet, eight-legged stalk-eyed freaks with serpents growing out of their faces. They were taking over the planet.

His insides screamed, but he could not, because his mouth was full of reptile, the slimy, gut-twisting thing that was probably laying its spawn in his belly. He could feel the eggs hatching; they were already spinning their webs just above his navel.

'That's good,' said some numbskull. 'Nearly done now, Mr Dyson.'

Chattering. They were still clacking all over the room, dark red against white walls, creeping, chirping, congregating, noise louder and louder. The snake dragged itself out of Joe's body and he retched as it crawled away.

There were more people around him now, every single one wearing a giant red spider. 'They're on you,' he managed, his voice bruised. 'All over you, everywhere.'

'Delirium,' announced the man. They gossiped on about rehydration and which ward and half-hour assessments, all the time ignoring the infestation around them. If people wouldn't listen, what could he do? He'd tried to warn them, but nobody wanted to listen.

He finished up in another cell, walls soft, padded like a mattress. They left him there on his own, just popping in from time to time to listen to his heart and take his blood pressure. In torment, he writhed away from the red things, tried to beat them to death with his hands, railed against his containment and his gross misfortune. Nothing could be worse than this, nothing in the world.

But then the purple things arrived . . .

Five

Mark loved the shop. He often went down there when everything was quiet, content to root around among bits and pieces, especially those in which his mother had taken a particular interest. Antiques were probably in his blood: like the two previous generations of the Richards family, he was intrigued by the past, though his mother was to blame for his areas of special fascination – clocks and porcelain.

In this age of teak, plastic and G-plan geometrics, Mark Richards liked to look at real furniture, beeswaxed, shining, and bearing the marks of age with dignity. He lingered, ran his fingers over a rosewood chiffonnier, admired an eight-day Nottingham long-case clock that had measured and witnessed seconds, hours and days since 1830, its dial decorated with wildflower designs, its construction twin-sourced, oak and mahogany.

In one of six rosewood chairs, he sat and gazed around his father's sleeping empire. How long since this place had been open for a full day? he wondered. A month, six weeks, more? It was true to say that antiques-dealing could be a long game, that rooms at the back contained queues of stuff that would not come into its own for ten or twenty years, but the place needed a reveille, a reopening, some fuss, some attention.

For a start, the *fin-de-siècle* Paris bronzes were in want of a wipe, as was a small cluster of Liberty buckles, while a Dutch secretaire was positively filthy. It was nice, too, about 1790, ebony and brass inlays, shelves, cupboards, a spindled gallery at the top. Shame to let it moulder. Nice. His English master had ordered the class not to use that word, so he would use it. Nice.

His fingers itched to pick up and clean some Lambeth and Burslem, a few bits of Liverpool porcelain, a Spode vase, all neglected, all wretched. But he had to go home and meet Grandmother Rabbit, who had run away from her own home and who would, perhaps, move into Coniston for a while. Well, it all promised to be very . . . exciting: a rabbit, Tilly Povey and a boy with no heart, toast, scrambled eggs and small-talk at the kitchen table. Perhaps Aunt Stella would arrive to break the monotony. Such a warm-hearted, sweet soul, Aunt Stella was. He grinned. Stella was honest, at least. She mended broken people for a living and made no effort to be what she was not.

Dad was still away, was not allowed visitors. Aunt Stella and Dr MacRae continued in their efforts to get him out of the hospital and into a private place, but what were they going to use for money?

How long would the cash last? Would they be forced to remortgage Coniston so that Dad could rave in luxury? How safe was Coniston?

It was in that moment that Mark began to understand something: his heritage mattered, his dead mother mattered, this shop damned well mattered. He could not stand by in idleness while Richards Antiques went to the wall, all these pieces snapped up for a song, the place closed only to reopen as yet another shoe shop. According to Mrs Povey, Bolton had more shoe shops than Soft Mick, whoever Soft Mick was. This was the sole antiques outlet in the centre of England's biggest town.

Well, it was too bad. With nine O levels tucked under his belt, Mark had returned to school, had entered the lower sixth, was studying English literature, French and history. For what reason? To end up teaching in some school where he would advise his pupils against using the word 'nice'? To gain a daft gown and a silly hat that he would wear just once for the photos? Where the hell would that get him on the map? He had no wish to teach, to practise medicine or law, nurtured no desire to become an eternal student, a don, a master of this or that. Beautiful things were all he wanted, things that needed a home in which they would be appreciated.

He would be seventeen in a few months. He knew more about antiques than his father realized, was an avid reader of auction manuals, knew what to look for, knew where the future lay, and it didn't lie in nests of matt-finish teak tables and long sideboards – no. The future lay in the past: it lay in that oval-dialled German clock, in the Worcester porter that sat in a corner on the surface of a seventeenth-century oak coffer, so deceptively plain, that coffer, so sturdy, so alive. The future lay in the hands of a dead woman who had embroidered her baby's bed linen so beautifully that it hung on the wall, too precious to be touched ever again, behind glass, preserved and perfect.

The future lay not in stuff stolen to impress a father, oh, no. He needed a good suit of clothes with a waistcoat, crisp white handkerchief in a top pocket, some fine Italian shoes polished to a mirror finish. There would have to be help, of course, someone to clean the place, a sales assistant or two. Then there was the other idea, the restoration side. What was the name of that man? Worked in a barn up in one of the villages, had a healthy respect for injured items.

And Mark needed to clear out a storeroom. Yes, a decent, solid desk, a chair, a sofa for visitors, a book in which to keep the histories of patrons, a list of their interests. Coffee, tea, little biscuits. The place needed life breathing into it, some energy, some hope.

So, the schoolboy who had entered the premises prepared to leave as a man. He would not run away, would not give up just because his mother was dead and his father was weak. He fingered the soft down on his chin and grinned. He must shave more often, must toughen his skin so that the hair would have to work harder to grow, would thicken into a beard. He thanked his mother for the darkness of her hair, because he had inherited it and dark people often looked mature at an early age.

He sat for a while and thought about his parents. In recent weeks, he seemed to have developed to the point where he had begun to understand a little about Molly and Matthew. Like characters from some Shakespeare play, they had loved too much, too completely. 'Whilst I am too sensitive and must grow up immediately,' he told the dusty air. He had to cope, had to fettle, as Mrs Povey would have put it.

Mark Richards picked up his school satchel, stained with ink, worn at the corners after years of being kicked around corridors and cloakrooms. Inside, Guy de Maupassant shared space with Geoffrey Chaucer and a dirty old man called Henry VIII. Mark the student was no more, and the real learning was just about to begin, though he would probably retain his interest in dead writers and defunct kings for the rest of his life. Mother would have approved, he felt sure, because she had known all about hard work and dedication, and that was nothing to do with awards, certificates, *The Miller's Tale*, the beheading of Henry's wives.

He locked up, turned to walk homeward. It was all decided. Let them try to force him to remain at school – yes, let them. He was a man with a future and he strode towards it, heart singing, decisions made. Richards Antiques would reopen very soon.

* * *

Emily Dyson shook all morning. She trembled as she washed and dressed, fidgeted her way through breakfast and lunch, was like a cat on hot bricks as she travelled with Tilly Povey on the 45 bus from Tonge Moor to town. Tilly tolerated this behaviour until they changed buses for the short journey up Chorley New Road, then she snapped. It was like being in the company of someone with St Vitus' dance, all involuntary movement and no sense. 'He's only a lad,' she said, as they got off the second bus. 'Anybody'd think you were on your way to Buckingham bloody Palace.'

'I can't help it.'

'Course you can.'

'How?'

Tilly took a deep breath and prayed for patience. 'Just tell yourself you're as good as anybody else. Hold yourself tall, no rounded shoulders, look every bugger in the eye and get on with it.'

But Emily knew she wasn't good enough for Chorley New Road. This was where all the doctors and dentists lived, all the lawyers and folk with their own businesses. Nobody round here clocked on. These people didn't obey rules, they invented them. They had Venetian blinds and lined curtains, central heating, nice furniture, cars, holidays abroad.

'Will you straighten that face?' asked Tilly. 'You'd stop a clock, honest. Try to look cheerful.' No, that was asking a bit much. 'Oh, God, just look a bit less depressed, will you? Anybody'd think you'd lost a shilling and found a tanner.

We're visiting a sixteen-year-old lad, for goodness' sake. Can you not just take it as it comes, Emily?'

'No. No, I can't.'

Tilly sighed so deeply that she felt it in her shoes. What the hell was she going to do with this woman who had become so precious in such a short time? Yes, Emily had just lost her daughter, had destroyed her house, had finally turned on a pig of a man, but Tilly suspected that Emily had been like this for years, defeated, unambitious, sad. This was the real Emily, the one Mark called Rabbit. 'Where's the fighting spirit gone?' she asked. 'The mood you had on you when you got rid of the stink of him?'

Emily shrugged. 'Happen it went up in flames with the rest of me life.' She stopped, grabbed Tilly's sleeve. 'I don't want to be here, I don't want to be near a daughter I neglected, or with a grandson I don't know.'

'What do you want, then? A bloody good thump with me handbag? Now, just you listen to me, Emily Dyson. Things are going to be all right. You've got me, haven't you? Eh? Look at me when I'm talking to you. We're going in that bloody house and we're going to sort Mark out.'

Emily felt like a leaf in the wind, a member of the autumn dead, ready to be swept away with all the other dried-out stuff. It was too much, all of it. She wanted a rest, a think, time to get herself sorted out. She wanted to go back to the Co-op, back to her own house, back to— No, not back to him, never that. 'All right,' she said resignedly, 'let's get it over with.'

They entered the house at the rear, were greeted by a lonely dog who fussed so happily that even Emily laughed. 'She likes me,' she exclaimed.

'Course she does,' replied Tilly, 'and she's half pedigree. Mind, we don't know what's in the other half, but who cares? Come on, sit yourself down and I'll make a brew.' She stared at the dog, as if trying to work her out. 'Greyhound,' she decided aloud. 'See? Back legs keep trying to overtake the front ones. Aye, I reckon Bess's dad did a few laps at Bolton dog track, Emily.'

Emily settled at the table, a rapturous canine by her side. 'She loved this house, did Molly. I remember her telling me that. She said it were a plain house on the inside, plain, but good-natured, a fit place for all her beautiful pieces. Eeh, Tilly—'

'Don't start, you'll have me skriking and all. See, that dog's all but talking to you. I wonder where Mark is?'

Emily stroked the ebony head and thought about Molly, that lovely girl who had married at seventeen, who had been cut down at thirty-five, everything to live for, cancer gripping on to her until she had rotted away. She'd had a good marriage, though. And now the poor man had gone out of his mind by all accounts and was locked away for his own good. So, next on the list, there was Mark to contend with, a lad she didn't know. He was probably posh, too, all Bolton School and proper talking.

'He'll be at the shop,' said Tilly. 'He likes the shop.'

'Does he?' Emily didn't know anything about her grandson, hadn't known much about her daughter, was not well acquainted with Stella, the doctor across the road from here. Where had all the years gone? And how could she ever quantify the damage done by Joe Dyson? 'What does he want to do when he leaves school?' Emily asked now.

'I don't know,' replied Tilly. 'Ask him yourself – here he comes.'

Mark entered the kitchen, was almost knocked over by Bess, who was bent on celebrating all over again. Once free from the dog, he greeted his grandmother. She still looked a bit rabbit-ish, but she was trying to smile, so that was a slight improvement.

Tilly watched them both, saw the shared discomfort. 'Been to the shop?' she asked him.

'Yes, and I've been thinking.' He placed himself in the chair next to Emily's, reasoning that if he sat there, he would not have to look at her, would not be in a position in which she might stare at him.

'Thinking?' asked Tilly. 'Well, there were no notice up outside the town hall. What are you up to? You've no right thinking without making an announcement. What, then?'

'I'm giving up school,' he pronounced, feeling that since the present company had no vested interest in him, he could use no man's land as a test site for his bombshell. He paused, waited for the storm, waded in again when nothing was said. 'I am going to turn the business round.' Then, for good measure, he threw in some bait. Perhaps these two ladies needed a vested interest after all. 'I shall want help from both of you.'

Tilly moved across the kitchen faster than sugar off a shiny shovel. She raised her left hand and used the digits as counters. 'Right, young fellow-me-lad. For one, you're not leaving school. For two, what are you telling us for? For three, you are *definitely* not leaving school.'

He stared full into those intelligent eyes. 'How do you propose to force me? Strait-jacket? Armed guard? Sedatives? I'm rather large if you intend to drag me there every day.'

Tilly opened and closed her mouth, putting Mark in mind of a newly landed trout. 'You can't just leave,' she managed finally. 'It's not right, it's not proper, you can't do it.'

'And who, exactly, will stop me? Dad? From what I hear, he needs someone to decide when he must wake and eat. Aunt Stella doesn't give a damn what I do, as long as I stay out of her hair. My mother isn't here.' He slid his eyes sideways, saw Rabbit's hands tighten into fists. 'Do you propose to ask Grandmother Dyson?' He swung round and looked at Emily. 'You, perhaps, are in charge of me now, because you're my only relative here today. What do you think?'

What did she think? Did she think at all? 'Give me a minute, let me take this in,' Emily replied. She mulled it over for several moments, wished that the responsibility for an answer could be placed on someone else's shoulders. 'You can always go back to school,' she said, 'but if that business goes down, you and your dad will both be in Queer Street.' She lowered her chin, pondered again. 'There's always night school, Tilly. Let the lad have his head. I think he knows full well what he's letting himself in for.' She met his eyes. 'I'm not much use, but put my name down on your list of helpers.'

'Gladly,' he answered. 'Now, Mrs Povey . . .'

But Mrs Povey had climbed on to an eighteen-hand charger and was carrying the flag into battle. Mark should be grateful for the chance to stay at that 'gradely' school till he was eighteen. He should thank his lucky stars for the chance of an education. There was university, and how many got the opportunity to do a degree? Finally, she made a remark about his mother spinning about in her resting place.

'Below the belt, Mrs Povey. You've taken a step too far and I can see you know it. The decision is made. Tomorrow morning I shall not go to school. I shall be at my father's desk upstairs in the spare bedroom he calls his office, will be going through books and papers. You may, if you wish, bring the police, the fire brigade and the coastguard, but I shall not be going to school.'

Tilly suddenly realized that she was looking into the eyes of a man. He had some growing to do, in both physical and emotional stature, but he knew exactly what he was doing. Mark was trying to save this house and its inhabitants. She blinked away a disobedient wetness in her eyes; he was taking on so much, too much for a boy of his age.

'My mother was married when she was just

months older than I am now. She was learning the trade from the age of fifteen when she first got a job with Dad. Some of us are forced to grow up early. I have no idea how much money Dad has, but it can't last for ever. Someone will have to see a lawyer about all that, probably Aunt Stella, because my father is not fit to look after the business, and I'm too young to be considered responsible enough to take over the finances. But, whatever happens, school is in the past. I can sit here, eat, drink, draw, or I can make use of myself.'

Silence reigned in the kitchen for a few moments. Emily and Tilly looked at each other, looked at him, both realizing that this was no teenage tantrum. He had thought it through, had reached a decision that seemed sensible to him. Tilly, who would have given almost anything for the chance of an education, retained strong reservations, yet was aware that she could do little to influence this young man's mind. Emily, on the other hand, saw the sense in his intentions and agreed with him totally. The shop needed attention and Mark was the last man standing.

'We'll have to see what your auntie has to say,' muttered Tilly. She couldn't see Stella Dyson taking this lying down.

But Emily knew that, no matter what her remaining daughter said, Mark's schooldays were over.

The purple things faded to pink after a day or so, though the red ones persisted for a little longer, gradually disappearing into tiny folds in the padded walls. Getting rid had been hard work, especially when his hands had been pinned inside the back-to-front jacket he sometimes wore. They put that on him when he wouldn't accept his injections, so he gave up in the end, allowing them to do just as they pleased – there were three of them, anyway, big ugly buggers who overcame him in seconds, so there was no point in trying to save himself.

The shakes started. He had a force-nine headache and his limbs would not take orders. Even his spine rattled when he moved, while his skin crawled and both eyes burned because of all the watching for the red and purple creatures. But exhaustion won in the end and he fell into a deep sleep, waking just occasionally when food and drink arrived.

Then the doctor came. He brought the guards with him, of course, as he was a weedy, be-spectacled specimen, all brain, no brawn and an accent that had been manufactured from cut glass. Or, as Joe Dyson would have put it had he been in complete charge of his own tongue, the doctor was a weedy bastard with a gobful of marbles and no guts.

'How are we today?' asked the doctor.

'All right.' He would have to be all right, because he wanted to get out of here, needed a couple of pints to line his stomach, then a meat pie and a drop of Scotch. 'I'll have to get back to work,' he slurred.

'Not yet.'

'Why? I've windows need doing.'

The three male nurses stepped forward. They had seen it all before and were preparing to protect their leader.

'You're an alcoholic,' the doctor said.

'Don't talk so daft.' Joe drew himself up to full height. 'I like a drink, but I can stop.'

'If you could stop, Mr Dyson, you would not be bleeding from certain orifices in your body. Your liver is ready to disintegrate and disappear down the lavatory. You will not be allowed to leave this hospital until you're in a much improved state. If necessary, I shall have you certified.'

Joe looked the man up and down. If the two of them had been alone, he could have beaten this midget to a pulp. Alcoholic? Joe Dyson an alcoholic? That was absolutely ridiculous and, had his tongue been in better shape, Joe would have said so. 'Sod off,' was all he managed.

The doctor opened a notebook. 'The police have been to your house and have interviewed your neighbours. Your wife had reached the end of the road, Mr Dyson. Alcoholism affects whole families, whole neighbourhoods. We know that you have been an abusive husband and father. This is all because of drink and you must stop. Apart from all of that, you are dying. This hospital is your last chance, your only chance.'

Joe smiled. Dying? Was he hell.

But the monotone continued: 'You cannot get through a day without a drink. Once you begin to drink, you're powerless to stop. When you have to stop due to lack of money, you sweat, feel sick, you shake, you become depressed. Oh, and I'm sure you've had panic attacks.'

The smile began to fade.

'To feel happy, or even normal, you now require alcohol. At this point in your life, drinking is not a leisure activity, Mr Dyson. Without a drink, you would fall off your ladders.' He closed his book. 'Now, you will rail against all of that, will deny everything, because drink is a clever substance. It forces you into denial. Right.' He turned to the male nurses. 'These gentlemen will escort you to a ward. You will remain here voluntarily, or I shall use my authority to keep you here against your will. There is no longer alcohol in your system. You will now begin a life without beer or spirits on the menu. You may co-operate, or you may choose to remain here alone, in this padded cell, under restraint. Am I clear?'

Joe nodded.

They led him away through a maze of corridors, stopping now and then to open doors, always locking them again as soon as they reached the other side. Good God, he was in an asylum. This was where they brought lunatics, folk who had lost their minds. They arrived at last at a ward called Churchill and he was ushered through into a space containing about twelve beds. In the centre of the room, two long tables were surrounded by chairs in which a few men sat, some reading, two playing dominoes, another trying to piece together a jigsaw.

'There's been a mistake,' mumbled Joe.

'I know that,' said the biggest nurse. 'Your mam

and dad made it about nine months before you were born. Now, shut up and put up, or you'll be dealt with.'

He was shown to a bed with a green coverlet and a locker by its side. It matched all the other beds except for the one next to him, which was occupied and, therefore, untidy. Joe perched on the edge of his mattress. He tried to think back over the last few days, attempted to piece together what had happened and how he had finished up among the insane. He was not mad: he had gone for a drink somewhere, had been arrested – it was all a mistake. Dying? What a load of rubbish these doctors talked. He had piles, that was why he bled a bit sometimes. God, he could have murdered for a pint of Magee's or a drop of Scotch.

The man in the next bed turned over, opened his eyes, closed them again.

Joe blinked. He recognized that face, had seen it recently. Where? When? Was this another drinker from the Starkie, or was it someone whose windows he'd cleaned? Bugger, his memory was like a sieve. He looked down at his grey cotton trousers, at the soft-soled slippers with which he had been issued. Like a prisoner of war, he was dressed to blend in with the rest of these poor beggars.

He dumped the slippers, lay on his bed, tried to imagine what life in here was going to be like, books, jigsaws, nothing to drink, grey mashed potatoes to be eaten with a spoon because knives and forks were not allowed. They would cut up his meat before delivering it, would expect him to listen while doctors and nurses told him how to live. It was all bloody mental – they were the mad ones, these hospital folk. He closed his eyes and drifted off to sleep.

Matthew Richards waited, kept his eyes tightly shut, knew when the evil being in the next bed had gone to sleep, because the snores were deafening. Molly wasn't coming. Molly was dead, would never come. All that business was straight in his head now, though he could not manage to revive the desire to continue alive. He needed sleep, eternal sleep, wanted to enter the gateway through which Molly had travelled.

Yet he was feeling something else now, a rage that simmered just beneath the surface of the larger pain. Because the fates had conspired to deliver into Matthew's hands one Joseph Dyson, father of the woman he had adored. He looked back through the years, had no trouble remembering the beginning of his marriage, though recent events tended to live in the shade.

She had been fifteen when she had entered his life, fresh-faced, straight from school, just a pretty child, no more than that. For almost two years, Matthew had watched over her, had protected her as if she had been his younger sister. The father had arrived, usually on a Thursday, which had been Molly's payday. The cash had been ripped from her hands and Matthew's heart, already on the brink of capture, had begun to nurse a terrible hatred for Joseph Dyson. The upshot had been that, until her marriage, Molly had worked for next to nothing, because the creature who had fathered her took almost every penny she ever earned.

Both parents had been required to sign a document allowing Matthew to marry their teenage daughter. Emily had been delighted to give her consent; Joseph had milked the situation, had sold his daughter for twenty pounds and two bottles of low-grade Scotch. So that had been Molly's value, just a couple of pints of alcohol and a few weeks' beer money. Her husband had never forgotten the cruel behaviour of Joseph Dyson.

Matthew allowed his eyelids to rise, then fixed his gaze on the vision in the next bed, hanging jaw, nose as bright as a beacon, the threads of alcohol poisoning visible on that ugly face, a network of destroyed blood vessels. 'Take this slowly,' he whispered. 'No sudden moves, Matt, go easily now.'

Determined to take his time, Matthew Richards turned away to face in the opposite direction. He needed the chance to think, to work on a plan. Because murder should not be taken lightly and, of course, he needed his sleep.

It was Friday morning. Emily had listened to Tilly's rantings, was now fully aware of her hostess's attitude. Mark should stay at school, should be grateful for the chance, would be better off at university, could be a lawyer, a doctor, something proper; anybody could serve in a shop. If Tilly had only been given the chance, she would have been in London now, damn and blast these bloody politicians, they hadn't the brains to find their way out of a wet paper bag, it all wanted sorting out by gradely folk with no stocks and shares.

'Oh, Tilly, shut up,' begged Emily.

'Hey, listen, you,' cried Tilly, 'we've got Kennedy and bloody Krushchev ready for daggers drawn, and here we are, piggy in the middle – and Macmillan sacking everybody except the tea-lady, by the way. Then there's bloody Mosleyites traipsing all over London flying the Nazi flag—'

'Oh, give over, Tilly. I've enough on moving to Chorley New Road without you going all political on me.'

'Politics,' announced Tilly haughtily, 'is life.'

'And so's Chorley New Road,' replied Emily. 'And my daughter doesn't know I'm moving there – unless Mark's told her – and my head's busy, so please stop it.'

Tilly suppressed a grin. At least Emily looked in danger of developing an attitude and that was a sizeable improvement. 'All I'm saying is that your Mark is a young man with chances and he's going to let it all go for the sake of a few chamber- pots and some old chairs.'

'Leave it, Tilly,' warned Emily. 'No use upsetting me or him. It's time I pulled meself together. This is my chance, love. My five kiddies got there on their own, their dad drunk and me at work – and there's nowt I can do about that. But I can stand by Mark. He can always study later on. This'll happen give his dad summat to get better for, a reason to come home.'

Tilly decided a change of subject might be a

good idea. It was time for Emily to move out of here, though no one had caught sight of Joe Dyson in days. He would be back just like every other bad penny, would find Emily eventually. At least it would take him that bit longer if Emily lived at the other side of Bolton. 'Have you packed all your stuff?'

'Aye, such as it is.'

'Well, if you work with Mark, he might fix you up with a few clothes.'

Emily froze. 'Work with him? Nay, Tilly, I can only clean up.'

'I'll be doing that,' insisted Tilly, 'because he asked and I said yes. I think he wants you more on the sales side.'

'Heck. I don't know anything about old stuff.'

'Oh, give over,' laughed Tilly, 'we've only to look in the mirror to know all about old. Any road, there'll be prices on things. Then you can read them books, the ones he reads.'

Emily was not sure and it showed. She dropped into a chair and tried not to shiver. Somebody working in a posh shop needed nice clothes, a good voice, an idea about what was on sale. She wasn't fit for it, because she'd done just the Co-op and mill work and usheretting. Oh, God, she couldn't do it.

'Don't start,' Tilly advised. 'I can see it in your face, all that misery, all that knowledge that you're fit for nowt – and that's your bloody husband's doing. Don't be frightened to say you know nowt about summat. That's how learning starts, from nowt. That's what learning is, Emily. It's finding out about new stuff, asking questions and listening.'

'Aye, I know that.'

'And you're as good as anybody. You can read proper, can't you?'

Emily nodded.

'If you can read, you can cook, knit, sew, sell stuff, do anything. So think on and don't look so mawpish.'

'I'll try.'

Someone knocked at the front door. Both women froze, then Tilly spoke. 'Stop where you are, I'll get rid of whoever it is. Put a brew on and find me a gingernut. I'm peckish.'

Emily went into the scullery, filled the kettle, located biscuits, tea, sugar, cups—

'Emily?'

'What?' She noted the tone of Tilly's voice, swung round to find her standing in the doorway with two members of the police force, one male, one female. 'What?' she asked again. 'What is it?' Oh, God, hadn't she lost enough with Molly? Was God punishing her yet again for having been such a terrible mother?

'You'd best come back in here and sit down, love,' said Tilly.

Emily stumbled through the doorway and into Seth's rocking-chair.

The policewoman approached her. 'Is Joseph Dyson your husband?'

'Yes.'

The young woman placed a hand on Emily's shoulder. 'He's had an accident. He was found badly injured early this morning in the hospital. He didn't recover, I'm afraid.'

Emily swallowed. 'Hospital? Which hospital?'

'Prestford,' said the male constable.

'But . . . but I didn't know he was in hospital.'

'She left him,' Tilly explained, her voice unusually quiet.

'That's the mental hospital,' said Emily. 'That's where Matthew is, isn't it, Tilly? What was Joe doing there? I know he's a drinker, but why did he finish up in that sort of place?'

The policewoman explained about the arrest, the delirium and the removal of Joe Dyson to the psychiatric hospital. 'He was seeing things,' she explained, 'and he'd gone too far. The doctor said his liver was just about finished after all those years of drinking. They have a consultant there, one who specializes in alcoholism. Your husband was very ill even before his fall. I'm sorry, Mrs Dyson.'

Emily turned away from the other occupants of Tilly Povey's kitchen. She stared deep into the coals, her body rocking slightly in the old chair, a hand to her mouth, her forehead set in lines of concentration. She remained like that for several minutes, while the officers shifted from foot to foot, while Tilly waited for her friend to react. After a while, Tilly went to finish what Emily had started, thereby fulfilling her own need to be doing something. The way Emily was sitting, so still, no emotion, well, it wasn't normal, wasn't natural. So Tilly brewed the tea and waited for the storm to begin.

But there was no storm. When Emily had completed the process of digesting the new information, she stood up, walked to the table and helped to distribute the teacups. 'He won't be missed,' she said, before biting into a gingernut. She smiled at Tilly. 'Well, what did you expect? He was no good and he's dead. I'll still go and stop with Mark for a while. Oh, and our Phil wants me to meet somebody called Annie, lives on Thicketford Road. Looks like he's getting ready for settling and not before time.' She smiled at the police. 'Sugar?' she asked, a smile decorating her face. 'And please, help yourselves to a biscuit.'

Stella Dyson didn't know whether to be flattered or annoyed.

Dr Simon MacRae was never away, was always dropping in at her flat for the slightest reason, mostly to talk about Matthew and Rutherford Hall, the private rest home to which Matthew would be moved within the next few days. But Simon was beginning to wear the air of a puppy desperate for a home, and Stella had never before been the recipient of such devotion.

And now, this bombshell. It appeared that the man who had fathered her was dead, had died in a bathroom on Churchill ward in Prestford hospital. 'You say he had the bed next to Matthew's?'

'Yes,' answered Simon. 'Of course, no one realized that the two of them were connected, though there's no need for that to be significant. I found out by researching the dead man's address when I was told his surname was Dyson. Even that was told to me in conversation while I was asking about Matthew's condition. I'm sure that Matthew was in no fit state to recognize his father-in-law, so he'll probably have slept through the whole business. Oh, I am sorry about your father, Stella. So soon after poor Molly, too.'

'What?' Distracted by the news, Stella shook herself. 'Oh, that doesn't matter. He was the worst man I ever had the misfortune to meet.' No, her main concern was for Matthew. Once his relationship to the man in the next bed was discovered, would the authorities want to question him? Oh, it didn't bear thinking about. 'How did he die?'

'His skull was fractured in a fall – he banged his head as he went down.'

'I see.'

He waited for more, for tears, but her mouth remained closed and her eyes stayed dry. 'So, your father's death does not trouble you?'

'Er . . . no, not at all. He beat us all regularly, beat our mother, too, spent his money on drink, so our mother had to work . . . Get Matthew out of there today, Simon.' She wasn't sure why that was important, yet she insisted on it. 'Please, get him moved now, within the hour.'

'Well, there is a place available, but have you any idea of the cost?'

'Matthew is wealthy,' she snapped. 'Sorry, I'm distraught. But I don't want him in there now. If he finds out that his father-in-law died there, it may push him further into depression.'

Simon leaped into action. He was now so

fascinated by this young woman that he would have done almost anything to please her. 'Are you now in charge of Matthew's finances?'

She nodded. 'Yes, the lawyers have that in hand. I shall need money for Mark, for the house bills and so forth . . .' It occurred to her that she had not seen Mark for a few days. She slept at Coniston, but spent her days here, either working or in her flat, while her nephew was always in bed when she returned to the house across the road. She must speak to him about his father, about the death of a man who had never really been a grandfather—

'What about the funeral?' Simon asked.

'Which funeral?' She pulled herself up. Something was bothering her, something on which she needed to concentrate. 'I shall not be going,' she told him. 'I imagine that my brothers, too, will stay away.'

'And your mother?'

Stella raised her shoulders. 'Who knows? Even she finally turned on him.' A begrudging admiration for Emily Dyson had started to flower inside Stella's head. That meek, self-effacing mouse had finally found some sinew, it seemed. 'I must see my nephew. The school telephoned to say that he has been absent.'

There were not enough hours in the day. Stella was doctor to hundreds, aunt to just one, but the hundreds left little space for the boy. And her concern for Matthew's welfare took a lot of energy. Always full of life, she was below par these days, slightly out of sorts, often distracted. No wonder, she told herself now, because life kept happening, was as relentless as April rain, never-ending, intrusive, a nuisance. 'What next?' she asked.

'Who knows?' He made for the door, stopped in his tracks, turned. 'You have had a great deal on your plate. How about a night at the Hallé? I can get tickets – there's a Beethoven programme at the Free Trade Hall very soon. I believe Malcolm Sargent is conducting. We could perhaps have dinner, too . . .'

'Yes,' she said, though the delivery contained distinct elements of absentmindedness.

'Next week?' he suggested. 'Friday?'

She stopped chewing her thumbnail. 'What? Sorry, I was miles away.'

'Of course.' He chided himself for being pushy at a time that was plainly trying for her, then let himself out of the flat.

Stella dropped into an armchair. No. Surely this was all coincidence? Her father had finally succumbed to years of imbibing, it seemed, had been strait-jacketed and dragged off into the hospital, where, by some awful quirk of fate and after the drying-out process, he had been deposited in the bed next to Matthew's. Ridiculous. What was a liver-damaged raving lunatic doing in a ward with depressives?

She bent an elbow, leaned her aching head against her open palm. What was that film? *Casablanca.* Of all the psychiatric units in all the world, Joseph Dyson had wandered into the one from which she had tried for days to extricate the man she loved. Did she love him? Or had she just wanted what her older sister had owned? Could she possibly love a man who was currently enjoying rather more than a passing acquaintance with insanity?

Questions, questions, a spinning head and a stomach that felt . . . not quite right. Her chin shot upward in a movement that was almost involuntary, causing a crick that burned hard. Mrs Janet Fishwick. Oh, yes, how Stella had smiled about Mrs Janet Fishwick, a patient who, ten years into her marriage, had arrived flushed and excited at the surgery some weeks ago. There had been no children, yet Mrs Janet Fishwick had suddenly declared herself pregnant. 'It happened last Monday,' the patient had said, 'but I feel different already.'

Stella had smiled, her colleagues had smiled, and Mrs Janet Fishwick had cried when, two months later, her suspicions had been proved right. Stella got up, walked to the mantel and stared at herself in the gilt-framed mirror. Not quite right; not quite herself. She was queasy, moody, odd. No, surely not? Oh, God, no! If . . . She swallowed, tasted bile, a taste that was becoming familiar to her. Gastric reflux, symptom three, page twenty-seven, title *The First Trimester*, American author, second year at med school . . .

Holy Jesus, this was not happening. It was only days ago. Mrs Janet Fishwick. She was not going to be another Mrs Fishwick, surely? But she didn't like eggs any more, was going off certain brands of tea, had begun to turn away from the sight of anything fried. Did she want children, anyway? Would she love a child enough to . . . enough to give up medicine, enough to stand out as a single parent? She was a doctor, for goodness' sake, should have known better – knew better now, of course she did.

The white face reflected in the mirror looked grim and rather tired. To how many young girls had she given that lecture – go to Family Planning, tell them you're getting married soon, get a cap, a coil? Dozens. Unwanted children were not happy children – Stella knew that because she had come from that category.

An organized woman, Stella had to wade through a lot of packaging in her mind before remembering what she had to do today. She had a late afternoon surgery, a few calls to make and a nephew to find. Yet she continued to stare at the blanching face in the mirror. 'Do not say goodbye to yourself,' she whispered. 'Stella is still here, no matter what.' And there was always the other option: there wasn't a doctor in England who didn't know where to go to offload an unwelcome passenger.

Matthew probably didn't remember the love-making. For him, Stella had been Molly returned from the dead, a dream, a final straw to which, in desperation, he had attempted to cling. Everything had always been Molly, right from the time when he had scraped her up from the gutter only to stand her on a pedestal in his heart. Jesus Christ, how had Dr Stella Dyson managed to be jealous of poor Molly? Because Molly's arrival at comfort had been easy? Because Stella had clawed her way up via years of hard work and deprivation? Was that it?

Even in childhood, Molly had defended her younger sister. She had protected Stella from bullies, from their father, from hunger. 'What have you done?' she asked herself aloud. 'Jealous of a sister whose husband adored her even when she was just skin, bone and pain? Wanting what she had just because she had it, needing to win, to carry the cup in triumph, lap of honour, I am the greatest?' Yet Stella stopped short of self-loathing because that was the area in which Matthew currently resided. 'Forgive me,' she begged, the words addressed to Molly.

She combed her hair, so like Molly's had been, applied lipstick to a mouth whose shape imitated Molly's, though it lacked some of the fullness. She coloured the pale cheeks, bones like her sister's, though slightly sharper, looked at the completed job, tried to smile. But the result was pale and watery. Compared to Molly, she was a very ordinary specimen.

Mark first, she decided crisply. The calls could wait, because Stella Dyson needed to do the decent thing. She walked out into a day that was designated as September, though the chill bit through to her bones like a surgeon's knife. As she crossed the road, it occurred to Stella that the ice came from within herself and that only time would thaw her out.

Six

Jack Richards, product of the longest-serving regiment in God's chosen country, was not pleased. An active member of several gentlemen's clubs in London and in the North West, he depended on his past, was proud to have been an officer in the Coldstreams, that group of men on whom Britain had relied for centuries. As he often said when in his cups, the Coldstreams could be taken for granted, could be depended upon. He dined out on his military history, lived in accordance with it, could be brutish and stubborn about it, could not have lived without it. And now . . .

Guardsmanship was not for the lily-livered or the faint-hearted. The law was that there should never be acceptance of the less-than-perfect; nothing could be flawed. Guardsmen themselves were perfect and, by association, so were their families. And his son was second-rate. Jack Richards, an officer and a gentleman, was about to lose face.

Feeling decidedly the worse for wear, Jack

replaced the telephone receiver, turned round to face his wife, said nothing for several moments. In his book, the best was the norm; anything less than best was subnormal, unacceptable, gross. His chest tightened. 'Should have put him in the regiment, earache or no earache. That would have stopped all this nonsense.'

Irene stared at him. Sometimes it was best not to question Major Jack.

He drew a weathered hand through thick white hair, propped himself against an armchair. Discipline. It was all about discipline and Matthew was plainly incapable of directing himself in a decent and proper fashion. She had spoilt him. Not while Jack had been about, oh, no, she would not have dared. But Major Jack suspected that his beloved had weakened the child during periods of separation, while her husband had been defending king and country.

'What is it?' asked Irene. Jack looked positively sick, had turned a greyish colour, was uncertain of his feet. 'Jack?'

'They can't come to dinner as we planned,' he achieved eventually. 'Neither of them. That was Mark. He says Matthew is in a mental hospital. A mental hospital, Irene. For goodness' sake, never had anything like that in the family before.' It was monstrous. Matthew Richards had shown no inclination for the military, had been exempted from service because of some namby-pamby ear problem and was currently languishing in a hospital for the clinically insane. It was incredible.

Irene swallowed the last drop of tea and shook

158

her head. She could not allow herself to be visibly disturbed because that would upset Jack. She had to remain calm at all costs, as that was what her husband expected of her. But she had to admit to herself that she was worried, even though she was unable to divulge that information to her husband.

'God,' he muttered, as he reached for the tantalus.

Irene watched while he poured a whisky that must have measured at least quadruple. They were both drinking too much, were using alcohol as a hiding place. Determinedly, she remained seated, did not allow her concern to show, but she was changing, had started to change after the death of her daughter-in-law. Instinct told her to go to her son; experience forced her to stay with her husband.

Matthew had always been such a steady boy, no great shakes at his books, granted, but level-headed, a gifted businessman, sensible, predictable. Admittedly, he had made a foolish mistake in marrying that girl, but he wasn't the sort to go to pieces. Oh, goodness. She had invited Lucy Pemberton, a woman Jack considered suitable for his son, and she mentioned this. With Jack, the saving of face was paramount.

'Put her off,' ordered Jack. 'Put everything off. Must get to the bottom of this devilish business – we can't have our son in a lunatic asylum.'

'Quite.' Irene got busy with the niceties, calling friends who had been coming over supposedly to cheer up Matthew and his son, cancelling the caterers, making notes as she went along, careful not to mention the nature of her only son's illness. 'What now?' she asked her husband, when all the calls had been made. Jack would know what to do, because Jack had always known what to do. In theory, that was . . .

'Damn foolishness,' spat Jack. 'If he'd never got himself involved with that girl, he would have kept his head. I must go along and heave him out of the wretched place, Irene. No, no, you stay exactly where you are. No place for a lady, my dear.'

She wanted to go with him, but knew better than to quarrel. When one married a guardsman, one married security. Jack made all the decisions and she went along with them. That was the natural way, yet she wanted so badly to visit her son, to reassure herself that he was still there, was still Matthew. 'I should like to come with you to the hospital,' she ventured. She had done as Jack had asked, had put everyone off, but, no, he would do the rest of it his way, as ever.

He had picked up the phone and was asking the operator for the number of Prestford hospital. Irene knew that the man was far too drunk to drive, but never once since her marriage had she argued with him. From the very start, Major Jack had made it plain that a guardsman could take on the world and win. So, could he achieve victory with this one?

He broke the connection and sank into the armchair. 'Well, he's leaving the hospital today, Irene. And would you like to hazard a guess at his final destination?'

Irene shook her silver head.

'Rutherford Hall,' he announced.

Irene Richards squashed her relief, forbade it to show, because the major was clearly displeased.

'You know what that means, of course? He'll be on our doorstep. How many from Eagley village work at the Hall? Eh? More than a few. By tomorrow, the whole area will know that our son is a raving lunatic. This is too much.'

So, the brave, bold soldier was retreating. What would he do? Irene wondered. Would he shift to London until the fuss died down? Because this was worse than the Napoleonic problem, than the Crimea, than his regiment's inch-by-inch progress through North Africa and Europe. This was his good name.

'It really is too bad,' he muttered.

'Yes, dear.' Was Matthew truly insane? Perhaps he had suffered some mild form of collapse – after all, he had been incredibly fond of that girl. Irene closed her eyes. Were she to tell herself the absolute truth, she might even have allowed a certain admiration for the wife of her son. Molly had pulled herself up, had taken over a great deal of the business once Matthew had instructed her, had become quite an expert in her own fields.

'This has been a shock,' said Major Jack, his hand straying once again to the Georgian whisky decanter. He poured himself another hefty measure and downed half of it in one greedy gulp.

Irene was at a loss. Almost desperate to see her only son again, she knew better than to anger the major. She cleared her throat delicately. 'Perhaps you should go to town for a while, my dear. See your comrades, relax, play some cards. The horses will be fine, because Taylor will take good care of the stables. Let me think something up.'

'Think what up? Even with your imagination, this is a bridge too far. If he had played his part in the second war, we could have put this down to malaria. Oh, yes, I've seen some chaps with that, don't you know, ghastly business, raving like wild dogs, repeat performances the rest of their lives. But this is no mosquito bite, oh, no. This, my dear, is sheer lunacy. There's no bottom to the boy, never was.'

As ever, Irene avoided anything approaching confrontation. With Jack, everything was black or white, no shaded areas, no room for compromise. He lived by the rules of the barrack room, the mess, the battlefield. Jack was always right because he was Coldstream, and there was no room for negotiation.

'May go off for a week or two,' he said, after a while. 'Catch up with Manny and Mac, see how old Ironsides is getting on. Bit of a reunion, perhaps. Are you sure you won't come?'

'I'm sure,' she said. London provided little of interest as far as Irene Richards was concerned. She had scant tolerance for the empty-headed wives who had survived the passage of time, harboured no interest at all in the geriatric diehards who had served alongside her husband. Irene's needs were few and simple; she required horses, beautiful furniture, happy company and the occasional rubber of bridge. 'It will all be a nine-day wonder,' she reassured him. 'By the time you get back, the village will have found someone else to discuss. You go off and enjoy yourself – I shall think of something. Many mental problems are rooted in physical illness. Just give me time to think of a plausible complaint.'

He grunted, emptied the glass.

Yes, as usual, Irene was the one who had to deal with the delicacies. Major Jack careered through on his charger, scattered the enemy, looked at maps, deployed personnel, told jolly stories about his prowess, about the brilliance of his blessed regiment. But when it came down to the knives and forks of life, Irene always had to cope. Yes, he had ridden roughshod in Shermans and even in Churchills, but he had not the delicacy of balance required to negotiate the high wire. That was all up to her, was probably the territory of many women married to these very decided men.

'I shall go today,' he said gruffly.

So, he was raising the white flag, the symbol of defeat, of submission. She, a member of what was called the frail sex, would take up the muddied standard of battle, would step alone into no man's land, mind working far more quickly than his ever could or would. Major Jack would go to London, would drink himself senseless, though not before he had recounted his exploits to those who would not hear, as they, too, were talkers rather than listeners.

She dropped her chin, hoped that he would not see the smile that tugged away at the corners of her mouth.

'Pack me a bag, old thing,' he asked.

Old Thing got up and walked upstairs. She stood at the window of his bedroom, grateful that he now slept alone, that she, too, had a space designated solely for herself. Yes, it had been a strange life, one in which he had appeared to lead, one in which she had been in charge where it really mattered.

She reached for his case, opened drawers, packed enough things for a couple of weeks. Strange that a man so organized should have no idea of how to pack for a few days in London. He could do webbing and dubbing, spit and polish, knew how to shine his medals. A trained killer, he understood all about arranging death and glory, had no idea at all of how to live. Poor Matthew, what a father he had endured.

She left the case for him to carry downstairs, because the rule was that women carried nothing heavy. Yet she had carried him thus far; she also bore the knowledge that, without her, Major Jack would have amounted to nothing. He would travel by train, she thought gratefully, would be deposited by her at Trinity Street station in Bolton. From that point, he would bore anyone and every-one in sight, the old soldier who lived in a past heavily decorated in medals, heavily gilded by his own drink-fuelled, though limited, imagination.

'Shall we be off?' he asked. 'Get the earlier train, call in at Manny's house, might even bum supper if I'm lucky.' He went off to fetch his case.

Irene put on her musquash and waited for him. She had spent decades waiting for him and it was, perhaps, time to stop.

Emily Dyson, newly widowed and nervous, placed

her scant belongings on the kitchen table in her grandson's house. She owned two skirts, three blouses – one torn – several aprons, some under-garments and two cardigans. The navy coat and hat she wore with her one pair of shoes, so a solitary paper carrier had been sufficient to carry all her worldly goods.

Tilly hung her own coat in the scullery, then joined Emily at the table. 'He'll be upstairs,' she said, 'going through them blessed catalogues. Get your coat off, then I'll take you to your bedroom. There's a nice bathroom, old-fashioned, them lovely black and white tiles, big bath. If you heat enough water, you could soak right up to your chin.'

Emily swallowed. 'That'll be nice.'

Tilly asked God for patience, then led the way upstairs.

It was daft, thought Emily, but she had scarcely visited the upper floor of her own daughter's house. There were lovely things everywhere, paintings, vases, old tables, figurines. Molly had had a good eye, because everything was arranged beautifully against a backcloth of very plain wallpaper.

Her room was at the front, the middle of three bedrooms that overlooked the road. It sported an oriel bay with stained-glass flowers here and there, a big bed, wardrobes, a small settee, drawers, lamps, pretty cloth on a bedside table. 'Now,' declared Tilly, 'tell me this isn't the lap of luxury, Emily Dyson.'

Emily gulped, brought to mind the up-ended orange box that had served as furniture next to her bed in Eldon Street. It had held a book or two, Joe's teeth in a jam jar, a cup of water. This was heaven in comparison, but some folk didn't belong in heaven. She felt like a weed in a rosebed, unwanted and in danger of being dug out.

'I wish you'd straighten your face,' said Tilly.

'I'll be all right.' These words were designed to convince herself, not her companion. She looked through the window, eyes straying left until they rested on the house that contained not only her daughter's home but also her place of work. 'Has Stella been sleeping here?' she asked.

'Aye,' answered Tilly. Stella had slept at Coniston, but that was the sum total of her contribution to the household. She hadn't done a hand's turn for the boy. If it hadn't been for Tilly, Mark would not have enjoyed a hot meal in days. 'She'll go mad when she finds out he's left school. It's her they'll tell, you know, with Mr Richards being in hospital.'

Emily nodded. 'Should be me from now on. I'm his grandmother and I'll be looking after him.' She lifted her chin determinedly. 'I don't mean I want to go behind our Stella's back, but he needs a mother. I'm old, but I can still be a mother to him. Molly were too ill, Tilly. And Matthew – well, Christ knows what's going on in that man's head. I know one thing for sure, he worshipped my daughter, so I'm with him and all. No matter what they need, I'll try to be good enough, I will.'

Tilly cleared her throat. 'Come on, love, time we got a move on. I can show you where

166

everything is, then we'll sit down and put the
world right over a cuppa.'

On the landing, Mark tiptoed away and shut himself in the study with Bess. He suddenly felt more
settled and better cared-for. It seemed that Rabbit
might have teeth, after all, and he was glad about
that. Sometimes it took tragedy to bring out the
best in people. Clearly, Grandmother Rabbit was
rather more than two-dimensional. He patted his
dog. 'We'll get there, Bess. By heck, we will.'

Stella ran through from the back garden and into
the kitchen, stopped dead when she saw her
mother. 'Hello,' she said awkwardly, 'have you
seen Mark?'

'I think he's upstairs,' replied Tilly. 'I'll go and
fetch him.'

Stella placed her bag on the table and sat
opposite her mother. 'How are you?' she asked.

'All right. You?'

Stella felt a long way from all right, but she
couldn't say that, was unable to confide in her
mother about the symptoms she was experiencing, nausea, aversion to many foods, silly cravings
for others. It was all in her mind, anyway, because
there would be no symptoms yet. Mrs Janet
Fishwick, on the other hand . . . That was where
Mrs Janet Fishwick could stay, on the other hand.
This was all due to nerves, Stella told herself
repeatedly. 'I am fine, thank you,' she replied
eventually.

'You know your dad's dead?'

'Yes.'

'Same hospital as Matthew, too.'

'Yes.'

It was like getting blood from a stone, thought Emily. Yet why should Stella be different from this? She had spent a childhood being cared for by a sister just a little older than herself, had been forced to toughen up in order to fight her way through to where she was now, qualified doctor, good education, a future mapped out.

Mark and Tilly entered the room. 'Hello,' he said, to his grandmother and his aunt.

Stella looked at him, wondered what he was up to. 'You've not been to school,' she accused.

'No,' he replied coolly, 'I've not been to school.'

Emily coughed. 'He's left,' she informed her daughter, 'because he wants to run the shop. Me and Tilly are going to help him get it sorted out before it goes to the wall. He's got it all planned out and he's been upstairs studying what he'll need to know.'

Tilly squashed a grin and stepped out of the scene, picking up a duster before making her way into the hall. Once there, she dusted, all the time with an ear cocked towards the kitchen. With every fibre of her thin being, she willed Emily to hold her own, to remain strong. Although Tilly did not approve of Mark's decision, she respected it: the boy was growing up, was ready to start his own journey through life.

'Preposterous.' Stella leaned forward in her chair. 'Have you any idea at all of the struggle I had to get where I am? I worked in the UCP, at

Lyons, at that little café down by Gregory and Porritt's, opposite St Patrick's.'

'To get your dream,' answered Mark softly. 'That was your dream, Aunt Stella, not mine.'

But Stella waded on. 'In London I sold shoes, clothes, food, newspapers. I worked in nursing-homes, at a post office, in Marks and Spencer. Whereas you, here, at the best boys' school for miles, just need to go and come home. And, even though your dad is comfortably off, you'll get a state scholarship, or a Bolton scholarship – even an exhibition scholarship. All you need is to apply yourself to your books.'

'It isn't what I want,' he answered.

'You have your father's support.' Stella's voice rose in pitch. 'And state help, too. There's no need for you to save and scrimp as I did—'

'He isn't you,' interrupted Emily.

'Then isn't he lucky?' yelled Stella. 'Because I had to do it all alone, no encouragement from anyone, on my knees to the council for help, night school, jobs all over the place, no family to back me, no Bolton School for me.'

There followed a short silence, then Emily spoke again. 'I'm sorry that I didn't own a shop in town, Stella, that I was at work all the time, but that is how it was. There was no money. Your dad was an alcoholic. And, anyway, that's your story – Mark has to write his own. He doesn't want Bolton School, doesn't want your dream.'

'I'm in charge while Matthew's away.' Stella's voice climbed all the time, was in danger of shattering glass. 'It's up to me.'

'All right.' Emily's voice shook. 'All right, then, you take him to school and you make him stop there. I'll be here to cook and cater for him, so you can be in charge of the education side.'

'I shall walk in at the front door of school and out at the back,' said Mark. 'No one can make me stay. Aunt Stella, I have my national insurance number and I'm willing to work. Whatever you say, I shall not be going to school any more.' He walked away and stared out of the window, Bess shadowing his every move.

Stella gripped the edge of the table, all ten knuckles showing a brilliant blue-white. 'I've had enough,' she told her mother. Then she burst into tears, picked up her bag and left the house.

'Bugger,' said Emily.

'I agree.' Mark came back to the table, paused, sat down. There was clearly rather more to this woman than he had ever expected. 'I don't want to call you Grandmother,' he said. 'May I call you Bunny?'

'I suppose so.' She was trembling so hard that she bit her tongue.

'It's not like Aunt Stella to cry,' he said. 'I've never seen her upset before, even when Mother died. Shall I go after her?'

Emily shook her head. 'No, love. She's my daughter and I'll go and see her later on. Right. What do you fancy for your tea, eh? Anything in particular?'

'Bangers,' he answered immediately, 'with mash and baked beans. And for afters, tinned pears with runny custard.'

'Eeh,' smiled Emily, 'I can see you're a lad after

me own heart. Come on, you can peel a couple of spuds. Now, have we got enough milk for custard? Where do you keep your brown sugar? Have you ever tried custard with brown sugar? And I'll drain the syrup off the pears, then nothing'll curdle. Do you know where I can find a jug?'

In the hall, Tilly Povey wound up Molly Richards' grandfather clock. The eight-day mechanism groaned, then she swung the pendulum that would start up time all over again. It was a new beginning for Coniston. She listened to the clink of cutlery against china and she thanked God. The clock chimed the quarter. Bunny was home at last.

Alice Povey needed the money. She was taking a fortnight off work, which was her due, but she had farmed herself out, had got a job that paid a damned sight more than she got at the infirmary. She wanted things, a new coat, a decent pair of shoes, a few luxuries for her bedroom in the flat at the bottom of Chorley New Road.

So she was on her way to Rutherford Hall, a home for the mentally disturbed – the rich mentally disturbed. She passed her old home on her way up to Eagley village, peered from the top of the double-decker into the front room of number 301 Tonge Moor Road. Mam would be out, of course, because there had been all that trouble up Chorley New Road, poor Mrs Richards finally giving up the ghost, the lad needing looking after, the husband getting himself carted off to Manchester.

There was no sign of life at the old homestead, so Alice concentrated on her destination. At the age of twenty-seven, she was a fully qualified sister in charge of a men's surgical ward. While she loved her work, Alice had always been fascinated by psychiatry, so this was her chance to earn a great deal of money while taking a closer look at the possibilities. And, by working nights, she would be quids in as well as better informed, since night work paid more.

The bus pulled in at the terminus. Alice got off and walked the last few hundred yards, turning in at the entrance of an imposing mansion, sweeping driveway, beautiful grounds, peacocks crying from the lawns. This place had been sold to a group who offered discreet containment for members of well-to-do families, people who were out of order, not ticking over properly. The private clinic provided a full range of treatments including drug therapies, electro-convulsion and counselling.

Twilight was descending as she approached the house, but the area was lit by many electric lamps. After the small frisson of fear that visits many when a new venture beckons, Alice steeled herself and strode with resolve towards the front door. She was here for just two weeks, was filling in for a sister who had gone abroad, so she comforted herself with the knowledge that this was hardly a life sentence. If she didn't like it, she could leave and enjoy the holiday she was supposed to be taking. It was a place she had never visited before, as her brief interview had taken place in an office in town. Oh, well, in for a penny, in for a pound, as Mam would have said.

When she reached the top of the steps, a dis-embodied voice spoke. 'Name?' it asked.

She looked around. 'Alice Povey,' she replied, wondering what the hell she was doing talking to a closed door. She was carrying on like an inmate, but she kept her cool, just about. A buzzer sounded, the door opened, and she stepped into Paradise, carpet as thick as a spongy-grassed summer meadow, lovely furniture dotted about, plants and ornaments everywhere.

A uniformed man sat at a desk. 'Right, Sister Povey,' he said, smiling at her. 'Matron left your photo, so I know who you are. Here, these are your keys. Nurse Beddows will be along in a moment to show you your duties.'

She took the keys and sat on the most comfort-able sofa she had ever met, burgundy plush with scatter cushions in the same material. She'd never thought of that, having cushions the same as the furniture, but it looked so classy. Perhaps she'd think about that for the flat she shared with two other nurses. And the carpet, no colour, really, sort of greyish-beige, a deep, deep pile. Like some-thing off a Hollywood film—

'Hello.'

Alice looked up. 'Hello.'

'I'm Doreen Beddows. I do three nights a week, and thank God you're here. Have you done this before?'

'No, but I've done maternity and that can be a bit crazy.'

Doreen laughed. A plump woman in her late

thirties, she oozed warmth and friendliness. 'Done your midwifery, then?'

Alice nodded.

'Well, if you've seen post-natal depression, that'll help a bit. But we've some serious cases here – what's your name?'

'Povey. Alice Povey.'

'Right.' Doreen placed herself beside her new colleague. 'There's no titles here. Some of them are near-aristocratic, so we let them all use our first names. The chief, Dr Masefield, he thinks informality is best. The patients call him all sorts of names, but that's another story. Now, you've come at a bad time, so this is going to be a baptism of fire. We've a new patient arrived today and Dr Masefield wants him watching and drug-free if possible. So you'll have to do the watching, because we've a lot on tonight – we're full to bursting. Now. Take a deep breath because you might need it. Ready?'

Alice nodded.

'Right, follow me.'

As they moved along corridors carpeted only slightly less luxuriously than the entrance hall, Doreen delivered a monologue about relief time, where the kitchen was, who else was on rota, how to attract colleagues should a situation get out of hand. She pointed out the door behind which the doctor on call was in bed, 'Don't wake him up unless you have to,' showed her which keys were which, then abandoned her at a door marked 47B. 'Here you are, love, he's all yours. Notes at the bottom of the bed, watch his blood pressure and heart-rate, and may God have mercy on your soul.'

Alice inhaled deeply and walked into the room. A young nurse nodded, put a finger to her lips, then went off to fulfil her own duties. When she had removed her outer clothing and pinned her starched cap in place, Alice turned and picked up the charts hooked on to the end of the bed.

Her patient was Matthew Richards of Coniston, Chorley New Road, Bolton. He was in a foetal position, on his side and curled up tightly, eyes closed, but obviously awake. Every muscle in his face was tense; he was listening and waiting; he was also her mother's employer.

She sat down in a straight-backed chair near the bed and picked up the notes. A professional to the core, she could not help gasping when she took in the significance of what she was reading. It was unbelievable. She knew this man, should perhaps wake the sleeping doctor and explain the circumstances. Impartiality would not be easy; remaining here unafraid was going to be almost impossible. Without completing her reading, she put down the notes and mopped her forehead with a handkerchief. The central heating was on too high, she was hot—

'Who are you?'

'Alice,' she replied.

He sat up, hair tousled like a child's. 'Are you spying on me?' he asked.

'No.'

She *was* spying on him. He had confessed, had told everyone what he had done, but all they did was watch him, day in, day out, even during the night now. 'They moved me,' he said.

'Yes, from Prestford to here.'

'Because that was where I killed him.'

Alice bit down on her lower lip. This man was a murderer and she was incarcerated with him, dared not leave her post. What was he doing here? Could the rich get away with murder simply because of their money? Was this all it took, a move to a private facility, out of sight, out of mind, out of reach of the police? Surely not?

'I had to kill him,' he said.

Alice picked up the notes and read them to the end. Matthew Richards was out of his mind. By the time she reached the end of the report, his insanity was clear. 'How did you kill him?' she asked.

'They don't let you have knives. All you get is a spoon. They cut up the food before bringing it. So I had to use the dressing-gown cord.'

'You strangled him?'

He nodded.

'With a dressing-gown cord?'

'Yes.'

'That isn't true. The man died because he slipped and banged his head, broke his neck. It was an accident.'

'I did it.'

He could not have done it. According to the notes, Matthew Richards had become agitated late on during the afternoon, so distressed that he had been sedated and put on watch. He had remained in his bed and had not woken until after the accident had happened. Nevertheless, he had repeatedly insisted that he had killed the patient in the next bed.

'Why did you do it?' Alice asked.

'He hurt Molly. Molly was his daughter.'

She gripped the sides of her chair. Molly Dyson's parents lived in Eldon Street, back to back with Mam and Dad. So that bad creature was dead and good riddance. But Matthew Richards was in no way responsible for the death of his father-in-law. On one-to-one watch at the time of the death, he could not possibly have left his bed, sedated or not, because every slightest move would have been noted. 'You didn't kill anyone,' she insisted.

'Why will no one believe me?' he asked.

'Because you were in bed asleep when the death happened.'

He lay back. They had to believe him. Had to. It was as clear as day, the ward, the walk past the sister's office, the corridor, the bathroom. He could feel the cord in his hands, heard the neck snap—

'It was a dream,' Alice told him. 'Drugs can do that. And if you wanted him dead, if you wanted to kill him, then that was in your mind while you were asleep. There was a mess in the bathroom, Mr Richards. Your father-in-law slipped in the mess and cracked his skull. His neck broke at the same time. You were not there, you were in bed. The notes are here. The hospital wrote all this because the staff knew that you would continue to insist on taking responsibility.'

Matthew's hands clutched the covers and he almost screamed. Why were people so stupid? Couldn't they see that it had to be true, that he needed it to be true? Someone had to pay for Molly's suffering and her father had been the most evil person in her life. The killing of Joseph Dyson was a sensible sin, a necessary one.

'Do you remember Tilly Povey?' she asked.

'Tilly irons,' he replied.

'That's right, she's the best ironer in town. Well, Tilly is my mother. Joe Dyson is . . . was our neighbour. Can't you see? Everybody hated him. It isn't just you, it's the whole neighbourhood and half the town.'

'I remember doing it,' he persisted.

This was going nowhere. Alice stood up, measured heart-rate and blood pressure, tidied his bed, made sure that he was settled. If this argument went on for much longer, her patient would get no rest at all. 'Sleep,' she ordered.

He dozed on and off, ranting occasionally, weeping, crying out the name of his dead wife. Apart from two short breaks during which the younger nurse took over, Alice Povey spent the whole night in the company of Matthew Richards. At the end of her shift, she felt as wrung out as a used dishcloth. She left him with coffee, which he drank, and toast, which he ignored.

In the entrance hall, she met Doreen Beddows again. 'Bad night?' asked Doreen. 'Is he still confessing to a murder he couldn't possibly have committed?'

Too tired to answer, Alice nodded.

'Oh, well, that's nothing,' said Doreen cheerfully. 'Wait till you get Mr Barlow. He thinks he's an engine driver, plays puffer trains all over the ward. Mind, he is eighty-four, so he has trouble stoking his boiler, never manages a full head of steam.'

Alice laughed wearily, then surprised herself by asking, 'If Mr Richards is still on watch, can I have him again tonight?'

'I suppose so,' answered Doreen, 'but why?'

'I'm going to get through to him,' declared Alice, 'if it's the last thing I do.'

Stella opened her door. 'Oh, it's you,' she said wearily. 'Come in.'

Emily entered her daughter's flat. She removed her hat and placed it on a stand just inside the door. It was a nice place, furniture plain but good, living room a decent size, red and black carpet, a cheerful clock ticking on the mantelpiece.

'Sit down,' invited Stella.

Emily sat. Of all the awkward moments in her life, this came very near the top of the list. She had rehearsed what she was going to say, but had been distracted by Mark, the discovery of whom was giving her great pleasure. He was no spoilt brat from the good end of town: he was just a lad who wanted a listening ear and a friendly companion.

Which was what Stella had needed all those years ago. And not just Stella – Philip, Tony, Eddie and Molly, they had needed a mother, too. How did a person make up for all that lost time, years in the mill, years at the cinema? How could she explain the exhaustion that had kept her from reading to them, helping them, loving them?

'Would you like tea?' Stella asked.

Emily could have been anyone, just a casual acquaintance, a colleague, a neighbour. Did she want tea? 'No, thanks. I've come to see you, not to drink tea. I wanted to know how you are.'

'I'm fine.'

'No, you're not.'

Stella knew that her eyes were almost wild as they darted all over the room, lighting on anything that might keep them at a discreet distance from her mother, the bureau, a table, a different chair. She bubbled inside, felt like a roaring cauldron into which a coven of witches might drop the components of a spell at any second. There was something wrong with her, something huge yet tiny, and she was falling apart.

'You need to talk to me, Stella,' said Emily.

The younger woman's shoulders sagged. 'I always needed to talk to you. We all did. It's too late now, Mam.'

'It's never too late.'

Ah, another of those trite little sayings that meant everything and nothing.

Emily tried again. 'I can see suffering in your face, love.'

Stella boiled. 'There was suffering in my sister's face – did you see that? Did you see Tony's grief when his baby was born dead?' Her mouth opened wide and sobs crippled the next words. 'Did you ever see anything? Where were you when I got my first period, when I had my first date and the boy tried to force me? When Eddie left home and we never heard from him for months?

You should have made time. There's always time.'

Emily remained where she was: she knew that if she crossed the room to offer comfort she would be rejected, even pushed away. She closed her eyes, as if cutting out vision would also remove sound, but the hysteria continued.

'I know it was hard. Living with him was a nightmare, Mam. But we needed you, needed you so badly, and you were never there.' The words stopped and Stella dropped into the other armchair. It was going to come out and she couldn't stop it. And the miracle was that in spite of enforced estrangement, she trusted her mother absolutely. Her core, the place in which unshakeable instinct was born, knew that Emily Dyson would never betray her.

Emily waited, hands folded in her lap, heart aching because she could be no more than blotting paper, a silent, almost inanimate witness whose ability was limited to the absorption of emotion. This girl had to turn to her, was desperate. But Emily could not help, could offer no encouragement, because it was all for Stella to do. At least the yelling had stopped: the girl was simply sobbing now, elbows on drawn-up knees, head in those delicate hands. Oh, God, she was a beautiful woman, not as soft-featured as Molly had been, but elegant. Even now, reduced to the attitude of a child, Stella Dyson retained a dignity that would never be dented, whatever the occasion.

Stella lifted her head and out it poured. 'Oh, Mam, I've done a terrible thing.'

'Have you?'

The dark head nodded quickly. 'You see, I don't know about love.'

Emily was unsurprised. That household in which the five kids had dragged themselves up, the place Emily had recently destroyed, had been a centre of fear and uncertainty. It was a shame that she, the mother of that family, could not feel shock now, when it was all coming back through one of the innocents, one of those underfed, poorly clothed and neglected infants.

'I always wanted him. The same as I always wanted what Molly had.'

'Molly never had anything,' ventured Emily. 'None of you did.'

'She had goodness, Mam. She had real beauty and she had acceptance. Molly was calm.'

'You're usually calm.'

'Not inside, Mam, never inside.' She dried her eyes. 'In the first few days at med school, we got corpses to work on. They do that right away to see if the students can face it. We ended up with a lot more corpses, people all over the floor, men dropping like flies.'

'And it didn't bother you?'

'Of course it bothered me. But there's a place in me where I can go – a bit like an air-raid shelter. I can concentrate, but feel detached. That's where I went while I dissected the dead. To be a doctor, you have to find that place, otherwise you'd get upset every time you failed. A doctor's failures finish up under the ground or in smoke through a crem chimney. I protect myself.'

Emily understood that perfectly and she nodded encouragingly.

'But I think that place was always there,' continued Stella, 'and so was the jealousy. I wanted what Molly had, a man who cared so much that he was blinded by love. I wanted to be like her. No, no, it isn't even that, it's more. I wanted to *be* Molly.'

'But you're a doctor, Stella. You got what you wanted. I know you had to go the long way round, but what you have you worked for, did it all by yourself. The fight you put up, doesn't that make it even more important?'

Stella took a deep breath, shuddering as the air left her body. 'I wanted him, Mam. And after she died, after the funeral, I took him.' She drew a hand through her hair. 'He thought I was Molly because my hair came down. He called me Molly. She's dead, but she still has him, Mam. It was at the start of the breakdown. I knew he wasn't right, but I let it happen. In fact, I made it happen. And I feel . . . different.'

Emily held on to herself, folding her arms as if the movement would contain all the bewilderment she was experiencing. She had come here to get to know her daughter; now, she knew too much. But this was how it had to be, how it should always have been.

'Mam, I think I'm pregnant.'

The older woman blinked several times. 'But . . . but that doesn't make any sense, love. You wouldn't know, couldn't, not yet.'

'I have a patient who knew within days and we all laughed at her.'

Emily, feeling decidedly unsteady, rose to her feet and crossed the room. She placed a hand on her daughter's head, could not remember touching her in years. The hair was soft, smooth, very thick and beautiful. 'I just want you to know this, Stella. I'll be here. This time I'll be here, and for as long as God spares me, I'll be here. No matter what. I mean that – no matter what.'

'I'm scared,' whispered Stella.

'Well, don't be. Tell me where all the stuff is and I'll make some tea. I'm glad you told me. I think it's time for you and me to get to know one another. We'll be all right, love, all of us, you, me, Matthew and Mark. And Tilly and all – she's nearly family.'

Stella waved a hand towards the kitchen. 'It's all on the lower shelf.' She mopped her face once more. 'And, Mam?'

'Yes, love?'

'Thanks.'

In the small kitchen, Emily stood for a while, her hot head pressed against the glass in a cupboard door. Perhaps it had all been saved up for now, for when she would be truly needed. Hating him, she boiled the kettle, set cups on a tray, found some crackers and cream cheese. Hating him, she plonked sugar and milk next to the cups, rattled in a drawer for a couple of spoons. Well, he was dead and she wasn't.

In the end, she had won.

Seven

Alice Povey had indulged in a good think.

Too restless to sleep properly, she had spent the day concentrating on Matthew Richards, wondering about his illness, trying to identify, from her very basic knowledge of psychiatry, a disease that might cause such delusions. There was shock, of course, which was capable of inducing some terrifying behaviours. Shock was a reaction rather than an illness, a result of something that had happened outside the patient. He had lost his wife and he had adored her. Yes, he could well be traumatized.

But could shock make him believe that he had actually killed someone, that he had taken the cord of a dressing-gown, had used it as a garotte? She had telephoned Prestford hospital, had gathered that there was no possibility of Matthew Richards having left his bed when Joe Dyson's accident had occurred.

Dementia? Yes, that could start in a forty-year-old, though it was rare. A single psychotic episode? God, she wished she'd hung on to those bloody books, but she had done what all nurses did, had sold them on second-hand as soon as the course was over. She had not intended to move towards psychiatry, but now she would have given the contents of her purse for those two or three volumes.

Schizophrenia, manic depression, anxiety ... what? He could talk quite reasonably for much of the time, had expressed himself well, was not coming out with a load of nonsense all the time. How clear could dreams be? The drugs he had been given to quieten him, might they have produced delusions as strange as this one? Was it possible to dream so clearly, to remember every tiny detail, right down to the cord used as instrument?

It was no use, she had to talk to Mam. This might not be strictly ethical, but Tilly Povey had always ignored the rules. Mam was one on her own; God had broken the mould after Tilly, and Dad had been heard to opine that it was a good job, because more than one Tilly might have caused a bloody revolution weighty enough to make the American Civil War look like a tea-party.

Alice got herself ready for the night's work, but set off early so that she might break her journey on Tonge Moor Road. She could have walked up to Coniston, no more than a quarter-mile away from her flat, but it would have been wrong to talk to Mam there, in the house belonging to the subject of discussion. So she arrived at 301 just in time for tea, was glad of the plate of silver hake, potatoes and peas.

Mam sat opposite her. 'Well?' she asked.

God, the woman could probably have seen through the walls of a lead casket. Without a word having been spoken, the mother knew that the daughter had something on her mind. 'Tell me about Matthew Richards,' said Alice, after a few seconds.

'About him? What do you mean "about him"? He's very nice-looking, he likes roast parsnips and he has a shop in town.'

'Mam!'

'What?'

'I'm looking after him. He's up at Rutherford Hall, a private place for people with mental trouble. It's all right, don't start, I've not left the infirmary. It's my fortnight off and I thought I'd have a look at mental illness, see if I'm interested. Oh, and I'll get a fortune for ten nights, so that'll help as well.'

'And he's there?'

Alice nodded.

'Poor man. He's never done a tap of harm to anybody, kept himself to himself, minded Molly and did all he could.'

Alice placed her cutlery on the plate. 'Thanks, Mam, that was lovely.'

Tilly cleared the dishes and took them into the scullery. Through the open door, her strident voice arrived in the kitchen. 'Why? What did you want to know about him?'

Alice counted to ten. 'Could he kill, Mam?'

Tilly's reappearance was swift. 'Kill? Matthew Richards? Nay, I've seen him open the window to let a bluebottle out.'

Alice was using a spoon to make patterns in the sugar. 'He says he killed Joe Dyson.'

'Eh? Bloody hell, give that man first prize. In fact, he should go to the Palace for an OBE or some such.' With a tea-towel clutched in her hands, Tilly lowered herself into the chair opposite her daughter's. She could sense the girl's deep disquiet. 'Nay, love, he couldn't have. It's not in him.' Tilly pondered for a few moments. 'I don't know, though, Alice, he worshipped Molly Dyson, you know – I could see him landing out at anybody who damaged her . . . No. What do they think?'

'They said he couldn't have because he was knocked out at the time on barbiturates. But he's so clear about it – I mean, he insists. I'm hoping they've got this right and he couldn't have done it, because he seems such a nice man.'

'He is.'

'He's so sad, Mam.'

Tilly kept to herself the knowledge that this nice man had been so devoted to his wife that he had completely neglected his sixteen-year-old son. That was the trouble with obsessive folk, people who loved one other person intensely. There was no room for anybody else, even for their own kiddies. But he wasn't a bad man, not at all: his only crime was that he had loved too much and too exclusively.

'Where's my dad?'

Tilly made a noise that sounded like 'humph'. 'How the bloody hell should I know? He sent a message up before with Ted Moss – that's the one who works with him, wife has big thick eyebrows and a bum the size of Lancashire – said he's doing overtime. Anyway, I shall give him the benefit of the doubt this once.' She grinned. 'He's saving up because he owes Ted a fishing rod.' Her brow knitted as she looked at her daughter. 'Give over worrying about Mr Richards, Alice. He's got to go through it, whatever it is.'

'I know. And I know he's not always going to be ill, but only if we can stop him thinking he killed Molly's dad.'

'Just do your best for him, love.'

'I will, Mam.'

Tilly told Alice all the news, about Emily destroying the house, about her moving to Coniston to care for Mark. 'So Mark's left school and he's going to open the shop again. Anyway, you want to take it easy, madam. Remember what they taught you about getting involved with patients.'

Alice jumped up, kissed her mother and went to catch the next bus. Mam was right, she mustn't get involved . . .

Irene Richards followed the nurse along the corridor. It had taken her a while to pluck up the courage to come, because although she badly wanted to see her son, she was fully aware that many Eagley villagers worked here and that the major would not be pleased if he found out about her visit. But this was her son. She had reared him, comforted him, had guided him across the stepping-stones of childhood.

While the major regarded the antiques trade as a decent hobby into which he could retire after service, the business had always fascinated Irene, had become the centre of her life, and she had guided Matthew towards it. The shop had been hers: she had returned north years before her husband's retirement, had prepared the path for him. Matthew's father considered that a real man would not have gone into the antiques business straight from school: a real man would have served his country first. *Ergo*, Matthew was not a real man.

'There you go, Mrs Richards,' said the nurse. 'He's sedated this evening, so don't be surprised if he hasn't much to say for himself.'

When the nurse had walked away, Irene stood for a while with her hand resting on the door-knob. She would not weep. The wife of a major in the Coldstreams did not weep . . . Was that all she was? A wife? He was away and life was wonderful, or would have been had Matthew not been ill and in this place. And why was Major Jack away? Because he could not face the fact that his son was human rather than superhuman. Matthew was not Coldstream material and was, therefore, imperfect.

She entered the room and was pleasantly surprised by the interior. The furniture, though modern, was substantial, light in colour, quite cheerful. Matthew, however, looked far from happy. His eyes were glazed and he lay motionless, no reaction when she spoke to him, his breathing even, limbs still.

'Matthew?'

There was still no response, not even a flicker of recognition. Had they made him like this? Was he sedated so that he would make no fuss, no noise? She noticed the line of perspiration on his upper lip, the darkness beneath his eyes. He looked absolutely dreadful. Without further hesitation, she rang the bell that hung by a cord over his head. Something was terribly wrong here, and she intended to address it.

A white-coated man came in, stethoscope drooping from his neck. He looked at Irene, then advanced on the patient. 'Ian Masefield,' he said. 'I was passing, heard the bell. I'm the chief psychiatrist here, but staff and patients call me Head Case – among a plethora of other names, some quite unpleasant.' He peered into Matthew's eyes. 'Good God,' he exclaimed, before turning to grab the notes from the foot of the bed.

'What is it?' asked Irene, fear beating a huge drum in her chest.

'Years since I saw this,' remarked the doctor. 'Fascinating.'

'What?' The tone of Irene's voice left little space for gentility.

Suddenly Matthew opened his mouth. 'No knife,' he announced, 'just spoons – what the hell? They're coming for him. Have you seen them?'

'Absolutely fascinating,' repeated Dr Masefield.

'Bess?' shouted Matthew. 'Come on, Bess.'

Irene dropped into a chair, because her legs refused to bear her weight for one more second.

She had walked into a nightmare and could no longer support herself.

'Hallucinations.' There was triumph in the doctor's tone. 'Such a low dose, too. This explains it.'

'Explains what?' Irene asked.

'The murder. The murder that never was. You see, he hated that man. He imagined that he had killed him, even saw himself doing it. And all the time it was a reaction to a barbiturate. Is he your son?'

'Yes, I—'

'This has to go in a paper.'

Matthew glared at the doctor as if he detested him. 'They put me in here. Have you taken my shoes? There's no moon tonight.'

Irene felt as if all the air had been drawn out of her lungs. She closed her eyes and leaned back. This was the worst moment of her life thus far. Her child was lost. He was here, yet not here, alive, yet not. Perhaps this was what she had feared, because truth was often unacceptable. She found her voice. 'What do you mean by murder?' she asked the doctor.

At last, the man awarded her some attention. 'Ah, well, he has convinced himself that he killed the man who occupied the bed next to his in Prestford hospital. There was a connection between them, apparently. I think the name was Dyson and he was being treated for alcoholism. Related by marriage, as far as I can gather.'

'Molly's father, I imagine.'

'The reaction to sedatives has been interesting.

192

He has been confused, hyperactive and has suffered hallucinations, we think.'

'I see. I am so pleased that my son was available for your experimentation.'

But the man did not react to the pointed remark as he was too engrossed in his own train of thought. 'The problem now seems to be the underlying depression and anxiety – so debilitating. How can we make him understand which is dream and which is reality? Yes, very interesting.'

Irene was confused. The person from whom she wanted answers was sitting up in bed, the eyes of a madman burning in his white face. Only he knew how he felt. How could this pleasant, rather chaotic young doctor help? 'So, what will you do?' she enquired of Ian Masefield.

'Counselling, good food, exercise and care, Mrs Richards. I feel that ECT would not help in this case.'

'ECT?'

'Ah, sorry. Electro-convulsive therapy. I would say that's inappropriate at the moment.' Finally he looked at her properly. 'Mrs Richards, I beg you, don't despair. From what I know of your son, he's a decent man who has had an appalling time. He dedicated his life to that poor lady and she was very ill. This is a rare man, you must be proud of him.'

She was. He had no medals, no awards, no history as a warrior. The battle Matthew had been engaged in, the war against death, would never be won by mere mortals. There had been no standard-bearer to lead the way, no trumpeter, no tales to tell in a mess hall, no comrades to support him. Matthew was the silent hero, the truly brave man. Coldstreams? God save her from them and from the emptiness of their lives.

The doctor left, only to be replaced almost immediately by a pleasant girl, quite tall, with long brown hair swept back and contained within a starched cap. She had a well-ordered, if rather ordinary face, though the green-grey eyes were lit magnificently as soon as the smile switched itself on. 'Have you been crying?'

'Not really,' replied Irene, 'although this has, of course, been something of a shock.'

'Well, it would be. You're his mother, aren't you?'

'Yes, I am.'

'He will be looked after, you know. And Dr Masefield just told us no more barbiturates – there's an allergy. I'm Alice Povey, by the way. My mother's been working for Mr Richards for years. Tilly, she's called, but it's really Mathilda.'

'So you know my son?'

'Never met him until last night, but I've seen him in the shop when I've been passing.'

'Are you talking about me?' Matthew asked.

Alice laughed. 'See? He'll be all right. Don't worry, they know what they're doing here.'

Irene rushed to Matthew's side. 'Yes, we were discussing you. How are you? Would you like something to eat?'

But his eyes were fixed on Alice. He remembered her, yet could not place her. 'Would you get me a cup of tea, please?' he asked.

Alice went off to fetch tea for Matthew and his mother. In the kitchen, she recalled what her own mother had said over the years about Mr and Mrs Richards Senior: so correct, so county set, all brogues and horses. But Mrs Richards did not seem to fit that picture. She was ordinary, normal, though extremely well dressed. Like any other mother, she was afraid for her son, keen for him to get better. She spoke perfect English, carried herself elegantly, yet she was nice, approachable.

She returned with the tea, saw the mother standing with her arms wrapped around the son.

'We did love Mark,' he was saying now. 'It was just . . . we were so close that he sometimes felt . . . And then she was so ill. Oh, my son, my son.'

Alice watched while the mother comforted her one and only child. He was an adult, yet he was still a boy to this woman. That was all Matthew needed, a bit of comfort, some love, to know that he was cared for. As she placed cups and saucers on the over-bed trolley, Alice noticed a single tear making its way down Irene Richards' cheek. Someone loved him and he was going to be all right.

Even Tilly was all of a dither, which fact on its own was enough to make the day special. She had her best coat on, too, in a shade of brown lighter than her usual garb, not quite so sensible and with an imitation fur collar. There was a small lift to her shoes, nothing dramatic, no winkle-picker toes, no stiletto heel, but still rather raunchy for Tilly, light tan to match her handbag. She also sported fifteen-denier stockings and even a hint of pale pink lipstick.

Another sign that this was a red-letter day was that Tilly Povey's hairnet was nowhere to be seen. Mark had a discreet word with his ally, the grandmother he referred to as Bunny. 'Her hair's naked,' he whispered.

Emily dug him in the ribs. 'Behave yourself,' she chided quietly. 'Me and Tilly haven't seen stuff like this before, not this much of it, any road. It's like Aladdin's cave.' She gazed round the shop, eyes widened in wonderment. 'I don't know where to start.'

Tilly, too, was bewildered. There must have been about fifty clocks for a kick-off, then paintings all over the walls from half-way up right to the ceiling, hardly an inch between them; figurines, tea-sets, cupboards, desks, bits of jewellery, stamps, thimbles, dolls . . . 'Bloody hell,' she said, 'and it's a right mucky mess, too. I'll have to bring my Seth and we'll get all this stuff down off the walls for a kick-off. Cream paint, I think – what's that carpet doing up the wall?'

Emily had been here once before, so her knowledge was superior by about an hour and a half's experience earlier in the week. 'That's tapestry,' she replied proudly, 'part of a set. The rest's at Leasowe Castle on the Wirral. That's been around since just after Shakespeare.'

Tilly could see which way the wind was blowing, so she tried to take some of it out of Emily Dyson's sails. 'And I've been around since breakfast, but I'm not bragging. Right. Where do we start?'

'We don't,' replied Mark. 'This is our initial visit, like a baptism. I've a bottle or two of wine in the back and some very nice sandwiches. We have to talk.'

Tilly looked at Emily, Emily looked at Tilly. The lad was so smart in his grey suit, plain tie, gold hunter stretched across his waistcoat. The watch was his pride and joy, a gift from his mother on his fifteenth birthday. He looked nothing like the street lads, those hordes who congregated on corners while the girls strutted about; Mark had his own style, was making a statement about who and what he was. Strangely, no one mocked him when he walked along Deansgate and Bradshawgate, because he looked like a young Gregory Peck, handsome, self-assured and very much a man.

'He looks twenty,' commented Emily.

'He looks gorgeous,' said Tilly.

The 'gorgeous' one dragged them through to the rear of the shop, where they negotiated a path through yet more piles of antiques, things that were not yet ready for display. 'We'll clear this lot,' he said. 'It will go into secure storage down by the railway station. The insurance man will be along later to discuss that. So. Here is the office.' With a flourish, he flung open a door to reveal a medium-sized room carpeted in red and furnished with good, solid pieces, a sofa, several chairs, a desk, bookshelves and cabinets.

'Lovely,' sighed Tilly, patting her naked hair. She sat down and looked at the spread on Mark's desk, her mouth watering in anticipation. 'Is that what I think it is?' she asked.

'Smoked salmon,' answered Mark. 'Only the best for my two favourite girls.'

Yes, thought Emily, this grandson of hers would go far. He had the looks, the charm and the patter, could probably have sold Manfredi's ice-cream to Eskimos without any trouble at all. She was so proud that her heart lifted every time she looked at him.

'Customer notes will go in there.' He waved a hand at a filing cabinet. 'And in the other side, we'll keep a list of searches, based on items in which a customer has expressed interest. Going along again to the next drawer, we marry what the customer wants to a broader field, pieces similar to his sphere of interest – if he likes Stubbs paint-ings, he may extend into equine figurines.' He looked at their faces. 'Worry not, all will become clear,' he reassured them. 'Collectors of antiques are compulsive and impulsive. They are easily excited and eager to invest. Sometimes they are too eager.'

Tilly picked up a sandwich and bit into it. She was starving and not one to stand on ceremony. 'Not bad for raw fish,' was her delivered judgement.

The shop bell sounded. 'Anybody there?' shouted a man's voice.

Emily looked startled. 'Is that our Phil?'

Mark laughed. 'We're keeping it all in the family, Bunny. Mrs Povey is, of course, an honorary member.'

Phil Dyson entered, Annie Hurst picking her way behind him. 'Come in,' urged Mark, 'but don't fall over anything until we're better insured.'

Annie was introduced to everyone. Emily had not met her before, had been too busy for a visit. She liked what she saw, a gentle-faced woman with soft hair and pretty brown eyes.

The man and the boy discussed policies and secure storage while the women listened in wonderment. Too young to have full responsibility, Mark made it plain that every transaction he conducted would have to be confirmed by his aunt, as Stella held the reins while he pulled the cart. He was not ashamed of his youth, was not proud of it: Mark was simply Mark, a straight thinker and a straight talker.

Emily watched her two boys together. They spanned two generations and a gulf the width of the Grand Canyon, but were sidestepping the past and bestriding all difficulties as if they had never existed. And she realized that she was happy, that the unfamiliar sensation in her chest was attributable to pure joy. If only poor Matthew would get better, the hole in her life would be almost darned.

Irene Richards had no intention of stepping out of her son's life. She had visited him every evening and was beginning to notice an improvement in him. He no longer raved about murder, though he remained quiet and withdrawn for much of the time. He was up and about now, was allowed to wander about Rutherford Hall, had maintained the status of voluntary patient.

Major Jack was talking of coming home, would be back within the next couple of days. A woman who had always kept herself in good order, Irene felt as wild as her son must have felt when under the influence of the barbiturates for which he had displayed no tolerance. She did not know what to do, where to turn. It would be back to the same old routine, all activities dictated by Jack, he issuing orders, she carrying them out; so far, he had enjoyed the privilege of rank, while Irene had been very much a member of the ordinary file of non-commissioned personnel.

For the first time since her husband's departure, she poured herself a hefty measure of gin – a desperate measure, she joked inwardly. But this was no joke, because mutiny was never pleasant. 'I shall be court-martialled,' she informed the empty room. 'Lucky if I don't get shot.'

For days, she had mulled over the possibilities, but there were no possibilities, not in the real sense. Her time in recent days had been divided between her two loves: her son and her horses. The third love, her home and its beautiful contents, was suddenly an insignificant contender.

The rediscovery of Matthew had been little short of miraculous. Her son, who had never been quite up to scratch in Major Jack's closed book, was edging his way forward, was no longer crawling on his belly to avoid encountering the hail of bullets he had once expected. His chin was out of the trench and he had almost ceased to look for trouble; inch by inch, he was nearing the point where he might advance gingerly into uncharted territory.

'The major will try to keep him away from the world,' she muttered. 'Rather a dead soldier than an injured one, because who wants to carry that burden into new pastures?'

Oh, God, what was she going to do? Should she run now, get away while the commanding officer was enjoying his rations? She had her own money, a secret stash created many years ago when she had first entered the world of antiques. The thought of moving on was both exciting and terrifying, because she had not been single for over forty years. Yet everything had to change. Soon, her son would be well enough to step back into society, would need support on a larger scale and, no matter what, Irene could not abandon him.

She put on her coat and prepared to do what her husband had done many times: she would drive when her head was rather less than clear, because she needed to talk to someone. And the only person she had in this cold world was her grandson, a boy not yet seventeen, someone she had not seen since Molly's funeral. He and his aunt Stella visited Matthew in the afternoons while Irene always went in the evenings, so their paths had not yet crossed.

If she departed now, she could see the boy and be back in time for her usual visit. Her hands trembled as she picked up the keys to the car. Perhaps she could talk to Stella Dyson, Matthew's medical sister-in-law. Perhaps she would change her mind and divert to the town centre for a shopping session. Whatever, she needed to get out now, wanted to be occupied, because her thoughts were not the sort of company she wanted to keep today.

As she drove past the elegant gates that bordered the property known as Rutherford Hall, Irene's sinews stiffened both in reality and in the metaphorical sense. Her son was in there, while the real idiots were on the outside, free to come and go as they pleased. It was time to redress the balance, though the plans in that direction were as clear as the mud of Flanders . . .

Stella Dyson had missed her first period and was absolutely certain about her condition. No longer finding Mrs Janet Fishwick amusing, she now realized that she and Mrs Fishwick were two of that small number of women who know almost from the start that they are pregnant. The physical side was inconvenient, because she was experiencing discomfort in her stomach, yet that paled into insignificance when she considered the longer term.

It was her mental condition that worried her now. She swung from one despair to another, afraid of abortion, afraid of shame, even afraid of childbirth. Her mind was fixed on her job, because only through application was she able to take her mind off her problem. It was grim and she could not make a decision.

Mam was a boon, coming across several times a

week to sit with her, to listen to her fears and worries. Visiting Matthew was not helping, of course. He knew who she was, probably remembered nothing about their brief coupling, was certainly in no state to take responsibility for his actions. Anyway, it had all been her fault: as always, she had seen what she wanted and gone for it. There was no excuse for her behaviour and the shame she felt made a huge contribution to her unease.

Her bell sounded and she went to let in this latest caller. It would not be Mam: she was at the shop with Mark and Tilly, was preparing to be dragged into the relaunch of the business. Even the name was to be changed to Matthew & Son, while the interior would be ripped to pieces and there was little she could do about any of it. Had she put her foot down, her nephew would now be sitting at home with nothing to occupy himself. Also, she had not the energy for foot-stamping, so she was allowing life to roll along beside and outside of herself. How could she criticize anyone? The mess she was making of her own existence was proof enough that she could not organize anyone else's.

It was Simon MacRae. He was becoming more confident all the time, was edging nearer to the first date, the first kiss and all that other tedious stuff that seemed to be imperative before mating. 'Come in,' she said, a layer of false enthusiasm painted on to the words.

He had brought the most hideous cactus in Christendom, a phallic article with spines all over it. 'Meet Fred,' he said, before thrusting the dark blue pot into her hands. 'He needs water very rarely, but he responds to kindness.'

Stella allowed him to carry the thing upstairs. 'Where would you like it?' he asked, merriment shining in the green eyes.

And she decided there and then that she would marry this man immediately, because that would save a lot of trouble. All she needed now was to find an explanation for her haste. She took the ugly plant from him, placed it in the hearth and kissed him. The experience was not unpleasant, though he tasted of strong mint toothpaste with just a hint of cigar keeping the Macleans company. His response was positive and she submitted without giving any trouble, allowing him to peel off her clothes and worship her body. It was interesting to watch his reactions: she noted how he trembled like a virgin, how his heart-rate changed, the sounds he made when he climaxed.

So, that was that. She was pregnant, the baby was Simon's and it would arrive a few weeks early.

'I love you,' he declared.

'Good,' replied Stella.

He began to run his hands through her hair and she wished that he would stop. Matthew had done that. As far as she was concerned, any man would have sufficed just now, but she had fallen lucky, had netted a doctor.

'Do you love me?' he asked.

'Of course I do,' she answered. 'Otherwise that would not have happened just now, would it?'

He angled his arm and supported his chin on

his cupped palm. 'Fred brought us together,' he said. 'Fred could be our best man.'

She looked at the plant. 'I don't think he'd look good in a morning suit,' she said, 'though he might be allowed at a register-office function, plain clothes, no fuss, just a carnation pinned to his chest. What do you think, Simon?'

'I want the church bit,' said Simon. 'It's only once, I hope, so let's do it properly. Yes, a choir, some bells, our mothers weeping. And Fred must be there, of course. Spring, summer?'

'Yes.' She smiled, though her mind disagreed. They would be married within weeks, and that was that.

'You can't do that, Stella.' Emily's eyebrows almost disappeared into her hairline. 'It wouldn't be right. You can't marry the man just because you think you're having Matthew's baby.'

'Oh, but I can.'

'What about love, though?' Emily asked.

Stella managed not to laugh. 'Did you love Dad? At the start, I mean?'

Colour arrived in the older woman's cheeks. 'I thought so.'

'And where did that get you?' asked Stella. 'You finished up with a drunken bum who beat the living daylights out of you every time his beer money dried up. That didn't exactly work out as a dream marriage, did it? No. At least Simon is a decent man, one who won't damage me or the child. Look, Mam, I don't have a lot of choice. Matthew is ill, I am pregnant, and Simon wants to marry me. He has taken me out several times, he is excellent company, so where is the harm?'

'It's dishonest,' insisted Emily. 'And the baby, if there is one, will be born at the wrong time—'

'The baby will be premature.'

'So you've . . . you've already been with him?'

'Of course I have – I had to. He has plainly wanted to marry me for ages. He is an honourable man, who would not abandon a woman who carries his child. Does it matter whose baby this is? As long as Simon thinks the child is his, where's the harm? It will get two parents, a good home and a decent education – who's going to know the difference?'

'You are.'

Stella sighed, clasped her hands between her knees. 'And you will know.'

'Yes.'

'And you won't betray me?'

Emily shook her head sadly. 'Do you need to ask that? I know I wasn't much of a mother, but I'm here now and, like I've said before, I'm going nowhere, not while I'm needed by you and Mark.' She leaned forward in her chair. 'Listen to me, Stella.'

'I'm listening.'

'Marriage is hard. Ask Tilly – and she's had a good marriage. It's the same person, day in and day out, year after year. The things you like about him now will become irritating – the way he laughs, the way he eats, all that. In the end, it's about friendship, because the fancy stuff goes off like milk left in the sun. All that fairy-story business is just that – tales for kids. Do you really think Cinderella lived happily ever after? Did she heck as like. Oh, it were all right when she had them dainty little feet to shove in her glass slippers, but what about when her bunions got sore, when she needed her corns shaving by a chiropodist?'

Stella could not stop the smile now. She had never known Mam have so much to say for herself: the woman had opinions, she was bright, she was sensible, even imaginative. 'Simon and I don't have any glass slippers, Mam.'

Emily raised her shoulders. 'That's as may be, but that clock still ticks and strikes twelve times at midnight. What do you do then, when it all turns back to pumpkins and mice, eh?'

'And we won't have a coach, either. There won't be all that to lose, can't you see? I don't love him, but I like him. There's no fancy business, Mam. Can't you grasp what I mean? What doesn't shine can't tarnish.'

The mother of this expressive young woman closed her eyes, tried to shut out what she had just discovered, but she could not. The sad thing was that Stella made a lot of sense, yet Emily could not manage to think along the same lines. What sometimes made good brain sense did not make good heart sense, though who was she to try persuasion? Yes, she had gone blindly into marriage with Joe; yes, she had loved him. And yes, that same man, having suffered a fatal accident, had ridden unmourned to his grave.

'It will be all right,' Stella insisted.

Perhaps the girl was right. Could a marriage

built on necessity really work? 'But you think he loves you.'

'He does,' replied Stella. 'He's been hanging around like a sick puppy for months, since long before . . . before Molly died. He has the love, I have the sense. Will that do?'

Emily opened her eyes. She didn't know, was too weary to wonder about it. Her life was full, enjoyable, but very busy. What with supervising signwriters, cleaning, painting walls, learning, getting leaflets printed, she was steeped well past her eyes in responsibilities. 'God knows, I'm not happy about this, Stella.'

'God's just another story from Hans Christian Andersen, Mam, but we don't need to go into that. Now.' She jumped up, rubbed her hands together. 'Tea and toasted tea-cakes, I think.' She went off into her kitchen.

Emily stared at a hideous plant on the hearth. It was a recent addition, just about the ugliest thing she had seen in some considerable time. Fred, Stella had called it, said it was her firstborn. Well, with all those spikes and prickles, Emily hoped that the delivery had been by Caesarian section, because the mother of that thing would have needed knock-out drops.

'The wedding will be soon,' called Stella from the kitchen, 'a lot sooner than Simon thinks, of course, so we must make sure you have something decent to wear.'

Yes, that was Stella, practical even when in the tightest of corners. 'Mark's going to buy me some things,' answered Emily, 'for when the shop opens.'

Stella appeared in the doorway. 'No, Mam, this will be something special, to make up for all those years when you had nothing. It wasn't easy, was it?'

'No. No, it wasn't.'

'How do you fancy sugar pink?'

Emily smiled. 'How do you fancy a thick ear?'

So they ate tea-cakes with far too much butter, drank tea until it was time for Emily to go home to Mark. And, in those short hours, they realized that they were making up for lost time. At last, mother and child had come together.

There had been no one in the first time she had visited Coniston, so it was a matter of girding one's loins again, this time without the help of gin. The gin had to stop: everything had to stop.

Irene looked around her drawing room and sighed. So many pieces, so much history, what a great pity this was. She ran a hand over a table on which the marks of a long-dead axe showed, over a case clock, over a mantelpiece saved from another farmhouse that had been demolished by man's utter carelessness. She had no idea of where her life was going, no real idea why all her personal belongings were in the car. But she had to go, because the step she had taken was drastic.

He would be on a train now, would be ready to come back into this house with tales of Manny's invalid wife, Mac's gambling, Ironsides' arthritic knees. He would also deliver the usual litany, who had died, who was about to die, who should have died because he never got a medal.

The major's horses, really hers, were gone. She

had sold them all for cash to a reputable Cheshire breeder, had wept buckets when her favourites had been boxed and driven away. But Major Jack was as hard on his mounts as he was on his son, so Irene had felt unable to leave them in his care. She had given up her horseflesh, her home, its contents; she was losing her friends, her bridge and her mind, because only a fool could drive away from all this.

'It's for Matthew,' she told a brass-framed mirror that contained glass so old and flawed that she scarcely recognized her echo on its surface, so distorted were her features. Well, at least the dogs were all gone. Monty, Winston and Bertie, two English retrievers and a Welsh collie, had died some time ago. She could not have left them and they would have been too old to settle elsewhere.

So. One of the heroes of North Africa and Europe was on his way home. He would expect a meal, a listening ear, a willing servant to unpack his case so that the char could do his washing tomorrow. He would seek his virtuous wife, would discover her treachery as soon as he found the pages on his pillow.

Dear Jack,
I realize that this will come as something of a shock, but I do not know how I might soften the blow, so I must deliver it quickly and efficiently.

I am leaving you and shall probably be gone before you get home. This letter may be a coward's way out, yet I dare not stay, as I am not in a state fit enough to withstand your righteous anger.

During your absence, I have visited Matthew almost every day. For many, many years I have stood by while you have called him worthless, but I can tolerate that no longer. He is a sick man who improves slowly with each passing day and I intend to support him through the pain he is enduring.

I have been a foolish woman, because I have heeded your every demand and command, but I shall take no more orders from anyone in the future. Matthew is now the centre of my life and I intend to recompense him for the neglect he has suffered so far.

You will rant and rave now. You will worry about the reactions of friends and neighbours, many of whom have visited our son, most of whom have wished him better. As for myself, I have finally discovered who I truly am and what I wish to do with my own future, whatever its duration. It is with great reluctance that I have sold the horses I bought for you, but I cannot trust you to treat them humanely, especially now, with your temper boiling.

This house, bought with the legacy I received from my parents, is in my name only. As you have left paperwork to me exclusively, I have guarded my own interests and make no apology for that. My lawyer tells me that my case is watertight and that I may have you evicted if I choose.

I choose not to do that. The divorce will be swift, discreet and without fuss as long as you comply with the following:

1. You will not try to find me.

2. You will stay away from Matthew.

3. You will dispose of no items from the farmhouse.

4. You will keep no more horses on my land.

5. You will care for my property and maintain it in good order.

I grant you permission to lease to surrounding farms any or all of my acreage. Such leases will be limited in duration to a maximum of four years. I have appointed an overseer for both house and land. He will call on you periodically to ensure that you are adhering to the rules above. Every piece in the house has been photographed and catalogued for future reference.

With great regret, I now leave the farm I have loved. I do this in order to rid myself of your company so that I might enjoy life elsewhere.

I wish you no harm and trust that you will remain in robust health.

Sincerely, Irene

She had no need to reread the letter. It had taken a whole evening to compose and correct and it would be followed swiftly by a document from her lawyers. Why was her heart beating so fast and so loudly? This was only property, just things. Yet saying goodbye to such cherished items was cutting her deeply and she found herself near to tears.

She locked up the house, turned to face the car. There would be no one to pick him up at Trinity Street, no one to bring him home to a house in which he had been little more than a non-paying guest, because his wife was the one with the real money. Still, with his pension and rents from the land, he would be able to afford his whisky, at least.

When Irene Richards started the engine of her vehicle, her spirits began to lift. How many people in their sixties got the chance of a fresh beginning, the opportunity for rebirth? She was so fortunate: she had reasonable health, a son who needed her, an excuse to continue alive. Because of her station in society, the purchase of another house had been hastened by friends in certain circles, a solicitor, an estate agent, a furniture dealer. Yes, she was lucky.

As she passed Rutherford Hall, she smiled to herself. 'Soon, Matthew,' she promised. Yes, soon her son would be home.

Mark flicked through a magazine. Sitting here while his father slept was no fun, but he persevered out of a sense of . . . was it duty? Was it? He was reading an article on Blenheim Palace, was studying photographs, found himself wishing that he could get his hands on some of those paintings.

'We loved you.'

Mark's head shot up so quickly that he cricked his neck.

'We always loved you.' Matthew closed his eyes again.

The son rose to his feet and walked towards the bed. His father was sound asleep. 'Thanks,' whispered Mark. Then he swallowed his tears and left the room.

Eight

Stella Dyson watched the furniture van as it pulled up across the road. It was destined for The Briars, a property next door to the one owned by Matthew Richards. Slightly smaller than Coniston, The Briars was a Victorian brick building with gables, windows set in sandstone surrounds, very tall chimneys and a garden that was wild. 'Probably full of briars,' commented Stella, just before biting into her apple.

It was her day off, so she pulled a chair to her window and sat idly, her eyes fixed to events across Chorley New Road, her mind riveted to small complications like pregnancy, when to tell Simon, whether he would believe her and what to do about a certain patient who was showing symptoms of glandular fever.

All the furniture carried into The Briars was new, high quality and solid, but definitely straight from the showrooms. Was this a recently married couple? If so, they were well-to-do, because there was nothing shabby about their purchases. She settled to wait for her new neighbours, fascinated by their choice.

Then the Bentley arrived, grey, sleek, probably purring like a contented cat. A woman stepped out of the car, elegant, beautifully dressed, her clothing making an understatement so subtle that it oozed money. She was handsome, with neatly coiffed silver hair and the bearing of the well-born. Good God! Stella jumped up, dropped her apple, cursed. This was the last of the Golden Delicious and she was watching her weight . . .

It was Irene Richards. Wasn't it? Stella stood so close to the window that her breath clouded its surface. Yes, that was Matthew's mother. What on earth was she doing here? They had a farm north of Bolton, a place near Eagley village. According to legend, the woman had taken years to furnish it with stuff so valuable that her insurance policy was fabled to be a hair's breadth from the National Debt. So . . . so what was happening?

The men carried in sofas, chairs, tables, beds, wardrobes. Another van arrived, this time from a department store in Manchester. From that, many boxes were transported inside, then a television set, a radiogram, some large, transparent bags that appeared to contain fabrics – curtains, other household linens, perhaps. It took over half an hour for everything to be transferred to the inside of the house, then the vans drove off, the front door of The Briars was closed, and it was as if none of that had really happened.

Stella blinked. No, it was real, because there stood the grey Bentley and here came Irene Richards again. The woman climbed into her car, reversed, widened the space between car and pavement, then swung into the driveway. She parked, locked the vehicle, went inside once more. Stella scratched her head. Nothing had been said, surely? She hadn't missed anything, hadn't forgotten, was not losing her mind.

Mam would have known, wouldn't she? Mark, too. There had to be an explanation. Stella hastened to get her coat, picked up a handbag and a bunch of keys, left her flat and crossed the road to Coniston. She walked round the side of the house, her eyes fastened to the wall between the two properties, ears pricked and ready for noise.

Tilly Povey was punishing a large amount of bread dough in the kitchen, was heaving it about as if bent on murder. 'Hello, Dr Dyson,' she said cheerily, 'Mark's at the shop with your mam. If you'll hang on a minute, I'll make you a nice cup of tea. This bread only wants another few minutes' rest and it'll be ready to divide.'

Stella sat at the table. She and Tilly were still trying each other for size, though the newly revived relationship was definitely improving. 'Tilly?'

'What?'

'Call me Stella, will you? I get enough doctoring across the road – it's nice to be myself sometimes.'

'All right.'

The visitor stared silently at her own hands as if waiting to find an answer in that tight tangle of digits. 'Tilly?'

'What?' repeated the housekeeper.

'Did you know that Matthew's mother seems to have moved in next door?'

Tilly dropped her dough into a huge, blue-rimmed enamel resting bowl, then covered its surface with a piece of muslin. 'Nay, they're country, Stella,' she replied. 'Must be somebody as looks like her. She wouldn't want to be living here so close to town, nowhere to ride her horses, no space for a stable in yon back garden.'

Stella nodded thoughtfully. 'I would have said exactly the same thing until about an hour ago. I still don't believe what I'm saying, but it's the truth, because I saw it all. It was definitely Mrs Richards.'

Tilly joined Stella at the table. 'But . . . why?'

'I have absolutely no idea. But you must find out, Tilly.'

The older woman frowned. 'Me? Why is it always me that has to go into the unknown? Eh? Were I born with the word "daft" printed on me forehead? It's the same at home, "Send our Tilly" every time some new bugger moves in on our block. You go, Stella.'

'Tilly—'

'Don't be wheedling. I've bread and flour cakes on the go here, some for Mark and Emily, some for me to take home. If I go piking off next door, me yeast won't get looked after. You have to watch yeast, you know, it's got a mind of its own.' She lifted her chin. 'Bread-making is an inexact science and you have to show your dough who's boss.' She paused. 'I wonder why she never said owt, though. I mean, that's a right peculiar carry-on, saying nowt then moving all that way.'

'New furniture, too. Brand new, straight from the factory.'

'Eeh,' exclaimed Tilly. 'I've never heard of any of the Richards lot buying new – they always have second-hand.'

'Antique, Tilly.'

'Aye, that's what I said. Well, this is a turn-up. Let me put the kettle on while I have a think.'

Stella's gaze landed on a batch of newly baked maids-of-honour. 'Take her a cup of tea and a cake, Tilly, act surprised when you recognize her.'

Tilly froze, hand in mid-air as she reached for cups. 'I'm no good at being surprised, you can ask my Seth. I've not been surprised since Macmillan told me I were having a good time. I never knew I were having a good time till then. Aye, that were a bit of a shock, I must admit.' She sniffed meaningfully. 'Bloody southerners,' she muttered, before continuing with her task.

To hide a huge grin, Stella brought a hand to her face.

'You know I'll do it, don't you?' Tilly swung round to face her guest. 'You know I can't stand this sort of thing, that I can't go home till I find out what's going on. You're taking advantage of my nature, Stella, but not my better nature.'

'Yes.'

'Oh, well,' sighed Tilly, 'at least I know where I am with you, so I suppose that's summat to be grateful for. Right. So I pretend as I noticed somebody moving in next door, only I don't know who she is until I see her.'

'That's it.'

'And I'm taking a cup of tea and a cake by way of welcome.'

'Yes.'

'Then I go all surprised, drop the cake and the tea and—'

'No, forget that bit.'

'I'll do me best.' Tilly poured tea into one of the best cups, a Doulton with roses outside and in, then found a saucer and a matching side-plate. Armed with cake and hot drink, she waited for Stella to open the door for her. As she walked out, Tilly threw the last words over her shoulder: 'Watch that bread,' she snapped, 'and if it goes wrong, you can make the next batch.'

There were three large bedrooms and one small one, though Irene had furnished just the master at the front of the house. Carpets had been laid yesterday and the split-second timing of the whole exercise had left her exhausted. She had bought a house in days rather than weeks, had equipped it from scratch, right down to condiments and bed-sheets. She had fooled herself into believing that the house was a mere investment, that she would let it to tenants, but no. Here she was with new furniture and carpets and . . . and, for better or worse, here she definitely was.

Almost tired enough for tears, she sank into one of her new chairs in the living room and wondered what she had done. Yes, it was an interesting house, no, she would not have chosen to live here, yes, she was here to be near Matthew, no, she did not want to reside on a main road. God. It was too late to go back: the major would be home, too much explaining to do – and she owned this house now, lock, stock and flaking paint. So, all that remained was a son in hospital, several pairs of curtains to hang, a bed to make – and what would she not give for a nice, strong cup of tea?

Someone rattled the doorknob and she forced herself to answer. A thin woman stood there, hair-net tight about greying brown hair, flowered apron wrapped like armour around the slight form. In her hands, she bore crockery, Doulton, Irene thought. 'Is that tea?' She reached out an eager hand and took the cup. 'You've saved my life. Do come in.'

Tilly followed Irene Richards into the house, which had stood empty for some time. It had that neglected look, rather decadent and sad, as if no one cared whether it lived or died. They reached the kitchen and sat on a pair of new chairs whose legs were still wrapped in cardboard.

'I'm Tilly Povey,' said the visitor, 'and you're Mrs Richards. Really, I'm supposed to pretend I don't know who you are, but I've bread rising, so I haven't time for all that carry-on. Anyway, I work next door for your son, but I had no idea that you were moving in here.' She glanced around the kitchen. 'Everything's new. I thought you went in for old stuff just like Mr Richards does.'

'Time for a change,' said Irene, between sips. 'The tea is truly wonderful and thank you for the cake. I shall eat it later.'

Tilly was getting nowhere fast. Madam-next-door was going to be wanting some answers and then there was the bread.

'I didn't tell anyone about my move,' said Irene.

'Oh, I see.'

'I wish *I* saw,' Irene admitted, her tone sombre. 'Followed my instincts rather than my head, I'm afraid.'

'Right.' The bread could be near the top of the bowl by now. She had to divide it, make two one-pounders, half a dozen flour cakes and, if there was any left, a fruit loaf for Mark. And there was still a bit of ironing. Tilly decided to come clean. 'It's Stella,' she confessed, 'Dr Dyson, Mr Richards' sister-in-law. She lives and works across the road and she saw you moving in, so she came over and sent me to find out why you're here. So I'm asking. Why are you here?'

'How much time do I have to find the answer to that question?'

'About two and a half minutes, no injury time added on.'

Irene found herself grinning. This Tilly Povey woman was a character, unafraid and rather eccentric, amusing and terribly outspoken. 'My husband disowned our son, because mental illness terrifies him. I have come to Chorley New Road so that I might help when Matthew comes home.' There. It was out in the open and it needed to be.

'That'll do,' answered Tilly. 'Is it all right if I tell her that? Only I'm thinking about me bread, you see. It's not that I don't care, because your son did his best for Emily's Molly. Mind, he could be closer to his own son, but never mind, 'cos there's none of us perfect. So I'm bothered about what happens to Mr Richards, only I'm bothered about me bread, too.'

For the first time in years, Irene Richards was helpless with laughter. This woman should have been on the halls, ought to have been used to entertain troops during times of conflict: she was a tonic, a tease and an absolute hoot.

Tilly watched the laughing neighbour. She hoped this wasn't the hystericals, because she hadn't time to cope. 'Are you fit to be left on your own?' she asked. 'Only I've got me—'

'Your bread to bake. Yes, yes.' Irene dried her streaming eyes. 'I shall come along later to explain myself. Mrs Dyson will be there this evening, I take it?'

Tilly nodded. She'd heard about the high-born being a bit high-strung, and this one was strung as tightly as a chicken trussed and ready for the oven. 'Are you sure you'll be all right?' she asked dubiously. 'Only Stella's a doctor, I could send her in to give you the once-over.'

'I'm fine,' Irene insisted.

'Good,' said Tilly, her tone demonstrating deep uncertainty. She left the cup, saucer and plate, making her exit rapidly. If Stella wanted to know anything else, she could do her own dirty work or wait till later on.

Tilly slammed the back door of Coniston in her wake and stared hard at Stella Dyson. She marched to the table, whipped the muslin off her dough and prodded to test the consistency.

'Well?' Stella asked.

Tilly sniffed. 'It'll do. I might even get a fruit loaf out of it.'

'Stop being deliberately obtuse, Tilly, you know what I'm talking about. Come on, out with it.'

Tilly pretended to ponder. 'Oh, I see what you mean. Her next door? Is that what you're on about?'

'Yes.' Stella's teeth were gritted.

'Right, I see. Well, it is Mrs Richards, yes, she has moved in and, yes, it's so that she'll be near her son when he gets out of yon place.'

'Ah.'

'But.' Tilly waved the deadly knife with which she intended to cut the dough into portions. 'But don't send me back because she's as daft as a bucket of frogs. In fact, she could swap places with her son because she's madder than he is. Hysterical, she was, laughing for nowt.'

'Oh dear,' breathed Stella.

Tilly greased her pound tins. 'Naw,' she said, after some contemplation. 'Her's all right. Has a sense of humour, so she'll do for me. Now, Stella Dyson, bugger off home while I concentrate on this here bread.'

Stella laughed, picked up her bag and buggered off as instructed.

Major Jack walked into his house. She had not come to meet him, had left him stranded at Trinity Street station, and he was not pleased. Fortunately, a taxi had been standing by, so he had not been forced to wait too long. He dropped his bags in the flagged hall. 'Irene?' he roared.

His voice seemed to echo and return to him. Had she gone out? Surely not – she had been told that he was coming home today, knew which train she should have met. Was she ill? He wandered from room to room, finally going out into the yard to look for her in the stables. Had she had an accident in the car? He hoped not, because that car was his pride and joy. This really was too bad.

The stables were deserted. When he saw the empty stalls, an uneasiness crept into his stomach. The casual staff who worked with the animals were nowhere to be seen, but Irene had always done some stable work herself – found it relaxing, liked the company of horses. The absence of employees was not a worry, as they came and went in accordance with instructions, but were all the horses out? There was no equipment in the tack room, no litter around, no droppings.

A shiver ran the length of his spine and he felt a dart of fear in his chest. Something was dreadfully wrong here. There was still ample daylight, but the beasts were usually in by this time, ready to be fed, dried off if necessary, made quiet for the night. He turned, his eyes scanning the lane, ears eager for the sound of hoofs, heart beating faster.

Well, there was nothing he could do. The best course of action would be a measure of Scotch and a bite to eat. Perhaps she had left him something in the refrigerator, a snack, or perhaps she had left a note to explain this atypical behaviour. Was she ill? Was she in hospital? He stopped next to the last stable, the one nearest the house: this was no longer a stable but a garage in which the

Bentley was kept. He opened one door, saw space yawning in front of him, no car, no clue.

Well, if she was driving, she wasn't ill. She could not have had an accident because the police would have been here by now. And if she wasn't ill or hurt, she would surely be back in time for supper. Travelling on trains was tiring, he was hungry, thirsty and his wife was missing. She had never gone missing before. She had no right to be AWOL today of all days, when he had so much to tell. Poor old Ironsides in hospital, his missus in a home, some form of dementia discovered when she had been found naked in the middle of Knightsbridge with a frying pan and a packet of Lipton's tea – where was Irene?

He went inside, picked up the kettle, put water in it, stood it on the cooker. Right. Coffee. He had no idea how to make coffee, had never had occasion to concoct the stuff. Ah, well, whisky would suffice. With some cheese and a packet of crackers, he settled in his chair by a cheerless grate. So, what had happened to the char? No fire, no meal prepared, no welcome.

He drank himself towards the hem of stupor, retaining just enough equilibrium to drag his body upstairs. In his room, he managed to get to the bed, where he collapsed and fell asleep, still wearing the clothes he had donned that morning in Chelsea. His last thoughts were of the horses and the car. Oh, yes, and his wife was missing . . .

Alice placed a blue mug on the trolley that spanned Matthew's bed. She was leaving

Rutherford Hall soon and she would miss the place. The staff displayed camaraderie, supported one another without question and worked damned hard. In fact, Alice was quite happy working in the area of psychiatric medicine and was seriously thinking of diverting in its direction.

He was seated by the window and was looking out on a beautiful area of garden. The peacocks had gone to bed, sad cries silenced for another day. Stray beams of light left behind by a setting sun reflected on clouds above a hilly horizon. It was all so peaceful, so unreal.

She would miss him. There was something so lost, so vulnerable in this man and she had spent a great deal of time in his company during her spell at Rutherford Hall. 'Hello, Matthew. Shall I bring your cocoa over there?'

He turned. 'No, thanks, Alice – I shall be going to bed in a moment.'

She joined him and sat in the chair that was a twin to his. 'I love the moors,' she said, her eyes fixed on those disappearing rays of light. 'I can't imagine living in a flat place.'

'I know,' he replied. 'It's amazing how we take such beauty for granted. Of course, the moors made Bolton, brought the cotton here, because the damp is trapped in the town and damp is what cotton needs. That's almost finished now, of course. All these man-made fibres, cheaper cotton goods from Asia – Bolton is going to need a new direction.'

'Yes.' She looked sideways at him. 'You'll be out of here soon.'

'I know. And so will you.'

Alice took the next step carefully. 'You live on Chorley New Road?'

'I do,' he replied. 'The house is called Coniston.'

'I live in a flat at the town end, right next door to the nurses' home.'

'Ah.' He stood up. 'Perhaps we shall catch sight of each other, then.'

She wanted that, wanted it more than anything. Wanted him. And she could not work out why. He was very attractive, which helped, but it wasn't just that: it was who he was, what he was. 'Will your son be carrying on with the shop?' she asked. 'Or will he go back to school when you're home?'

He smiled thoughtfully. 'He'll never go back, Alice. I'm very impressed by him and was glad to hand over, I must admit. Yes, he has talked to me during his visits. Stella is supervising as best she can, but Mark is very much at the helm. He asked if he could change the shop's name.'

'He has,' she said. 'It's Matthew & Son. There's a new sign outside, gold on green. Very nice.'

'I know. He wanted to see his efforts rewarded right from the start. So I allowed him his head. That is one determined young man, very interesting to talk to, suddenly an adult. I wish I knew him better.'

'You will,' she promised, before walking to the door. 'You'll have all the time in the world.'

'Of course I will,' he lied. When she had gone, he drank his cocoa and prepared himself for bed. It had been easy in the end: regaining his sanity had not been a problem. Now, he knew exactly how to act, how to walk to the drummer most people heard. It was one step, one hour at a time, go in a straight line, no running, no loitering, head up, stride on.

But he would not be going home, oh, no. Matthew Richards needed to be alone, wanted a fresh start, a clean sheet. His son deserved a new life, a chance to make his own way. It was time for Matthew to move on. The past was Molly and the future was not, so the path had to be away from the places he remembered, the years he had shared with her.

As a murderer, he was not fit to be a father, had never been a parent anyway. Yes, Mark would be healthier away from him.

He lay down, fell asleep within minutes. His torture was over and he was no longer in acute pain.

'Right,' said Tilly. 'Emily wants our support and that's why we're going. Look at me when I'm talking to you. Straighten your face and your tie – Seth!'

'What?' He was fed up. He'd done a hard day's work on early shift, wanted a nice snooze in front of the fire, yet here he was, dog's dinner, best suit, hanky in the top pocket, and it was only Wednesday. He had never dressed up on a Wednesday for as long as he could remember. His shoes hurt, his trousers were tight and the shirt collar felt as if it might cut through his neck like a hot knife slicing butter.

Tilly gave him one of her looks. She would never work men out if she lived to be a hundred and five. Now, women were different – they were normal. Put a woman in nice clothes and she blossomed, looked five inches taller, three inches thinner and a damned sight happier. Men were the opposite, and this man was as opposite as a man could possibly be. Dress him in greasy over-alls and a flat cap and he was blissful. Best suit? No chance. He wore the air of the terminally insulted, looked downtrodden, uncomfortable and definitely at odds with the world. 'Stand up straight,' she ordered.

'I am straight, it's the bloody clothes that's crooked.'

'There's nowt wrong with the clothes, it's you,' she replied. It was a big night for Emily. The lady next door, Matthew Richards' mother, was coming round to introduce herself properly. 'You know Emily doesn't take things in her stride,' she told her husband.

'Well, I wish I could stride,' he complained. 'These trousers are splitting me difference and, as for the shoes, I'm crippled.'

It was hopeless. She had done her best to bring him up properly, but he was always at odds with clothes. No matter what she did, he never looked right. The clothes didn't seem happy, either. They sat on him unwillingly, as if they cried out to be reunited with their rightful wearer. 'Why can't you look like somebody owns you?'

'I am owned,' he replied, 'and I don't know why you don't put me on a lead and have bloody done with it. I wanted a quiet night in, a Guinness from the outdoor licence, watch a bit of telly. It's a shock, is this, enough to give me a heart-attack. I've had no chance to work me way up to it.'

'Aye, well, you can work your way up to the bus stop and shape yourself. We have to be quick because she never said what time she were coming. Mrs Richards, I mean. The more of us the merrier, then Emily won't feel stared at.'

Seth would feel stared at. He didn't know what use he would be, but Tilly had put her foot down. For such a thin woman, Tilly was very heavy-footed, heavy-handed and loud in the voice department. He was going, she had decided he was going, and that was that. 'Come on, then,' he said resignedly. 'Let's get it over and done with.'

She picked up her handbag. 'You should be grateful that I'm taking you out. There's many a woman would have given up on you years ago, but you know me, I'm not one as gets beaten easily. I persevere.'

'I noticed,' he answered gloomily.

The air of misery sat on him all the way down Tonge Moor, through town and up Chorley New Road. By the time they reached Coniston, he looked like a man ready for the gallows, feet moving reluctantly, head bowed, eyes haunted.

As they crossed over from the bus stop, Tilly grabbed his arm. 'Right, you,' she hissed, from between tense lips, 'I want none of them stories from work and forget all about fishing and false teeth.'

'Yes, miss.'

'And try to smile.'

'What for?'

'Because I said so. Now, if you're good, I'll buy you a pint on the way home – we can stop off at the Wheatsheaf. And I'll do you tripe and onions tomorrow.'

He cheered up at once. 'Can we have bread-and-butter pudding for afters? With custard?'

She awarded him a look that might have curdled paint. 'Don't push your luck, Seth. I do have my limits.'

Resigned to his fate, he followed her limits up the path and round the back of the very smart house that was her place of work. Never mind, he thought. This looked like a house where they might have a drop of brandy and a nice sandwich. He could live in hope, he supposed. So he straightened his shoulders, pinned a smile to his face and hoped for the best.

Stella watched Tilly and Seth Povey crossing the road. It was plain that Mam had sent for reinforcements, though Seth Povey looked as if he needed armour himself, very hangdog and long-suffering, going like a child reluctantly to school. She remembered the Poveys from her childhood, of course. Most children had avoided Tilly, but Molly and Stella had known better than to do that.

Mrs Povey had never said much, but the little woman had often made too big an apple pie, too much bread, or, 'Here, eat these pears before they go off.' She had been kind without sentiment, generous without altruism. Then Stella had disappeared to better herself and had been forced to learn Tilly all over again. The past was never mentioned, yet Stella knew, just as Molly had known, that Tilly Povey had kept the family from starvation.

Yes, Mrs Povey was a good woman, as was Mam. The likes of this generation would probably never be seen again, such humour, such strength and sheer, dogged determination. Tilly had gone out to work sometimes, but had held her family in a vice-like grip, no room for mistakes, no quarter given, no straying from the path she had designed for them.

Emily Dyson, on the other hand, had found it necessary to use her limited strength differently, working two jobs in tandem, no time for herself, little enough for her children. He had knocked her down literally and figuratively, bruising her body and her soul, yet she had jumped up again each time, her goal the feeding and clothing of her children.

Stella placed a hand on her belly and thought about the cluster of cells that had developed inside her womb, wondered how she would feel about living with a human so frail, so completely dependent. She had visited the father of this embryo several times, had watched his marked improvement, had noticed that his eyes remained haunted when he thought no one was looking at him. Matthew remained a closed shop, a place that would not open for business until his wife's memory had drifted away of its own accord. He remained sad, though he hid his feelings well. So. Was the definition of sanity just that? Did the sane contain their pain? Was that the only difference?

She took a sip of tea, then lifted up the packages she had stolen a few days ago from that antique jewellery case in the largest bedroom at Coniston. Guilt stayed her hand for a while, but eventually she allowed her fingers to unwrap the first of the parcels, the one tied in blue ribbons. These were the earliest letters, were yellowing slightly, their pages dried and crisped with age. She had to look, had to know, had to enter the secret that had belonged so exclusively to her dead sister. Such love, such utter devotion: seldom apart, these two had still needed to write their need for each other.

Moments later, she was locked in, eyes riveted to the words she read, head reeling from shock and astonishment. So physical, so needy, so down-right honest. Matthew's letters to Molly were similar, few holds barred, expressions plain, their physical passion displayed here with a boldness one would never have expected from either party.

God. Stella leaned back against a cushion, her head filled by what might have been termed pornography had the circumstances been different. So that had been it, then: here was the secret, the centre of it all, the reason behind their unmistakable closeness. Yet no. She recalled finding them in the rear garden of Coniston, he lying on a blanket, Molly idling on a swing bought for their son, each reading Keats, a verse from him, one from her.

They hadn't needed anyone else. The

membership of their club had been limited to two, books closed, no further applications to be considered. How many times had Stella approached them only for their conversation to stop as soon as she had stepped within hearing distance? Mark, their only child, had been treated with kindness, had been furnished with all the equipment needed for a happy childhood, but he had not belonged.

The third and final bundle of letters was the most telling. Here came the pain, then the hope, cancer excised, cancer reawakening. Christie's, radiation, pills, loss of hair, a shorter style, I love you, I love you. They would beat it. They would go to America and find a cure, would stamp out the element that threatened to separate them. Frail handwriting, tears extending the words in blue drips down a page. She had raged, had not gone softly, though none but a reader of these notes would have known that.

Stella blinked back the wetness in her eyes. Speech had not been enough: they had needed to write down their thoughts, had wanted to commit their love to paper. She swallowed. He would never find another Molly, would probably not seek one.

America had held no promise. They were quieter now, the messages mostly from him. As she scanned back, Stella was surprised to discover that Molly's earlier writings demonstrated a literary brain, an ability to express herself on paper in a way that showed talent and knowledge. So little Molly, the frail, gentle and beautiful daughter, had been a gifted live-wire, one who had chosen to show her abilities only to him, the one man she had ever loved.

The final letter was from him. Written just weeks ago, days before Molly's death, it was bleak and very moving.

My Darling Molly,

It has come now, is no longer a spectre whose form is unclear. You will never speak to me again and I already mourn the voice I loved. Death is by your side and he will reach you long before I do. The pain will be over, sweet girl. No one will read this last letter, another message for your eyes only, eyes that have not managed to see for several days.

Yes, I remember it all, right from your first day at the shop, your frightened eyes, that father who ruined your life continuing to do just that. Please do not fear for me, because I shall always have your love and that will keep me strong while I wait to join you. Perhaps you were right about Stella, although I cannot agree with you, even partially. I could never love her as I have loved you, so I hope that now, while you are so close to your last hour, you will forgive me if I continue to ignore your wishes. She may have some of your features, but she has none of your warmth and I shall not want her to take your place as you suggested.

Think of me sometimes, my sweetest, dearest girl. Know that I have loved you absolutely and that I shall never find so wonderful a person as you. Remember Wilfred Owen and that poem?

> *Go forever children, hand in hand.*
> *The sea is rising and the world is sand.*

> *Molly, you were my life-raft. Continue so and*
> *visit me in the dark midnight, touch my soul*
> *and bear me off to be with you.*
> *Matthew.*

Stella's tears joined his and damped the page
all over again. So, that was love. Molly had adored
him so thoroughly that she had tried to pass him
on to the next sister. Yet Molly had known Stella's
empty soul, had discussed with her the possibility
of happiness, had argued that a sad childhood did
not mean loneliness for ever. 'But your love didn't
stretch to encompass Mark, did it, Molly?' Perhaps
that was where the deficit lay, in the area of
parental affection.

Stella Dyson retied the bundles and placed
them in a drawer. She would return them to their
rightful owner at the earliest opportunity.
Matthew had stated his lack of interest in her; to
pursue him any further would be foolish. So,
tomorrow would be engagement day, a nice
solitaire, dinner at a restaurant, Simon deliriously
happy, Stella knowing that she was carrying the
child of a man who could never belong to her.

She knew now what love had been for them, for
Matthew and Molly. It was probably different
for everyone, no set rules, no compulsory factors.
Living without it was something Stella understood
perfectly; she was even good at it, was excellent at
hiding the fact that she minded.

Simon, then. Good man, clever doctor, would

do well as a family practitioner, as a family man. But could she fool him? Would she be able to produce this so-called premature baby and present it as his own? And did it matter? How many could prove beyond a shadow of a doubt that the name on a birth certificate was absolute proof of parentage?

Ah, well. Her own company did not please her at the moment, so she dried her eyes, combed her hair and prepared to go across the road. A meeting between Mam and Mrs Richards promised to be interesting. And Tilly was there, so there would be plenty of amusement to be had.

Tilly and Seth sat at the kitchen table, he tense because he was in his glad-rags, she tense because he was tense. It felt strange to be here at night, because this was her day place, the house in which she earned her money. Nights were spent at home with Seth. Her eyes slid sideways until she achieved sight of him. God, he was in a right state, face like a smacked bum, fingers pulling at the collar of his shirt – had he shaved properly?

They had been deposited here by Emily, who had disappeared to put the finishing touches to her appearance. Piles of sandwiches sat under damp muslin, then a trifle with real cream on top. Tilly sniffed. After coming close to her this afternoon, she didn't reckon Irene Richards to be the trifle type. 'Leave your collar alone,' she hissed.

He gulped, hoped that his Adam's apple wouldn't cave in under the pressure. As ever, Tilly had used enough starch to stiffen a mile of cloth and he felt like a prisoner who was serving a lengthy sentence for a crime he had never committed. It wasn't fair. If she wanted to take him out, she could at least treat him to his local pub, a pint, a meat pie and a game of darts.

Tilly tried to remember why she had brought him. Oh, aye, because it was going to be just women. The presence of a man often softened the stronger sex, the gender usually labelled as weaker and fairer. Well, some use the daft lad was going to be if war broke out. Mind, she didn't see Irene Richards as a warrior type – she was just posh and Emily was terrified of posh.

Mark wandered in, stopped, had a good look at Seth, then placed himself opposite the couple. Tilly looked funny: she was dressed up, but in a very bad mood. The man Mark took to be her husband appeared to be in pain as well as in his own very bad mood. 'Hello,' Mark said.

'Hello,' replied Seth.

'Is your collar tight?'

'It is, lad. It's like a noose. She puts that much starch in, it feels – ouch.' He turned on Tilly. 'No need for that. No need to go kicking me under the table.'

The boy fixed his gaze on Tilly. 'No kicking,' he scolded. 'Mr Povey is a visitor. Why have you come?' he asked Seth.

'She made me,' confessed Seth. 'Because both your grandmothers will be here. Happen they're expecting handbags at dawn – you and me can be seconds and Tilly can hold the coats.'

'I can't think why she's moved in next door.'

Mark shook his head. 'I'll be surrounded,' he said mournfully.

'I'm surrounded,' sympathized Seth, 'and there's only one of Tilly. Still, I wouldn't swap her. I daren't – she'd find me and kill me.'

Tilly had had enough. She stood up, glared meaningfully at her husband, then swept out of the room. Seth would be dealt with later, and the Wheatsheaf would not form part of the equation. She walked into the dining room in which Molly Richards had breathed her last, thought how clinical the stripped bed looked, wondered when they could all set to and bring back the original furniture. Eeh, this was a sad world, Mr Richards struggling to get his brain straight, his mam rolling up next door after giving up a whole way of life for his sake.

Then there was Emily, poor scared little mouse, upstairs at this moment and probably rehearsing whatever she was going to say to Irene Richards. Stella, who seemed lost, living across the road and being courted by that other doctor – what was his name? Mark, the child who had grown up at a gallop, tycoon in embryo, education abandoned, the world his oyster. Seth, fed up in his suit, Alice trying not to care about Matthew Richards, oh, God, what a mess.

Tilly sensed that her daughter was on the brink, was ready to fall in love with the man she had been nursing. 'Oh, Mrs Richards,' she said, the words whispered towards the stripped and plumped-up pillow, 'what a state you left us all in. I don't know when he'll get over you. I don't know how you both managed to leave your son feeling so alone. And there's more to your sister than meets the eye – I can tell she's troubled. Then there's your mam, feels she's not good enough for anything, upstairs now trying to hide her feelings under a new frock. Your ma-in-law's not much better off, can't tell whether she's coming or going. I wonder what her husband thinks about her moving out, eh?'

Tilly stood at the window, saw Dr Stella Dyson walking up the path. Oh, well, time to face the music. And if Seth started talking about what was written on the lav walls at work . . . She grinned, squashed a giggle. No, perhaps Seth's daftness might be useful, might break the ice. Aye, there was good in everyone, even in Seth Povey.

No, especially in Seth Povey . . .

Nine

Everyone except Irene had left.

It had been a chaotic evening, Seth and Tilly the entertainment, the rest playing the role of audience, Stella and Irene performing the middle-class ritual that accompanies new acquaintance – the weather, government policy, please pass the milk.

Now, with Mark in bed, his grandmothers got on with the task of knowing one another, each woman increasingly amazed by the experiences they shared. 'I was never actually slapped,' Irene Richards was saying now, 'because that would not have been right, you understand, for an officer in the Coldstreams. His cruelty was far more subtle, harder to identify. All the money is mine, the house is mine, Matthew's business was initiated by me. But Jack is the man. The horses were his, because horses belong to a man. Yet all documentation was in my name, Emily, so I sold them.'

'You didn't.' Emily put a hand to her throat.

'I did.'

'He'll go mad. Ooh, Irene, imagine. He comes home, no wife, no car, no horses—'

'Wrong order,' Irene stated baldly. 'It should be, no horses, no car, *then* no wife. I dismissed all the staff – they were only casuals, you understand. I did all the cooking unless we were having an occasion. Occasions are too much for me now, as I have a wee touch of arthritis in my hands. We had a lady come in twice a week, but I was the one who kept order.'

Emily gulped. 'It's a bit like what I did, I suppose, when I'd had enough.'

'Slightly less dramatic than burning furniture, but just as effective, I hope.' Irene smiled. 'Emily, did you know that my son confessed to the murder of your husband? Nonsense, of course.'

'I heard summat of the sort,' replied Emily, 'but even if he had killed Joe, I wouldn't have blamed him. Joe was rotten right through, you see. All he cared about was his drink – he was diagnosed as an alcoholic just before he died. They said he were dying anyway.' She bit her lip: she had said 'were' instead of 'was'. 'Irene?'

'Yes?'

'Will you want a bit of help next door?' Thus Emily Povey dismissed her husband – his life and his death meant nothing to her: she preferred to talk about curtains and carpets. 'I could come in and help you sort out – Seth said he'd give you a hand, too. And I know Tilly would.'

'It would be nice to have the place tidy before Matthew comes home. He doesn't know about my move, by the way. I have no intention of becoming intrusive – I just want to be on hand in case I might be needed.'

'Same here,' said Emily.

They bade each other good night, then Irene went home.

Emily sat for a while in the kitchen, wondering how they could make Irene's house countrified so that the poor woman might feel at home. She wouldn't want any of these new-fangled fitted kitchens, no. A nice big table and some heavy chairs like Matthew had, a pot sink, a big cooker. Mind, she had gone all modern with her furniture, so perhaps she wanted a big change all round.

So, the bullying happened in posh houses, too. It wasn't just coal-miners and cotton-spinners who put their families through hell, then. It seemed that Mr Richards had always despised Matthew because Matthew had suffered from . . . what was it? Otitis something-or-other – an ear complaint. Unfit for the army, poor Matthew had been unfit for his father, too, just not good enough.

Well, he'd been good enough for Molly, that was certain. Aye, he was a nice man. She'd seen how nice he was these past few days when she had visited him with Mark. He and Mark hadn't a lot to say to one another, but that would be sorted out. Matthew Richards was just an ordinary bloke who had adored his wife. He hadn't killed anybody. That had been all in his mind. Some medicine had made him poorly, so his thoughts had been mixed up.

She washed and dried a few cups, set the table

for breakfast, hoped Irene-next-door was all right. Eeh, fancy that, her calling a posh woman by her first name. And when she thought about the major with no horses, no car and no wife, she found a little smile on her face. Well, he would get his comeuppance, wouldn't he? If he put horses first, then it was time he saw himself at the bottom of somebody's list.

Emily put the kitchen lights out, then allowed Bess to follow her upstairs. She was good company, was Bess, a nice-natured dog, one you could depend on. In the act of closing her curtains, Emily's hand stayed itself. Across the road, Stella was in her living room, staring at herself in the mirror. She'd been quiet tonight, thoughtful. Was she having second thoughts about marrying Simon MacRae? Was she thinking about abortion? So tense, the girl had looked this evening. If only Emily could go over the road and tuck that poor child into bed. Years late, of course. The tuckings-in and the story readings should have happened long ago.

Too late to worry now, new things to think about, the shop to open, Irene to settle, Mark to care for, Matthew on his way home. She blew a kiss to her daughter and closed the curtains.

Bess was on the bed. 'I've warned you,' said Emily.

Bess knew all about people. She curled herself up, showed the whites of her eyes, smiled. It worked. She watched Emily as she walked off towards the bathroom, then closed her eyes, listened to running water, fell asleep.

When the woman returned from the bathroom, the bitch had become a fixture. But there was something comforting about a dog, even if you had to twist your legs nearly inside out to get into bed. Emily angled herself this way and that until she was more or less in bed, just the odd elbow sticking out and a bit of a draught around one ankle.

It occurred to Emily Dyson in that moment that she was almost happy, and the knowledge came as a shock all over again. She had Stella nearby for now, troubled, but within reach. Matthew would soon be home and Mark was wonderful. Even if she had to move out of Coniston, she was going to have a proper paid job at Matthew & Son, where there were several upstairs rooms that might be suitable for a flat. Most of all, her children were settled – even Phil was on the brink of marriage. Oh, and there was no more Joe Dyson. That fact on its own was worthy of a champagne toast . . .

He raged. Stuck out in the bloody countryside, the nearest shop over half a mile away, no car, no horse, no wife, no breakfast.

Jack Richards came downstairs more swiftly than he had intended, feet sliding from under him, spine crashing against the steps. He heaved himself up, cursed, staggered into the hallway. She had not arrived home, had not telephoned, had left no message.

Right, he needed to muster the troops. The troops. Where had they come from? Irene had been in charge of all that kind of thing, domestic arrangements. She had even organized stable staff, so he had no idea of what to expect in the way of help. His back hurt, one of his knees felt slightly twisted and his head was like a lead balloon, floating yet heavy.

'Buggeration,' he cursed.

After several abortive attempts, he managed to get some coffee brewing on the stove. He raked out the kitchen fire, riddled about to find paper and kindling, got a few feeble flames on the go, located milk, sugar, bread and jam. Where the hell was Irene? He paused, a hand half-way to his mouth, huge doorstep of bread and jam poised in mid-air. Matthew. That would be it, oh, yes, that would be the cause of all this. Jack had gone to London, had turned his back for a short time, had granted her the opportunity to consort with that spoilt boy.

But there was no note, no sign, no message.

He munched his way through two shives of stale bread while he considered his options and his needs. The latter were few – he needed food and someone to cook it. Oh, and he needed an explanation about his horses – he saw through the window that the stables continued deserted. Options. Well, he could stay here for a while without needing to shop, might manage for a day or two on the contents of the larder and the refrigerator, was in possession of some whisky, but what about later on in the week? He could go and look for her, phone the police, ask friends. No. Asking friends would involve a loss of face. Should he sit it out?

Irene, damn the woman, because she was the biggest question mark. She had never been a troublesome filly, had turned into a biddable mare – but where the devil was she? Had she been abducted by a gang? Had a whole string of horses been kidnapped? Was the stable to be held to ransom? God, his imagination was running away with him. What would the colonel do? No, he did not need advice: Jack was a master tactician, had negotiated a route through Tunisia, had dominated Sicily, had dragged ranks through Italy, had even tamed a couple of American platoons. Where was the bloody ransom note?

Wait. The boy might have the answers. She had gone against her husband's expressed wishes, had visited their son – lily-livered brat, he was. As for the horses, could they be away at a show? So. He must swallow his pride and make for Rutherford Hall, which was rather a long way to walk. There was a bicycle in an outhouse, but he had come down rather heavily on his coccyx earlier on and would need a cushion on a bicycle saddle.

He finished his catch-as-catch-can breakfast, found a sturdy walking-stick, donned tweed coat and cap, set off down the hill to the loony-bin. The further he walked, the crosser he became. Had Madam done as she was told, there would have been no need for this. She should have been there waiting for him, should have made sure that his needs were catered for. Damned women, not a brain between five of them.

Eventually, he reached the ornamental gates

that fronted the Hall, stopping for breath as soon as he was inside the grounds. This was ridiculous. What on earth was he going to say to the white feather he had spawned? Irene really had gone too far. He had stopped being concerned for her safety, because he had heard nothing to suggest that she was hurt or ill. The kidnap theory seemed rather over the top in the cold light of day so . . . So what? He did not know what to think.

'Onward,' he muttered, before negotiating the drive.

The front door was closed. He pressed a bell. 'Yes?' said a voice that belonged to nobody.

'Major Richards,' he barked.

The door opened and Jack stepped inside. So this was how the crazy people lived – knee deep in carpets, plants everywhere, expensive furniture, subtle décor. Bloody idiots should have been thrown in the glasshouse, half-rations, no tobacco, no parole. Oh, yes, he would have got this lot back on their feet in no time, needed to pull themselves together. Mental illness? It was for pansy-boys and women, not for real men.

A female greeted him, asked how she could help him.

'Here to see my son, Matthew Richards,' he said quietly, knowing that several locals worked at Rutherford Hall.

'You are Mr Richards, too?'

'Of course,' he replied. 'Has my wife been in?'

'Not today, not yet.'

Ah, so Irene had been visiting. Well, it was time for some plain talking. 'I wish to see my son immediately,' he said, spine straight, back hurting, feet red-raw after all that walking.

'Certainly, sir. Follow that corridor until you come to Room 47B. If he isn't there, he might be in the garden or in the day room, or, if he is in therapy, you may have to wait in his room. Thank you.' She returned to her notes, replacing spectacles on a very sharp nose.

Jack set off to find Matthew's room, suddenly apprehensive about what he was going to say. He had not seen the boy for several years – well, that awful funeral didn't count, so much weeping and wailing, dog howling, Matthew kicking everyone out of the graveyard. This was no longer a boy, of course, must be about forty by now. Jack's footsteps slowed. It had to be done, had to be said, no point in avoiding the issues now.

Without bothering to knock, he flung inward the door of 47B and strode into the room.

Matthew looked up. 'What do you want?' he asked.

Jack faltered. There was no respect, not even a greeting from the man.

'I don't want you here,' said Matthew, his tone quiet. 'Please go.'

The major was determined to be unimpressed. He closed the door and approached his son. 'I am looking for my wife . . . for your mother.'

Matthew continued to remove items from a drawer. 'She isn't here,' he said. 'Of course, you may look in my bathroom and under the bed, if you wish, but I can assure you that I am not concealing her.'

The major lingered uncertainly next to the bed on which his son's belongings were spread. 'Leaving?'

'Yes.'

'Ah. So you are . . . better, then?'

'Yes.'

Matthew went into the bathroom to retrieve toiletries.

'Good,' said Jack. This was a damned awkward bag of tricks. He did not want to go down on his knees, had no intention of appearing vulnerable while in the presence of someone who indulged himself to the point of nervous collapse. 'You have seen your mother?' he asked.

'Yes.' The voice floated through the open doorway, was quickly followed by its owner, sponge-bag clutched under an arm. 'If Mother has left you, Father, then I am pleased for her. You are and always have been an absolute pig of a man. I have asked you to leave here. If you do not go, I shall remove you.'

Flabbergasted, Jack sat down abruptly in the bedside chair.

'Go,' said Matthew, a harder edge to his tone.

'I just came to ask if you knew of Irene's whereabouts.'

The younger man raised his shoulders. 'She may be visiting someone else. I know that she is well because I spoke to her on the telephone not fifteen minutes ago. I suggest you go home and wait there because I have no idea of where she might be.' This was the truth. Mother had made a few vague noises about change, had mentioned nothing imminent.

There was a timbre to his son's voice, a new severity. Jack decided to try once more. 'The horses are gone. The farm is deserted, no char, no food, no word from her.'

'Really? Then perhaps my mother has come to her senses at last. She has lived long enough with a fool. As a father, you were an insult. As a man, you understand only bullying and you mistake that for strength. A trained killer is what you are, Father. You killed the love in me when I was a child and now, with my own son, I find myself incapable of communication.' He waved a hand towards the door. 'Here, they taught me to understand myself. All my failings are from you.'

Jack struggled to his feet. 'How dare you?'

The dam opened. 'How dare I?' roared Matthew. 'How dare you ask how I dare? Because I am your son. And I have killed. Yes – yes! I am a killer just as you are. They have tried to convince me that I did not kill, and I have pretended to come to my senses. You gave me anger, you gave me hatred. Beyond that, you gave me nothing at all. Molly taught me love. She is gone now and the love died when she did. I have no use for you, so please go.'

'How dare you?' repeated the red-faced visitor.

'Careful, Father, or you'll suffer a fit of some kind. You've turned the most extraordinary shade of puce.'

Jack stepped forward and raised his stick.

The younger man caught the weapon and held it firmly. 'Never again,' he said, his voice dangerously quiet. 'You're feeble now, weakened by age and stupidity and drink. I could take this stick from you and use it, so be sensible for once and get out of my room. Now.' The final word arrived loudly and clearly.

Jack Richards backed away until his son released his hold on the walking-stick, then he swivelled on his guardsman's heel and marched out of the room.

Matthew sank on to the bed, his whole body shaking as badly as it had some days earlier. He was fine – he was. This had been a nervous break-down brought on by the death of his wife, made worse by the killing of Joe Dyson. He must not falter now because of Jack Richards, the big man who had never grown up, who had played toy soldiers all his life. 'Damn him,' he spat quietly.

The door flew inward. 'Matthew?' It was Dr Masefield. 'That, I take it, was your father. We could hear you in the therapy room.'

'Yes, that was Major Jack,' he replied.

Ian Masefield approached his patient. 'Don't allow him to set you back. We've been through all that with you and with your mother, who happens to be one fine lady. Your dad never grew up, Matthew. That's why some of these people make a career of the forces, because they couldn't manage life on the outside. We talked about this, about how they move from one family to another, boarding-school to forces, swapping this set of rules for that set of rules.'

'Yes.'

'Soldiers are often children acting out the

games of infancy. Not always, I have to say that – and God would have to help us if we didn't have these defenders of our rights. But, Matthew, that old man is soaked in self-praise and alcohol. Let go. Please let go.'

The seated man bowed his head. 'It's so hard without her, Ian. I'm another who never grew up, you see. Most men love their wives, but Molly was everything to me. Perhaps it should have been different. I have a son I don't know, because I was so wrapped up in her that I—'

'You were wrapped up in cancer, Matthew. It happens.'

Tears hovered on his eyelashes as he spoke. 'She wasn't just a wife, she was my best friend, Ian. She was sun and moon, she lit my life and directed the tides. Climbing back isn't going to be easy, but only I can do it.'

'Strength is knowing your weaknesses,' Ian Masefield told him. 'Strength is knowing yourself inside out and protecting the inner child. Many's the time I've seen someone going to the wall after the death of a parent. It takes time, Matthew.'

'I know.'

'So, what are you going to do?'

Matthew knew exactly what he intended, but he would not discuss it. He had thinking to do, arrangements to make.

'Your mother is coming for you?'

'Yes. Later this afternoon.'

'You need only pick up a phone, Matthew, should you ever wish to talk to me.'

'Thanks.'

When the doctor had left, Matthew stood up and walked to the window. There was something so calming about the rise and fall of those moors, gentle slopes, almost maternal in shape, the comforters, the cradle. So, the letter he had prepared for Mother must remain here because he could not send it to the farm. Had she left the old goat to his own devices? Why had she said nothing? 'Why are you saying nothing?' he asked himself.

There was a journey he must make now without help, no map, no compass, no companion. In an hour or so he would leave this place, would empty his personal bank account, would buy transport for himself, would leave behind the town in which he had lived and loved.

For his mother and his son he had left a message, had taken the coward's way out. There had been too much talking, almost too much help. Words had crowded out feelings: there had been funeral words, words of wisdom from the mouths of his mother, his doctor, his night nurse. Yes, Alice Povey. He smiled for a moment . . .

Empty words in therapy sessions, consoling words from the doctors. Oh, these patients, these wounded animals whose cries he had heard in the night, whose hands he had held during group sessions. Jesus, so much pain caused by man's inhumanity to himself. He was well. His thoughts ran in straight lines again, few diversions, traffic-lights on green, no roadworks. At the end of his road there was a roundabout in need of demolition, but he had to be alone, had to . . . Had to leave a note for Alice Povey.

Time. He wanted time, time to himself, time for yesterday, clear out the filing cabinet, no interruptions. Mark had his grandmother Dyson and Tilly, the mother of his night nurse. Alice would be back at the infirmary soon, would be tending broken bodies at the expense of fractured minds: she had a gift for counselling, a talent that should be used.

On a day in late September, Matthew Richards wrote his goodbyes then prepared himself for his next journey. Time to move on, time to put his world into some sort of order.

Jack Richards was exhausted beyond measure. To and from Rutherford Hall in one day and on foot was too much: a journey of that length after a fall had been a foolish mistake. He came in through the front door of Eagley Farmhouse, noticed immediately the musty smell that settles in matured dust. How long had she been gone? Had she stopped the char at the same time or had the house been neglected for many days?

Whisky. After a generous double, he felt better, but knew that he should go up for a change of shoes. Where did she keep his slippers? For now, he seethed. Still no horses, still no Irene, no messages, no bloody lunch. And that son of his – no, of hers – was a nasty piece of work. Hadn't he said he was a killer? Some such nonsense anyway, baloney spouted from a source that remained clearly insane. God, what a mess this was.

The clock had stopped. No Irene to wind it, of

course, no home-made soup for lunch, no bread brought warm from the village bakery. Still furious, he dozed, only to wake half frozen in the fireless room. Stiffened by the chill and by his earlier fall, he dragged his weary body into action, lit the fire, then went upstairs to find his slippers.

As he rooted about under the bed, he found a sheet of paper, lifted it and realized that Irene had left a note after all, that he must have dislodged it when falling into bed the night before. So, here it all was, the betrayal, the perfidy of the female, so much deadlier than the sting of any male. She had gone. After over forty years, during which time he had protected her, his wife had taken it upon herself to desert him.

He read the document twice, noting how she had tied him up so neatly, so perfectly. There would be no more horses, no more entertaining, very few creature comforts. There was a small pension and, of course, he could lease the land. Her land. Realizing the extent of his powerlessness, he sank on to the bed. Who would clean, cook, wash his clothes? How could he manage the household all by himself? Life as he had known it seemed to be slipping away, had been pulled from beneath his feet by the hand of a woman whose companion he had been for over four decades.

How could she do this? Did he have any redress? Irene would use the family lawyer, he supposed, a man who was a part of their social circle. Any attempt to sue his wife would surely be abortive, since she was the indisputable owner of the house, the farm, the car. In one fell swoop, he had been reduced in status: he was now no more than a non-paying guest in his own home.

Friends – did he have any? There were those who played bridge and those who rode horses. Without a horse to his name and with no partner for a contract four, he was no longer a member of his own set, a group he had created and cultivated carefully over the years. He was stuck here, in this house, on the edge of a village, no wife, no status, no future.

The situation was worse than grim. There was no one in whom he could confide, nowhere he could turn for help and advice. His mind floated back to London, his second home, the city from which many of his comrades hailed. But he could not run back there, tail between his legs, begging-bowl outstretched . . . He had to find Irene, had to plead with her, appeal to her better nature. But her letter forbade that. To be forbidden by a woman, to feel forced to heed her order, that was an uncomfortable feeling.

Well, it had to be tackled, faced head on like the Hun or the Jap or those terrible Americans who had shown up too late. This was another of life's irritations and he would meet it bayonet at the ready, gun loaded, whatever it took. Where did she buy the meat? How would he get to town with no car? Could he afford a skivvy to come in once a week? What about renting out the stables?

He would do this, by God, he would. There was nothing in her instructions to indicate that he must not take in lodgers, nothing to forbid the use of outbuildings. This was another war, and wars were there to be won.

Love was a luxury that could not be afforded; it was also something Stella Dyson did not understand. Her affection for Matthew Richards had dwindled within weeks: she had no further need for him and he was not suitable, partly because he did not want her, mostly because he was ill. So she had passed herself along the line to the next possibility, Dr Simon MacRae.

The arrangement made sense. He adored her, needed her and proved all that with a half-carat of clean white diamond, enough flowers for the Chelsea Show and by spending every moment of his free time in her company. She was a fortunate woman, but would have to play the rest of her hand cleverly.

She now wanted Matthew's child, but not because she loved him. Molly had always regretted Mark's solo status: she had wanted three sons, Mark, Luke and John, so this would be Molly's secret son. Or daughter. A girl could be Marcia, Lucia or Joanna. It was strange how Stella had settled, as if pregnancy calmed her: she had ceased to worry about herself. There was some vague concern about timing, but all would be well, as she assured herself repeatedly. Strange how she had developed this loyalty towards her dead sister; perhaps Molly had needed to be dead to win her sister's unqualified love. It was all very complicated and, in the long term, was not deserving of too much thought.

At this particular moment, she was thinking mostly about love, wondering about its qualities and constituents. Across the road at Coniston, her own mother would soon lie asleep, probably pinned down by a black Labrador-cross. She had married for love and regretted it. Similarly, the occupant of the next house, Matthew's mother, would enjoy her solitude, a husband of about forty years abandoned in Eagley, love forgotten, dispersed, drowned by time and a million tears. So what was the value of love? Better, surely, to marry a friend?

There had been consternation today, because Matthew had disappeared. He had taken up his few belongings, had headed off by himself, just a note apologizing to his mother and his son. Poor Irene. She had uprooted herself for no good reason, was currently having her bed-time cocoa in her son's kitchen, would be moaning about her mistake, no doubt. Love was madness, then. The one person among her circle who had enjoyed true love was now suffering, had taken off by himself to lick wounds too deep for general treatment. If love inflicted that sort of damage, then Stella would be best off without it.

She switched off the light, walked into her bedroom, lay down and fell asleep within minutes.

Emily poured out the cocoa. 'He might turn up tomorrow,' she said, intending to comfort a neighbour who was fast becoming a friend. 'Remember, he's not been well, Irene.'

'No explanation,' Irene said. 'Just a short note

about needing to be alone for a while. What is a while? A day, a week, a year?'

'Who knows? He might not know himself. If you'd told him what you'd done, buying next door and all that, he might have come home.'

Irene shook her head. 'That would have been the wrong reason, Emily. He has to find his own way back.' She sipped her cocoa, picked up a biscuit and took a bite. Was it Jack's fault? Had his visit caused Matthew to shy away from his family? No. When the staff had told her about Jack's intrusion, she had lost her temper almost to the point of seeing her lawyer, but something had stayed her hand. Matthew had been careful to say little about his intentions for the future. He had signed over the shop accounts and the domestic purse without trouble, had given the reins to his sister-in-law without so much as an eyelid batting in protest. No, his decision had been made days ago.

'So you may have moved for nothing,' said Emily sadly.

'That isn't true, either,' replied Irene. 'Even after this short time, I'm beginning to sense a . . . well, a sort of freedom, I suppose, a release.'

'Really?'

'Oh, yes. Jack dominated my life, you see, filled every moment of every day. He spilled into each waking second and made me miserable. It was all so regimented, coffee at a quarter to eleven, lunch at one thirty, supper at six. He would stand with a watch and time me.'

Emily gave a half smile. 'I once read that a wife

260

is in an ideal place for murder – the kitchen. A little bit of extra in his dinner, and off he goes. Mind, that was before they knew how to trace poisons.'

'We are wicked women,' said Irene.

'Yes,' agreed Emily, 'and isn't it wonderful?'

They had already discussed with Mark the implications of Matthew's disappearance. Sadly, the boy had expressed no surprise: it was almost as if he had expected this to happen. 'Poor boy,' muttered Irene now. Neither woman needed to state Mark's name, because they both felt a great sadness on his behalf. His existence would not draw Matthew home; his existence had not kept his father from temporary insanity.

'I wonder where he's gone?' mused Emily now.

Irene finished her biscuit and drummed her fingers on the table. 'Somewhere isolated, at a guess. Dartmoor, the Lake District, the New Forest – who knows? I think he will not wish to be in a busy place, Emily. Whatever, unless he has a large amount of money, he will be forced to work or to come home very soon. Body and soul need to be kept together – even for the most romantic amongst us.'

'He must be lonely,' said Emily.

'Without Molly, his world has gone,' answered Irene. She raised her head and looked directly into the eyes of Molly's mother. 'We thought she wasn't good enough, but she was. She loved him. I'm so sorry.'

'So am I. But it's him we've to think about. Molly is out of it and better off. Her suffering must have been terrible. Only what he's going through – pain in his heart and soul – even morphine couldn't fix that.'

Irene glanced at the clock. 'I must go, because the decorators start tomorrow. Thank you for being here. These past few hours have been appalling and I don't know what I would have done without you.'

'Any time,' said Emily.

Irene left the house to go next door. She would get no sleep tonight because her mind was filled with pictures of her son, colours dredged from a dark palette where the world was cold and uncaring, where suicide or self-neglect were the norm. But she was helpless, so she did what generations of waiting women had done: she went through the motions and pretended that all would be well tomorrow.

Alice Povey sat in an empty room. This was her last night at Rutherford Hall and she was unhappy. She had enjoyed the work and would miss many people, but the one she would miss most had occupied this bed for two weeks and now he had gone. Soon her refreshment break would be over and she would return to her duties, but for now she wanted to be where she had last seen him, where she could remember his voice.

Falling in love – well, half in love – with a patient was against the rules, but her heart could not read nursing manuals. Anyway, surely love took longer than two weeks? How could she be sure after so short a time? But her heart could not tell the time, either. He had left a newspaper folded neatly on the locker. By tomorrow, the room would have been cleaned and nothing of Matthew Richards would remain, so she picked up the paper, realizing at once how silly she was to be retrieving a souvenir, a keepsake from a man who had deliberately disappeared.

Then she saw the advertisement, a neat ring inked around it in blue. Her heart missed a beat: she knew where he was. She should tell Dr Masefield, Matthew's family, his general practitioner. Pacing about, Alice tried to clear her head. No, no, she could tell no one. Were he discovered, he would probably disappear again immediately, perhaps permanently.

She stopped pacing, sat down again. How best to deal with this? God, what a dilemma. Well, the best decision was to make no decisions. She ripped the section out of the newspaper and placed it in a pocket with the little goodbye message he had left for her. She would find him eventually. It was best to leave him for a while to get his bearings, let him settle before appearing on the scene. 'He trusts me,' she told her reflection in the mirror that had shown his face until earlier today.

Alice left Room 47B and went back to her duties, her footfalls a little lighter than before. If it was her last act on this earth, Alice Povey would find the man she had begun to love.

Matthew Richards emerged from the bed-and-breakfast place on Bury New Road, closed the door behind himself. There was a chill wind today, the sort that cut right through a person. But as a man who was already deeply frozen, Matthew did not notice this extra layer of cold. He opened the door of the red Mini he had bought yesterday, climbed into the cramped space and turned the engine over.

He wondered whether this day marked the true commencement of insanity, as he was about to embark on a project that seemed at best eccentric, at worst an act of extreme lunacy. But his mind, such as it was, had been made up some days ago and he had turned in circles many times, had wondered what to do, where to go. Then that advertisement had placed itself in his hands and he had followed the fates blindly, feeling that Molly had sent him in this obtuse direction. Time, he reminded himself.

Town remained the same, except for the antiques shop on the corner of Deansgate and Bradshawgate, its corner door facing Churchgate. Here, a needle-shaped monument marked the place where the severed head of an Earl of Derby had once been displayed in a township notorious for its leanings towards republicanism. The sign Matthew & Son gleamed in gold paint against a background of bottle green. Mark was on his way, then, would probably make a decent fist of the job.

He drove up Deansgate, turned right at the fire station and headed towards his home. Coniston was not a place he particularly wanted to see, though it happened to be on the route he was forced to take. The house slumbered, curtains closed, two pints of milk on the doorstep. He parked at a discreet distance, fixed his eyes on the front door, remembered that awful day some weeks earlier when Molly had made that final journey down the drive, stop, pull out, turn right, head towards Heaton cemetery, himself, Mark and Bess in the first car.

There had been a few eyebrows raised when the bitch had been put on board, yet who could have denied that faithful servant the chance to say goodbye to her beloved mistress? And, in the event, Bess had turned out to be one of the few real mourners. Poor Mark. After this respite, he must go to Mark and explain a few things, but just now he was too raw.

A deep unease crept into Matthew's chest when he looked at his sister-in-law's house. Something jagged sat in his conscience, a sharp thought that was not even a thought: it was a feeling of guilt that he could attach to no particular event or circumstance yet it remained throughout his drive to the cemetery. Something untoward had happened during those twilight days and he could recall no detail.

He swung the little car into the graveyard, parked it, got out and walked the last few hundred yards. Ah, there she was, still no headstone, the earth advertising recent disturbance, brown, clotted, a small hillock the only monument to mark her place of rest. The stone would be of the best Italian marble, simple, just a rose carved into a corner, a small built-in vase for flowers, her name emblazoned in gilt.

He knelt by her side, assuming the pose that had become too familiar during recent months, she prone on her bed, he on his knees, sharing, while he still could, the air that she just about managed to breathe. She was still now, would never again need oxygen, medicine or comfort. Dear God, she had been his very soul. And there was nothing here apart from clots of soil and a few decaying flowers.

But he had to say the words here, because no other place on the globe marked her existence, just three and a half decades on a planet whose life spanned millions of years. 'Molly,' he began, 'I have to go away now. Mark needs me, but I am not here yet and I don't know what to say to him. You were a good mother until the illness began, but I was never a good father. I was so wrapped up in you that I scarcely noticed the poor boy.'

With the heel of his hand, he dashed away a tear cold enough to form an icicle. 'I shall make it up to him, Molly. They explained to me what had happened, all about my own development having been arrested by my father's disappointment in me, but that is a poor excuse for my neglect of our son.

'You know what I have done. We both had poor fathers. Mine is alive and living the life of Riley up in the hills. Yours I dealt with. A lot of thinking to do, Molly, but I can't do it here.

'Please watch over them all while I'm away.'

He stumbled to his feet, almost losing his balance, was nearly on top of her grave when he finally righted himself. Yet the need to join her in reality was fading fast. There were reasons why he must remain alive. One of those reasons was his son, a second his mother, but other unclear factors were present and he could not yet grasp them.

So, he had to go now to another location, a place where only the weather and the beasts made noise, where he could be useful and thoughtful simultaneously. A hard road. Yes, until he could justify himself, he would need to be away from the madding crowd.

He left her there under a grey September sky, simply turning away to take the first few steps towards his solitary future. The rebuilding of Matthew Richards was about to commence.

Ten

There was open land as far as the eye could see, though it was quilted, divided up into portions by dry-stone walling that rose and dipped with the lie of the earth, like a padded bedspread of many greens, its sections unequally stuffed, imperfections making it perfect.

This was Matthew Richards' new home and place of work. He had always loved Yorkshire and, since the breakdown, his need for solitude had dictated his destination, because he wanted time and space in which he might think. He hadn't expected to get the job, as he had not worked with livestock for many years, not since Mother had abandoned cattle to concentrate on horses and antiques, but the farmer here must have mistaken desperation for eagerness. So, three months into his training as a shepherd, Matthew was about to be abandoned to the elements in this rough and wonderful county.

Enoch Braithwaite, Yorkshire born and bred, had spent his middle years shepherding in Northumberland, the result of which circumstance was an accent all his own and a vocabulary that spanned both counties. At the age of eighty-two, he was finally succumbing to pressure, was travelling north to live with his daughter. When asked about his future, the grizzled ancient just bared his gums and spat out a solitary word, 'Bugger,' so Matthew had stopped mentioning Enoch's reluctant retirement.

There were three dogs, all male, all black and white Borders. The old one, Tammo, was to retire with his master, but the others, Benny and Jester, were now Matthew's dogs. Their relationship was simple: Matthew told them what to do and they did the right thing, which was not necessarily in accordance with Matthew's orders. Enoch saw the solution and stated baldly, 'Let the dogs teach you, you'll soon catch on.' Satisfied with that, Matthew journeyed with Enoch towards the old man's last days in Yorkshire.

For almost three months, the two had shared with their dogs a place called the shepherd's hut, a one-roomed abode that seemed to be at least fifty per cent fireplace. Built of local stone, the building was large, dry and heated by logs delivered every other week by the farmer. There was an oven, a grill that dropped over the fire, and a zinc bath on the wall outside. Toilet facilities were left to the imagination of the tenant, though Matthew did not miss the niceties of life. He did miss his mother and Mark, however, and was glad about that. He missed a certain night nurse, too, but he was settling on the whole.

Towards the end of his time in the Pennines,

Enoch expanded one night. He opened his heart and a bottle of Scotch donated by the farmer, its purpose to dull the pain of Enoch's retirement. 'Long time,' he began. 'Me and sheep, we go back. Tons of wool. Me dad, grandad and great-grandad were sheep men, too. Enough wool to make cloth for the whole of Yorkshire.'

'Yes,' agreed Matthew. Enoch was usually economical with words, but there was always a first time.

'Daughter,' spat the old man. 'Bugger.'

'So I gathered.'

But Matthew's interjection was ignored. 'Sooner have me sheep and me dogs, because you know where you are with the beasts. Women is different.'

Coming from Enoch, that was almost a parliamentary speech. Matthew waited until the old chap had poured himself a second hefty measure.

'Tups are still out. You get two tries, then that's your lot on the ewes. Separate 'em about New Year, make sure you get your lambs in spring, not summer.'

'Right.'

'And I've shown you your walling.' He gave Matthew a look of begrudged admiration. 'You took to that, didn't you? Soon as your tupping's done, get your tups out. They'll be daft for a day or two, then they'll settle. Keep them separate. Get them lambs borned early, no stragglers. And see to your walls.'

'Right,' repeated the younger man.

'Walls is everything. Without walls, there's no

sense.' He leaned forward expansively, was plainly warming to his subject. 'Sheep is stupid,' he pronounced, 'but clever in another way. They'll go all out to make your life a misery, because that's their job. They get lost, get killed, get mixed up with other hefts up yon on the hill and they do it all on purpose. A heft is a herd on a hillside – did I tell you that?'

'You did.'

The old shepherd spat into the fire. 'I've been watching you,' he said, 'and I reckon you're here for a reason, nothing to do with sheep. Oh, you'll be all right with them. But there's a look on your face I've seen meself when I've looked in yon cracked glass.' He waved his pipe at an injured mirror above the jug and bowl on the washstand. 'Seen that look in me own eyes, I have. You're running, aren't you? Same as me, run away from life.'

'Yes.'

'From a woman?'

'In a way, yes.' He was running not from the memory of Molly, but towards a place where he might deal with the loss.

'Bugger,' muttered the aged shepherd. 'Now, take my Monica. I'd pay you to take her, I would, I would. She's an old woman, sixty if a day, not led a healthy life, fat as a pig. But she makes me go and live with her. Hmmph.' He spat again with an accuracy that was admirable. 'When did she become the boss? That's what I want to know. I brought her up, now she's in charge and that's not right.' He sucked noisily on his pipe.

'Age has disempowered you,' said Matthew.

'Disembowelled me, more like. Thirty years I've been here. And now, Farmer Jenkinson decides I'm too old, gets in touch with Monica and I'm going to be carted off like a sack of spuds.'

'Bugger?' asked Matthew.

'Too right.' The pipe stabbed the air with the next words. 'She lives in a bloody bungalow, fitted carpets, television, all that. There's not a field to be seen, no sheep, nothing to look at. I'll be dead within a month.'

'Don't say that.'

'I have said it, too bloody late, and that's what they'll say, too, when they carry me off in me box, "Oh, what a shame, he should have stayed shepherding." I wanted to die here, Matt, here, where I belong. Nothing wrong with up yonder, but here, you see, this is God's own land. Yorkshire. Specially this side, tucked up to the mountains, the backbone of England.'

The whisky was oiling these aged wheels very well, thought Matthew.

'Matt your real name?' the old man asked now.

'Yes.'

'Apostle.'

'That's right.'

'And what have you done? What's the sin you're running from, Matt? Nay, I've watched you all these weeks and I can see there's something. I won't tell a soul.'

'It's my own sin to know,' replied the younger man carefully. 'Something I can't talk about yet. My wife died after many years of suffering. It left me ill. So I have come here to think, that's all.'

'Farming's in you?'

Was it? Was anything in him? 'My mother came north with me to Lancashire before my father left the army. She bought a farm and I helped out for a while. Then she specialized in horses, showing and breeding. At the same time, she sold antiques. I have a mixed background.'

'No daughter?'

'Just a son,' answered Matthew.

'Good. Bugger.'

The aged man nodded off. Matthew removed the pipe and the glass from his hands and wrapped a tartan rug around his legs. So weathered, that face, grizzled by time and poor shaving, mouth toothless, hair thick and white, a battered trilby hat beside him on the floor. Monica would not be happy with this old reprobate; he would not be happy in a dormer bungalow with fitted carpets and traycloths.

This was Matthew's tenth week at Hillside Farm. Even after such a short time, he felt the difference in his skin, as if the wind had whipped and toughened it. His right hand was callused already, hardened by the way he gripped his stick, that vital piece of equipment he used to get up and down the hills and crags. He liked sheep. They simply existed, grew wool, gave up their wool, then filled their bellies.

'And shoot the foxes.'

'I thought you were asleep.'

'Well, you know what Thought did, eh? Followed a muck cart, mistook it for a wedding.'

This statement was followed by a huge snore. Matthew would miss Enoch, yet he needed to miss him, needed to be stripped right down to his own core, just himself against the elements. Could he shoot a fox? Could he strangle a man? Would Joe Dyson have slipped, had the cord not been around his neck? Would I have finished the job if he hadn't fallen? An accident? Perhaps . . .

It was time for bed. Nine o'clock was as far as the day stretched because it began early, was born in darkness, dogs sniffing to be up and out, fire to stoke, ashes to remove, water to fetch and boil. He undressed and crawled on to the cot that had been borrowed for him. Soon he would be fully qualified and fully responsible; soon he would be the shepherd.

Tonight was to be the night. Stella made herself extra beautiful, took great care with hair and makeup, made sure that her engagement ring was dazzlingly clean. Her main hope was that Simon would not recall the date of their first mating, that he might be vague about the timing.

But he was a romantic, had even remembered their first monthiversary, flowers, champagne, a night at the theatre. She was nervous. The tale of Mrs Janet Fishwick, now a legend in the practice, hovered on her lips and she prayed that she might deliver it slowly, because gabbling would give her away. 'Learn to lie,' she ordered her reflection.

The results of her labour were pleasing, though she would never be as pretty as Molly. As ever, she compared herself with her dead sister, the only person on earth whom she had truly loved and admired. But her nose and chin were too sharp, her hair was not quite so thick, her body was finer, less gentle.

He was here. He let himself in with the key she had provided, stood back in pretended amazement, told her that she was beautiful. She bit her lip.

'Darling, what is it?' he cried.

She lowered her eyelids slowly, looked at him through lashes whose thickness had been assisted by the application of three layers of mascara. 'Don't be cross,' she begged.

'I could never be cross with you.'

Stella took a deep breath, but no sound emerged. He had such an open face, so innocent. Large green eyes, that squared chin donated so often by writers to characters who would need to be brave and good. 'I . . . er . . .' Frantic now, she searched the recesses of her soul for a statement that might make sense when attached to the words she had already delivered.

'What?' His eyebrows raised themselves.

'Present,' she managed finally. She crossed the room to open the drawer of a small sideboard. Inside, she found a purple box. 'I didn't wrap it,' she said. 'It was to be your wedding gift from me, but take it now, please.'

He pulled off the lid and lifted out a small pewter casket, raising the top to reveal a pair of solid silver cufflinks, the centre of each decorated with a Chinese health and happiness sign in 18-carat relief. 'Lovely,' he exclaimed, 'hand-made in Knightsbridge, too. Thank you.' He kissed her.

Panic bubbled, rose in her chest until it filled her head, too. Was she a complete fool? Simon was here for a purpose, had been cultivated deliberately – she had always known that. Yet now, at the eleventh hour, with an embryo that had become a foetus, with a foetus that would be a baby inside six months, her legs would not attempt this final hurdle.

He drew away from her. 'Out of sorts?' he asked.

She nodded.

The doctor inside him came to the rescue, took her pulse, said she felt hot, prescribed a rest and a nice cup of tea. She lay on the sofa while he covered her with a light blanket, watched him bustling about with the small details of life. This was a good man; she was not a good woman; he deserved the best; she did not deserve anything.

He kissed her and left her. She felt very alone and angry with herself, because it had all seemed so simple, so logical. She was pregnant, she needed him; he was in love, he needed her. A baby was a baby and all it required was security, which factor was provided quite easily by a pair of parents. It was within her power to furnish those parents – all she needed was the ability to tell a small lie, which, when measured against the back-cloth of the planet's troubles, was less than a speck of dust in the Sahara.

Yet she had, in the past few minutes, demonstrated quite clearly her inability to carry out that one small task. Tomorrow? Would she be more capable after a night's sleep? 'Know thine enemy,' she whispered, into the darkened room. Yes, she knew her foe, all right, and it was herself.

What were her alternatives? Abortion at this stage? Have the baby and give it away? Run from Bolton, have the child adopted, return after . . . after what? After going on a course? After an illness? Oh, God. Physician, heal thyself, said her mind. But she could not marry Simon, or so it seemed. He was a handsome and pleasant-natured man, would soon be snapped up by some woman who came with no complications, no lies.

'I am changing,' she whispered. Hormones were the possible cause, yet the alterations in herself were radical, as if she had just emerged from adolescence to step on to the first rung of adulthood. She was thirty-three years of age, for goodness' sake, was an independent, educated woman, a physician, a doctor who could hold up her head with the rest. She was not spectacularly clever, would never discover a cure for anything, but she was capable of keeping people ticking over, could manage diagnosis, treatment, care.

'Oh, shit,' she muttered.

The fire flickered, quiet music played on the radiogram, cars swished by outside. Sometimes there had been no fire, sometimes very little to eat. Emily Dyson had rushed through the house at the end of her shift as a cotton-doffer, had rinsed her face, had set off again for the cinema, scarcely time to greet her children. Molly. Oh, Molly. Bread and jam from Tilly Povey, pennies stolen from Joe Dyson while he snored drunkenly in his chair, errands for old ladies, a shilling found outside the library, what a red-letter day that had been.

Stella Dyson lay in her pretty room, tears coursing down her cheeks as she mourned the other girl-child, that pretty sister who had shared the shilling without question, without hesitation. Even her husband had been shared in the end, because Stella had fooled him, had snatched attention from him when her sister's body had scarcely cooled.

She was a bad person. The time had now arrived when she must give an account of herself, must know herself thoroughly. Because no matter what happened from now, life was going to change completely, either with Simon or without him. Stella. Star. Yes, she had been the celestial body destined to rise and survey the globe from a position of loftiness. Margaret. Molly. Daisy. A flower bound to the earth, rooted, beautiful, visible to all, touched by many, always treasured, now lying beneath the soil that had nourished her. Molly rested under the stars, yet was not beneath them.

She slept fitfully, watched Joe Dyson applying the buckle end of his belt to the bared skin of her brothers, saw Emily, white-faced and terrified as she insinuated her own body between child and weapon. They waited in the hospital while Eddie's arm was set in plaster, while Phil's broken ribs were strapped, while Tony's shoulder was pushed back into its socket. She ran with Molly, feet dragging her away from the fury of their father.

Molly on her wedding day, beautiful in white, the handsomest man on her arm. Stella, lonely in that house of pain, going out to earn secret money, night school, waitressing, a room in town, studying, avoiding both her parents, running, running. Why hadn't Molly taken her to live with them? Naked love on a hearthrug, bathing together, all written down in letters, no room for Stella, no place for a third party. A love so hot, so raw that it had spilled on to paper. Yes, that was love . . .

She woke, knew herself. Lonely and abandoned, Stella Dyson had resented her sister, so the love had been mixed with other emotions, though it began to shine through now. Molly, dear Molly, that wonderful person whose child lay now in the belly of her sister, yes. So. That was it. The unborn cradled inside Stella Dyson belonged to both sisters; there was no father and there could never be a father.

This was going to be a lonely road, and only Emily had known that. How Mam had watched her lately, how she had hovered, few words, just feelings carried across rooms, across this wide road, across time, space and many dimensions unknown to man. Mam did know her daughter after all, knew Stella's main stem, her root, her honesty. 'Oh, my God.' Thus emerged Stella's first prayer, borne on wings of sorrow and isolation. 'Molly,' she cried, 'please, please don't leave me this time.'

For the rest of her days, Stella would never be

sure about the next few minutes. Was she asleep, awake? Had she been in some kind of trance? But Molly came to her, not transparent, not floating above the floor, but substantial, alive, surrounded by Wild Roses, a perfume she had always favoured. 'Don't cry,' Molly said. 'Remember the shilling?'

'Yes.'

'We shared that. Now, we can share our daughter. Think of her as ours for now, but when she comes, know that she is just yours. She will be your strength, Stella. And I am with you.'

'But – no, you aren't here any more.'

Oh, that laugh, pure, visiting every note in the octave, not quite a giggle, not quite a burst from the belly. 'I am very near,' said the visitor.

'Where shall I go?' Stella asked.

'To Tilly,' came the immediate reply. 'Tilly and her daughter will help you. Matthew, too. This will be a wonderful child, just yours – my niece. Not Marcia – that is too like Mark. Joanna. That is a good name.'

Cars continued to travel up and down Chorley New Road. Bess was about – Stella heard the dog's bark. Her friendly clock continued to mark the passage of time, a floorboard creaked under the foot of a sister who could not possibly have been here. 'Where is Matthew?' Stella asked.

'His secret. He will be found.'

'I'm so sorry.'

Again, that laugh. 'No need,' Molly said, 'and tell Mark I loved him.'

Stella blinked and her sister had gone. She sat

up, stared hard at the spot on which Molly had stood, willed her to come back. But nothing happened, because nothing ever did – this was nonsense. There was a place in the human soul, an area triggered by half-sleep, not quite a dream, not quite reality. In that space, Molly had lived for a while.

Stella lay down again, took a deep breath and there it was, Wild Roses, clear and true, too strong to be imagined. And in that exact moment, far too early for it to be a possibility, Joanna moved inside the womb.

He wasn't showing any signs of improvement. He even managed to make a new shirt look old because he insisted on being hunched up, like a kid who refused to look smart on his first day at school. He wanted Christmas in his own house. If he couldn't be in his own house, he would sooner visit family. A man could break wind among his own, didn't have to be watching his aitches, could undo his braces and his waistband after eating too much.

Tilly glared at him. She'd got herself all decked out in new, right down to her vest and knickers. Even her brassière was blue, as were her blouse, her suit and her shoes. But Tilly believed in doing things properly. She wasn't one for half measures, because half measures meant half living and she entertained every intention of making her mark on this earth right up to and including the day of her departure.

Seth returned the glare. 'I never even got consulted,' he complained.

'If I consulted you about every little thing, Seth Povey, we'd still be wondering when to get wed. You even managed to look a mess then. How was I to know you went through the whole service with your shirt flap down to the backs of your knees, eh?'

Seth glowered, but said nothing. If he started on about the wedding day, she'd be off like a bullet, how drunk he'd been, how Ted Moss, the best man, had been even more drunk, how her new husband had shown her up by nearly fainting on top of the vicar. He couldn't bloody win, so he'd be better not to enter the contest.

'Where's the presents?' she asked.

'In the hall.' He would have to use the correct knives and forks, no chewing on a leg, no warm goose-grease running along his wrist, no flaming Christmas at all. She'd gone posh, though she wouldn't admit it, always carried a hanky even when she didn't have a cold, had started getting her hair done in a shop, took a drop of sherry before her evening meal. She'd be having saucers next news, proper cups with only a drop of tea in them, no mugs because mugs were common.

'Straighten your face,' she told him.

'Would you like me to iron me shoelaces?' he asked.

'I've already done 'em,' came the swift reply.

He glanced down at his feet, would not have been surprised if she had, indeed, ironed the laces. She'd worked her way up to place mats, big oblong things with photos of London on them, Tower Bridge, Trafalgar Square, Buckingham blinking Palace. A tablecloth was good enough for gradely folk, something homely with a checked pattern on it, but, oh, no, Tilly Povey was on the way up and he was being dragged along at the back, as per usual. It would be serviettes next news, only he would have to call them napkins.

'Seth, have you no ambition?'

'No.'

'Do you not imagine a better life?'

He thought of an answer, but swallowed it.

'I only want things nice,' she said.

'We're all right as we are,' insisted Seth. 'I got you a new washing-machine, didn't I? And that good iron. What more do you want? A couple of servants to do it all for you?'

'No,' she answered. 'Like I said, I just want things nice.'

He wanted things easier, but he was swimming against the tide, so he gave up with all the grace he could muster, which was not much. 'Let's get it over with, then.'

Get it over with. He didn't know how lucky he was, lovely dinner cooked by a wonderful woman, a lady who would pick them up in a nice posh car, who would drive them home tonight, pleasant, intelligent company, waited on by their betters, Queen's speech on a big telly, comfortable chairs to sit in.

He made one last effort. 'When she comes, tell her I'm ill in bed. Then I'll cook that chicken and we can have our own . . .' His words died: if looks could have killed, he would have died with them. He knew, just as he had always known, that this much-loved wife drew the maps. She had inked in his path away from crime, had pointed him in the right direction, had seldom steered him wrongly. 'Tilly?'

'What?'

'You know I love you, don't you?'

Colour rose in cheeks too thin to enjoy this decoration. 'Aye, but stop where you are, no kissing and manking about, because I spent ages on me hair.' She composed herself. 'Happy Christmas, lad,' she whispered, 'and I love you, too.'

Christmas Day. Alone at last, Matthew Richards stretched out his arms as if he sought to embrace the whole of this, the biggest county in England. He breathed in clean, sharp frost, admired the sugar-coated hills as they glistened, a light sprinkling of snow reflecting the rays of a low-hung sun. It was truly the finest Christmas card he had ever received, and it had cost no one a hard-earned shilling.

Benny and Jester played, chasing each other, seeking to dissipate that first burst of energy with which they were burdened each morning. A bird of prey hovered, called, swooped to pick up food. The quiet sheep were invisible, probably hard against walls, would be waiting for fodder. For the first time since Molly's death, Matthew felt truly alive.

Inside, he stoked up the fire, found a frying-pan and opened the pack of sausages he had bought yesterday in Huddersfield. He fed the dogs, brought water from the well, began a day like every other. No Christmas here in the land of sheep.

The door swung inward. 'Matt! Merry Christmas!' It was Tom Jenkinson and his wife, Bella. The large, red-faced woman gave Matthew a kiss, then planted a basket on the table. 'There you are, Matt, a little cake, some mince pies and a nice dinner – just stick it on top of a pan of water and steam it nice and hot.'

Tom, less exuberant than his wife, placed a bottle of port and two envelopes next to Bella's basket. 'Little drink and a few bob extra for you there, Matt. Oh, and a Christmas card – I should have brought it up the other day with your logs, only it slipped my mind.'

'Come for your dinner,' pleaded Bella. 'This is the first chance we've had to show off our handsome shepherd. Enoch was a treasure, but he was no oil painting. You could have two dinners – save that one for later.'

'Thanks,' replied Matthew, 'but I've a couple of animals that want watching – one lame and the other with a cut mouth.'

'Oh, well,' sighed Bella, 'I must wait for another time to brag about you, then. When the women round here find out how good-looking you are, there'll be no peace to be had.'

They left in a flurry of renewed seasonal greetings. Matthew turned his sausages, looked out to make sure that his dogs hadn't wandered, watched the Jenkinsons' tractor as it edged its way back down to their farmhouse. He ate breakfast, finishing off with a delightful mince pie, pastry so thin as to be almost transparent. They had brought him a card – that was nice of them.

He opened the first envelope, found two five-pound notes and a card from the Jenkinsons, a Santa on a sleigh pulled by sheep. So, what was in the other envelope, then? He turned it over, saw the Bolton postmark, sat down suddenly in Enoch's chair. Oh, God. Not three months had elapsed and they had found him. How solicitous they would be, come home, we shall look after you, you need family at a time like this.

'Bugger,' he said, without thinking. Oh, yes, he was beginning to understand old Enoch's frustrations.

He lifted the envelope and placed it carefully behind Enoch's rack of pipes. Monica had forbidden him to take his pipes: she had declared herself unwilling to bear the smell of shag in her carpets and curtains. Poor Enoch. He had probably been right, might well be dead within the month. The envelope glared at him. A small area of false safety sat in Matthew's consciousness, as if leaving the envelope sealed would kill it off, would wipe it out of existence. Nonsense, of course.

There was work to be done, the supervising of newly tupped ewes, the feeding of tups, which would soon need tempting away from the flock. He carried on with his job, dogs ducking and circling, sheep maa-ing stupidly while he checked a lame tup, while he attended the cut mouth of a young ewe. And still that white envelope sat in his head, was the biggest thought he had as he settled hundreds of his charges.

Bugger. It would have to be done. Lunchtime beckoned and he called in the dogs, led them over rocks and down slopes, glad when flatter ground arrived to make his journey easy. When he got back to his home, the dogs were waiting for him, tongues lolling excitedly in expectation of food. He built up the fire, fed Benny and Jester, put his dinner to warm.

Then, when the act could no longer be postponed, he reached for the envelope and slit it, using the knife with which he would eat Bella Jenkinson's food. There was a card that bore a standard snow scene, carollers wrapped in scarves and hats, a lantern on a pole, glitter glued to roofs and pavements. Slowly, he opened it. It was from Alice Povey.

The stupid smile was on his face before any thought had visited his brain. Alice. So easy to talk to, such a pleasant girl. Then his mind clicked into gear – how had she found him? A letter tumbled out and he spread it on the plastic tablecloth.

Dear Matthew,

I hope you are well and that you receive this card and letter. Please forgive me, but I found a newspaper in your room and knew that you must have applied for the job of shepherd. If you did not get the job, then I am wasting my time, but if anyone else reads this, it won't matter, I suppose.

Everyone was worried, though I am pleased to hear that you wrote to your mother and your son before leaving. I shall be going to your house for

*Christmas — so will Mam and Dad. There will be
the three of us Poveys, Emily and Stella Dyson, a
doctor called Simon MacRae, Mark and your
mother.*

*Your mam bought the house next door to yours,
the one called The Briars and has been living there
for about three months. She left your dad at the
farm and, according to my mother, Irene has
nothing good to say about him. It turns out that
your mother is the one with the money, so your dad
has to stay put and do as he is told.*

*I have put my address at the top of the letter and
I do hope that you will write to me. If you do, I
shall send you my telephone number. The infirmary
put a phone in because we are all nurses and are
sometimes on call, so if you get to Huddersfield — I
looked on a map and that is your nearest town —
please phone me. I am not putting the number this
time in case my letter doesn't reach you.*

*I often think of you and I send you best wishes
for Christmas. Do not worry, because I shall never
betray you. You needed to get away and I shall not
tell anyone where you are. I do hope that you will
find time to write to me, Matthew.*

From your friend, Alice Povey

He was still smiling stupidly as he put letter and
card back into their envelope. He was glad that
Alice would be having Christmas at Coniston,
pleased, too, about her parents. Mother, though?
Had Mother given up everything to look after
him? Oh, people went too far in their efforts to
help others. But perhaps that move had been

necessary. Major Jack Richards had never been an easy man. Mother had held herself in check, forever playing the dutiful wife, the perfect hostess. Matthew had watched her often, had realized that her embarrassment had been acute while Father had ranted on about the war, which seemed to have been won by him, Field Marshal Montgomery and a couple of others who deserved no particular mention.

Well, Matthew might have been the catalyst, but Mother would surely be happier away from that irascible rogue. Should he write to Alice? Yes, of course he should. He placed the letter behind Enoch's pipe rack and rescued his Christmas meal from the fire. It was delicious, the stuffing mouth-watering, turkey done to a turn, vegetables cooked but firm. Mrs Jenkinson's culinary prowess had already been advertised by Enoch, but now Matthew was in a position to judge for himself.

Replete after two helpings of cake and a strong brew of Yorkshire tea, he settled to doze by the fire. For the first time since her death, he did not dream of Molly. This time, his mind pictures were of a pretty young woman with long brown hair and green eyes. And he needed to count no sheep.

Emily Dyson was in her element. With the help of Tilly, Seth, Irene and Mark, she had reinstated the dining room. All Molly's things had been kept, of course, as Emily had not wanted to dispose of anything without Matthew's permission, but sideboard, table and chairs were back in their rightful place at last.

She hadn't hung streamers. According to Irene, streamers were all right for children, but something less garish would be appreciated by adults. And, oh, what progress Emily had made. She had embedded candles in logs, had made snow from thick white washing-powder mixed with a little water, piling it up on the logs' surface, then some holly, a sprinkling of glitter, a few silver bells. From the ceiling hung a white-painted branch, blue baubles dangling from its arms. This had been the best fun for years.

Her table was a masterpiece, everything in white except for candles, blazing scarlet in shallow silver holders. She had chosen red serviettes – no, napkins. According to Irene, the two-ply disposables were acceptable at Christmas. Crystal glassware sparkled after much polishing, silver cutlery reflected dancing flames from an open fire. Oh, this was going to be the best Christmas ever.

Except for Stella, that was. Emily's daughter had been quiet of late. Not that Stella had ever been a loud child, but she had always seemed to know where she was going, had been aware of what she wanted. These past few days, Stella had been withdrawn and thoughtful, as if she couldn't make up her mind about life.

Mark strolled in with a box of crackers. 'Where do you want these, Bunny?'

'Are they red?'

'Yes, ma'am.'

'Sideboard.' This one was growing up fast. Seventeen in a few weeks, he had the bearing of a man twice his age, had grown in stature and in confidence, would soon be ready to open his shop. Yet Emily knew that inside, he was hurt by the behaviour of his father. No one had heard from Matthew since the day of his vanishing act and Mark scarcely mentioned him these days. 'Are you happy, son?'

Strangely, he was. He had Tilly every weekday, Seth some days, Irene most days and he lived with Bunny, possibly the best grandmother in the world. 'I am happy,' he replied. If he couldn't have parents, he was content with the people he had collected in recent months. 'I am happy,' he repeated to his grandmother.

Emily blinked away a tear. In one sense, it seemed sinful to celebrate Christmas here, using the very room in which Molly had died, yet it was the right thing, it was what Molly would have wanted for her son. 'She would have been a good mam if she hadn't been ill, Mark.'

'I know.'

'When they were kids, she looked after your aunt Stella like a little guard dog. I was hardly ever in and they had to see to themselves, but I never worried about my girls, because I knew they'd look after each other. Well, Molly did the looking after. She did what she could for my boys, but they were older – they never needed her like Stella did. You've got to remember that Molly had already been a mother because she'd brought her sister up.'

'Don't get upset, Bunny.'

Emily swallowed the sorrow and continued, 'I often wondered if that was what laid my Molly low. It was a hard childhood, Mark, very hard for two little girls trying to cope with a drunken father and a mother too worried about where to hide her money to be bothered with the kids. Then she got ill and I didn't dare even visit her. He would have followed me, would have carried on drunk all over this house, trying to get money out of your dad.'

'I know. And none of that is your fault. Come on. It's Christmas.'

'Yes, it's Christmas.'

'Has Gran gone for Tilly and Seth?'

Emily burst out laughing. 'Never mind, lad, we can call it our good deed for next year.'

'I like them,' Mark protested.

'So do I.' Emily composed herself. 'But he's really fed up now. He reckons she's making her way up to finger-bowls. When I saw him last week, he said, "Her'll be putting the mop bucket on the table next news, just so's we can rinse our hands between courses." Reckons she's gone posh and says it's all Irene's fault. And he'll be in his best clothes again.'

'Wriggling about until he looks as if he has fleas,' Mark concluded.

'And thanks for inviting our Phil – it's a nice wedding present for him and Annie. They've decided to stay down Thicketford Road and they're using Phil's savings to do the place up. Aye, I'm glad Phil's settled.'

They went together into the kitchen, checked the bird, the bacon-wrapped sausages, the vegetables. Emily realized that they worked well in tandem, Mark automatically supervising one half of the cooking, she attending to the rest. It was as if she had known this grandson all his life – a pity she had needed to skip a generation to arrive at this.

They sat down simultaneously, he with a beer and lemonade shandy, she with her ever-present cup of Horniman's. 'We're all right, you and me, aren't we?' she said.

He laughed. 'Eeh, we are that, lass.' His Lancashire accent was far from professional, but she laughed anyway.

Things were hotting up. Seth, sufficiently comfortable to feel at home, had reduced himself to dangling braces, shirtsleeves and a looser belt at his rather expanded waist. 'You can't do that!' he yelled at Irene Richards.

'Why not?'

Seth was righteously indignant. 'Look, you can't mortgage a public facility. The waterworks isn't a building.'

'Oh, it is,' Irene protested. 'I've seen a waterworks and it had several buildings.'

'That's right,' agreed Phil's Annie. 'They have sheds and stuff like that.'

'You can have a bloody shed in your bloody back yard, but nobody'll give you a mortgage on it.' Seth was warming to his subject, was heating up to boiling point, in fact. 'Look, I pay me water rates, right? And you give me water. Now, you can't go mortgaging that because I own it.'

'Specially after you've drunk it,' said Phil.

'Not the water, you load of flaming nutters.' Seth drew a hand through his hair. 'The works, the place, the public facility. Sorry, Irene, you are out, you are bankrupt and that's an end of it.'

'Shame,' said Tilly mournfully. She had consumed enough sherry to be past worrying about Seth and his clothes. 'It's her game,' Tilly continued. 'She fetched it with her from her house.'

Seth turned his attention to his wife. 'Oh, aye? Mrs Flaming Rockefeller? Bad enough having table mats covered in London, now you own half the flaming city. Who said you could build hotels on Mayfair before putting houses there first? Eh?'

Tilly dragged herself up until her spine was rigid. 'You what? You want me to build decent houses then pull 'em down and replace 'em with hotels? What kind of a banker are you? No wonder the cost of living in London's so high. I wanted hotels and I got hotels. It were my money, so shut up.'

Emily came in with coffee, set it on the table and started another row. Her tray had covered the Old Kent Road, knocking down four houses in the process. Tilly moaned on about the homeless at the poor end of town, Mark crawled about on the floor looking for the top hat, which had been his movable piece, while Seth declared himself unwilling to do any further business with women.

It was stalemate. Mark found his piece,

suggested Ludo and was set upon by Tilly, who beat him about the head with a Christmas cracker. Alice Povey declared her father to be unreasonable, then poured coffee for everyone.

Emily sat in a corner and soaked up the warmth. Without a doubt, this had been the most wonderful Christmas of her whole life. Tilly and Seth were in their element, pursuing a hobby they had practised to a highly professional level – the art of argument. Their daughter, Alice, had struck up a friendship with Emily's daughter, Stella, while Irene had let her hair down and had shown herself capable of holding her corner in any quarrel. Phil and Annie were getting on well with their nephew, while Mark was relaxed and happy with everyone.

Stella's young man had not arrived, was reputed to be on call, but Emily had her doubts. Although she had conversed quite well with Alice, Stella was holding back, was not quite on form. It was as if she needed to be separate from Simon, from her mother, from everyone.

Emily felt no surprise about this, as she understood Stella's directness and honesty. To fool a man into marriage was an underhand act, and Stella was having difficulty with her conscience. Had she told Dr Simon MacRae the truth? Was she considering raising the child alone? There could surely be no choice more difficult. Although the world was changing, an illegitimate child was still frowned upon, as was its mother.

'Bunny?' cried Mark.

'What?'

'How much would you pay for a house on the Old Kent Road?'

'Nowt,' she replied automatically. No, in spite of Stella's problems, in spite of Molly's death and Matthew's disappearance, Emily would not have left Bolton for all the tea in China. 'I'm happy where I am,' she concluded. And that was the truth.

Eleven

Dear Alice,

I am sorry to have taken so long to reply, but I am in charge of some very stupid sheep here. Thankfully, my dogs, Benny and Jester, have more sense than I do, so we have managed to rescue some who seemed bent on suicide. Or would that be sheepicide? Whatever, this is a hard winter.

I was so glad to hear that you enjoyed Christmas at Coniston and, yes, it would appear that your mother is still the same, bless her. She was with me for four years before Molly died and she kept the place ticking over while I and the nurses tended Molly. I have to tell you that Tilly is an ironer beyond compare – if you ever want something old to look new again, give it to Tilly. I am sure you know that about your own mother.

I was shocked at first when you told me that my mother had bought The Briars, but it is perhaps for the best as my father, a consummate bully, had ruled her for years with a rod of iron. So there we are, back to ironing again! Yes, Mother holds the purse strings, though it never felt like that and, yes,

*she could buy and sell Major Jack tomorrow,
but she is not a cruel woman, so I assume that my
father will continue at the farm for the foreseeable
future.*

*When I last wrote to you, tupping was over.
Then I had the task of separating males from
females – not easy, but Benny and Jester did it all
and I just hung around trying to look intelligent.
Lambing has begun. Stupid again, these sheep
drop their young all over the place and the dogs
have to sniff the lambs out. There have been few
born dead, fortunately, but the foxes have begun to
prowl and were killing two or three newborn lambs
each night. I had to shoot dead two of those
beautiful creatures. The moments when I killed the
foxes were among the most dreadful of my life so
far, but I had to protect the lambs.*

*When all the sheep are safe and tagged, I shall
begin to mend and maintain the walls, something
I really enjoy. It is like making a jigsaw, but without a picture to follow. Walling is my hobby and I
find myself quite content when I am involved with
stone. It has a kind of warmth, as if it is alive.
When I wall, the dogs become dogs again and run
about like silly pups – they know when they are
working and when it's playtime. We take dogs for
granted and treat them as pets, but a working dog
has great dignity.*

*When I shot the foxes, it felt like murder. They
were just small wild dogs feeding themselves and I
was haunted for many nights afterwards. The
other nightmares, the Molly dreams, are gone. This
place is wonderful for a person who needs to start*

again. There is just me, the land and the creatures. The walls I build are of a material taken from the land, so it is all a great circle, but with sense to it, nature feeding nature, everything coming down to Mother Earth and the gifts she has for us. Silly, I suppose, but that's how I am working things out.

I am pleased that you are visiting Mother, Mark and Emily. Emily had a hard life and she deserves the best of everything. Mark needs a mother and he now seems to have three: Bunny? – what a name – my mother and yours. I am pleased that Stella is engaged to be married. Simon MacRae is a decent man who did all he could for my dear Molly.

The time will come when I shall return to Coniston to see my family. It is difficult to know how far ahead that time is, but it will probably be at least six months, as I need to see my first lambs on their way and I am looking forward to the shearing – still a great deal to learn. Perhaps I shall visit in the summer, but I am not yet sure about anything.

Thank you for being there when I was at my spectacular worst and for keeping me company during those hours of darkness. I enjoy your letters and hope that you will continue to find time to write in spite of the busy life you lead. What happened to the kidney patient? Did he pull through? I was glad to hear that the boy with the burst appendix is out of danger. Are you still considering a move towards psychiatric nursing? There are no bandages or sutures for the human mind – the healing of the invisible has to be harder.

I look forward to hearing from you again.

With every good wish, Matthew

Alice read the letter twice, then placed it in a box with the other she had received from him. He had communicated again with Mark, Irene and Emily, had found a way of getting the letters posted in the North East, so he was certainly bent on keeping his location a secret. It was all part of the healing process, she supposed. Sometimes, a patient was his own doctor, and this one had certainly written a prescription for himself, time in the wilds of West Yorkshire, a job to keep him busy, nature his friend and his healer.

This was Alice's day off. Her flatmates were at work, so she had the place to herself. She and three other nurses shared the upper floor of a large house at the town end of Chorley New Road, a bedroom each, two living rooms, bathroom and kitchen. Today Tilly was to visit on her way up to Coniston. Alice moved everything into its proper place – Mam was famous for having the eyes of an eagle and would surely make comment on any untidiness.

But Alice need not have worried because when Tilly arrived she was far too concerned about other matters to notice cup-rings on tables or used plates shoved under a chair. 'Hello, Mam.' Alice gave her mother a peck on the cheek.

'I'm getting to the bottom of things today,' Tilly announced.

'Good.' Alice knew that Mam would tell the tale at her own pace.

'Been going on weeks now.' Tilly dropped into a chair.

'Has it?'

Tilly nodded vigorously, almost dislodging the famous hairnet. 'It's nearly spring.'

Alice had already noticed that, though she made no comment.

'Stella's finished with yon doctor and it's summat to do with that. Emily's a cat on hot bricks, can't keep still for five minutes together, keeps emptying drawers and filling them up again. That shop opens again next week – she's been painting and decorating, learning stuff about antiques, helping Mark to interview a driver to pick things up for the shop, going daft, she is.'

'I see.'

'Do you? Well. I wish I could blinking well see. There's summat funny going on – not ha ha funny, I mean strange. Emily's like a toy that's been wound up too tight. I reckon her spring'll go any day now.'

'Have you talked to Stella, Mam?'

'No, I haven't, but she's at the back of it. Emily's over that road every night – Mark told me. She's fifty-nine, Alice. She can't go bouncing around as if her elastic'll carry on stretching like it did thirty years ago. I'm worried.'

'I can tell,' said Alice. 'Do you want me to go and talk to Stella?'

Tilly shrugged. 'I don't know. And I'm not used to not knowing. If this goes on, me and Emily'll finish up where Mr Richards was, God help him. And where the bloody hell is he now, eh? Piking off like that, just leaving us all to cope.'

'He had to go, Mam.'

Tilly rounded on her daughter, stared hard at

her for several seconds. 'You know where he is, don't you? You got on very well with him while he was up at that private place.'

'I don't know anything except this, Mam. He's a good bloke, and if he's disappeared, it's because he's had to. You've no idea how ill he was. There were times when I wondered whether he would ever find himself. That's what mental illness is. It's forgetting who you really are and hating what you've turned into. Nobody understands it. Few people care. Psychiatrists hardly know what they're on about, because the only people who know what mental illness is are those who have been there, who have suffered. So leave him alone, because you don't know what you're talking about. None of us knows.'

Tilly looked at her daughter and knew who Alice was. Alice was Tilly all over again but with an education. 'I'm so proud of you,' said the mother.

'Leave him, Mam. Don't try to find him.'

'All right.'

'Trust me,' begged Alice.

'I do, love. Now, get that kettle on before I die of thirst. And who's supposed to have dusted that bloody bookcase?'

'Gillian.'

'Fetch me a duster and some polish. Eeh, you young girls, you've no idea.'

Alice could not be bothered to remind her mother that she was twenty-seven years of age, a nursing sister with her own ward. Reduced to infancy yet again, she set the kettle to boil, found duster and polish, took the line of least resistance.

* * *

The time had come. He was standing here and he was demanding an answer. And she owed him the truth, the complete truth.

'Look,' he said, 'I know you were upset at Christmas and perhaps I was a little too keen to make love to you – I apologized even though I backed off. I didn't force myself upon you, Stella. I apologize again now. Are you ill? Why bolt the door? Why give me a key and then lock me out?'

Stella took a very deep breath. 'I don't love you,' she said.

He dropped into a chair, the strength leaving his body so suddenly that he almost gasped. 'We're engaged, for goodness' sake.'

'Yes.'

'Then when did you stop loving me?'

The whole truth. 'I never loved you. I've never loved anyone. There was a time when I wanted my brother-in-law, when I imagined that what I felt for him was love. But, except for Molly, I really have never loved anyone.' She pondered for a few moments. 'My mother – I feel something for her, I suppose. But my whole life has been about getting as far as I could in my chosen career because I could never be Molly.'

He blinked slowly. She was a stranger, a woman he had never known, because she had been acting a part, no more than that. 'Why did you want to be Molly?' Even now, he ached to comfort her.

'Because Molly was good and beautiful, the nearest to perfect I have ever seen. I wanted to be her, I loved her, but a part of me resented her

303

perfection. I wanted what she had. She had Matthew. So when she was dead I took him. On the day of her funeral I took him. My hair fell out of its pins and he thought I was Molly. I could have stopped him, but I didn't.'

Simon MacRae was a mature man, a practitioner who had seen many kinds of illness, whose first duty was to be diagnostician. This woman was ill. She was a doctor and she was ill. The disorder was not a reactive one: she had not gone to pieces because of a death, a shock, a sudden alteration in circumstance. Oh, no, her craziness lay in her calm, in her ability to stand aside and calculate, to manipulate, to shape life so that it would fit her requirements. He had been just another piece of her modelling clay.

'I know what you're thinking,' she said now.

'Then you're very clever, because I scarcely know what to think.'

'Nonsense,' said Stella. 'You have pigeonholed me under the miscellany we call personality disorder. Well, sorry, no prize for that, Doctor. There was, perhaps, some arrest in my emotional development during childhood. My psyche, however, is in good shape, because I prostituted that part of myself during my training – earned money as a guinea-pig to some top psychos in London. I was a paid victim of researchers – many students were. Sane, Simon.'

'Really?'

'Yes. Would you like to see my certificates? No psychosis, no neurosis, brighter than average and quite stable. The Molly thing is a little dream that got left over from my youth. I indulged it once.'

'You slept with your dead sister's husband?'

'Yes.'

'When he was insane?'

'When he was disturbed, yes. Had he been in any other state, he would not have looked twice at me.'

'Sleeping with him made you closer to her?'

'Possibly. It also made me pregnant. I was using you to cover my tracks. Then, when it came to the hurdle, I couldn't jump. Sorry, I'm mixing metaphors. Simon, I'm pregnant. In approximately five months, I shall give birth to an illegitimate child. I'm sorry that I considered fooling you in order to make life easier for myself and the baby.'

He could scarcely breathe. Here stood the woman he loved – and, yes, her belly was slightly distended – telling him about herself and Matthew Richards. Good God . . . 'This is crazy behaviour,' he managed to say.

'The behaviour may be crazy, Doc, but the patient isn't. Now, I suggest you run away like a good little boy while I make some life-altering decisions. As an unmarried mother, I cannot remain here in general practice. Would you go now, please? I have some notes to make.'

He stayed where he was, fingers steepled against his mouth. He remembered that night, heard Matthew's screams, recalled how the man had fought until the sedation had kicked in. So Stella had made love to Matthew that very night, had entered the madness with him. 'How could you?' he asked.

'How could I what? Make love to him? Comfort him, comfort myself? I was a virgin until that night. I don't know the answers. None of us knows the answers. The truly insane are those who pretend to have the solution to the puzzle we call life.'

'You're a cold woman.'

'Yes.'

He nodded. 'And yet not. No, you're capable of great passion.'

'Then you know more about me than I do.'

He stood up and walked to the door, suddenly anxious to be away, needing to think, not knowing what he needed to think about. Angry, upset, hurt, confused, he closed her door quietly.

Inside the flat, Stella Dyson dropped on to the sofa and wept. She, too, was bewildered. She didn't love anyone, would never love, yet she felt chilled and alone once that front door had closed. 'Just the two of us, Joanna,' she informed her little bulge, 'because your other mother is dead, your father is God alone knows where, and I just lost your stepfather.'

Major Jack Richards had found his niche in life. The discovery had been born of necessity, as he had needed to eat in order to remain alive. Reared to follow instruction without question, he had spent days with his nose buried in Mrs Beeton and her fellows. Any fool could cook as long as he could read.

And Jack was no fool.

The only stumbling block was Irene. He could not open a small restaurant without her permission;

also, planning would have to be agreed with the local authority, so he had been stymied for a while. But need, being the mother of deed, came up with her own idea. Paying guests. With three spare bedrooms and a couple of extra sitting rooms, Eagley Farmhouse had a future.

The choosing of potential housemates had taken a degree of thought. He wanted men, real men with history, people who had come through war bloodied but unafraid, gentlemen in every sense of the word. Fortunately, the military magazines to which he subscribed carried advertising columns, which facility had enabled him to choose his house guests with care.

He decided to stick with the upper echelons of rank and file, those over whom he might hold sway, so his companions were two sergeants and a sergeant major from a variety of regiments, none of them Guards. Irene had done him a favour; he was in his element, had his own club here, three drinking companions, three sets of ears and a car belonging to one of his men.

Just one element was missing from his life: he had no horse. Those empty stables reminded him daily of all he had lost and he struggled to come up with a plan that might make sufficient money to allow the purchase of a decent mount. The land had been let via Irene's agent, a bespectacled piece of near-humanity named Colin Martindale. He drove a Morris Minor, drove Jack up the wall, was forever checking furniture for scratches, took upon himself the task of passing on land rents paid by local farmers for the use of Eagley's acreage.

Rooting through Irene's bureau, Jack found that he had endowments via the Prudential Group. These had been set up by his departed wife, and Jack immediately saw in them the potential for providing himself with a good gelding, a hunter, he hoped. With this in mind, he telephoned the Prudential office in Bolton and was informed that a representative of the company would be with him that day.

He opened the door to find a short man with sandy, receding hair and unremarkable clothes, the trousers indented at the ankles by bicycle clips. 'Richards, Major.' Jack held out his hand and noted a strong grip in the palm of his visitor.

'Phil Dyson.'

The name rang a distant bell, but Jack, too eager to make progress with business, dismissed the notion. He wanted money and he wanted it yesterday. 'Come in.' He led Phil through to the main drawing room, invited him to sit, offered whisky.

'No, thank you. I've just got a moped and I have to have my wits about me. It's amazing how close cars come when you're on a bike.'

'Quite.' Jack poured himself a measure of his favourite tipple. 'Bit of a mess,' he said, once the glass was half emptied. 'Wife had to go off, sick relatives, didn't want to bother her. She took care of household matters – I'm Coldstreams, retired. Need some cash, had to pay out a massive amount for the wife's unfortunate family, so just a temporary hitch.' He thrust some documentation under Phil's nose. 'Any chance of realizing some cash out of this lot?'

Phil hid his amusement. Having spent Christmas in the company of Irene Richards, he had enjoyed a slightly better than passing acquaintance with the true circumstances surrounding the dissolution of this marital alliance. It was simple. Irene despised her husband with a passion she kept under control, but which shone through every little comment she made about this bombastic, shallow fool.

'Well?' asked Major Jack.

'Just a moment, please,' replied Phil. A fast reader, he could tell at a glance what was what, yet he derived untold pleasure from keeping this false aristocrat waiting. 'Small print, you see, but it will take me no more than two minutes to cut through.'

'Red tape,' blustered the major, struggling to his feet to recharge the glass. Carefully, he hung on to his very short temper.

Phil continued to fight a bubble of merriment that threatened to erupt. Oh, God, wait until he could tell his Annie about this. He looked up, noticed the malice in Jack Richards' eyes. 'Several hundred on each, sir,' he said, controlling his voice with difficulty. 'I shall give you a receipt for the policies, then I shall return in a few days with your money.' He cleared his throat. 'Of course, if you would care to allow these to mature for another few years, they will bring far more.'

'No,' blustered Jack. 'The money is needed immediately. The costs of nursing are so high these days. Only the best, you see. Thought I might buy a horse with the small change, after I've done my duty, naturally.'

Phil Dyson could not wait to get out. He would have to tell his mother about this, would have to make sure that Irene found out. To have the old goat pretend that his marriage was all right, that his poor unfortunate wife had been called away – oh, what a scream.

'Then I shall expect you soon,' concluded the major.

Phil got to his feet. 'That you will, sir. Don't bother to see me out.' He fled the scene with all the dignity he could muster, then laughed all the way down Tonge Moor.

As soon as Phil had left, Jack Richards was on the phone. Armed with a thorough knowledge of local stables, he knew exactly where the best horseflesh was raised in these parts. Excitement bubbled: he could already feel the wind in his face, the power of the mount beneath him. Oh, yes, he would soon be on his way again . . .

His men would be home soon and he would commandeer the car, would make the rounds of local stables until he found the right mount. He was going to be the Galloping Major again and he was content with his lot.

Simon MacRae paced about his consulting room. He was disturbed to the point of acute restlessness, felt as if his nerves should be visible, unsheathed wires poking out all over his body. Stupid.

She wasn't suitable. He had reached the age of thirty-six without finding anyone suitable. Then, out of the blue, he had fallen head over heels for a woman who was absolutely perfect, slim, good figure, a cloud of dark hair, eyes as near to violet as he had ever seen. She was clever, sensible, humorous, full of wit and wisdom. Oh, God. He dragged a hand through a mop of unruly brown hair, wondered how he could possibly have been so stupid.

Her sister, Molly, had been his patient. Another lovely woman, she had lacked Stella's edge, had been softer, quieter, far too angelic to be true. Even when riddled with pain, Molly Richards had sought to inflict no suffering on the man she had adored, had begged for more morphine. And Simon had given it to her, had increased the dose until her body had broken down beneath the weight of it. Like many physicians, he had killed the agony, had concentrated on palliative care, knowing that his generosity would terminate the life of his patient. It had not been euthanasia; it had been the murder of cancer.

Stella. Even now, cast aside by her, treated abysmally and so casually, he continued to want her. Even while his mind called her unacceptable, his heart refused to listen. It was too late, he was too far gone, too tied up in her. She was the other half of himself, a person he remembered from the future – was he the mad one here? No. It was her pragmatism that had always appealed, her matter-of-factness, her ability to face life without dressing it up in pretty colours. And all that was clearly illustrated by what she had done and by what she had failed to do.

Stella Dyson had been too honest to go through with her plan. He had no doubt that she had worked everything out right down to the smallest detail. She was like that. He had watched her poring over volumes for the slightest clue, searching to match a symptom, a drug, a hint that might help her deal with a patient. She was what she was and he could not stop loving her.

'Give yourself time,' he whispered. But there had been time. The cooling had begun in December, when she had ceased to respond, when she had asked him not to go to Coniston for Christmas dinner. His pain had begun then, too. 'Jesus,' he cried into the empty room, 'why her?' He wanted a wife, a child, a mortgage, a family of his own. Bachelorhood had been fun, but it had run its course and he was done with it.

Surgery would begin shortly. He needed to pull himself together so that he might concentrate on his patients, couldn't do his job if he didn't find a solution to this dilemma. Right. A plan. She, too, needed time, needed to get away from work so that she might think. 'Calm,' he ordered himself. He could feel his blood pressure rising, knew that he was making himself ill. 'Heal thyself,' he snapped.

He snatched up the phone, dialled. 'Stella?'
'Yes?'
'I want you to come on to my list, to be a patient of this practice – I can put you under one of the other doctors' names. I have a plan.'

She did not answer.

'You need time to think. None of this will go away, Stella.'

'Too late for abortion,' was her terse reply.

He tucked the receiver under his chin, picked up a pencil, snapped it in two. 'I'm not suggesting termination, Stella. I want you to go away. I can give you a reason – anaemia, anything – just a chance to get away so that you can concentrate. This is a child, a person, the son or daughter of Matthew Richards, your child, too. You can't travel this path alone, Stella.'

She was breathing evenly, no quickening in the rhythm.

'Please be our patient. Please, Stella, let me bring you through this.'

'All right.'

He heard a click, knew that she had severed the connection. He replaced his own receiver, felt control trickling back into his body, knew that his heart-rate had returned to normal, that the temporary hypertension had cured itself. Oh, how he loved her. No matter what her faults, her mistakes, her difficulties, she was the one.

He poked his head out of the doorway, saw them all sitting there, the faithful, those who believed that a doctor could make them well, could make life bearable. He nodded to his receptionist. 'Two minutes, Audrey. Just let me wash my hands before I start on this little lot.' He winked at the nearest, a small boy with a flushed face. 'Soon have you right, Billy.'

Back in the privacy of his consulting room,

Simon MacRae washed hands and face, dried himself, picked up the first package of notes. Billy Riley, one of six children, underweight, full of life, that life in hands that had just been scrubbed with carbolic and a stiff brush. And he still wanted to marry her.

The day of the grand opening had arrived. Tilly, magnificent in her Christmas suit, was in charge of coffee, tea and biscuits. Emily, flapping even more under the weight of additional responsibility, hovered nervously between miniatures, glassware, clocks and china. In her handbag, an item to which she was almost glued, sat notes that might jog her memory regarding what was what, prices and dates. This was one of the most terrifying days of her life.

Irene was the queen today. She needed few lists, no dates, no prices, because this was second nature to her. While Mark was the manager, Irene was the true brains, as her knowledge of antiques seemed boundless. She had arranged the podium, a large area near the biggest window on which bargains were set. On these pieces, the shop would make little money, but they were there for a purpose. People might just buy something more valuable after purchasing a cheaper article.

Tilly approached Emily. 'You'd better tell me what's up, love. You're in enough of a sweat to break something – stay out of the road of them pots.'

Emily stepped away from a pair of Imari vases and a Hans Coper goblet. She was in the wrong place: she should not be near breakables. Her daughter was breakable, too . . .

'Emily?'

'I'll be all right. Go and brew your tea.'

Irene, too, knew that all was not well with Emily. She drew a duster over a mahogany teapoy and a George III washstand, which items had been marked down because of a few scars. As she cleaned the podium pieces, she kept one eye on her new friend, wished with all her heart that she could help the unhappy woman.

Phil Dyson's Annie turned up, knocked at the locked door and was let in by Tilly. 'Nearly time,' said Annie excitedly. 'How's my mother-in-law?'

'Terrible,' replied Tilly. 'I think we're going to need a conference.'

'Shame,' said Annie, then went first to tell Irene about Jack and the cashed policies.

'I'm sure he'll be buying a horse and he's not to keep a horse,' said Irene crossly. 'He's not fit to own one, cruel man. I shall have to deal with that. It's in the agreement – if he keeps an animal, I shall have him turned out of the house.'

'He did mention a horse.' Annie regretted having upset Irene on this special occasion and she said so. 'I wouldn't have told you, only . . .'

'Thank you,' said Irene firmly. 'Nothing Jack does surprises me. But I'm a great lover of horses and he should not be allowed on the same planet as those wonderful beasts. I'm glad that you told me – please thank Philip on my behalf.'

Annie crossed to where Emily stood, hands twisting together, handbag dangling from an elbow, forehead tramlined with worry. 'Hello, love,' said Annie. 'Phil says he'll try to get here later on. Are you all right?'

'Er . . . yes, I think so.'

'Do you want me to help you? Only I can stand here with you and pretend I know what's going on – my mother always said I could talk the back legs off a dog. I can ask Mark or his other grandma for help if we get stuck.'

Relief flooded into Emily's tense body. 'Eeh, love, I'm glad our Phil found you. It's very kind of you, is that, to offer to help me. Yes, I'm a bit nervous. Bolton's famous, so I'm told, for collectors and they all know what they're looking for. I'd be grateful, Annie. You can run about and ask Irene or Mark when I get stuck. Oh, God, they're opening the doors. Hold my hand, love.'

A relative newcomer to the Dyson family, Annie felt that she could not yet question Emily's state of mind, though the poor woman did seem to be very upset. According to Phil, his mother had wanted to see Stella settled and was distraught because Stella and her doctor boyfriend had ended their relationship, but something told Annie that there was more to this situation than met the eye.

Mark was standing on top of some library steps. 'Just a moment,' he shouted.

The small crowd stood still. Irene smiled to herself – this grandson certainly had presence, although he was not quite seventeen.

'Welcome,' Mark called. 'Welcome to the opening of Matthew & Son, previously known to many as Richards Antiques. As you will see, we are three stores knocked into one, so we manage to keep large amounts of stock and we take orders for people who are searching for specifics.

'Now, at the rear of the shop, we have an office where anyone is welcome to discuss his or her needs in the field of antiques. A renovation service will be offered very shortly – we have a professional cleaner of paintings and a furniture restorer on hand to attend to pieces requiring those services.

'You will notice that we have several worthy items on offer today – my grandmother, Mrs Irene Richards, though quite old, is not one of them, but she is on hand to answer any queries. You will find some early nineteenth-century Swansea pottery, some Doulton Lambeth stoneware in excellent condition, a George II dropleaf table, two Cumberland tables and a magnificent lady's desk, French, mid-nineteenth century.

'Victoriana abounds and is cheap, but will become valuable as the years pass. Don't miss the small stuff, belts, bangles, handbags, miniatures. Beds, including several four-posters, are upstairs and, believe me, they took some carrying. Behind glass, we keep jade, ivory and jewellery set with precious stones. Please feel free to have any of those pieces valued. Mr Preston across the road at the jeweller's is capable of assessing them and is happy to help in that sphere.

'Coffee and tea are available behind the shop for those who require refreshment. Thank you for coming, and enjoy browsing.'

During the ensuing ripple of applause, Mark's two grandmothers glanced at each other. They were proud of him, proud and happy, because Mark Richards had definitely found his niche.

Emily settled to her task and was amazed by the helpfulness of customers. They told her what things were worth and she was delighted to find that they were, on the whole, honest and accurate in their assessments. Phil's Annie got distracted into teddy bears and dolls' houses, did a roaring trade in price-marked old dolls.

Across the road, next to a monument commemorating the beheading of an earl, a man stood. He had parked his Mini round the corner and had come all the way from Yorkshire to watch the opening of Matthew & Son. There was not much time, as he had left his lambs in the care of a farmhand, but Matthew had wanted to see the other half, the '& Son'. Alice Povey had told him in a letter that today was the day and he had been unable to stay away. This was a good sign, surely?

The sight of his familiar stamping ground brought to Matthew a mixture of emotions. He ached when he thought of Molly, when he remembered the two of them working in the shop, often engrossed until midnight while they categorized pieces, while they cleaned and sorted out the tangles created by customers. But this was his town, all right, Preston's, Henry Barrie's, Ye Olde Pastie Shoppe, ice-cream parlours, the civic buildings, the markets, the Pack Horse. God grant that he would soon miss his home more than he missed Molly, that he would grow to need his son.

How grand the lad had looked in his smart suit, waistcoat and fob watch, neat shoes, hair cut well, bearing almost adult. Matthew had also seen Emily, Irene and Tilly, was reassured that the son he had abandoned was not alone. But he had to get back to the rough land behind Hillside Farm, had to look after that flock. Tougher now, Matthew Richards had learned to skin a dead lamb, to use that soft fleece on another lamb to fool a bereaved mother into adopting an orphan. There was fight in him now, the beginnings of new life that had come into the world with the sad creatures he bottle-fed, with his daily battle against the elements. Yes, he had done the right thing.

Soon Bolton would be his place again, but for now he belonged to the wilds. After one last look at the throng inside his shop, Matthew turned on his heel and walked back to the car. He could do this. He could come back to life, but in his own good time.

Obeying Molly was silly, yet it made sense. It was silly because Molly was dead and could never have been here. The smell of Wild Roses could easily have been imagined, while the rest had probably been a dream, but there was sense in getting help, a support system consisting of women.

What had Molly said? Tilly and her daughter, Alice. Stella had talked to Alice at Christmas, had found her sensible, intelligent and quick-witted. Mam already knew, of course, but strong scaffolding was going to be an absolute necessity. These were trustworthy women and Stella needed them.

Simon continued faithful, annoyingly so, yet comfortingly so. Her attitude towards him was mixed and that confused her. She had always been able to delineate people clearly and quickly, was swift to recognize a patient who pretended to be ill, even when her knowledge of that patient was minimal. Simon was a separate issue, one she would deal with at a later date.

The doorbell sounded and she allowed in her mother and Tilly. The latter was in one of her moods, because her husband had gone drinking with Ted Moss, the best man who remained unforgiven after thirty years. 'Seth'll be maudlin,' she complained, 'maudlin and fretful. I can't be doing with him when he's miserable. Hello, Stella.'

'Come in.' Stella led the two women into her sitting room. 'Have you told Tilly?' she asked her mother.

'She has,' replied Tilly, 'and don't be worrying, you know we're on your side. Did he take advantage of you while he was out of his mind?'

'No,' said Stella easily, 'quite the reverse. It doesn't matter how I got into this condition, Tilly, but I wanted you to know because Mam has been allowing this to make her ill. I need advice. So does she. And I've never forgotten how kind you were to me and Molly when we were young. I'll leave the door on the latch, because Alice is coming.'

Emily removed her coat, took Tilly's and draped both across a chair. The sheer relief of offloading her worries to Tilly had pushed her close to tears. She felt like a wrung-out dishcloth, no bones, no substance. But Tilly was strong; Tilly always knew what to do.

'Mam, it will be all right. Simon's going to help – he insists. I'm going on to his list and that will give me a chance to get away. He will recommend rest and recuperation for a few months.'

Emily gulped nervously. 'Stella?'

'What?'

'The baby. When you've had it. What will you do?'

Stella had closed the shutters on that one. The answer was that she had no answer and that was unlike her, too. She could not see beyond the next few months, had given little consideration to the birth: her main aim was to get away, because patients and fellow doctors must not be allowed to see her increasing girth. 'Mam, I don't know. That's another story altogether. I'm different. I can't think as far ahead as I could.'

'Hormones,' declared Tilly. 'I've read about them and they're a bugger. Oh, and I've told our Alice,' she added, blunt as ever. 'She's got somebody with a burst stitch or summat, but she'll be here when she's got him sewn up again. He were doing wheelchair races with another patient. Men.' She spat the word. 'No bloody sense, no bloody idea.'

Stella smiled. The thing she loved about Tilly was that this little woman was very decided. She knew her own place in the world, knew her strengths, her weaknesses – and she took no prisoners.

Emily went to brew tea. That was something she could do, an activity that seemed sensible in the face of all the confusion in her mind. Poor Stella. She was in a right pickle, but at least there were others to share the worry now.

Alice let herself in. 'Hello, Stella,' she announced, before pulling off her raincoat.

'Have you stitched him up?' asked Tilly.

'The doctors have,' came the sharp reply, 'and I asked them to fasten his gob at the same time – what a fuss. Aren't men babies?'

Everyone agreed with that. They drank tea and talked about the shop, men's surgical at Bolton Royal, Irene's new kitchen, her anger because her estranged husband had bought a horse. Silence arrived. Alice placed her cup and saucer on a side table. 'So, you're going to leave us for a while, Stella.'

'Needs must,' replied Stella, 'and I may not come back. But I can't project that far, so I'm just feeling my way. I do know this – only with safety-pins can I fasten my skirts. Another few weeks and I shall be showing properly. Simon's trying to work something out.'

Alice was not happy. Matthew Richards was one of the nicest people she had ever met, and she felt as if everyone here conspired against him. Yes, he had run away, though not as a coward might have run. Matthew had done the right thing. He knew that he was still incapable of functioning within the framework of his normal life, so he had gone off to cure himself. Simple. And now here sat four women who discussed the future

322

of his child without so much as a mention of him.

'Simon still wants to marry you, I'll bet,' Tilly was saying now.

'I can't think about that,' said Stella.

Alice decided to voice her concern. 'What about Matthew? This is his child, too.'

'We can't tell him,' replied Tilly, 'because we can't bloody find him.' She glared at her daughter, was still sure that Alice knew his whereabouts.

Stella shook her head thoughtfully. 'No, this isn't his child, Alice. He scarcely knew what he was doing. It's just his sperm, that's all.'

Emily, who was not used to such plain speaking, picked up cups and began to pour more tea.

Tilly called the meeting to order in her usual blunt way. 'No need for details. All we need to know is that Emily's Stella is expecting and we don't tell anyone. We know, Simon knows, and that's it, it goes no further, not even to Irene.'

'Especially not Irene, not yet,' Stella insisted. 'If we want to be really pedantic, this is her grandchild. When it's time, I may tell her, but I must be the one to do that. It's a case of thinking caps now, girls. Simon can get me out of work for a few months – anaemia, something of that nature. It will be difficult, because this is a small country and the medical people are tightly knit, so we will have to be very discreet.'

'Where will you go?' asked Emily.

Stella had no idea. She talked in vague terms of places in the south, of nursing-homes on Jersey and the Isle of Man, even Ireland.

At this point Alice had little to say. She knew that

she should support Stella and would do her best not to betray her, yet she felt pulled towards Matthew. He should know, should be given the chance to have a say about the future of this child. His letters proved that he was much better, but would news of a baby send him over the edge again?

Tilly watched her daughter. 'Alice?'

'What?'

'Are you with us?'

The trouble with Tilly was that she knew just about everything. Sometimes, Alice feared that her skull was transparent, that Mam could see right through into her innermost thoughts. 'Of course I'm with us.'

'Right,' said Tilly. 'We all go home and think about it. And let's see what Simon comes up with.'

That night, Alice slept fitfully. She could not get him out of her mind, could not bear what was happening. Stella didn't love him; Stella seemed to love only Stella and the memory of a dead sister. What was the right thing and was there ever a right thing, a clear path?

When she rose the following morning, Alice Povey knew one thing. As her mother's daughter, she could not let this lie. Like Tilly, she had to know, had to get to the bottom of things. She had to see him.

Once in the hospital, she juggled rotas, called in a few favours and collected a few days' leave. She was going to Yorkshire.

Twelve

The horse was Loganberry, black as night, so dark that she seemed slightly blue when standing in sunlight. There was an arrogance about her, as if she considered the whole world to be beneath her. She was a goddess among minions and it showed. Treading ground, the whites of her eyes on show, she blew angrily down her nostrils, disdain oozing from every solid ounce of her structure.

This was not what Jack had intended to buy: he would have preferred a gelding, but the mare was magnificent, broad and tall, elegant legs and that special bearing that comes only from the best bloodlines. She was on trial, was being tested and assessed until the money came through.

He saddled her, ran expert hands over the taut neck, felt the nervousness that accompanies all good mounts. She would perhaps be a little feisty, but he would break her, would get her to submit to him. A horse needed to know who was in charge, so the first lesson was about to begin.

Loganberry eyed him warily. She disliked him,

did not trust him, and she let him know that, snorting furiously when straps were tightened. This was going to be a painful ride and she had no intention of tolerating pain. He yanked on her mouth, bruising flesh that was used to tender hands.

Jack walked to the rear of the stall to pick up his whip. He brandished it, determined to let her know that he was master, slapping the weapon against his boots, enjoying the animal's reaction. Oh, yes, she was ready for him, but he was more ready. After this initial ride, she would know her rightful place in Jack's scheme.

The first kick was vicious. It floored him immediately, his right leg whipped from beneath him as if it were a twig attached to a sapling. He hit the floor heavily, was struggling to get up, whip waving, face red with fury. But she broke completely from slack tether, bringing both front hoofs hard on to his stomach. Winded, he rolled away into hay, tried to get outside her reach, but he was cornered.

She reared, fearsome noises blowing down that aristocratic nose, feet beating the air, temper hot. He felt one huge, crushing pain in his back, then he passed out. The mare danced on the mortal who had tried to be her master, turning away only when he became completely still.

Then she swung round and strolled with quiet ease through the stable doorway. She was free and he was routed.

Simon placed his bag on Stella's table. He was

now one of her doctors so he had to tread carefully, yet as her friend he remained determined to help her through the maze she now faced. She was looking so drawn, seemed to have lost weight, only her abdomen showing a slight increase in girth.

'Thanks for coming,' she said.

'Blood pressure in a moment,' he told her, 'but a cup of tea to start, I think. Then we have to work our way through the medical stuff.'

'That's the easy part.' She pushed a strand of lank hair from her face. Stella was a woman who did not bloom in pregnancy. The early months had scarcely affected her, yet now, at the half-way mark, her skin was pasty, eyes dull, hair lifeless. But the part most diminished was her brain. As a doctor, she needed to think clearly; as a woman, she wanted to crawl away to consider her future.

He brought two mugs of tea from the kitchen. 'You are going on a holiday, my dear,' he said. 'And we have no need to justify that. Your haemoglobin is slightly low, so I'm telling no lie when I pronounce you anaemic. Now, the question is, what exactly do we do with you? Oh, and what are your long-term plans?'

She raised her shoulders. 'Easy. Don't know and don't know.'

'Have you thought about the future?'

Stella laughed, though there was irony in the sound. 'Yes, I've thought. I've also appointed thinkers – my mother, Tilly Povey and her daughter, Alice. And before you ask, no, they don't think that you're the father. I told them the absolute truth, no salad dressing.'

Simon's heart lurched. It was her refusal to use 'salad dressing' that endeared her to him. She probably interpreted her need for truth as a weakness, but it was, in fact, her strength. Had she been able to live a lie, he and she would have been married by now. And the most stupid part of him wished that she had been able to lie. No. Had she found the capability to be deceitful, she would not have been Stella.

'Please, Simon, don't ask me what I'm going to do with the child, because I can't even think about it.' She paused, lowered her chin and concentrated. 'And here sits a female doctor who has seen this several times. I lecture teenagers on how to avoid pregnancy, yet look at me, in my thirties and in a pickle. God, I'm stupid.'

'No, you're not. Had you been stupid, you'd have aborted weeks ago. Did you consider that?'

'Yes.'

'And?'

'Again, don't ask. If my brain could kindly kick into gear, then I might reach some answers. And I find the job hard. I can't say I'm worried because I'm not anything – it's almost as if I've stopped existing.'

'Euphoria?'

'No, just nothing at all. I'm empty. I seem to have moved out.'

She was describing shock, yet she was not in shock. Deep down, this woman was terrified, so afraid that she had shut herself away in a safe place, had allowed an emergency mechanism to click in. Stella Dyson was brave, almost reckless, because she knew very well that her problem could have been solved quite easily. 'You're still in there,' he told her.

'Hope so. May have a daughter or son to rear and a new life to start, Simon. I can't see myself carrying on here in Bolton with a fatherless child whose sire lives just across the road. That's if he comes back.'

Simon kept his counsel. A practice just outside Huddersfield had applied for Matthew's notes, so the father of this baby was somewhere in West Yorkshire. 'He'll come back. He has a son here.'

'He always had a son,' she answered quickly. 'They both had a son. When he was small, they spent time with him, seaside, parks and so forth, taught him to read and count. Then, when Molly's first illness arrived, that was the end of their parenting.' She paused. 'To love like that, in such an all-consuming way, must be terrifying, yet wonderful.'

'Not good for Mark, though,' said Simon.

She thought about that. 'When he falls in love, if he does, he'll know what love is, because he saw it. Perhaps, in a strange way, it will have strengthened him. And he may well make a good father, too, because he has learned from his own childhood. Hard to say.'

Simon did the necessary checks, placed his hand on her child, wished with all his heart that this could be his baby. Why had she told the truth? Stella looked far from her best, yet he still wanted her and, no, this wasn't just sex. He needed to look after her, and not just as a doctor. A kind of fury was building inside him, frustration, annoyance with the world, with the fickle nature of fate—

'Sit on it, Simon,' she whispered.

'On what?'

'On whatever's going on in your head. Your face is too open.'

He swallowed. Was she psychic, too? 'I'm your doctor now.'

'I'm aware of that,' she answered.

'Do you think I'm likely to forget my place in your life? Have you any idea what torture this is for me?'

'No, I have no idea at all.'

Oh, God. Perfect temperature, blood pressure spot on, just a slight drop in oxygenated cells – did she always have to be perfect? He almost laughed at himself, because the poor girl was in far from perfect shape, dark smudges under her eyes, skin pallid, hair limp and oily. 'You look absolutely dreadful,' he told her now.

'Thanks. Next time I need a little friendly encouragement, I shall phone the undertaker. Simon?'

'What?'

'Would it be terribly unprofessional if you were to take me out?'

'Yes.'

'Right,' she said, 'let's do it. A ride in the country, the wind in my hair, get the old sense of proportion back.' She laughed at him. 'Look, they

330

all know we were engaged – there will be talk already because I'm on your partners' list. Let's allow them to see that we remain the best of friends.'

'You're a demon.'

'Yes. So buy back my soul. Come on, you're off-duty and so am I. A ride on the wild side before I consign myself to obscurity. Please.'

He conceded, just as he always would where she was concerned. In that moment, he felt that he would always be there for her, that even when she moved on to another place, to another doctor, he would be waiting. For what? For her to love him?

She went for her coat and he sat very still, felt foolish and confused. He had been rejected out of hand, had returned as one of her doctors, was willing to wear any costume at all just to earn a place in her life. Was he a man or a mouse? 'Squeak,' he said, under his breath, as she re-entered the room.

'Where shall we go?' she asked.

He shrugged, thought of Sunday School and Bible study – 'Whither thou goest, I will go . . .'

'Simon?'

'Yes, ma'am?'

'Rivington. Let's see if we can climb to the top. Come on, I'm pregnant, not ill. We can stop for fish and chips, lots of vinegar, eat them with our fingers. A glass of beer in a pub. We have to talk. I must get out of Bolton very soon – this practice will need a locum, so they'll want notice.'

'Oh, all right.' He grabbed his scarf, owned the suspicion that he would have jumped through hoops of fire had she demanded that. Then he pulled himself up short and cursed his selfishness. Stella would be going to a new place, a town where she would know no one. If she wanted to run around outside, then he would arrange that.

Stella walked out of the flat and blinked the mist from her eyes. She would miss Bolton, her mother, her colleagues. Most of all, she would miss the gentle soul who walked behind her. So devoted, so transparent, he was. And she could offer no comfort because she was empty – wasn't she?

Alice Povey had passed her driving test at the first attempt in 1960, though her experience since had been negligible. And Gillian Cawley's old banger, a Morris Minor of uncertain temperament, was not the ideal chariot in which to make the journey over the top and into the wilds of Yorkshire. Yet she had to go.

Trains were all very well but, from what Alice had been able to discover, the farm was four or five miles outside Huddersfield and the bus service was not a frequent one. So it had to be the car. She walked round it, saw the rust, thought the tyres looked all right, hoped that the brakes would work.

Oh, well, even if she survived the journey, Mam would kill her when she got back. Yes, Mam would go ballistic, but Alice had given considerable thought to her proposed actions and she could see no other way of appeasing her over-active conscience. She had to see him. She could not tell him in a letter that he was about to become a father, needed to look him in the face first. Also, she would have to judge his state of mind and that could not be done with pen and paper. He might not be fit to be told, but she would take her chances.

Back in the flat, she picked up a small case and said goodbye to Gillian, who was busy going blonde. 'I hope you don't lose your hair,' she said.

Gillian sniffed. 'And I hope you don't crash my car.'

Alice snatched up the keys. 'If I get to Yorkshire, it'll be nothing short of a miracle. Don't forget to pay the paper bill and remember I don't like wreaths. Oh, and I want burying in Tonge cemetery, not up Heaton.'

Gillian stuck out her tongue and carried on reading instructions.

Terrified, but armed with the address of Hillside Farm, Alice set off on her momentous journey. Part of her mind told her she was daft; the rest insisted that she was doing the right thing. The bubble of excitement in her chest was nothing to do with wanting to see Matthew Richards again. No, she was just apprehensive about driving, that was all.

Phil Dyson parked his moped on the driveway of Eagley Farmhouse. It was a brisk day, cold, but bright, and he had enjoyed the ride from Thicketford Road up the moor to Jack Richards' place. Well, it was Irene Richards' place, but she no longer lived there.

In his pocket, Phil carried a cheque for three hundred and seventy pounds and another for two hundred and ninety. This bounty was supposedly required for sick relatives of the major's wife, although in truth the ill-tempered old buffoon would probably be buying a horse with it. Irene Richards was not best pleased, or so it seemed. According to her, Jack was not fit to own a goldfish and she would find a way of putting a stop to his behaviour.

Oh, well, there was nothing Phil could do about the misdeeds of his client. He had come to make a payment and, beyond that, he could do no more.

The door was opened by a man sporting a moustache and a copy of the *Daily Express*. 'Can I help you?'

'Is Major Richards in?' asked Phil.

'No. He went out about half an hour ago to try his new horse for size.'

'Ah.' Phil had other clients to see, but could leave the cheques only with the owner of the policies. So Mrs Richards had been right – the old blunderbuss had, indeed, bought a horse. She would drive him out of house and home once she knew the truth.

'Should be back any time,' said the man. 'I'm Stephen Hartley, by the way, one of the major's house guests.'

Irene wasn't pleased about the lodgers, either. The chances of her furniture being damaged had now been greatly increased, especially if the major's friends were as fond of drink as he was.

334

Phil hovered uncertainly, then made his decision. 'I'll go round the back and see if he's there.'

'Fair enough.' The man closed the door.

Phil walked along the side of the house, realizing as he approached the stables what a valuable property this was, bigger than it seemed from the front, with an enormous rear yard and half a dozen stables. He crossed the cobbles, looking through each doorway until he reached the end. The place was as silent as a graveyard . . .

A groan reached his ears. Inside the stable furthest from the house, a heap of humanity lay on the floor. Phil froze for a while, then rushed inside. The man was in a position that seemed impossible, one leg obviously broken, blood seeping through his clothing. Squatting down, Phil checked that Jack Richards was breathing, remembered reading somewhere that a patient in this state must be moved only by experts. 'Wait there,' he breathed, realizing the stupidity of his words the moment they were born.

He dashed across the cobbles and flung open the rear door of the house. A different man was washing dishes at the kitchen sink. 'Can I help you?' he asked, dishmop in hand, a flowery apron making him look thoroughly ridiculous.

'Ambulance. Phone.' Phil's breathing was all over the place. 'He's in a right bloody mess.'

'Who?'

'The major. Go on, get to that phone. Tell them one leg is definitely broken and he's lying funny – we daren't move him.'

The paying guest ran off, apron fluttering

around him, dishmop still clutched in his hand. Phil's own legs were threatening strike action, so he lowered himself on to a stool. He could have killed for a brandy, but there were circumstances more desperate than his own.

The man returned. 'On its way,' he said. 'I'm Doug, by the way. Are you all right?'

Phil nodded. 'I am, but he isn't.'

The lodger divested himself of his feminine garb. 'I warned him,' he said. 'That horse is a mad bugger if ever I saw one, whites of its eyes on show all the time. Do you think it was the horse?'

'I would say so, yes. And he does have a reputation for cruelty to horses. Looks like he bit off more than he could chew this time.'

The man ran outside, leaving Phil to his own thoughts. The other lodger, the one who had opened the front door not ten minutes ago, came downstairs and entered the kitchen. 'What's all the fuss?'

Suddenly too tired for words, Phil waved a hand towards the back door. A third man came in and followed his fellow lodgers out into the yard. This was a bit like Crewe station, Phil pondered irrelevantly. How long would an ambulance take to get all the way up here? Even with a flashing light and a bell, progress would be at rather less than lightning speed. He could have killed for a cigarette. This was one of those times when it was easy to regret having given up. The tap was dripping. Heating milk boiled over on the stove.

Phil rescued the milk pan, then, for some reason best known to his subconscious, began to wash the dishes in the sink. Shock did some funny things to folk, he thought, as he applied a pan scrub to a fish-slice. Someone had eaten bacon. He swept broken eggshells from the drainer and put them into a bin. Would they need hot water? No, hot water was for a baby. This baby was a nasty old man who had probably been bludgeoned by the flailing hoofs of a terrified horse.

Time stretched itself through fifteen more minutes. The three men outside did not return. Phil made a pot of tea, poured himself a cup, added three spoonfuls of sugar for shock. It tasted terrible, but he was following orders he had read years earlier. The ceiling was beamed. A row of shiny copper pans hung from one of the beams, of which there were seven. The man might die at any minute. Phil hoped that the three men had not attempted to move him. That tap wanted a new washer. There were twenty-seven cookery books on the dresser.

Somebody would have to tell Irene Richards. No, not over the telephone. Whatever had happened between Irene and Jack, the fact remained that they had been married for over forty years. If anything of this nature ever befell Annie, he would kill himself. Phil and Annie were like a pair of gloves accidentally separated and kept in different drawers for ages. The flowered apron was on the floor.

Annie helped out at the antiques shop sometimes. Irene and Mark had given her an old spinning-wheel, one that had been used by a child. Ages ago, before the mills, cotton had

337

been spun in cottages. It took about ten families to spin enough cotton for a weaver, so even the kiddies had been forced to spin. Annie had put the wheel next to the fireplace. The couple sat sometimes and stared at it, thinking of the wizened children who had used it.

There had to be something wrong with the clock and with his watch. Where was the horse? One of the cookery books was about cake decoration. A whole book devoted to icing. Fancy that. He was shaking inside, felt as if all his innards were rattling about. More tea. Another cup, another two sugars. Eagley was a long way out of Bolton.

It arrived. Phil heard it bouncing on the cobbles. Somebody shouted, was obviously guiding the ambulance into the yard. Doors slammed, feet pounded on the yard's uneven surface. Tears sprang to Phil's eyes and he didn't know why. The man was despicable and his wife was lovely. A nursery rhyme beat its way through his head, 'Horsey, horsey, don't you stop, just let your feet go clippety-clop' – God, where had that come from?

He was crying. No sound, just wet stuff leaking down his face. Good job he had never fought in a war. There had been talk of him being called up, but his job had been essential. He would have seen a lot of bodies in the war, many severe injuries, blood and gore. Silence from outside now. They would be putting Jack Richards on to a backboard, a very hard stretcher, possibly with no padding. The man would have a collar round his neck.

338

The back door opened and Stephen Hartley walked in. 'Are you all right, mate?'

'Just shock.'

'Looks like his back's broken. No sign of the horse, but it had to be the culprit. Shall I get you a brandy?'

'No, thanks, I have to ride my bike.'

'Nothing you could have done for him, son.'

'I know.'

Phil stayed with two of the men until the ambulance had left, its progress slow because of the bumpy ground. The third man had accompanied Jack Richards to the hospital. There was nothing more to be said. Phil stood up, shook the men's hands and left the house. Now, he had to call on Irene Richards.

Alice Povey had never visited Yorkshire before so she enjoyed the privilege of that thrill that visits most Lancastrians when they go 'over the top' for the first time. The words 'magnificent', 'fierce' and 'spectacular' proved too mild for the vision that awaited her once the car had coughed its senile way over the pass. Awestruck, she left the vehicle under a hanging rock where it kept company with a large sheep, who appeared singularly unimpressed by the noise of the sadly misfiring mechanism.

'Top of the world,' muttered Alice, as she turned this way and that, her eyes widening while they absorbed beauty that was simply too wonderful for ordinary words. Yes, Lancashire was pretty, but compared to this it was mild, much gentler, certainly a great deal warmer. She tightened her scarf, gathered her coat closer to her body. Oh, she could live here, yes.

There were several seas named for colours, Red, Yellow, Black, but here lay the Green Sea, mile upon mile of it, sometimes soft, sometimes sharp, rising, dropping, a slight breeze causing a ripple on the surface of the grasses. She could scarcely breathe for joy as her gaze followed the spread right up to a drunken horizon, its contours impossibly pleated, so wild, so wilful and free. This was why he had come here: the area was elemental, untamed, was a place in which a man might find his soul.

Dark tendrils stretched across acres, those age-worn walls of which Matthew was so fond, their constituents hacked from the very land they marked. Shadows in clefts were black, then the land rose improbably, thrown up by the hand of God, green on green, yellow with purple, colours that threatened to be blindingly bright when summer arrived.

A lone curlew swooped and called; sheep maa-ed their stupidity into the air. This was not Brontë country but, oh, it might have been. Here was a perfect setting for a Heathcliff to lose his mind, for another man to regain his. 'I want to stay,' she murmured, before sitting on a bald rock to eat her sandwiches and to drink coffee from a flask.

Alice had found God's county; she had no need for Devon and Cornwall, no desire for prettiness, pasties and pixies. Yorkshire was real, was terrifying, exciting. The air was so pure that it cut into her lungs, scaldingly cold, activating her brain so that she was truly alert. To live here, to walk here, to open one's eyes every morning to such beauty – why had she not known about this? The sheep was studying her, its expression baleful.

'Hello,' she said.

It nodded its head and turned away, plainly unimpressed by this foreign intruder. With a certainty born into its feet, it climbed over rock and mound, no thought required, its only desire greener grass. From animals like this filthy creature had come a wool industry so huge, so powerful that its owners had fought tooth and nail to prevent the importing of vegetable wool, now known as cotton. Side by side, divided by the Pennines, these two counties had existed in war and in uneasy truce; in the end, the similarities had outweighed the differences and they had all produced cloth. Thank God for that, thought Alice. Even a Lancastrian could survive here now.

A nervousness began to rise beneath the joy. She was suddenly afraid of the size of her commitment – what would Matthew Richards think when he saw her? And what was she doing, anyway? To cross the mountains was one thing; to cross the divide that separated one human from another was a different matter altogether. People wanted inner space. The way they lived, walled away from each other, keep off the grass, no trespassers – all that was merely an outward expression of a deeper need, the desire for individuality. And here she

341

sat, little Miss Bossy-boots with a Thermos, some greaseproof paper and the audacity to interfere with a man's life.

Should she go back? If she did, it would be a downhill start, no effort for the asthmatic Morris that had already breathed its temper through two counties. No. She had come this far and she wanted to see him anyway, would enjoy visiting his way of life, seeing his sheep and the bits of stone walling about which he enthused.

She went back to the car, picked up the map and plotted her way to Huddersfield. The sheep now stood above her, on the rock under which the car's bonnet was parked. Where else might one park a Morris Minor beneath a sheep? Where else could one feel so embraced, yet so free? Alice made up her mind there and then that this was her place. She had seen no city, no town, no person; this sheep, this rock and this vista were enough. Although a Lancastrian by birth and by culture, she adopted Yorkshire as her second home – and Yorkshire did not seem to mind in the slightest.

Rivington was fun, even in cold weather. They reached the folly at the top, both breathless, no energy for laughter or for speech.

A slight colour had returned to her cheeks, whipped up by a frisky breeze with no sense of direction. He noted the improvement, thought she should migrate to the coast, somewhere quiet with soft sand on which she might walk daily. No, no, he could not part with her. When he finally managed to absorb some oxygen, he spoke. 'I'm not really your doctor,' he said, 'you're on Mike Harris's list. I'm standing in for him.'

'I see.' She tightened the belt of her raincoat.

'Because I can't be your official doctor, Stella. I still love you.'

'Oh.'

'So I'm not your practitioner. You're my partner's patient.'

'Right. Shall we find something to eat?'

He didn't know why he was trying, because she would not listen. He didn't even know what he was trying to achieve . . . As she turned to descend the hill, he grabbed her arm. 'There's still time. We can face this together, Stella. Get married, tell people we've been married for weeks, whatever. Or tell the truth, let them know that we jumped the gun. Better still, move on, start elsewhere.'

'Not your child, Simon, not your problem.'

'And if I want it to be my problem?'

'No.' She walked on.

'Stella!' His tone was raised, sounded almost angry. 'I'm offering you stability, security, a place for the child.'

She swung round. 'And your own head on a plate. I can't think. Did you not understand earlier when I explained that? I'm empty, used up, exhausted. Simon, I would marry you in a flash if I had any sense, but that's the whole point, isn't it? No sense. You're talking to someone who just wants to enjoy the day, because today is all there is. Find me somewhere, Simon. Tell your partner to announce my anaemia and post me off to Switzerland for recuperation.'

'Switzerland?'

She almost growled in frustration. 'Switzerland on paper, somewhere in Britain in reality. Just do it. I'm not hungry any more, so I ask you to take me home, please.'

He followed her down the path, would have followed her to South Africa. But she was the conductor and she had to call the tune. And she could not call the tune, because her music had dried up. Not a word was spoken as they travelled back to her home. He stopped the car, kept his eyes straight ahead.

She leaned across and kissed him lightly on the cheek. 'It has to be afterwards,' she said quietly. 'I have to wait till I get myself back, Simon. There's no explanation and I can make no apology, because I'm not choosing to be as I am now.'

'I wish I could know what you're going through, Stella.'

'Get me out of Bolton, please. And thank Michael Harris for me. He's a good egg.'

'I'll miss you,' he said.

She allowed that slow smile to flourish briefly on her lips. 'I miss me. Oh, I was so sure that I could go through with the charade, so hard-faced about it. Then something kicked in and I stopped being rational. I just hope my patients are surviving this hiccup. Make it soon, Simon.'

He swallowed painfully. 'Will you keep in touch while you're away?'

'Of course. I promise. No matter what, you and I shall always be good friends.'

'I hope so.'

And she was gone. He sat and watched as she closed the car door, as she closed the door that led up to her flat. The chill cut right through him, though this ice owed little to the actual temperature: it was loneliness. He drove off, turned right into Mornington Road and entered the surgery. She needed time and he needed her.

Phil Dyson left his moped outside the shop and dashed in, heedless of anything except the need to find Irene Richards. Annie was there, too, polishing some Indian brassware while Irene showed a customer how to activate a secret drawer inside a bureau. 'Phil,' cried Annie.

But he did not stop. He fled across the shop and took Irene's arm. 'Mrs Richards, I—'

Unused to being interrupted, Irene stopped mid-flow and looked into the stricken face of Emily Dyson's son. 'Your mother is upstairs, Philip.'

'It's you I want.' He apologized to the customer, then led Irene away. He didn't know how to express what had happened, had no idea how to take the edge off it. Did she need the edge taking off? 'It's your husband, Mrs Richards. I went up to give him the cheques for those endowments and . . . he was in one of the stables, on the floor. They've taken him to the infirmary.'

Irene blinked slowly, as if she had not understood the message.

'I think he got a horse and the horse got him,' said Phil. 'He was in a heap on the floor. Somebody sent for the ambulance and one of his lodgers went with him. He was a mess.'

Irene's hand travelled along the back of a *chaise-longue* and she supported herself determinedly. 'Is he alive?'

'He was then. About half an hour ago. But he wasn't moving.'

'I see.'

'So . . .' Phil ran out of steam. He glanced across at his wife, tried to smile at her, failed miserably. Mrs Richards continued to stand in exactly the same position, no movement in her, no attempt to speak.

'Are you all right?' he asked her.

She was not all right. Her prime emotion was fierce anger, fury directed at a man who was not even there. He had taken up the whip again, she felt sure of that. How many times had she rubbed salve into a wounded horse? How many hours had she spent comforting a frightened beast? She inhaled deeply. 'Was the animal there?'

'No. One of the men in the house said the horse had looked a bit wild.'

Irene took a deep breath. 'It had to happen eventually,' she said softly. 'So, the animal must have bolted after dealing with him.' She heaved herself up, seemed to gain about two inches in height as her composure returned. 'My car is outside, Philip. I wonder, would you be so kind as to accompany me to the hospital?'

He nodded. 'Of course. May I use the phone? I must tell my boss what has happened so that my customers can be dealt with.'

While Irene brought her coat, Phil phoned his employers, then told his wife what had occurred. 'Tell Mark,' he advised her. 'Where is he?'

'Out,' she replied, 'looking at some stuff in a house up Deane. Oh, Phil, are you all right? Shall I come with you to the infirmary?'

'No.' He would rather have stayed away himself, but what could he do? It was Prudential policy to look after customers in situations such as this; in a sense, this was a part of his job but, oh, how he wished he could get out of it. 'See you at home later on,' he told Annie.

She went off to explain the situation to Irene's abandoned customer, then carried on with her own tasks.

Phil led Irene Richards out of the shop. Except for a small twitch on one of her eyelids, there was little difference to her appearance. As ever, she was beautifully dressed and wonderfully composed. He sat in the passenger seat while she drove round the corner and up to Chorley New Road. They turned into the infirmary car park and stopped before she spoke again. 'I knew I would never get away from him. These few weeks of freedom were far too good to be true. Now, Philip, I have to visit a man I care nothing for, am forced to act the dutiful wife simply because he cannot conduct himself properly. Damn the Coldstreams. Damn them for encouraging him to judge himself perfect.'

Phil thought she was being a bit hard on the regiment, but he kept his lips closed. She was the one who had suffered; she was the one who must cope with what had happened today. He climbed out of the car, walked round to the other side and helped her to her feet. As he took her hand, he could not help noticing that she was trembling.

When Irene had been identified at the reception desk, she and Phil were led away to a small side room containing just a table and some chairs. She sat down, looked around her, placed her gloves inside a good leather handbag. 'This is a bad-news room, Philip. Shortly we shall get a cup of tea. After a decent interval, a doctor will come to talk to us. Thank you so much for being here, I'm terribly grateful.'

'Don't mention it,' he answered.

As predicted, tea arrived, carried in by a very young trainee nurse who fled as soon as the saucers hit the table. 'You see?' said Irene. 'Tea and tears, though I don't know who is going to provide the latter.'

Phil drank his tea, trying to prevent the cup rattling in its saucer.

Irene left hers on the table. She had no need of tea: all she wanted was an answer. Her eyes were fixed on the upper part of the door, which had a glazed panel; through that she watched the comings and goings in the reception area.

A doctor arrived, young, handsome, but with his face arranged in sympathetic mode. A stethoscope dangled from his neck and his shirt would have benefited from an introduction to Tilly Povey's iron. 'Mrs Richards?'

'Yes?'

The man crossed the room and sat beside her,

his body turned sideways so that he could look straight at her. 'It's too early for a full assessment, but it is clear that your husband broke his spine.'

'I see,' was her only answer.

'He took a bad beating, I'm afraid. His right leg is badly crushed and he will need some X-rays.' He paused, waited for comments or questions, received none. 'Would you like to see him?'

Irene did not answer right away. Did she want to see him? The reply was undoubtedly no, but that false politeness with which mankind is blessed reared itself. This was her husband, a man with whom she had lived for a very long time. He had not changed: she was the one who had allowed major structural improvements to her foundation. 'Yes, please,' she lied.

She rose, as did Phil, but Irene smiled at him. 'Wait for me, Philip,' she said. 'This is something I must do alone.' Then she addressed the doctor: 'You may judge me to be cold, if you wish, but I have no interest in my husband. Our only son is away, so I am left to deal with this.'

'I see,' replied the medic.

'Frankly, Doctor, I am more concerned about the horse, his latest victim. Because of Jack Richards, my son had an appalling upbringing. Then, when Matthew became too old for ill-treatment, Jack took it out on animals. But, yes, I shall look at him for a moment. After all, he has no one else.'

The doctor glanced quickly at Phil, but got no response.

Phil, who knew all about abusive fathers, was

miserable on Irene's behalf. For the major, he felt little, because the man was clearly a coward and a bully. But this honest and decent woman was definitely in shock. Unable to leave the hospital, not wanting to stay, she simply obeyed the rules of polite society, the conventions imposed by the human race.

He flicked through a magazine, walked up and down the room, wondered what was happening to his clients. Annie was happy, anyway, had fallen on her feet with a nice little job at Matthew & Son. A broken back could kill a person. Think straight, he ordered himself, head all over the place, allowing himself to be distracted, needing to be distracted.

Matthew Richards. Yes, Phil suddenly understood the man. God, it must be so easy to go insane when given the right circumstances – the wrong ones, more likely. Phil had been deeply saddened by the death of his sister, but how must her husband have felt? Obviously devoted, Matthew had allowed everything to go to pot during Molly's final months, the business, the house, the gardens. How fragile life was. He closed his fists tightly and prayed that his Annie would remain strong.

The door opened and Irene Richards walked in. The nurse who had accompanied her stepped away to carry on with other tasks, leaving Irene looking very lost and isolated.

'Mrs Richards?' Phil stood up.

'Oh, Philip.' She sank into the chair she had occupied just minutes earlier. 'What a dreadful state he's in. They said very little, but it doesn't take a medical genius to guess that Jack will probably never walk again. No reflexes, Philip, no response. Bruising might heal in time, but his back is broken in at least one place, or so they think.'

He didn't know what to say. Sometimes it was better if a person died. Living with severe paralysis was not an option most would want to consider, but it depended on the scale, he supposed. Would the man be able to get about in a wheelchair, would he have the use of his arms, his speech?

'We have to wait,' she said, as if reading his mind, 'weeks, possibly months before we know how he will be.'

'I'm sorry.'

She exhaled. 'Thank you. I shall never forget today, Philip.'

'I haven't done anything.'

'Yes, you have. By the way, Jack is conscious.' Oh, yes, he had been conscious. If looks could have killed, Irene might have been on her way to the morgue at this very moment. It was plain that he blamed her for not being there, for abandoning him to a wild horse.

'Did he talk?' asked Phil.

She shook her head. 'But he understands what is going on around him, I'm sure of that.'

'He must be very angry,' said Phil.

Irene smiled wearily. 'I cannot remember a day on which he was not angry. Apart from these past few weeks, the only time I was happy was when he was away and Matthew and I had just each other.'

'That's sad.'

'Yes, it is. But, dear boy, you and I have work to do. Let's go, because we can do nothing here.'

As they drove back to the shop, Irene remained silent, yet Phil could feel the tension that surrounded her. He knew full well what she was thinking. If Jack Richards survived the accident, he would probably need care for the rest of his life. After a very short period of freedom, Irene was in danger of regaining a husband. And, of course, she neither needed nor wanted him.

He handed her over to Annie, Emily and Mark, left the shop, started his moped and went on with his business. And he still didn't know what to do with Jack Richards' cheques.

Thirteen

Tilly had gone all spread out. He could see that she was all spread out when he passed the front window, hands on hips, elbows stuck at angles like a pair of bent coat-hangers, face like a fit. From the stance of her upper body, he could imagine the lower part, feet set wide, legs looking as sturdy as puny legs could ever manage. Yes, she was definitely all spread out. Tilly in a straight line could mean trouble; Tilly spread out was as near world war as could be managed without a proper declaration.

Sighing resignedly, he entered the house and hung his canvas workbag on its usual hook.

She came out of the front room. 'Oh, so you're home.'

'No, I'm not,' he replied. 'I'm a figment of your overactive imagination.' Immediately, he wished he could bite back the words, because Tilly spread out was not a Tilly to be tangled with.

'Don't you come the funny stuff with me, lad,' she snapped. 'I'm not in the mood. If you're planning on joining that daft husband of Irene's in the hospital, just carry on this road and I'll see what can be done to oblige.'

He took off his coat and hung it with his bag. No chance of any bloody peace in this house tonight, then. As for a quiet pint in the Starkie with Ted Moss – no way. He fiddled with the straps on his overalls.

'She's gone,' Tilly announced.

'Irene Richards?' he asked. 'Where would she go? Mind, she hates the sight of him so—'

'Not her,' yelled Tilly. 'Not Irene Richards. Look at me when I'm talking to you. It's your daughter what's gone.'

Ah. So Alice was his daughter now. When she'd passed her nursing exams, she had been Tilly's daughter – the same when she had come top of her class in midwifery. When the kids did well, they were Tilly's. 'Do we live in the same house?' he asked now. 'You and me, like?'

'Eh?' Her brow was suddenly knitted. 'You what?'

'I said, do we live in the same house, Till? I get mixed up, you see, because you have good sons and a good daughter, whereas mine are rubbish. Only if I've come to the wrong address, just point me right and I'll bugger off.'

She bared her National Health dentures. 'Listen, you lummox. I went down to see our Alice about what happened to Jack Richards, thought she might have a book about broken backs and stuff, but the girl called Gillian – she's gone blonde and, ooh, she does look common – she said our Alice had beggared off in that Morris Minor of hers.'

'Right.' He felt as if he might just commit murder for a cup of Horniman's.

'Right? What do you mean, right? Have you seen the state of that car? It's held together with faith, hope and Plasticine. The only thing worth keeping is the number-plate. Where is she?'

Seth blinked. 'How the hell should I know? I've been struggling with a broken lathe for the past three hours, then I come home to this. She's twenty-seven, Tilly. If she were five years old and missing from school, I'd worry. But she can look after herself.'

'She's very thin,' insisted Tilly. 'A good puff of wind could blow her right through to next Tuesday. And I wouldn't put me worst enemy in that car. Where the hell can she be?'

'How the hell should I know?' he repeated. 'I'm a lathe operator, not a detective. If she's gone, she's gone for a reason. Has she missed her work?'

'No, she took a few days off, swapped round with some other sister.'

'Then she's gone on purpose. She's borrowed that girl's car and she's took off for a break. People do that, you know, normal people. They relax, have a rest, take a couple of days off.' He wished Tilly would take some time off, preferably somewhere warm. Like Brazil. 'Is me tea ready?' he asked.

'Your tea? Your belly, eh? Never mind that our daughter's missing—'

'Oh, she's our daughter now, is she? Coming up in the world is our Alice. A minute since, she only had a dad. But now you've decided to adopt her. Tilly, I'm tired.'

'Tired?' she shouted. 'I'm worried sick out of my mind, can't afford to be tired. Why didn't she tell me where she were going, eh? Answer me that one. She never even told Gillian and she's in her flaming car. She's up to summat, you mark my words, Seth Povey.'

'I am marking them,' he said, with exaggerated patience. He had been marking them for years. If he marked them for much longer, they would be printed on his soul in indelible ink. He would go to his Maker on Judgement Day with 'Look at me when I'm talking to you' stamped all through him like the words in a stick of seaside rock.

'We've got to find her,' Tilly insisted.

'All right,' he said, 'you hang on while I fetch the army out. Then, if you'd make sure there's petrol in me helicopter, I'll fly round for a couple of hours, see if she's at Blackpool. Oh, you get the dogs and search Moss Bank Park and the Jumbles—'

'Don't you get sarcastic with me, Seth.'

'Tilly!'

She stopped in her tracks. Seth was an easygoing fellow, but he had a breaking point and she had seen it only once. Their Stuart had been given a good hiding for pinching an apple from the greengrocer. Seth had dealt with the shopkeeper and with the rest of the apples. It had not been a pretty sight. Since that occasion, over twenty years ago, Seth had kept his temper, but she was taking no chances. She walked into the living room, took his dinner from the bungalow range oven and slapped it on the table.

'Stop worrying, woman,' he ordered. 'Our Alice likely has her driving licence with her, so if there'd been an accident, we would have been told. You can't go causing bother because a grown-up woman's gone on a jaunt. So let's hear no more about it.' He picked up his cutlery and attacked a pork chop.

Tilly made a great noise with the washing-up, crashing and banging, rattling cutlery on the drainer. It was all very well for men: they didn't worry like women did. A pork chop and a bottle of beer and the world was well, never mind about Alice messing about in a car that wanted scrapping, God alone knew where, probably broken down on a level crossing with an express train coming.

Seth listened to her rattling and chunnering. She was making enough din to alter the shape of Stonehenge, but he concentrated on his cabbage: a man needed his iron if he had to live with Tilly in a spread-out mood. She was drying now, breathing heavily. He looked at the sideways clock and noted the time. Tilly had been boiling for about ten minutes: another five and the steam would have dispersed, then it would be on with the telly and full speed ahead with the knitting needles.

She came in and plonked a cup of tea next to his right elbow. 'What if she's eloped?' she asked.

Oh, no, she was going into extra time. Where was the bloody referee when you needed him? 'Who'd elope in a clapped-out car?' he asked. 'If you're going to elope, you make sure you're in something that'll get you there.'

She clattered his cutlery into the twelve o'clock

position and lifted his plate. 'Sometimes I think you have no soul.'

Seth counted to ten, had little trouble holding on to his patience now that his belly was occupied. He had never known Tilly to be any different: with Tilly, you saw what you were getting and you got what you saw. Unfortunately. She was always wound up about something or other. If Tilly'd been a bit older, that Emmy Pankhurst would have needed to move over, because Tilly Crawford-as-was would have blown up Parliament. Aye, Guy Fawkes and his mates would have done a lot better if Tilly had been around,

'What are you thinking about now?' she asked.

Seth leaned back and surveyed the wife who might have changed history. 'Now, that's summat even you'll never know, Till. Nobody can get inside anybody else's head. No man is an island? That's another load of rubbish, because we all have our little hiding place.'

'You're getting on me bloody nerves,' she said crossly.

'I know.'

It was stalemate and she was forced to accept it. 'The news is on,' she said.

'I know.'

She switched on the television. 'I'll make us a fresh cuppa, you find me knitting.' She stalked through into the scullery.

Seth took another look at the sideways clock: injury time had lasted exactly ninety seconds. Not too bad, considering the circumstances . . . Good job she hadn't awarded herself a penalty, though . . .

Alice had wandered around Huddersfield all afternoon and had been impressed by it. There were good shops, a couple of decent market stalls from which she had bought clothes on the cheap, while the whole town was supervised by Castle Hill, a fort that dated back to Norman times. Wherever she went, she knew that the hill was watching her, as if it kept an eye on the town, made it safe.

She bought a little guidebook with maps, wandered round St George's Square, found the finest railway station in England. Someone in the guidebook referred to it as a stately home with trains, and Alice could not have dreamed up a better description. The town hall was equally impressive, while many of the buildings that had housed industrial nerve centres were ornate, almost Italianate in appearance.

It was pretty. She had ice-cream at D'Agostino's, wandered through the market hall, talked to people she didn't know, folk she would probably never meet again. The idea of Yorkshire people being dour and silent was dismissed within ten minutes, when a small group gathered to point her towards the ice-cream parlour, John William Street and New Street.

She knew that she was wasting time. Although she genuinely enjoyed her time in the town, she should have been somewhere else, needed to get to Stainthwaite before dark. The temptation to book somewhere for bed and breakfast was strong, yet Alice knew that if she thought about her mission, her reason for being here, she might well turn round and go home.

God, why the hell had she come here? Yes, Yorkshire was stunning, yes, the people were great, yes, Huddersfield looked like the sort of place in which she might settle one day, but all those things were just bonuses, happy accidents that had occurred by chance. She swallowed. Right, she could get into the car and drive home, or she could do that extra four miles out to the village where Mr and Mrs Jenkinson had their farm.

And that was as far as she would be able to get. Matthew kept his Mini at the farm because the rest of the journey had to be on foot or by tractor – even a tractor gave up for the final hundred yards. Pretty scenery was all very well until the practicalities had to be addressed. She was tired, hungry and thirsty; she was unhappy about what lay ahead; she wanted to see him, didn't want to see him. It was all none of her business, anyway, and she should have kept her nose out of it.

'Onward,' she said, through gritted teeth. She climbed into the car, noticed a hole in the floor through which she could actually see Tarmac. What was she doing? The slightest bump, and Gillian's pride and joy would probably fold up like cardboard left out in the rain. With determination that was more than grim, Alice set off towards Stainthwaite. She had come this far and it had to be done. And she should not have come at all.

* * *

Jack's condition was stable but his back was broken in two places and his chances of leading anything approaching a normal life were not good.

Irene sat in the car park attached to the Bolton Royal Infirmary. Next to her, Emily Dyson maintained an uncomfortable silence. This poor woman in the driving seat had a great deal on her plate, but she didn't know the half of it yet. Not only was her husband in grave danger of spending years flat on his back, Emily's daughter was carrying Irene's grandchild. Tilly knew about it, as did Alice, but Irene was in no fit state for more bad news.

'He won't walk again,' Irene announced.

'I thought as much,' said Emily. 'Our Stella didn't think a lot of his chances, either. Mind, she did say she knows of cases where doctors have been wrong. But you can't tell Matthew about it, can you? He should know what's happened to his dad.'

Irene raised her shoulders a fraction. 'It would make no difference, Emily. Jack never had much time for our son, and that seems to work both ways now.'

'But you need support, love.'

'I have you and Tilly and my grandson. You know, I had never been so happy for years. Back in the business, a house of my own, watching Mark using that fine brain, having you and Tilly for company. But it's as if some jealous god were watching me, waiting for me to stray towards happiness. Now this. What on earth is going to happen next?'

'None of us knows that, Irene.'

'They found the horse. She has gone back to her owners. Thank goodness she will not be shot. It has been judged an accident.'

'Right.' Emily had not loved her own husband, had hated him, in fact, yet she could not understand how Irene could want to protect a horse that had done so much damage to a man – any man. 'What about the house?' she asked now.

'The farmhouse?'

'Yes.'

Irene sighed heavily. 'Come with me, Emily. I cannot face all these decisions alone. Your daughter-in-law is helping Mark in the shop – let's go up to Eagley so that I can work out what must be done.'

'All right.'

'You don't mind?'

'Of course not.' Emily pondered the changes that had happened in her own life during recent months. She lived on Chorley New Road with a grandson she adored, had a nice job in a shop, mixed with people she would never have met had she not taken the marital home to bits. And Joe was dead. It was horrible feeling glad about someone's death, but she could not help herself. So perhaps she should understand Irene and her horses. Only a wife knew how cruel a husband could be.

They travelled in silence up Tonge Moor Road, each woman engrossed in thoughts too dreadful to be aired. Irene felt the tension returning to her body as the land rose steeply towards Eagley Top, her eyes sliding sideways when the car passed Rutherford Hall, the place in which she had re-acquainted herself with her son. Now, here was the village. She turned left up the incline that led to Eagley Farmhouse.

The two women climbed out of their seats and stood at the front door of Irene's home. She knocked. 'It is my house, but their home, Emily. They pay rent, so I'm not going to barge in.'

A man appeared from the yard. 'Hello?'

Irene walked towards him and gave him her hand. 'Irene Richards.'

'Bill Bright,' he announced. 'I'm round the back – would you follow me please? Steve and Doug are out.'

They pursued him round the corner and into the yard. He pushed the rear door inward and stood back to allow them inside.

'Good heavens,' exclaimed Irene, 'what on earth are you doing?' The kitchen was filled with furniture. 'Why is all this in here?'

'Secret recipe,' replied Bill Bright. A strong smell of citrus hung in the air. 'Found it in India. You see, wax builds and I take it off and start again.' He pointed to a small side table. 'Find a scratch on that, Mrs Richards. I have a strong interest in old wood and I do hope that my behaviour is not offensive to you – I meant no harm. I thought I would make myself useful in view of the . . . well . . . the circumstances.'

Irene examined the piece. 'Amazing,' she declared. 'I know for a fact that there was a scar on this leg.' She straightened. 'So, you're spring-cleaning?'

'Yes.' He smiled broadly. 'How about a cup of tea? I've made some bread, too.'

Irene managed a laugh. 'You'd make someone a wonderful wife, Mr Bright.'

'Bill,' he corrected her, a smile as shiny as his name visiting his face. 'How is the major, by the way?'

Irene steered herself past a small bureau, Emily in hot pursuit. 'Not good, Bill.' She sat down, as did Emily. 'His back is badly damaged, so is his spinal cord. He can speak a little, but feeding is difficult. There seems to be no sensation at all from the neck down.'

'I'm sorry,' said Bill. He came to the table, a large breadknife in his right hand. 'I don't want you to worry about us. There's Doug Allinson – he was Lancashire Fusiliers, sergeant, he has a son in Chester who'll take him in. Steve Hartley can go to his sister and I can look after myself. I have a bad knee, but I can do odd jobs, then I've a bit of pension—'

'No,' said Irene firmly. 'I won't have that, not yet. This house is not to be left empty.' She paused for a moment, drummed fingernails on the table. 'You may all stay for now, at reduced rents, and use the money from the acreage – I have no need of that.' She liked the man and made this decision from instinct. 'Eventually, Eagley Farm will go to my grandson, but he has no need of it until he is of age.'

Bill carried on buttering bread. 'So, what will

happen to the major when he comes out of hospital?' He looked over his shoulder at the two women. 'Because he'll want looking after, won't he?'

Irene could not afford to think too far ahead. Jack's wounds would heal slowly because of his paralysis, so she kept the long-term future on hold, in a place at the back of her mind, a compartment she chose not to visit too frequently.

Emily chipped in at this point: 'She doesn't know yet, Bill. Nobody knows. For a start, there have been some cases where people have got a lot better—'

'And many where they haven't,' interjected Irene.

Emily placed a hand on Irene's. 'We just have to wait and see,' she said. 'So it's no use making any decisions about that just yet.'

Bill nodded his agreement. 'Hang on while I make you a sandwich.'

Irene surveyed the small pieces in the room. She could identify quite clearly the items on which the man had already worked his magic. 'Bill?'

'Yes?'

'Have you got the recipe for this stuff?'

'Yes, I have.'

'And time on your hands?'

'That, too.'

She made her second quick decision within five minutes. 'Would you consider working at the shop? We already have a restorer, but this creation of yours is excellent – you might consider coming in for a few hours each week to clean up some of our stock.'

He grinned from ear to ear. 'I wouldn't mind,' he answered.

'And, Bill?'

'Yes?'

'Think about marketing it. There are six stables out there – knock down a few walls and there could be a workshop. Just take that into consideration. You may have the beginnings of an empire here.'

Bill grinned. 'An empire? Well, I don't know about that. Look what happened to the last empire – India's gone now. That didn't thrive, did it?'

Irene's next laugh was lighter. 'Ah, yes, but India gave you the secret recipe first and we must capitalize on that. Yes, Bright's Indian Polish. What a wonderful name. I think we can do business, Mr Bill Bright.'

Hillside Farm owned the craziest roof Alice had ever seen. It dipped and slipped, having a huge dent in the middle of the main ridge, then tiles that seemed to have shunted together in parts, rather like the carriages on a toy train that had stopped too suddenly.

Drunken outhouses leaned against the main building, as if they were too tired to stand without physical and moral support, while the dry-stone walls that surrounded the property were gappy at the top, like a row of lower incisors in need of a brace. The view was awesome, layered trees in greens and blues, a misty horizon with ghostlike ridges, sombre yet beautiful, a weak springtime sun dipping away towards Lancashire and the Irish Sea.

She looked at the house again, noticed an arched, recessed porch with a sturdy, studded door set into it. Right. What was she going to say? 'I have come to visit Matthew Richards. Please take me to him, because my car won't go any further'? Would they carry her up in the tractor? Would they ask her to stay at the farm until morning? Might they object to a young woman going to visit a man? Had she lost her mind completely?

A chicken walked over her foot and she stepped back.

'Sorry,' yelled a female voice.

Alice turned to see a large, red-faced woman bearing down on her.

'Bella Jenkinson.' She shook Alice's hand. 'You lost, love? Come in and have a cuppa. I'll just catch this daft hen first. She thinks she's in Colditz, keeps making a break for it. Tom says he believes she's organizing an escape committee.' She scooped up the bird in expert hands and marched off to the coop with it. 'Now stay in there, you bugger,' she yelled, before returning to Alice's side. 'Right, let's get you sorted, shall we?' She led Alice into the house.

The interior was a strange contrast to the outside, beautifully furnished, cosy, heated by a roaring log fire. As instructed, Alice sat in a fireside chair while Bella washed her hands and set the kettle to boil in the kitchen. Alice watched through the open doorway, noted that the kitchen, too, was clean and well equipped.

'So, what brings you here?' called Bella.

Alice swallowed her nervousness. 'I'm a friend of Matthew's.'

Bella hurried back to the living room. Visitors were sparse, as was gossip, so she was immediately on red alert. 'Matt, you mean? The shepherd?'

'Yes.'

Bella placed herself in the chair opposite Alice's. 'He's up in the hut, love. Well, it's not a hut as such, made of stone and quite cosy, really.' She left a gap for a response, was disappointed. 'He never said he was expecting anyone. Never had a visitor since he arrived.'

Alice inhaled a little more courage. 'My mother is a friend of the family. I've brought some news.'

'Ah.' The broad face was open and expectant. 'Not bad news, I hope?'

'Personal,' replied Alice.

'Oh, I see. Only I hope he won't have to leave. We had a lot of lambs this year and he's got his work cut out. I mean, we could manage, put a farmhand up there for a while, but Matt has a way with sheep. He's happy, see.'

'Yes, I know. He writes to me.'

Bella nodded. 'So you'll be the one who sent the Christmas card and the letters?'

'Yes, and I understand that I can't get near the hut in a car. So, if you would direct me, I had better set out before nightfall.'

'Eeh, lass, you can't go up there on your own. Wait till my Tom comes back with the tractor, he'll take you up. He's only a couple of fields away, so he'll not be long. Tell you what, I'll toast us a couple of crumpets and you can have some of my home-made butter. I don't do much in the dairy now, but I do make butter for my own table. You nip up and have a wash, sort yourself out. You'll want to look nice for Matt.'

'I don't need to look nice,' answered Alice, suddenly irritated by the woman's over-effusiveness.

'Take no notice of me,' said Bella. 'I don't see many folk up here, so I read when I have time – love stories and that – and I always like a happy ending. So if I had you down as Matt's young lady, I'm sorry.'

'That's all right.' Tired now, Alice was prepared to concede that the farmer's wife was probably lonely and looking for news.

'Er . . . the hut's just one room,' Bella said now.

'No matter,' replied Alice quickly, 'we go back a long way – and I might not stay.'

'You can sleep here if you like, go up first thing in the morning.'

Alice considered that option, decided that she should carry on to Matthew's place as soon as possible, because she felt unequal to the third-degree questioning she would doubtless receive here. 'I need time with him,' she said boldly, 'and I must get back to my job soon, so I had better go up there tonight.'

The usual questions were fired, what was her job, where did she live, what did she do in her spare time. Alice fielded them as best she could, then withdrew gratefully to the bathroom.

As she rinsed her face, she caught sight of herself in the mirror, found herself tidying her hair and wondering what he would think of her. Silly. She had come here for a reason. He was not free. Stella Dyson was going to have his child . . .

'I shall never understand you.' Simon MacRae stood in front of Stella Dyson's fireplace, arms akimbo, head shaking slowly from side to side. She had burnt her boats, had poured petrol on her whole life, had thrown a match into it – and from a distance that could hardly have been described as safe.

'Why?' he asked.

She studied him. Anyone would think the world was on the brink of war. 'Because this is what I am. This is the Stella Dyson you pretend to love.'

'It's not pretence.'

'Whatever you say, Simon. Just accept that I will always do everything my way, which is, perhaps, a good reason for my continuing with the single life.'

'After all we've been through,' he exclaimed, 'the plans we made so carefully, the steps you took to cover your traces.' He paused. 'What was said?'

'The truth.'

He paced up and down, an expression of total bewilderment on his face. The woman was incapable of lying, even to save herself. Sometimes lies were a necessary evil, padding against a world that could be cruel and unforgiving. 'Have you always told the truth, the absolute truth?'

'No.'

He sighed. She was even honest enough to admit having lied. The woman was hopeless. 'But what did you hope to achieve by this behaviour, Stella?'

'It isn't about achievement, Simon. This is about living with myself afterwards. You would have to be me to understand. And as you can never be me, you must accept that you can't get to grips with what I have done. What did you expect? For me to be on the run for the rest of my life?'

He sat down, but agitation made him mobile, so he jumped up again. 'And what did Shaw and Fletcher say?'

'Oh, it was interesting to watch,' she answered. 'Doctors, men of the world, people who keep things in perspective. Shaw actually blushed – that was an interesting reaction. Fletcher, well, older, wiser, he just said he was sorry. So I told him that it wasn't his fault and they granted me six months' leave of absence, told me I could keep the flat and asked if there was anything they could do on a practical level.'

'And?'

'And I said no, thanked them, came in here and packed my bags. You're making a far bigger fuss than they did. Will you keep still? I feel like the hub of the fairground big wheel with just one car circling me.'

He stopped his pacing, ran an uneasy hand through hair that had no chance of behaving itself today. 'So, will you go to Liverpool?'

'Oh, yes. It's one thing for my colleagues to know my business, but patients must be protected.

I doubt that I shall work here again. And I made it plain that the child is not yours, by the way.'

'Who cares?' he asked.

'I do.'

'Ah.'

Stella stood up, walked to him and took his hands in hers. 'Please, please forgive me, Simon. I'm the one with the problem and I know this has reflected on you, because many will believe that this is your child. We know the truth. All that matters is the truth.'

He blinked the moisture from his eyes. 'Now, just make sure that you stay well. I shall visit you in Liverpool and thanks for trusting me with the address. There's a beach at Crosby, walk on it, watch the ships coming in. See your doctor regularly and look after yourself.'

'I shall.'

There was little more to say. Simon felt a strong urge to shake her, kiss her, shake her again, wanted to declare himself for the fourth or fifth time, would have liked to move with her to Liverpool. But Dr Stella Dyson was a woman who must map her own route; all Simon could hope was that he might be awarded a small area on the chart. He kissed her and left her to her packing.

Tilly sat at one side of the bed, Irene and Emily at the other. He was flat, motionless, could see only the ceiling. When talking to him, a person was forced to lean across the bed to achieve eye-contact with him. As few wanted to look into those baleful orbs, he was reduced to listening to the radio or to reading via a system of two mirrors, the second righting the work of the first in order to have the script in the correct form. As this method depended on staff remembering to turn the pages, Jack Richards was not very well occupied.

Emily looked at Irene, tried to envisage the poor woman bringing home her husband and caring for him in a downstairs room of The Briars. It would be like poor Molly all over again, but in the next house. Irene had blossomed at Matthew & Son, had looked so happy until Jack's accident. Now, the strain was showing and she managed to look almost her true age.

Tilly was unusually quiet. Like Emily, she was concerned for Irene, was hoping against hope that Jack Richards would get better, but things were not looking good. He had no movement at all from the neck down and was giving the doctors no reason to believe that there would be any noticeable improvement.

Irene cleared her throat delicately. 'This must be terribly difficult, Jack, after such an active life.'

He made a sound that imitated a growl, but no words followed the noise.

'Now, you are suddenly completely dependent,' she continued, 'at the mercy of those around you. Like the horses were. Like my poor dogs used to be.'

Tilly's head shot up so quickly that she developed a hot crick in the back of her neck. There had been hatred in Irene's voice, a thinly veiled venom that even he could not have failed to notice. 'Irene, he's not a well man—'

'He broke the spirit of many a horse. And now it is as if they have collected together to remove all his power. Loganberry did this for all of them. Dreadful, isn't it?'

Emily didn't know where to look. She understood Irene's reasons for hating the man, but it didn't seem right to sit here gloating, nearly laughing at him.

'You are a dreadful man,' Irene continued.

'Hey, hold on a minute,' cried Tilly, 'you're not playing fair. He's in a bad way and—'

Irene stood and leaned over him. 'I hate you, Matthew hates you, everyone despises you . . .'

Emily noticed that Irene was not meeting his gaze, that her eyes were travelling downward all the time, were moving all over his body. What the hell was she up to? Was she trying to finish him off? 'Stop it,' she said.

Irene raised a hand and, for an awful moment, her two companions thought she was about to hit the man. But she pulled the cord over his bed, sat down and waited for a nurse to arrive. Then, cool as a cucumber, she showed the nurse what she had achieved. 'The right fist has tightened,' she said. 'Anger him. Infuriate him and he will move, I promise.'

The nurse looked at the hand, saw that there had been change.

'If there's anything at all left in him, keep him furious,' advised Irene. Then she rose and led her two friends outside.

In the corridor, the smooth, calm lady who was

always so self-contained, leaned her head against the wall and sobbed. Behind her, Tilly and Emily shunted into one another, each woman frozen by a sight they could not have imagined in any circumstances. Irene Richards had her breaking point.

They guided her outside, found the Bentley and got her into the driving seat. Tilly was crying openly, while Emily, too shocked for tears, had turned grey-white and was trembling. Today, the two women had seen a real heroine at work and they would never forget what Irene Richards had achieved.

'Come on, love,' urged Emily, 'we've a lot to do at the shop tonight, stocktaking, Mark said.'

Irene dried her eyes. 'I'm sorry.'

Tilly sniffed. 'You're brave,' she said. 'Next time my Seth gets difficult, I shall know who to send for. Mind, you'd have to be good with maggots, but that's Ted Moss's fault.'

Emily looked at Irene, Irene looked at Emily. And they simply entered that lunatic place known only to women, the zone where laughter is king, where the pain and the pleasure come together, where self-control and common sense take a nose-dive out of the nearest window.

Tilly pretended to be offended. 'It's all right for you two – you haven't got bloody maggots in your Tupperware. Oh, please yourselves.' She took a small paper package from her handbag. 'Mint Imperial, anybody?' Then she, too, began to laugh. People passing by looked into the car, probably wondering why three mad women were out and about late on a Tuesday afternoon. But inside that Bentley, bonds grew even stronger. From now on, these three would be inseparable.

He opened the door, staggered back, looked at Tom and . . . was it Alice Povey? It all flooded back, those nights when she had sat with him, when she had held his hand, when she had mopped his brow with a cool cloth. She looked good, blue jeans, a brown jacket, a silly corduroy cap made out of sections like a cake, button in the centre, neb worn to one side. 'Hello,' he managed. Why was she here? Did it matter? He was unbelievably pleased to see her.

Tom looked uneasy. His weight swung from foot to foot and he plainly felt out of place. 'I . . . er . . . shall I come back for you later?'

'No,' answered Matthew, 'I shall look after her.'

The farmer thought of a crude answer, swallowed it. There was a level to Matt the shepherd that was best left unplumbed, as if he had been used to a different life, a degree of privilege and education. 'I'll be off, then.'

Silence reigned as Tom walked away. Alice looked at Matthew, thought how well he appeared, relaxed, tanned and alive. She pushed her hair from her shoulders and waited for him to say something, was beginning to wonder whether she might spend the rest of her life standing on a mountain side with the wind cutting through her like a frozen stiletto.

'Come in,' he said at last. No, he did not need to ask for reasons: she was here and he was glad.

She walked past him into the large room, was immediately struck by the size of the fireplace. 'Big enough for Buckingham Palace,' she said.

Matthew closed the door. 'That fireside and an old jumper are all some of the lambs have. I have to be their mother.'

Alice looked around. She saw a table with a couple of dining chairs, a sofa, a rocker, an over-stuffed armchair, some rugs, a dresser with blue and white crockery stacked on its shelves. Two dogs were in the room, curled together in a cardboard box, not interested in the new arrival.

'Benny and Jester,' he told her, 'the best shepherds in these mountains. Sit down. How have you been?'

'Fine.' She suddenly felt awkward, a fish out of water – no, an intruder at a feast for one that had been planned for months. He had a whole life here, was organized, happy; he needed no one. She sat down, felt anxious to make herself less, as her mother would have termed it.

'Cup of tea?' he asked.

'Please.'

He busied himself, was plainly at one with his routine. Oh, she should definitely have stayed away. The purpose of her visit was forgotten for the moment, as she could not imagine discussing with this stranger the existence of a child in the belly of his sister-in-law.

He brought her the tea. 'There you are.' Sitting himself in the rocker, he studied her covertly. She looked so pretty, hair cascading from beneath the ridiculous cap, face freshened by mountain air. 'So, what brings you here?'

Alice managed not to choke on a mouthful of tea. 'Few days off,' she replied, 'so I thought I'd look you up. It's very pleasant in these parts.'

'Yes.'

It occurred to her that he had probably spoken to very few people since his arrival here. He displayed the ease of a man comfortable in his own company, as if he needed no conversation, no human contact. 'Your mother's well,' she said.

'We write,' he replied. 'I now have a postal address in Huddersfield and collect mail twice a week. I haven't heard from her for several days, but she should soon have the address of the farm, because I sent it yesterday. It's time for her and Mark to know where I am. I understand that she has left Father to his own devices and that he has moved old soldiers into the house at Eagley.'

'Yes.' She couldn't do it, was unable to talk to him about Stella. 'I miss Rutherford Hall,' she told him. 'Perhaps I shall go back into that type of work.' When he made no reply, she decided to ask him about sheep.

He laughed. 'Do you have all night?'

'Yes, yes, I do.'

He leaned forward, strong hands hanging between his knees. 'People entertain gross misconceptions about sheep, think they're nice, soft woolly things that wander about, sheep may safely graze, all that, baa, baa, black sheep. Not the case, Alice.'

'No?'

'No. They do stupid things very cleverly and deliberately. Get them to the gate, steer them forward, no, no, no. They stop about twenty feet away and have a meeting. They elect politicians and union leaders, the main aim being to avoid going through that gate. Sheep dip? They hate it. I was taught all this by a man as old as these hills. I chose not to believe him, but he was so right.'

She laughed.

'The Bible paints a picture of sheep following their shepherd, Alice. In reality, the shepherd is in the right place and the sheep are just south of Watford and preparing to march on Parliament. Without those dogs, I would be a total failure.'

'You should write this down,' she told him.

'Yes, I intend to.' He warmed his hands at the fire. 'Sheep follow nobody, so I have given up on the Bible. They start as sweet little lambs born in great numbers at twenty minutes past four on a Sunday morning. This mass delivery is carefully planned by the Ewes' Guild and the members want help from humans – they demand that. In fact, they want a brass band and a choir – I think they'll be writing this into their next contract. Oh, and they're working on a new killer tick that attacks men. It's hard work, believe me.'

She was fascinated. So this was the Matthew Richards who had been known to Molly, clever, interesting, amusing. 'You're going to write a book, aren't you?' The man was so alive, so wonderfully vibrant.

'Probably. I think people should be aware that they consume the enemy with their mint sauce.

There's one called Henry, bigger than the rest. I'm sure there's goat in his ancestry – he butts me. So I've called him a shoat.'

Alice found herself relaxing because he was relaxed. Clearly, there was no mental illness here. This was a chap who knew what he needed, who had his own cure parked in a corner in the form of an old typewriter and a pile of paper. He would write, might sell, might amuse others with his clever observations.

'Are you sleepy?' he asked.

'Yes. Not because I am bored,' she added hastily, 'but I've been wandering around Huddersfield.'

'No problem.' He dragged out the cot, found a pillow and a blanket, explained the primitive sanitary arrangements.

So it was that Nurse Alice Povey spent yet another night in the company of Matthew Richards. She lay on her makeshift bed, listened to his breathing, so even and untroubled, and she was happy because the man was well at last. As for her reason for being there – well, that definitely seemed unimportant.

She felt safe with him, guarded, unthreatened. Those sheep were very lucky to have such a man to take care of them. The fire crackled, the dogs whimpered through dreams of rabbits and foxes, and Alice drifted into the best night's sleep she had enjoyed in months. Oh, yes, here in this place, the sheep certainly could graze in safety.

Fourteen

She woke early and, for a few moments, could not remember where she was. But even inside the hut, the air came as a shock, driving through her system like an invading army, no prisoners taken, straight to the target, wide awake in seconds. She was alone: there was no Matthew, no sign of a dog. Beside her on the pillow she found a large sheet of paper.

Gone to contend with the stupidity of the masses. You may get visitors, two orphans who are continuing to use me as their mother. Remember that these sweet creatures will become expert criminals, so do not be taken in by their prettiness. Remember also that they were rejected by their real mothers, so they must be intrinsically unlovable.

The really cute one has the blackest face. He likes to get up on to your lap while being fed, thinks he is a human child. To that creature you must sing 'Baa, baa, black sheep' with feeling, especially when you get to the 'Yes, sir, yes, sir, three bags full.'

The second chap is a clown. He displays huge

dexterity, pulls teats off bottles, and I think he
could have a future in engineering, so have signed
him up to do nights in a local factory. He may not
like you. If he does not like you, you will know it –
did you bring a change of clothing?

I shall be back for breakfast at about 8 a.m., so
have the kettle on. The lambs' bottles are in
the hearth and my waterproofs are hanging on the
door. Take no nonsense from either of the orphans.
I have also left you some coffee in a Thermos.
Bacon and eggs are in the cold store to the left of
the front door.

Good luck. Matthew

She looked for the waterproofs and they were,
indeed, suspended from a hook on the door. Was
he joking? Would these lambs spit at her, urinate
on her? Still fully clothed, she jumped up, peeled
off her trousers, took clean underwear from her
handbag, changed, dressed herself hurriedly.
Waterproofs? At least they'd help to keep the chill
out.

Compromise. After all, she was a nurse so this
should be easy. Oh, no, they were already maa-ing
at the door, were knocking on it, for goodness'
sake. There had to be a plan. Quickly, she donned
the waterproof jacket, then the capacious
trousers, pulling them on over her jeans and
hiking them up so that the waistband sat under
her arms. They remained over-long, but that
problem was solved by pushing her feet plus the
trouser legs into Matthew's wellington boots,
which were about five sizes too large.

Bottles. Because of the size of the boots, Alice was forced to shuffle across to the hearth, making sure that the soles never left the floor; had she raised a foot, she would have lost a boot. She gave the sou'wester a wide berth, as she knew it would have cut off sight and hearing, since it was big enough for a head twice the size of hers.

Chair. With a bottle in each capacious pocket, Alice picked up a chair and slid her way to the door, the movement of her feet similar, she felt, to that of an ice-skater at her first lesson. Right, so if she wedged the chair in the doorway, she could be half inside and half outside, while the lambs would be definitely outside.

The blur of activity that followed would have been difficult to describe, but the eventual outcome was that Alice and chair were outside, while the lambs were not. She sat down in the straight-backed chair, exhausted by the whole business, watching helplessly while two greyish and black-faced creatures, apparently on springs, executed a very poorly co-ordinated dance all over Matthew Richards' quarters.

He was in charge of hundreds of these daft creatures. When their celebrations drew to a close, they homed in on her, each lamb clamping its jaws round the teat of a bottle. They were strong, pulling so hard on the milk that she seemed to be fighting to hang on to her arms. God Almighty, men's surgical would be a piece of cake after this.

The greedy reprobates syphoned the milk in seconds, then stood back to look at her, clearly expecting more. What had happened? She had been told to sing, to be nice to them. The animal with the paler face then performed his *pièce de résistance*, nipping the teat from the end of the container and shooting past Alice as if fired from a gun. Worried about what might happen if he swallowed it, she dashed off in pursuit, forgetting to shuffle and losing both boots before she had travelled three yards.

'One of those days, is it?'

As the huge trousers slipped down to her ankles, Alice looked over her shoulder and into the face of Matthew Richards. 'I shall never speak to you again,' she promised, with as much dignity as she could muster in the circumstances.

Matthew, a mischievous expression in his eyes, rescued his boots and walked into the hut. 'Fine,' he threw over a shoulder, 'and don't worry about the teat – he never swallows them.'

She stepped out of the trousers and, barefoot and freezing, followed him into the hut. 'Liar,' she spat, as she hung up the jacket. 'You told me I needed to sing. I didn't get time to sing. I feel as if I've done eight hours on women's medical.'

He was placing a frying-pan on a grill that spanned the fire. 'One egg or two?' he asked innocently.

'Those bloody lambs want locking up,' she advised. 'They're psychopaths. They almost had my arms ripped out of their sockets. Why do they call Jesus the Lamb of God? If God knows about these things, He must have realized that He should have used a different advertising slogan. They went mad.'

Matthew melted some lard. 'No, I was the one who went mad – remember?'

'If you'd been as insane as those two, you'd have been kept locked up for ever, certified and in a padded cell.'

He laughed. 'Their insanity will pass, as did mine.'

'Convince me,' she replied. 'Nobody in his right mind would live up here with that load of idiots. I like my bacon crisp. And what size are your feet? I was wearing a pair of canal boats.'

'Eleven,' he replied, placing bacon in the pan.

Alice kept her face fierce. In truth, she was delighted by the man, by his humour, his sense of devilment. The long note he had written proved that he was keen to communicate, to amuse. Furthermore, she was at home, which was utterly ridiculous. In a county that was brand new to her, in a place with no plumbing, with a man she scarcely knew, she felt as if she had spent her whole life among these hills. 'And don't break the yolk of my egg,' she ordered.

Matthew was smiling into the pan. Alice was great, was here, was so . . . so alive. She took things as they came, no complaints about the absence of a bathroom, not a hair turned when forced to share his sleeping quarters, no fear of him. Yes, she was very like her mother. 'How's Tilly?' he asked.

'Oh, God,' she breathed, 'don't start me off. My dad's taken up fishing.'

385

'Good. A man needs an interest.'

'He's more interested in the beer they drink while they catch nothing. He brought home a fish so small that Mam buried it with full military honours in her little front garden. Then there's the maggot box.'

'Oh dear.'

'She said he had to choose between her and the maggots, so he asked her if Tupperware did bigger boxes. And his new fishing rod cost over five pounds – that was after he'd replaced one of Ted Moss's.' She paused, wondered anew about her real reason for being here. 'Mam works for your mother now. And she looks after Mark – she helps in the shop, too.'

'Busy lady.'

'She always was. She doesn't know what rest is, thinks it's for the idle rich. Dad was talking about buying a little Austin van, but she put her foot down. Mind, if Dad really wants a van, he'll get one. She thinks cars are for lazy folk, too. Mam doesn't think like other people and, on top of everything else, she's gone posh.'

He paused, turned and looked at her. 'Posh? Tilly?'

Alice nodded. 'When you've finished your dinner, you should leave your knife and fork together, not parked at twenty past eight as she calls it. She has a cup and saucer for herself now, though Dad insists on his blue-and-white-ringed pint mug with tea so thick you could melt a spoon in it. Place mats, they're another bone of contention. And cubed sugar with silver-plated tongs. It's a phase – she'll get over it.'

He dished out the food and brought it to the table. 'How's my son?' he asked. 'I've worried about him lately.'

About time, too, thought Alice, though she kept her opinion locked away.

'After Molly became ill . . .' He paused, picked up a slice of bread. 'She was my life, Alice. It was as if we breathed for one another. He needed me, you know, yet I neglected him, cut him off, kept him at arm's length. My own pain was so huge that I never considered him.'

'He's surviving,' she said. 'In fact, he's thriving. I believe he's having driving lessons soon, when he's seventeen, so that he can pick up things he buys. There's a restorer working in the back of the shop, then Irene, of course, who has forgotten more about antiques than most have ever known. She's teaching him. Emily's there, doing her little bit, catching on fast. Phil Dyson married a nice girl called Annie, very capable – she does her share. My mam cleans and pokes her nose in, the same as ever.'

'I'm not needed.'

'No, I didn't say that.'

He smiled. 'I don't want to be needed just yet, but I want to know that Mark is all right.'

'He is.'

'Good.'

Alice chose her next words carefully. 'Stella – you handed the purse strings to her, didn't you?'

'Yes, I was too ill . . . you know how I was.'

'Well, your mother has taken over, because

Stella will be going away for a while. Liverpool, I think she said.'

'Really?'

Alice noticed that his expression gave nothing away, that he scarcely reacted to his sister-in-law's name. 'They're putting a locum in her place.'

'Stella's ambitious,' he said. 'I suppose she'll be going on a course that will improve her career.'

'Perhaps.' Alice's appetite was huge, so she polished off the meal, plus two slices of Bella Jenkinson's home-made bread plastered with the same woman's butter and jam. 'Wonderful,' she declared.

'The air makes you hungry. Would you like to come walling with me?'

She grinned. 'A date. How romantic. Will I need to wear the wellies and the waterproofs?'

'Wear whatever you like.'

Alice shrugged. 'Forgot my case, left it in the car at the farm, so all I had with me was a change of knickers. I suppose jeans will do?'

'In the absence of ballgown and tiara, yes.'

They drank more coffee, sat in companionable silence while their meal settled. He fed the fire, she read a few pages from a book about walling. 'Through bands, hearts, copes, cover bands – how do you learn all this?' she asked, after a few minutes had passed.

'By doing it wrong and putting it right. Like anything else in life. I can now make a wall stand.' He looked straight at her. 'It's about putting things right, elemental things – sheep, walls, myself. Then Mark. I had to start at the bottom, at

388

my own functioning, work up through this place. Keeping the sheep alive was part of it. The walls are a very important factor – I suppose I'm making life stand up again. I got lost, didn't I, Alice?'

'Yes, you did.'

'He was better without me while I was like that. I don't know whether I shall ever return to Bolton on a permanent basis, but I want to meet Mark all over again when I'm whole. It's not about drugs to calm me down, to mask the problems. It's about myself, about recognizing where I went wrong.'

She would not weep. Determinedly, Alice bit her lower lip and listened to the man, witnessed this stage of his journey back to full sanity.

'I stole his mother from him,' said Matthew now. 'She was dying, yes, but he should have been a part of her life and of her death. It would be easy to say that bad parenting from my own father affected me. Psychiatrists are anxious to fool us into shifting the blame across to someone else – anyone else. But where does the buck stop, Alice? With Adam?'

'I don't know.' Her voice was unsteady.

'It stops here,' he said. 'I am that boy's biological father, but have been no more than that.'

He was about to become a father again . . . No, no, she could not tell him about Stella Dyson's baby. There were still a few links missing in the chain-mail he was constructing and she was unwilling to enlarge the holes in his protective layer. 'You'll know when you're ready,' she advised him.

'Will I?'

'Oh, yes – you won't laugh when a visitor's trousers fall down.'

'I'm unused to visitors but, yes, I shall try to become civilized. Come on, we have walls to build.'

She pulled on her coat and her silly hat, followed him outside into a world bathed in spring sunshine, was happy to become another link in the chain-mail. This was a lovable man and she had better develop a protective covering of her own . . .

Matthew & Son was closed on Wednesdays. This was the day when stock was brought in by a casual driver, when stock was delivered to houses by the same means. But on this Wednesday a meeting had arisen almost of its own accord. In Mark Richards' small office, the clan had gathered, had squashed its members on to the sofa provided for the use of visitors.

Mark, at his desk, rather less grand than was his wont, was wearing jeans, an old jumper and an open-necked shirt, whose collar was less than pristine. He had stuff to move and was not on show, so he could be himself.

Tilly, Emily and Annie, parked on a two-seater sofa, were jammed together like sardines, no room for elbows, synchronized breathing an absolute necessity. Irene was missing.

'Shall I telephone?' asked Mark.

'Give her another five minutes,' answered Emily. 'She was at the hospital last night. Your grandad isn't giving her an easy time, Mark. He's blaming it all on her for leaving him and for selling the horses.'

Mark, who had been to visit his grandfather, remained unimpressed by the man. Yes, he was partially paralysed and, yes, that was sad, but Jack Richards displayed all the charm of an open grave in the rain. 'He's his own worst enemy,' he said now. 'Should be grateful that he can move his arms a little, because one of the breaks in his spine was very bad. His speech is quite colourful.'

'Irene calls it barrack-room talk,' said Emily.

Mark tapped on his desk with a pencil. 'This isn't like her,' he said. 'Something must have delayed her. Oh, I wish I could drive. Is Mr Bright coming in today?'

Emily blushed and shook her head. She liked the look of Bill Bright. Irene had plans for him: Bill was to come to the shop twice a week, would be provided with a van, would help out by cleaning furniture and collecting goods when there was too much business for the other casual driver to handle.

Tilly glanced sideways, noticed the colour in Emily's cheeks and smiled inwardly. Emily had suddenly gone all girlish, had started to apply a touch of powder and lipstick – and it was all because of a certain gentleman. Tilly was already beginning to consider what she might wear for the wedding. She had her nice blue suit, but every man and his dog had already seen that and she fancied something in mauve . . .

Only Annie was sure she knew what the subject

of this impromptu meeting would be. It was about Irene, who was looking so tired that each person here was concerned for her. They would be talking about Jack Richards, about what to do with him once the hospital let him go. Also, Irene needed relief now, deserved help. She had just the one son and he was missing, so it was up to the clan gathered here to come up with a plan. No one liked Jack, but all would be required to play a part now.

'He can't go back to the farm.' Annie brought to life everyone's thoughts in that short statement. 'From the sound of things, he's going to take some looking after and I for one am not happy to let Irene take the strain.'

Everyone murmured their agreement with that. Tilly offered her tenpenceworth. 'Our Alice might know what to do. If I could find her, like. She'll be able to ask about nurses who wouldn't mind earning a bit extra. 'Cos I reckon he might need round-the-clock attention. And Irene's not giving up this shop. She's come to life and look how happy she is among all the old stuff. It took ten years off her face till he had his accident.'

Mark cut in. 'She may be saying goodbye to Aunt Stella – she leaves for Liverpool tomorrow morning. Or she could be shopping.'

Tilly edged herself out of the sofa. 'Well, I'm starting my cleaning – you lot can please yourselves. No use sitting here doing nothing.' She marched off towards her broom cupboard, turned in the doorway, spoke to Emily. 'She doesn't know your Stella all that well. I can't see

Stella going out of her way to say ta-ra to her. Mind, there's nowt as queer as folk.'

Mark had been right: Irene Richards was in the company of Dr Stella Dyson. But these two women were not just saying goodbye.

Stella understood the nature of the human animal, was aware that secrets had a habit of leaking out, especially over a period of time. Sometimes she wondered about her own terrible need for honesty, suspected occasionally that she was simply offloading her own sublimated pain, spreading it about a bit, letting everyone have a share. She hoped that was not the case, wanted to be a 'clean' person, one who dealt in truth. That same Stella who dealt only in truth was now sitting at the table in Irene Richards' kitchen. 'I know you're having a hard time, but I also feel that you should hear this from me and not through the grapevine.' This woman's husband, Matthew's father, was lying in the hospital, just a few hundred yards away, with a broken spine.

Irene stared straight ahead, her eyes fixed blindly on the door. 'On the day of your sister's funeral, you . . . you and my son?'

'Yes. I have no excuse for it and I behaved abominably. I thought I loved him. I don't understand myself and cannot say why I did it.'

The older woman, shocked, swallowed hard before speaking again. 'You don't know what love is, do you?'

'No. I think I loved Molly and wanted to be like her. I now love my mother, but I've probably never loved a man. I cannot go away without telling you this, Mrs Richards.'

Irene allowed her eyes to rest on the visitor. 'And Matthew?'

Stella raised her shoulders. 'He probably has no memory of the event. He was at a distinct disadvantage. Were it an offence, I could probably be charged with rape. But the child – this child – is Molly's. That's how I've managed to rationalize my position. I don't know what will happen to me in the future, but I think I've decided to rear the baby myself.'

Irene lifted her right hand to show an envelope clutched tightly between stiffened digits. 'This morning I received a properly addressed letter from my son. I now know his whereabouts. But I shall not offer the address to you, because you do not deserve it; nor do you merit the ability to upset him. You are the most incredibly cold and calculating woman I have ever had the misfortune to meet.'

Stella did not react. Irene Richards might even be right, after all.

'You don't care, do you?' Irene asked.

'At the moment, I don't feel anything. There's knowledge, but no emotion. I must go away, because I'm a bad example to patients, not because I'm afraid. At first I felt fear, but the hormonal changes have stopped that. The ability to worry seems to have been eroded.'

'And you are carrying my grandchild.'

'I am, yes.'

Irene rose to her feet. 'Will you go now, please? I

394

should be at the shop, should be helping my other grandchild, the legitimate one.' She paused. 'I'm sorry – I should not have said that.'

'No matter, Mrs Richards. I feel neither pleasure nor pain and can deal currently only with truths and practicalities. I want nothing from your son, by the way, nothing from your grandson. My telling you this should not imply that I nurse any expectations for this baby.'

The older woman lowered her head in thought. 'No, I must apologize to the baby, because none of this should reflect on him or her. To you, I make no apology.' She raised her chin and looked straight into Stella Dyson's eyes. 'Leave my house now, please. I have many things to do today.'

Stella understood completely. She felt clean at last, had nothing to hide from the people who mattered. Matthew remained in ignorance, but his mental health had been uncertain and it felt right to leave him out of this for the time being. The fact that Stella's mother and her friends Tilly and Alice Povey were in possession of the truth no longer signified: the right thing had been done.

'Goodbye,' said Irene.

Stella left the room without saying another word.

Irene Richards pondered for a while, then decided what she must do. She now had the address of a farm in Yorkshire. It was time to speak to Matthew.

Alice was exhausted. Matthew had heaved about all the big stones, or skins, as he called them, and was currently struggling with ties, huge chunks of double thickness whose purpose was to span both layers of wall. Her job had been as filler, which task involved the packing of rubble between the twin layers that formed the structure.

It was clear that Matthew, whose status as a waller remained amateur, revelled in this task. He read books about the skill, for goodness' sake, knew that the construction of a chain-length could take a whole crew a whole day and could use up twelve tons of rock. He was not a builder: Matthew was a mere mender, someone who plugged the gaps in walls built by true experts.

He surveyed the results, hands pressing into the small of his aching back. 'The creation of these walls took real work,' he told Alice. 'And they can be destroyed in seconds by careless visitors.'

'And by sheep,' she said.

'Ah, but they are co-owners. Much as we damn sheep, these structures belong to them, too. The damage they do is acceptable. Mankind is the real problem, the destroyer. Are you hungry?'

'Starving.' She dropped the bucket of rubble and sat on a flat rock. There was real satisfaction in walling; she understood his affection for it, because he was able to see the fruits of his labour straight away, could weigh up which stones to use, how to place them. It was a simple, yet vital activity. Through employment such as this, he was finding his way back. 'Will you stay for ever in Yorkshire?' she asked him.

'I don't know. I have to get back to my son, and I don't mean just in terms of geography. Ideally, I should like to be up here through the winter and into spring, get the lambs through the worst, then off back to town – Bolton, Huddersfield, wherever. Let someone else do the dipping and shearing. I like the solitude—'

'You like to save life.'

He turned and faced her, squatted on his haunches, leaving just inches of space between them. 'He went for a smoke,' he said softly.

'What? Who?'

'The male nurse who was guarding me that night. When he left, I followed Joe Dyson into the bathroom and I killed him. I used the cord from the dressing gown. He cracked his head on the lavatory and died. So, remember that you shared a room with a murderer last night.'

Alice blinked. 'Good God.'

'Yes, I feel that I killed Molly's father. The cord left no mark because he slipped before I could tighten it. The man who should have stayed with me could not admit that he hadn't done his job properly. That's why I'm taking so long to get back into life. I suppose I was ill, anyway, but finishing off that dreadful man almost finished me, too. It's all so strange, because it was, in fact, an accident. He slipped. As I put the cord round his neck, he turned to look at me and he slipped. I did not tighten the cord – I had no need to, because he cracked his head as he went down. There was murder in my heart, though. Confusing, what?'

'You're doing penance,' said Alice.

He sighed heavily. 'There is no penance, Alice. There is no forgiveness for the dreadful thoughts

I entertained regarding my wife's father. No, I'm being selfish. I always wanted to write about animals and countryside, about the day-to-day fun and anguish that come with being a farmer or a herdsman. Here I get the material and the opportunity. Then I can go to him as a whole person.'

'To Mark?'

'Yes.'

They began the walk back, he slowing down so that she could keep up with him. She was walking with a killer, had shared food with him. And yet, no, he was not a killer. He had put the cord round the neck, but the rest had been an accident. He could not have known that Joseph Dyson would slip, could never be sure that he would have finished the job.

Acting on an impulse she could not deny, she slipped her left hand into his right, noticing straight away how he took a positive hold on her fingers and gripped them firmly. He needed a friend and now he had one.

Bella Jenkinson felt as if all her birthdays had come at once when the Bentley turned up. This was a quality car, the sort that was not often seen in these parts. And the woman who emerged so gracefully from the vehicle was elegant, the grey suit almost matching the car, accessories perfect, good shoes, bag and gloves.

Bella ran to the mirror and wiped a smudge of flour from her nose, noticing how plump she was, how ordinary, nose like a blob of Plasticine, eyes hiding in small seams of fat, cheeks far too plump, too red. Oh, why hadn't she worn something newer? Her cardigan was pilled, her dress as old as the hills, slippers worn and ragged. Still, she had another visitor and she would be grateful.

She opened the door.

'Mrs Jenkinson?'

Bella smoothed her faded apron. 'Yes. Would you care to step inside?'

Irene smiled and walked into the house. 'Charming,' she said. 'What lovely furniture you have – do you know that some of this is valuable? Excuse me, I'm being rude. I am Irene Richards, mother of Matthew.'

'Oh.' Bella swallowed. 'He's doing well for visitors.'

'Is he?'

'Yes, there's a family friend up there already – I think she said her name was Alice something or other. Please sit down and I shall make you a drink. Have you come far, Mrs Richards?'

'From Bolton. Only an hour and a half away even at my speed. I'm not a fast driver.' So, Tilly's daughter was here, the young nurse who had been so good to Matthew. A rush of gratitude flooded into Irene's chest. Someone cared about him, cared enough to put herself out for him. 'I need to see my son, Mrs Jenkinson.'

'And so you shall. My Tom will be here any time looking for his dinner. He'll get you up there in two shakes. Just you rest yourself and I'll make us a drink.'

While she waited for her cup of tea, Irene found herself automatically valuing a clock, a settle and some chairs. There was an interesting monks' bench, too, plus some Victoriana that was certainly worth keeping until people began to want it. And Matthew was not alone. Alice Povey – yes, she was a likeable, genuine girl. Irene smiled to herself.

The door opened and Tom Jenkinson walked in. Like his wife, he was always pleased to see a new face. Bella entered from the kitchen. 'This is Matt's mother. Mrs Richards, my husband, Tom.'

'Hello,' said Irene. 'I wonder, would you take me up to Matthew? It seems rather beyond this footwear of mine – not made for mountaineering.' She looked down at her black leather court shoes.

'Course I will,' answered Tom.

They drank tea, talked about the weather, about how well Matthew had done with his first season, about antiques. Irene left her card, told them that if they wanted to sell or buy furniture, they should contact her first. Then she left in the company of Tom Jenkinson, who promised to retrieve her from the shepherd's quarters later in the day.

As they climbed, Irene noticed, not for the first time today, that her ears reacted to the elevation, that the air was like clear water, refreshing and pure. 'So beautiful,' she said, as she gazed down on seamed fields and hills, a haphazard patchwork stitched together by walls.

'We get used to it,' replied Tom, 'just like Londoners take all those buildings for granted. I saw Big Ben, you know. I never saw anything more wonderful in my whole life. But down there, see, they just walk past it because it's always been there. This lot's been here longer than Westminster, so we're used to it. Visitors love it. That Alice loved it.'

'Did she?'

'Oh, aye. Said something about never wanting to leave. Your Matt loves it, too. We fetched him a second-hand typewriter the other week, because he says he is going to paint the mountains but with words. I like the way he puts that. He's a clever man, your son.'

'Yes, he is.'

'Natural shepherd, too. I can't imagine him staying, though. Maybe he'll stay till he's written his book, but I don't think he's here for ever.'

Irene made no reply, as she didn't know what to think. Matthew's exit from Bolton had been sudden and virtually unexplained, but now, as she remembered how disturbed he had been after Molly's death, she had no idea what to expect or hope for. Perhaps this was his real place of healing, so different from Rutherford Hall, unsupervised, liberated and so incredibly lovely. And was Alice Povey about to be a part of her son's future? If so, what on earth was going to be done about Dr Dyson?

Tom left her at the hut, told her that it would not be locked and that he would return in a couple of hours. While the tractor pulled away, Irene watched as her son hove into view, his hand attached to the hand of Alice Povey. Irene could not control the smile that visited her lips. Oh, yes, if only he could find someone, a sensible woman, one who cared. Alice cared.

They separated as soon as they saw the visitor, hands snatched apart as if burnt. Matthew stood for a second, as if he could not believe his eyes, then he ran to his mother, arms outstretched to welcome her. 'It's lovely to see you,' he said, into her hair. Irene noticed the swallowed sobs, returned the hug and waved a hello to Alice.

Inside, the pair sat at the table, while Irene, pleasantly shocked by her son's healthy appearance, settled herself into the rocking chair. Like Mark, he had followed his own path, had found what he needed and had proved his own judgement to be correct. His accommodation, though primitive, was cosy and well organized. At last, Matthew Richards' mind seemed to be mending itself. So. Must she be the one to impede his progress?

'I'm sorry,' he said. 'I didn't mean to worry you.'

'Don't apologize,' answered Irene. 'I bring bad news, I'm afraid, so let us get it out of the way now.' She looked at Alice. 'My husband is in the infirmary – I think the accident happened after you had left or while you were off-duty, because he's on your ward. He's badly hurt.'

'Sorry to hear that,' replied Alice.

Irene addressed her son now. 'He was kicked by a horse, Matthew. Your father's back is broken. There's some movement in his hands now, the right one in particular, but it seems unlikely that he will walk again.' There, that was sufficient reason to explain her sudden appearance here. 'I thought I had better make the journey to tell you.'

Matthew tried to be shocked, could not manage even to be sorry. His father was a misty figure, unreal and unreachable. The desire to know Jack Richards was long dead, because he had never been genuine or even tangible. Matthew had no idea what to say to his mother. Eventually, he managed a question: 'Does this mean that you will have to spend your life looking after him? That has already proved a thankless task. Imagine his fury if he can't move. What will happen to him and to you?'

'I don't know.'

Alice studied Matthew's mother covertly. There was more. With that instinct born in many women, Alice homed in on Irene's discomfort. Jack Richards was not the sole reason for his wife's long journey. 'How's Stella?' she asked.

The silent communication happened then, as the two women stared directly at each other. So much was said in those few wordless seconds. While Matthew worried about his mother's future, Irene and Alice simply absorbed each other.

He went out for logs. 'Who knows about it?' asked Irene, when the coast was clear. 'Exactly how many people are aware of the truth?'

Alice licked lips that were suddenly dry. 'Her mother and mine. And me, of course. I'm sorry, but we were pledged to secrecy. She's going to Liverpool to have the—'

'I know. I've known since this morning, when she told me. So my two good friends, Emily and Tilly, have kept this from me.'

Alice thought about that. 'Look at it another way, Mrs Richards, you'll always be able to trust my mother and Emily with a secret. They're honourable women.'

'And you? Are you an honourable woman?'

'Yes.'

'Are you having an affair with my son?'

'No.'

'Because he's still vulnerable, Alice. And he likes you – I could see that straight away. This is a very difficult and delicate situation. Stella Dyson is quite sure that he retains no memory of the occasion when he and she . . .'

'Had sex?'

Irene managed not to shiver. Young people these days were so direct, so careless with language. 'Yes,' she said resignedly. 'In fact, Dr Dyson takes full responsibility for what happened.'

Alice walked to the door, made sure that Matthew remained out of earshot, came back. 'She was as mixed up as anybody, Mrs Richards—'

'Irene.'

'Irene. I think Molly's death pushed Stella over her own edge. She says she can't feel anything, that she's gone numb, but I'm not sure about that. What I do know is that she's pushed everything away. When I look at her, I see a volcano waiting to erupt. And she can't live on the wrong side of truth. She intended to marry Dr MacRae, but found herself unable to bear the thought of passing off the baby as his. She has a lot of backbone.'

Irene closed her eyes, put a trembling hand to

her mouth. 'Oh, Alice, what a mess. I can't tell him.'

'I came here to tell him,' said Alice, 'so perhaps I'm less trustworthy than Emily and Mam. But, like you, I just can't bring myself to do it. He's almost standing up again and I couldn't take the legs from under him. Stella must feel the same, because I'm sure she was quite capable of finding him – she has one heck of a brain, you know. If she'd set her mind to it, she would have found him.'

The older woman wiped her eyes with a lace-edged handkerchief.

'Oh, I am sorry,' said Alice. 'You must be in a heck of a state, even without all this. You'd just settled, hadn't you? And Mam says you've done that house up lovely. Being disabled won't make your husband any nicer, but I suppose people would think you were terrible if you didn't help him now.'

'Precisely. And there is a sense of duty, of course.'

'Pity about that. From what I've heard, you deserve a break from him. He could be in hospital for a long time, Irene. Don't make any decisions.' Alice's heart ached for the woman. The Richardses' marriage had been a difficult one and Irene had waited years before finally allowing herself to rebel. This was a woman who would not have given in easily, one who believed in old-fashioned mores, in marriage, in perseverance. And now, with her new life and her new freedom, she had an illegitimate grandchild on the way, a husband in hospital and a son who was still finding his way back into life.

'I shall be all right,' Irene said now.

'I hope that's a promise,' answered Alice.

Matthew came in, threw logs on the fire, piled more by the side of the grate. He gave Alice potatoes to peel, Irene carrots to scrape while he sliced onions to go with steak. Through tears brought on by the onions, he looked at Alice and Irene, brushed the water from his face. 'Alice, tell Mother about the orphan lambs.' And the story was told all over again.

It was time. Stella looked around the flat she had enjoyed, her own little bit of the world, the place where she had been comfortable. She would not be returning and she would miss it. The armchair was overstuffed and it cuddled all who sat in it; there was a slight flaw at the right side of the mirror. Would the next tenant understand the door? Would he or she know that it stuck, that it needed an extra shove? The friendly clock was packed, because that was her own.

She had rented a small flat in Brighton-le-Sands, one of the several villages that comprised an area generally known as Great Crosby. The river Mersey was nearby, as were shops, as was the nursing-home where Joanna would be born. Less than fifty miles from Bolton, it was far enough away for her to feel safe. Feel safe? She was incapable of feeling anything.

Possessions. She had clothes, a few bits of jewellery, some pots and pans and a clock. She also had a passenger. Oh, why hadn't she married Simon? Life could have been so easy, so manageable. Here she stood, car keys in her hand, emotions frozen, time suspended, all alone and a new environment to face. She would miss Simon, the Poveys and her mother. She would miss the practice, the sound of traffic on the road, shopping in Bolton, her bed.

A house move during pregnancy was never a good idea – basic nesting instincts railed against it. She would have advised any female patient in her own position to stay put, yet she had to go, because she was a doctor. 'Physician, heal thyself?' she murmured. 'Oh, if only.'

The baby would be born in Park House, a private nursing-home run by Augustinian nuns. Her gynaecologist for these final weeks was to be a Rodney Street man, competent, uncritical, a good doctor. Her hips were narrow and the delivery might well be surgical. Her baby was active, sometimes tumbled about like a whole football team trying to equalize in the final moments of a match.

'Feel something,' she said aloud. 'For God's sake, feel something.' Had Joe Dyson really kicked all the stuffing out of her? Had her emotional base atrophied, could a bad father do this? She placed a hand on her belly. 'Molly says you're a girl – I do hope so. You'll have the best of everything, even if I have to work myself to a shadow.' Molly's child. Joanna was a prettier name than Joanne – and a Joanna would be for John, one of the four evangelists whose names Molly had wanted to use.

Onward, then, out into a cold world whose chill must be ignored – or dealt with. Let them judge, let them point a finger at a doctor who had allowed herself to become pregnant, let them criticize a woman who was incapable of killing an embryonic human. She had committed no crime, had hurt few of her fellows, was not guilty of anything gross, yet she would be condemned for the sin of fornication, would be an outcast, the subject of taunts and ridicule. There was a great deal wrong with this world . . .

After one last look at the life she remembered, Dr Stella Dyson stepped out towards the unknown. She took with her the memory of a wonderful sister, a friendly clock and a bank balance that would support her, just, to the end of her pregnancy. Beyond that, there were no directions.

Fifteen

Stella Dyson placed a folded towel on the concrete step and gazed out on to the Mersey. After three and a half months, the seascape was familiar and comforting. She watched as a tanker drifted lazily across the horizon, noted how still and sultry the day was. This was June and Crosby basked in full sunlight, slowed almost to a standstill by the merciless heat of Earth's star; even the children on the beach seemed lethargic, quiet, a few brave souls making sandcastles, most sitting still, ice-creams and lollipops clutched in sticky, sandy fingers.

She opened *The Times*, scanned the news. Valentina Tereshkova had become the first woman to circle the planet, John Profumo was on his way out, another example of ruin caused by dishonesty. Lord Milford sat now in the House of Lords, the first Communist peer to be accepted by that august body. Ah, well, there was one small sign of truthfulness winning through. Sir Winston, sixty years an MP, would not seek re-election, President Kennedy had sent in troops to quell race riots in Alabama, a Buddhist monk in Vietnam sat on the front page, his body writhing as he burned to death in the ultimate act of protest.

She folded the pages. What a world. What a place into which to bring a child. While man tried to extend his frontiers beyond the globe, the earthbound continued on courses of destruction, whites killing blacks, government ministers sinking to the level of gangsters. A pope dead, a new one elected; no foul play there, at least. 'It turns,' she said to herself, 'turns on its axis no matter what.'

Stella liked Crosby. A few miles north of Liverpool, it enjoyed an elegant decadence, a worn yet valuable appearance, old money mixed with new, pleasant people who kept their distance until required, a politeness that was truly appreciated by the newly arrived Dr Stella Dyson. She enjoyed the water, the mud-coloured sand, the shops. There was an old-fashioned courtesy here, a tendency to treat a stranger with respect. Yes, she would not mind settling in Crosby.

She rose with difficulty, right hand reaching automatically for the small of her back; she was huge, the skin of her abdomen now stretched so tightly that she felt like a bowl of Tilly Povey's bread dough, fully risen and ready to be divided into portions. And she was, indeed, about to be separated from her child by a surgeon's knife, since her pelvic girdle was judged too narrow for delivery, while her baby, Joanna, had parked herself determinedly in the breech position, head lodged just below the ribs, feet kicking wildly at her mother's bladder. Stella smiled wryly. She nursed a suspicion that Joanna was going to be a force to be reckoned with. Giggling without quite understanding why, Stella Dyson made her ponderous way homeward.

Mersey View no longer owned a view of the river. Early in the nineteenth century, a terrace of six houses had been built as holiday cottages for the rich, five-bedroomed homes that were quaint, like a child's drawing, front door square in the centre, large windows, tiny gardens. From these dwellings the young had dashed with their towels and their toys, straight from front door to beach, no traffic, no obstacle between them and the river.

Now, the view had gone for ever, because land had been reclaimed and built upon, while the road was bordered both sides, not just by houses but also by shops and other businesses. It was busy, anonymous; it was just what Stella had wanted. She waddled up the short path, slightly breathless after her walk from the beach. The front door, a thick piece whose hinges always complained about the weight they bore, groaned inward and allowed her into her temporary home.

The house had been made into two flats, one upstairs, one down. Stella, whose living quarters were on the ground floor, had been the sole occupant thus far as the upper storey was undergoing improvements, but she was happier alone. Apart from some banging and clattering by tradesmen, the final weeks of her pregnancy had been spent in relative quiet, just herself, the companionable clock, a radio, some books and a television set.

Fred the cactus, her first gift from Simon, still prickly, still phallic in shape, now graced the hearth. On the mantelpiece next to the clock sat two photographs: a rare monochrome portrait of the Dyson children, Philip, Tony and Eddie at the back, Molly and Stella in front. Then, in colour and framed in gilt, Molly stood alone, that wonderful face, a cloud of dark hair, eyes so large, so incredibly violet, a rare beauty frozen permanently behind glass.

The phone rang as Stella placed her keys on the coffee table. 'Hello?'

'It's me.'

It was usually him. Faithful as ever, Simon MacRae phoned twice a day, visited once a week. 'I'm just back from my walk,' she told him.

'I hope you aren't overdoing it in this heat,' he said. 'You've only a few days to go now.'

As she was the one about to go under the surgeon's knife, she was hardly likely to forget her date at Park House in a few days' time, but she bit back a sharp reply. This was the hand that had meted out liberal amounts of kindness, and she must not bite it. 'I am tired,' she admitted. 'Sometimes, I think I'm about to launch an ocean-going liner rather than a baby.'

'I'll have the champagne ready,' he said, 'as long as you promise not to christen the child with it – none of that God-bless-all-who-sail business. Still enjoying Crosby?'

'Very much. They even have an ice-age boulder

412

and a windmill – it's very quaint. And the water's so soothing – I sit for hours watching ships. Oh, I went on the ferry to Birkenhead – there's a good market. Please don't start issuing gale warnings, Simon, I didn't drown and I didn't go into labour at the baby-clothing stall. My case is packed and my blood pressure is perfect. Mr Barton is sharpening his scalpels as we speak.'

'And you will allow me to be there?'

'Of course, if you insist upon it. And, remember, they're to wake me right away – I have no fear of pain.' A strange excitement had arisen of its own accord, a definite need to meet this baby. At last, she was starting to feel something. 'She's slowing down, Simon, resting. I think she knows it's almost time.'

He laughed. 'I can't imagine what will happen if you have a boy.'

It was not going to be a boy: Molly had promised a girl.

'Stella?'

'What?'

'Your mother's getting restless. She's my patient now and is anxious to be there for the birth. Any chance?'

'Oh, for goodness' sake.' Stella found herself smiling again. 'Why don't you advertise the event in the *Bolton Evening News*? Sell tickets, half price for pensioners and the underprivileged. How is everyone?'

'Your mother is well, the rest I see little of. But that nephew of yours has been invited to join the Chamber of Commerce, the youngest man ever to be asked. Molly's father-in-law is about to be released from hospital. I met Mrs Povey in town and she was very fretful about the whole business. Irene Richards is not looking forward to having him home.'

'No.'

'And I'm told that she and Mark are to visit Matthew soon – they are both ready to be reconciled, father and son. I expect Mrs Richards will stay at that farm and leave the two men to get on with it.'

'She hates me.'

'Don't be silly, of course she doesn't. It came as a shock when you told her about the baby.' He sighed heavily. 'I do wish you were more sensible and less inclined to impose the truth on everyone.'

'I don't mind her hating me, Simon. It's better this way than it would have been had I kept quiet. Imagine the trauma had she found out in a few years. No, I still think I did the right thing.'

'I shall come tomorrow,' he announced now, 'and I shall sleep on the sofa. No objections. I have some time due to me and I have every intention of keeping you company until the birth is over—'

'But, Simon—'

'No negotiations, Stella. My mind is quite made up. If you go into labour, you will need someone with you.'

'Thank you,' she replied.

'No matter. 'Bye for now.'

' 'Bye.' She replaced the receiver. He was a good

man and she didn't deserve him. The puppylike devotion had ceased: he now loved her with a quiet determination that was becoming quite attractive. She could not manage to imagine life without him, yet she must, as she was determined to take full and sole responsibility for the daughter she carried. Turning, a hand pressed again into the small of her back, she looked at her sister's photograph. 'Just you and I, Molly,' she whispered. 'Like the day of the shilling, we share.'

Molly said nothing; she had said nothing since the day of the dream that could not possibly have been a dream, the day of the apparition that could not possibly have happened. Stella had never believed in God, yet she now began to suspect the presence of something, a being that existed beyond the limitations of man's senses. She did not want that being to be real, yet she nursed the uncomfortable notion that the earth was like a set table, an arrangement ordered by a divine essence and disordered by its own components, by mankind. Oh, surely she was not going religious? Yes, her confinement would be in the company of nuns, but was Christianity infectious? She hoped not . . .

Sense and Sensibility kept her company for ten minutes, Marianne Dashwood running about in the rain, Eleanor fretting just as Molly had worried about Stella. But even Austen could not stay the hand of Morpheus; Stella drifted away into sleep, dreamed of a sister and a shilling, of a handsome doctor and a cactus, of a beautiful child who would soon be Molly reborn.

'It's nowt to do with you.' Seth opened his news-paper and sank back into the rocking chair. He studied the football results and tried to ignore his wife, but she was rumbustious again. Did she never get tired? Was she going to continue energetic right into her dotage?

'Trouble with you, Seth Povey, is that you don't think.'

The Wanderers were going to need a push in the right direction, come September. Even bloody Blackburn had started to look in better shape.

'It'll cripple her,' declared Tilly.

He and Ted had been promised tickets for the first game of the new season at Burnden Park.

'Are you listening to me?'

Slowly, he lowered the paper. 'Till, I've been listening to you for donkeys' years.' He con-sidered that statement. 'No, I've been hearing you for as long as I can remember.' Had he actively listened, he would have been a headcase by now. 'A man likes to read his paper after a day at work,' he said. 'Don't you think I get enough noise in the machine shop?'

Tilly managed a full row of knitting before she spoke again. 'He never stops talking,' she pro-nounced. 'That Jack Richards could mither the legs off a table and chairs.'

Seth allowed his reading matter to fall to the floor. 'Then his wife has my deepest sympathy,' he muttered. 'It must be terrible to live with some-body who never shuts up. Nobody wants to live with somebody who never shuts up.'

She changed needles. 'That's what I said.'

'I bet you did.'

Tilly glared at him. 'And what do you call that thing parked outside our house?'

'Arthur,' he replied immediately. 'Arthur the Austin.'

'Hmph.' She clattered her way along the next row. 'There's that much rust it looks like frills round the wheels. And why is it two different colours?'

'Three, if you count the rust,' he answered. 'The red bit is off a red van. I shall get it done blue all over – you should be proud of being the owner of a vehicle. Nobody else on this block has one.'

'Nobody else has a box of maggots in their kitchen, but they're not jealous.' She consulted her knitting pattern. 'Something will have to be done.'

In the act of picking up his newspaper for a second attempt at reading, Seth paused and straightened. 'Leave my van alone,' he ordered.

'I'm not talking about your bloody van,' she declared crossly. 'I'm on about Mrs Richards. We shall all have to take turns, because she's not giving up that shop. They've got two nurses for nights and somebody else who'll do a couple of days. Then we must make a rota.'

'Leave me off your bloody rota,' he said. 'I mean that, Till. I don't mind fixing doors for folk, or mending the odd bit of furniture, but I'm not putting up with him – I had enough of bloody officers during the war. There we were, over the flaming top, blood and guts everywhere, while they worried about getting their dinner.'

Tilly awarded him one of her special glares, a one-more-word-and-you're-dead look that quietened him instantly. 'You know that's a lie, Seth Povey. I've heard you say they mucked in just like everybody else – they're not all lunatics, so straighten your face and put that kettle on. No. Wait a minute, I'll have a Guinness.'

Oh, heck, she was planning on some serious thinking: Tilly on Guinness was a full committee, including chairman, treasurer and the man who fetched the pies. By ten o'clock there would be a timetable to which all members, including absentees and abstainers, would be forced to adhere, come hell, high water or an afternoon's fishing. 'I'm wiping no bugger's bum,' he announced, as he stood up. 'That's it, Tilly, line drawn. I'm not doing it.'

She crossed him off her mind's list and carried on knitting.

Amazingly, Bess fitted in quite well with Benny and Jester. She nursed no delusions about herself, made no attempt to pass herself off as a sheepdog, was happy to stay by Mark's side while the other two dogs rounded up sheep whose stupidity seemed to increase with every passing day.

Another astonishing fact was that Matthew and Mark got along like a house on fire, each genuinely interested in the other's life, no awkwardness, few uncomfortable silences. On one level, they were like new acquaintances, each astonished by the other's qualities, both discovering similarities in their beliefs and attitudes. Yet they knew each other thoroughly, and a blossoming mutual respect was definitely a factor in their relationship.

But one little secret still existed and Mark knew that it had to be tackled. Grandmother Richards was at the farm, had left her two men to their own devices, so Mark manufactured his opportunity while he and his father sat on a large rock at the edge of a field. As he planned for the umpteenth time what to say, Mark realized that the secret was not such a small one, that it might well damage many people, yet he had to clear the air. 'Dad?'

'What?'

Mark gulped painfully. At seventeen, he was neither man nor boy, yet he enjoyed a maturity that enabled him to see clearly. Strangely, he felt that he had inherited this trait from Aunt Stella, whose tendency to face the truth squarely and with as little emotion as possible was almost legendary. He, too, liked truth, though his feelings could not be put aside, especially in certain instances. 'I used to steal those things – remember? How I would say I had saved to buy small antiques? They were stolen. Tilly put me straight.'

'She would,' replied Matthew, without hesitation. 'Tilly is just about the straightest person I've ever met, always calls a spade a bloody shovel, no nonsense.' He turned his head and looked at his son. 'I'm sorry you felt the need to do that.'

'So am I.' Mark swallowed again. Now for the big one. After two days in the company of this man, he had to risk everything, yet there was no way to avoid the inevitable. Dad was well, was whole. In fact, although he would never express it, Mark clung to the knowledge that his father was happier than he had been while Mother was still alive and ill.

'What is it?' Matthew asked.

'Please, please, hear me out, Dad. Let me get right through this without too many inter-ruptions, because I rehearsed it for days before coming here. It's not going to be easy for either of us.'

'I see.'

Mark inhaled. 'Oh, I hope you do see. It's about Aunt Stella.'

'Go on.' A coldness crept up Matthew's arms and along his spine. For some time, Stella had been a grey area, had dwelt in a place that visited him only at night, in the dark hours.

'This will be hard, but here goes.' The younger man placed a hand on Bess's head, as if contact with this beloved animal would empower him. 'You know, I actually forgot the event, the occasion I'm going to talk about, so I do under-stand something about the human mind and the illnesses it can produce.' He closed his eyes against a cruel sun. 'It was the day of Mother's funeral.' He cleared a dry throat. 'I lost – or perhaps threw away – a whole section of that day. It went out of my mind in an instant, packaged and gone.'

'Yes?'

'You became ill, Dad.'

'I know. I went into hospital, then to Rutherford Hall.'

Mark nodded. 'I took Bess out for a walk, needed to get away. After the scene in the cemetery, I was unhappy and wanted some air. But it was cold and Bess was shivering, so I came back after ten or fifteen minutes. You were upstairs. I left Bess in the kitchen and stood in the hall. I could hear you, could hear movement from your room. Afterwards, I decided that you were no longer my father. Even though my brain wiped out the memory, I hated you.'

'I see.'

Matthew didn't see – and there lay the problem. 'I crept upstairs. There were hairpins all over the landing. Aunt Stella was making noises and you were not, but I looked through the hinged edge of the open door and saw you both. Her hair was all over the place. I think you imagined that Aunt Stella was my mother.'

It all flooded back, as if a blind had lifted in Matthew's mind. Molly's things, scent, a lipstick, a powder compact. Scarves, stockings, a blouse . . . And Molly. No, no, that had not been Molly. Molly had just gone into the ground – dear God, what had he done? He placed his elbows on his knees and leaned forward, head in hands.

'I went into my own room, heard Aunt Stella going into the bathroom, gave her a few minutes, then followed her, stood in the doorway. And it all left me, was instantly forgotten. She was doing up her hair and my eyes met hers in the glass. We made toast afterwards and that was the end of it. No memory at all. Until a few days ago. Dad?'

'Yes?' He raised his head.

'Be strong.'

'I'll try.'

'She went away to Liverpool. I have a feeling that Dr MacRae knows exactly where she is, because he's been after her for ages – they were engaged for a few days.' Mark paused before the final assault. 'She was bigger, Dad. Around the waist and just below.'

'What?'

'I think she went away to have a baby,' said Mark, 'and I think the baby may be yours. The whole thing came back to me just recently and I decided to tell you.'

'Oh, my God.' Matthew jumped up and began to pace, Bess hot on his heels as he strode back and forth. 'Yes, yes,' he moaned. 'That's the thing . . . one of the things I've been half remembering in sleep.' He seized Mark's hands. 'And you? Promise me that you haven't been nursing this for months, that you really did forget it.'

Mark nodded. 'By the time I got to the bathroom, it was gone. I suppose the funeral had been enough for one day. Though I do remember you coming into the kitchen later with no clothes on. But you and Aunt Stella in bed together – it was as if that had never happened.'

'My God,' breathed Matthew.

'When it returned after all those months, it helped me to understand you and what you'd been through with your own mental illness. Now, Stella's a cold fish, Dad. She made it happen, I'm sure. And you – well, you were in shock and probably thought Mother was back and well again.

Aunt Stella got engaged, then broke it off. That's another clue, you see. She probably worked out that if she married Dr MacRae she could pretend that the child was his.'

'You're sure there is a child?'

'Watch Grandmother when she comes up later with Tom. Mention Aunt Stella's name. I know Grandmother has a lot on her mind with Major Jack coming home soon, but I'm sure she knows about this baby. She just won't talk about Aunt Stella. I think Bunny knows – well, she's Aunt Stella's mother. I have a feeling that Mrs Povey knows something, too.'

Matthew stood stock still, hands clenched as he pulled away from his son. Molly had often advised him to marry Stella after her own death. He could never marry Stella, but could not walk away now from a child, from his responsibilities. Yet he had distanced himself from Mark for long enough . . .

'Mark?'

'Yes?'

'What the hell am I going to do? Forgive me, please, forgive me.'

Mark smiled reassuringly. 'I've grown up a lot, Dad. I run a business now, with the help of both my grandmothers, and I'm not a child. The thing is, I'm so grateful for my education at Bolton School – it isn't wasted. There's no need to apologize. I owe you a lot.'

'No, your schooling is never wasted and your English is excellent.' He paused for a few beats of time. 'So you, too, were amnesic.'

'I suppose so. The mind switches off, doesn't it?

I think Aunt Stella switched herself off years ago, but that was deliberate.'

'Probably. Their father was a monster.' A dead and buried monster now, of course . . .

'So.' Mark stood up. 'Here comes our next pickle. I went to the doctor the day before yesterday and saw MacRae – pretended I had a sore throat. He said he would be away for a few days, so I asked him where he was going. He told me Liverpool at first, something about getting up to date with gynaecology through a man called Barton in Rodney Street. Then he let slip that he would be staying with friends in Crosby. I think Aunt Stella's in Crosby and that this Mr Barton is her specialist.'

'So we think we know the area.'

'Yes. And, Dad, I would bet Matthew & Son's takings for last month that Dr MacRae is going over there for the birth. He adores Aunt Stella. So, we find out where the nearest maternity hospital is, then try to discover whether a Mr Barton works there.'

'Clever, aren't you?'

Mark allowed himself a tight smile. 'I hope so. You see, Dr MacRae would never tell a lie – he isn't the type. He'll be learning something from Mr Barton, because he'll be there when the baby's born, so that was the truth.' He paused, shook his head. 'I hope I'm right. Then I've been asking myself why we need to know all this. I kept going round in circles, but I always ended up knowing that you had to be told. So, where do we go from here?'

'Home,' said Matthew decisively. 'Come along, son, there are arrangements to be made. The shop is closed for two weeks, you say? Good. I may need you and Mother. Right, we must tell Tom to get cover for the flock, then Mother will have to pack – we'll go back in the Bentley.' He stared at the skyline for a moment. 'What we do after that is anyone's guess.'

Sixteen

In the back of the Bentley with Bess, Mark was quiet.
Grandmother Irene, a woman of whom he was very
fond, was quiet, too; Matthew, not speaking, raged.
Although Mark could not see the details, he sensed
that his father's hands were clenched, that his jaw
was tense, that he was in a state of fear and bewilderment. Oh, God forbid that Dad should collapse all
over again.

As he clung to his dog, Mark wondered how on
earth so many people had managed to get so
many things wrong. Or had everyone really got it
wrong? Who could know exactly what was right
when everything had been so disordered?

The car sped over the top and began the
descent into Lancashire. Mark gulped; it was
almost as if Yorkshire had been safe, unreal, a
happy dream from which he would wake at any
moment. During the past few days, he had been
a child again, a free spirit attached to the hills, a
deputy shepherd, a son. He remembered the
drawings he had done during his own confused
time, a house on a hillside, a log fire, bread

toasted at that fire, Bess at his feet. Yes, Dad had given him all that. Oh, how he loved his father, how well he understood him now. Yet Mark had done this, had told the truth, had become another Aunt Stella, shame the devil, honesty at all costs.

'Stop it, Mark.' Matthew's voice was quiet. 'This is none of your doing.'

The man was reading his son's mind. 'I can't help it,' replied Mark.

Irene spoke up at last. 'Mark, you did what I could not. I was too weak, as was Alice, as was Tilly. What you've done is a very great act of love and I'm sure that your father appreciates that.'

Matthew's head turned sideways so quickly that the tension in his neck trapped a nerve. 'What? Tilly and Alice?'

Irene bit her tongue, though she knew that she had merely filled in the last few missing pieces of the picture.

'I told you I thought they all knew, Dad,' said Mark. 'But what could they have done while you were ill? I had to see you with my own eyes before talking about all this. No one wanted to put you back in hospital.'

Irene overtook a tractor. 'The girl – Stella – told me herself,' she said. 'Her actions when she became pregnant were deliberate. Molly's death seemed to affect so many people to the point of becoming unhinged. I was barely civil, told Stella exactly what I thought of her. Since then, I've had time to ponder my way through the whole shocking business.'

'And?' Matthew managed to imbue even this single syllable with a high degree of sarcasm.

She pulled over and stopped the car in an unmade lay-by, turned her head so that she could see her son properly. 'She's replacing her sister. At the time, she fancied herself in love with you. But, no, I feel that is not the case. I don't know what will happen if she produces a boy, but I'm perfectly sure that Stella is about to give birth to the sister she lost.'

'That's crazy,' exclaimed Matthew, 'crazier than I was, than my poor son was when he . . . when he forgot what he had witnessed. The woman must be certifiable.'

'I spoke to Emily,' she continued. 'Molly was mother to Stella, fed her, kept her out of harm's reach, taught her to read and write, even bought clothes for her at school rummage sales. When your wife died, Matthew, Stella lost her grip on life. Because of her nature, she kept all that inside – she does not allow feelings yet she has them – and she is going to suffer in a way that none of us is qualified to imagine.' She raised her chin. 'We must help her.'

A single tear made its slow way down Matthew's face. 'Molly told me to marry Stella. I can't.'

'Of course you can't. You love Alice Povey.'

'Do I?'

'Yes, you do.' Irene looked over her shoulder at Mark. 'My word, if you weren't already adult, this would be a shock for you. You're a good boy. I cannot tell you how proud I am to be your grandmother.'

Mark, who was feeling about five years old, awarded Irene a tight smile.

'So.' She placed her hands on the steering-wheel. 'We sit half-way between here and there, in the middle of nowhere, front wheels in one county, rear wheels in another, no idea of our destination—'

'Bunny will know where Aunt Stella is,' said Mark.

Irene nodded. 'She will, indeed. So, do we torture poor Emily until we get the answer? Shall we use thumb-screws? And what do we do about the answer? Is any one of us prepared to rush off to the bedside while Stella Dyson gives birth? Childbirth isn't easy. After delivery, a woman's mind can be in a precarious state. Shall we crowd around the bed and make her worse? Is that what you want, Matthew?'

'No.'

'Right.' Irene pushed her spine into the back of her seat, closed her eyes for a few seconds. 'Then why are we here? Where are we going?'

'Home,' replied Matthew.

'And would that be Stainthwaite or Bolton?'

'Neither,' replied Matthew. 'It would be Alice.'

Mark grinned and cuddled his dog.

Alice Povey knew all about patience and a great deal about patients, but she could not tolerate Jack Richards. Yes, it was a shame that anyone should be paraplegic, yes, he was in a bad state, but he had the nastiest attitude she had come across in all her years as a nurse. 'I feel sorry for your wife,' she told him, as she turned a page of his book. He could turn the pages himself with a bit of effort, but why should he try when there were servants around?

'It's her fault,' he snapped.

'Is it?'

'Left me up there without so much as a by-your-leave, no thought for me, dashed off to run that shop with her grandson.'

'Good for her.' Alice lowered her tone: she was here to preserve and improve life at all costs, should be an example to her juniors, was supposed to train new recruits to be kind, considerate and pleasant. 'I happen to know that you were forbidden to keep horses, that you are a cruel man.' She straightened. 'Some people get exactly what they deserve.'

'How dare you?'

Alice bit down on a smile. Mam's favourite saying was 'Look at me when I'm talking to you', and the major always asked people how they dared. 'You're like a record with the needle stuck,' she told him. 'I dare because I know what you are. I dare because I'm up here and you're down there with no horsewhip. So, have a taste of your own medicine.'

'My men will look after me,' he replied haughtily.

'Will they? Well, two of them have gone. The last one, Bill Bright, he and your wife have turned the stables into a factory. He's making B Bright Polish. Do you get it? B Bright, as in Be Bright? They're going to sell it because it's very good for old furniture. Bill's going to take on staff soon.'

'Is he, by God? Well, we shall soon see about that. How dare they?'

Alice shrugged. 'I don't know how they dare. Perhaps I'll ask next time I see them.'

'I shall ask them myself when I get home,' said Jack.

'Oh, you're not going home,' answered Alice. 'I think you'll be living in one of the front rooms at The Briars. Everybody's fighting about who should look after you. That'll be because you're such a nice man and an easy patient. They'll be queuing all the way down Chorley New Road for a chance to spend time with you, won't they? There'll be enough application letters to start a bonfire with.'

He glared at her.

'Hello, Father.'

Alice stepped back and collided with Matthew. 'Hello, Alice,' he whispered into her ear. She stepped away from him, swivelled and found herself blushing as she looked into his face. 'Er . . . hello,' she mumbled. 'It isn't visiting time – we've doctors' rounds soon.'

Matthew moved towards the bed. 'Father, how wonderful to see you looking so well.' He gave his attention to Alice. 'Yes, I overheard what you were saying, Sister Povey, and I agree. Wouldn't the Chelsea Pensioners take him?'

'Why should they?' Alice straightened her starched cap. 'They seem a nice enough bunch of men, wouldn't want to send them a bad apple. Anyway, red's not really your dad's colour, is it?'

'I suppose not.'

Jack was livid. He opened his mouth to deliver another 'How dare you?' but swallowed it because this nurse might ridicule him again. But how did they dare? He was an invalid, a cripple, would spend the rest of his days in a wheelchair, if not in bed, was a victim, a sufferer. They were walking away. 'Come back at once,' he shouted.

A trainee nurse arrived at his bedside. 'Mr Richards, we've had enough for one day. I'm telling you now, it's no good spitting porridge at me like you did this morning, because you'll just get it back, right in your face, if you do it again.'

Alice caught the words and smiled. But her heart beat with frightening quickness as she led Matthew Richards into her office. She had visited him several times, had stayed with him, now knew more about sheep than she had ever wanted to learn. Each time, he had remained the perfect gentleman; each time, Alice had been disappointed, because he was lovely and she was . . . she was fond of him.

They sat, separated by the desk that announced her official status.

'How are you?' she asked.

'Fine. Mark and Mother came across to see me. Mother stayed at the farm and spent her time explaining to the Jenkinsons how much they were worth in terms of furniture. Bella is going to sell some of it because she wants to go to Majorca. Tom will do as he's told, as usual.'

'So. What brings you back to this side of the Pennines?' asked Alice.

He fixed his eyes on her, said nothing more.

She shifted in her chair, stacked some papers, wished that he would not stare so steadily. He knew. Someone, possibly his mother, had finally found the courage. 'Well?' she asked. 'Is this a staring competition? If so, tell me the rules and I'll join in.'

'Stella,' he said.

'Oh. She's gone away.'

'To give birth.' This was not a question.

Alice folded her arms. 'Right. Have you come all this way to tell me off? Because if you have, get it over with. Only I have ward rounds in a minute, a couple of surgeons who are directly related to God. I have to put the red carpet out and make sure the brass band's tuned its trumpets. Don't look at me like that, Matthew, it's not my fault.'

'Did you judge me unfit to be told?'

'I gave up judging, left it to those who think they know everything – like my mother. So, who told you?'

'Mark did.'

'How did he find out?'

'Does it matter?' He leaned forward, elbows on the desk. 'Have you any idea how shocked I am? I don't know what to think, what to do, don't know what to expect of myself.'

'Well, nobody can help you with that, but I can tell you this much – Stella Dyson wouldn't marry you if you came with iced caviar on a nice bed of lettuce. She's convinced herself that she's having this child for Molly. She has some sort of fixation with your dead wife, as if she owes her something, or as if she wants to be just like her. It's from their childhood. So, if you're thinking of poking your nose in, don't bother, because she'll probably tell you to bugger off.'

'Will she?'

Alice nodded. 'Anyway, marrying you would be a mug's game for Stella, Matthew, because few women can compete with a sainted ghost – it'd be like going through life shadow-boxing. So, if you want my opinion, you'll stay right out of it.'

'It's my child.'

Alice looked at the upside-down watch that was pinned to her uniform. It reminded her of the black and green clock at home, time up-ended; she felt up-ended, too, because Matthew Richards would not stop staring at her. She looked up. 'No, Matthew, it isn't your child – not unless Stella wants it to be. It's hers. She's carried it and she's the one who'll have to have it cut out of her any day now. Yes, it's a Caesarian. She's going through it all by herself – you were just Molly's husband and you were as close as she could get to Molly. What are you going to do? Take her to court for custody? Bring the kiddie up on the side of a mountain with two dogs and a load of sheep?'

'No.'

'Then go home and get on with your sheep-dipping.' She stood up.

'Alice?'

'What?'

He inhaled deeply. 'Come back with me.'

She froze mid-stride, a hand straying on to the desk for support. 'What?'

'After God's surgical army has paid its visit, of

course.' He smiled uncertainly. 'No, I mean eventually. Come to Yorkshire and live with me. It's only four miles to Huddersfield and I can extend the hut – bathroom, a better well, a cess-pit.'

'You make it sound so attractive,' she replied, after a short pause. 'All my days I've hankered after my very own cess-pit. Then there's the joyful prospect of spending my life with sheep.'

'Alice—'

'What a day you're having, Matthew.'

He sighed again. There was a great deal of Tilly in Alice: once Alice got hold of a subject, she worried it to death.

'Here you sit, worried to distraction because Stella's about to have your child. So you've driven all the way across the mountains to propose cohabitation with a woman who is up to her eyes with your father and some surgeons who think they work in close collusion with the Almighty.' After this lengthy diatribe, she paused for breath, but only for an instant. 'My mother is right – men are beyond understanding.'

'I love you,' he told the desk.

'Good,' she snapped, 'because I love you, too. I don't care who you killed or didn't kill, because I loved you right away, when I first met you at Rutherford Hall. But if you think I'm piking off to Stainthwaite without a wedding ring, you'd best get your head tested again.'

'Could you fight a ghost?'

Alice Povey drew herself up to full height. 'I wouldn't have to fight a ghost, Matthew, because

435

I know who I am. I've always known who I am and I've never wanted to be like anyone else. Mam told me I was special because I'm her daughter. Mind, I was Dad's daughter when I was naughty, but that's Mam all over. Now, I realize that Molly was important to you and that you'll remember her every single day of your life. I'm not afraid of—'

The door was flung inward. 'Sister Povey?'

Alice looked at the intruder. 'Mr Carrington.' Her voice was as sweet as saccharine laced with cyanide. 'Yes, I know it's time for your round and I shall be with you shortly. This man has travelled from Yorkshire. He needs advice before his father is discharged from my care. I shall be a couple of minutes.'

Mr Carrington blinked a few times. It was plain that his relationship with the Supreme Being was temporarily uncertain. 'I have very little time,' he said.

'So have I, Mr Carrington.' Alice gazed levelly at the self-important creature who had imposed himself upon her. 'There are twenty-four patients in my care,' she said, her tone soft, 'and I'm keen to ensure that each man is prepared for discharge and that each family, too, is prepared. If you would kindly leave us for a few minutes – thank you.'

Mr Carrington left.

'Well, he didn't seem too pleased,' commented Matthew.

'Anal retentive,' she declared, 'that's one of the requirements of the job. Now, what are you going to do about Stella?'

Matthew sighed. 'The right thing – whatever that is.'

She nodded thoughtfully. 'We have to talk. Are you going to Coniston?'

'Yes, I shall be there this evening from about nine o'clock. Mother insists that we attend Emily's wedding. She had refused the invitation, as we were all in Yorkshire, but now we appear to be going.'

'Then I shall see you later.'

He rose and walked to the door, stopped, turned. 'I meant it, Alice. I do love you. If anyone had told me that I could love another woman, I would have been shocked. It has been a shock to me.'

'I know.' She joined him. 'A shock for me, as well. I'm not the type for sheep. And I could never marry a murderer. You know Molly's dad died by accident, don't you? What you can never know is whether you would have finished him off if he hadn't slipped.'

'True. Do I get a kiss, then?'

'Later,' she promised. 'I could never kiss anyone while Mr Carrington is close by. It would be like trying to enjoy a meal in the morgue.' She left.

Matthew returned to the desk and sank back into his chair. So, was this sanity? Molly was dead, her sister was about to give birth to his child, and he had just become engaged to Alice. He had no bathroom, few comforts to offer and he spent days out on the hills with the most stupid animals ever invented. But Bella Jenkinson wanted to sell up. If

Tom gave in – and he would – then Matthew would perhaps bid for the farm.

'Do I really want to spend the rest of my life with sheep?' he asked the other chair. He had two butters now, two males who hated him, a pair who seemed to have goat in their ancestry: there was the shoat and the geep, a nasty pair of rams who rammed him at every opportunity. But he couldn't lose Yorkshire and he couldn't lose Alice.

Had he proposed marriage just to keep himself safe from Stella? No. Life without Alice was a dinner with no gravy, dry, tasteless, no fun at all. And she was no substitute for Molly, had none of Molly's gentleness. At the end of the day, few women would aspire to a cess-pit and no electricity. He found himself grinning inanely, trying to imagine Alice at her mother's age, another Tilly, bossy, determined, stubborn.

Yes, he had found another treasure and was the luckiest of men.

It was dressing-up time again. Seth had taken the day off work and was now subjected to the ministrations of his wife, who was to be his fellow witness at the marriage between Emily Margaret Dyson, widow of this parish, and William George Bright, ex-soldier and manufacturer of B Bright Polish, patent pending. Apart from Irene Richards, Seth and Tilly were to be the only guests at the actual ceremony, but Irene had suddenly closed the shop for Bolton holiday fortnight and had gone off to Yorkshire, so it was all down to the Poveys.

438

'I know Emily said she didn't want a fuss,' complained Tilly, 'but she never said nothing about wanting tramps at the wedding. It's just us, Seth, we're all she's got. Have you shaved? Where's the ring? Even her sons are only coming to the house later on because they're all working, and her grandson's in Yorkshire with his dad – stand up straight.'

Seth glowered. He had been forced to act like a tailor's dummy once too often lately. And she'd thrown out a box of maggots 'by accident', just when he was getting to grips with fishing. 'You're choking me,' he gasped, as she forced the knot of his tie right into his Adam's apple.

'I will bloody choke you if you don't shape, you lummox. Now, look at me when I'm talking to you. Be nice. Do you understand that? You're the best man in a way. Well, all I can say is they've scraped the barrel. Thank God it's only register office, so you just hand that ring over when you're told. And if they want to take a couple of snaps afterwards, no pulling your face. All right?'

'Yes, Mother.'

Tilly walked to the mirror and righted her hat, which had slipped during her grappling session with Seth. She was in mauve, a nice little two-piece with a white blouse, navy shoes, bag and gloves, then a mauve and purple hat that would surely make every other woman in town green with envy. It was in Panama, none of your cheap straw for Tilly Povey, oh, no, she was going to do her best friend proud. It had a pretty bit of netting hanging from the shallow brim, a lovely touch, though it made her feel a bit cross-eyed when she tried to focus on something specific. But she didn't mind, because it was all in a good cause. Then there was the feather . . .

Seth told himself not to laugh. There'd been Royal Ascot on the telly last year, and he had seen better hats on the rich, famous and stupid, but he kept his opinions to himself. Old and wise, Seth Povey had learned the hard way that a man should never come between a woman and her hat. There was a secret bond between females and headgear, a sort of hallowed ground upon which only those with a declared deathwish dared to tread.

'I fell lucky with this hat,' she told him via the mirror.

He wanted to ask her which fence she'd failed to negotiate and had it been Becher's at Aintree, but he thought better of it. Her gob was shut as tight as a clam, so he simply agreed with her, yes, it was a lovely hat and, yes, she had been lucky when it had got marked down to half price. He would have to make sure that he stood on her right side at the registry, because that feather on the left was just the right length to get up his nose.

'We'll have to go soon,' she announced.

Seth gulped. She was planning on travelling by bus in a hat that needed two seats to itself. If she sat near the window on the left of the bus, her feather would get bent by the glass; if she sat near the aisle, he would get a faceful of bloody feather. Now, if they sat on the right-hand side of the bus, her feather would get broken by anyone moving up and down the aisle of the vehicle, whereas if she sat near the window on the right-hand side, he would get the feather . . . 'Take it off, Till,' he said. 'Your feather might get spoilt.'

She swung round and scrutinized his face. Deep in her soul, she knew that Seth hated this wonderful hat. He was ashamed of her. He ashamed of her? His suit was ashamed of him, for goodness' sake. But he had parked his expression in neutral. 'We could have gone in that van if it would start,' she complained.

'It'll start when it's fixed,' he replied. 'Just take the hat off, love. You don't want to be a witness with a bent feather, do you?'

She was beaten and she knew it. With huge reluctance, she removed the hat and placed it in its box, carefully curling the purple feather into its original shape. It took a large degree of self-control not to react to the sigh of relief that emerged from her beloved's lips. It would be a while before he got his tripe and onions – that much was certain. As for bread-and-butter pudding, he could whistle for that, too.

Someone knocked at the front door. 'See who that is,' she said, 'and don't touch anything, you might get a mark on your clothes.'

He was going on a filthy bus, for heaven's sake. Sighing again, he went to do her bidding. This was an unfair household in an unfair world – a man couldn't even hang on to his maggots with Tilly around. He opened the door to find Irene Richards on the step. She was dressed in a tasteful fawn suit and a hat that was featherless and sensible. 'But you're in Yorkshire,' he said, before thinking.

Irene smiled. 'I was, but now I'm here. The shop remains closed and I've left Matthew and Mark waiting in town. Is Tilly ready?'

'Tilly's always ready,' he answered quickly.

Irene laughed. The relationship between these two had been a source of amusement for many months.

'Come in,' he said. 'She's in pale purple and it matches her mood.'

Irene walked through the house and found Tilly still struggling with her feather. Having discovered its freedom, this lengthy item seemed reluctant to return to its original place of confinement. 'I've brought the car, Tilly,' Irene announced.

Tilly was ecstatic. 'I can wear me hat,' she cried, 'and, oh, it's good to see you. Did you have a lovely time? How's Matthew?'

'He and Mark are in town having coffee,' replied Irene. 'We came back from Stainthwaite this morning, so thank goodness that this is an afternoon wedding.'

Tilly stopped fussing for a moment. 'Matthew's here?'

'Yes.'

'And . . . does he know?'

'Yes.'

Once again, Seth Povey found himself in a world that spoke a language deliberately coded to exclude the male of the species. Did Matthew know what? That he was in Bolton, that his mother-in-law was getting married, that cod had gone up by twopence a pound? 'You can sit in the back seat on your own,' he told his wife. 'If you put yourself dead centre, yon hat might get there without being crippled.'

Irene bowed her head and pretended to study her nails. Tilly's hat was, indeed, dreadful, but its wearer was one of the finest women of Irene's acquaintance so diplomacy was required.

'You hate my hat, don't you, Seth Povey?'

Irene coughed away a bubble of mirth.

He pulled at his collar. 'Tilly, my love, you would look beautiful in a potato sack and with a stew pan on your head.'

Irene blew her nose delicately into a lace-trimmed handkerchief. Tilly's cheeks had taken on two spots of colour, a sure sign that she was on the brink of losing her temper. Trying not to laugh was extremely painful, so Irene fixed her mind firmly on her son's dilemma. Not only was he about to become father to Stella Dyson's child, he was also engaged to Tilly's daughter. But she would not pass on the happy news, as that was for Alice and Matthew to convey. 'We should go,' she managed. 'The wedding is at four o'clock prompt.'

'Aye,' agreed Tilly, who disapproved of register-office weddings, 'they get pushed through like summat on a conveyor belt.' She glared at her unfortunate spouse. 'Don't try and soft-soap me with potato sacks and pans. And comb your hair, it looks like a bird's nest.' She crammed the hat on to carefully regimented curls, sniffing as she watched Seth's attempts to organize his own hair. Even if she took him to Savile Row, he would emerge looking like a leper at a feast. Oh, well, such were the burdens a woman must carry through life.

Irene picked up her keys. 'We really should leave, because Mark and Matthew can't stay in the café for ever.' She was relieved that she had left them behind, as the Bentley would not have been adequate for five people and Tilly's hat. 'I am so pleased for Emily and Bill,' she added.

'So am I,' answered Tilly. 'I wonder if he's got his shirt flap tucked in. Did I tell you about our wedding, Irene, when this fellow turned up—'

'Yes,' chorused Irene and Seth.

Tilly pulled the veil over her face and walked towards the door. Behind her, Seth winked at Irene. 'It's a grand life if you don't weaken,' he announced, his tone innocent. He watched as his wife turned sideways to get through to the hall. 'They don't make doors as wide as they used to, do they, Irene?'

Irene shook her head and thanked God for people like Tilly and Seth, without whose presence the world would have been greyer, duller and free of long, purple feathers.

Stella sat in her living room, a book of poetry in her hands. She had never bothered much with verse, but she had taken a sudden shine to Keats and her lips moved as she read 'Ode to a Skylark'. It was exciting yet peaceful, a pattern made with words; she could almost hear the bird pouring its heart out into her flat. 'It's a bit like embroidery,' she told her companion, 'very well put together, a stitch at a time. Or a watercolour. You have no idea what the next shade is going to be but it all washes together beautifully.'

Simon made no reply. His mind was fixed on a telephone message he had received this afternoon from one of his partners in the Bolton practice.

'Have you read Keats, Simon?'

'What? I suppose so. I did an O level in English lit, and I think he was one of the poets we covered. Why?'

'He's full of soul.'

Soul? Stella had never bothered with soul. Stella had always been concerned with life's practicalities. The message had been simple. He was to telephone Matthew Richards at Coniston after nine o'clock this evening. So, the truth was out, Simon supposed. He couldn't tell her, not now – she was due to go into theatre tomorrow. 'Then I'm glad you found Keats, because he's keeping you in your chair, which is a damned sight more than I managed.'

She put the book down, wore the air of a royal personage who was about to make a pronouncement. 'I've been thinking.'

'You never stop thinking. I sometimes wonder when, if ever, you're going to wind down.'

Stella pretended to glower at him. 'This baby is nothing to do with Molly. Molly is all finished, isn't she? I think losing her was a dreadful shock, you know. Fancying myself in love with her

445

husband was a piece of nonsense I nurtured all through those final months of my sister's life. He was the last link. She was a particularly wonderful person.'

Simon found nothing to say. Many people had sung the praises of Molly Richards, but he had seen only a very ordinary woman, rather quiet and dull, nothing special. Her beauty had been remarkable, that was true enough, but she had been somewhat Mona Lisa-ish, no expression, no character in her face.

'They had a dramatic relationship,' she told him now, 'overtly sexual, needful, very honest.' Yes, those letters had said a great deal about Molly and her husband. 'And Joanna is not a part of that.'

He sighed, wondered yet again how Stella would feel should she be delivered of a son.

'This is my daughter,' she declared, her chin held up in an expression of defiance. 'She will be like nobody, she will be herself. I seem to be coming to my senses at last.'

Simon MacRae wondered about that. The love of his life, pragmatic and 'commonsensical', was reading romantic poetry, had dragged him round the Walker Art Gallery, was suddenly filled with a girlish frivolity that defied all reason. Sandcastles on the beach? Thirty-nine weeks pregnant and collecting shells, counting dead jellyfish, sitting fully clothed in the waters of a tidal river that was not exactly crystal clear? Hormones, he told himself firmly. And he still had to phone Matthew Richards.

'She will look like Molly, but she will have my brains,' she said now.

He glanced at the clock. 'Perhaps it's time for your bath.'

'I'm cleverer than she was, but she had the beauty.'

'That is a matter of opinion,' he replied. 'Yes, you are the brainy one, but I also find you the more attractive.'

Stella smiled. 'Well, she won't be attractive now, will she? Everyone is prettier than a dead woman.'

'I didn't mean— Oh, Stella, don't be so obtuse. Get into the bath and call me if you need help.'

She struggled up from the chair. 'Mam will be married now. Mrs Bright, how quaint. Almost Dickensian. What a wonderful honeymoon she will have at the Blundellsands hotel and at the nursing-home.'

'It is of her choosing. Now, go. This time tomorrow, you will be a mother.'

When she had gone, he picked up the phone and dialled Matthew Richards' number. It was time for Stella to give an account of herself, and he had been chosen as understudy. The star of the main feature was in the bath, but the show had to go on.

It had been a satisfactory wedding. The ceremony had gone off without a hitch – even Tilly's feather had settled down after a while, had stopped quivering and shivering all over the small office. Seth had not dropped the ring, no one had cried and Emily had looked wonderful in dusky pink.

Afterwards, they all returned to Eagley Farmhouse, Irene driving the Poveys, her son, her grandson and the hat. After a short debate, the latter passenger had been confined to the Bentley's boot, where it remained all through the buffet meal, which was taken in the dining room. Liberated, Tilly performed her party piece, a very good imitation of Gracie Fields singing 'Sally'.

As evening approached, Emily's family began to arrive, Tony and his wife, Nellie, then Eddie with Sally, Phil with Annie. Five grandchildren in assorted sizes completed the gathering and demolished the food within half an hour.

Bill, who had no family of his own, was delighted with the ready-made relations-by-marriage. He played with the children, delivered some army songs on his mouth organ, made everyone dance. Then, as his *pièce de résistance*, he treated the whole party to a demonstration of his polish. Irene watched with delight. She had invested money in Bill Bright and she would surely see a very good return.

Tilly, who had visions of a miracle cure for her Utility sideboard, managed to pinch a bottle of Bill's magic elixir. 'Well,' she told the assembly, 'if it can do so well for really old furniture, just think what it'll do for mine.'

Seth did a clog dance, though his best shoes were not really up to the job, then each child was press-ganged into singing, dancing or reciting. Everyone agreed that it had been a really good do, especially the children, whose consumption of jellies, cakes and sweets had been unrestricted.

It was almost time for the bride and groom to leave. Emily took Irene on one side. 'Er . . . we've made a decision, me and Bill,' she said, 'but I have to talk to you about it first. You know you said I could live here with Bill and that you'll look after Mark?'

'Yes.'

'Well, we've decided – if it's all right with you, like – that we'll take your husband in. He's used to this house and we can give him a downstairs room. See, Bill can manage him. We can get people in to help, but Bill will be out in the stables making his polish, so if Major Jack gets too much he can come and deal with him.'

Irene sank into a chair. 'Emily, do you know what you're taking on?'

'Yes, I do.'

'But . . . but you're gentle, my dear.'

'Up to a point,' replied Emily, 'but I'm not daft, Irene. There'll be help and plenty of it. You'll have to take your turn, so will Tilly – it's all right, I've asked her. If it doesn't work out, we'll think again. But there's folk in Eagley village who'd be happy to earn a few bob – and he can be left to himself in between times. You're not giving up that shop and neither am I. Major Richards will just have to fit in.'

Irene laughed, though the result sounded weary. 'He's a dreadful man. People have always fitted in with him.'

Emily pulled herself up to full height. 'Aye, well, he'd best not tangle with my Bill. He was a drill sergeant, you know, has a voice like a foghorn, if he wants to use it. Now, we'll have to go.' She dropped her voice. 'We're staying at a hotel near Stella – she gets the Caesarian tomorrow.' Emily glanced at Matthew. 'He knows, doesn't he?'

Irene nodded. 'Yes, he does. But he'll not be stepping on your daughter's toes, Emily. I think he feels a sense of duty to make sure that Stella and the child are safe, but no more than that. In fact, I shall go so far as to tell you that Matthew has plans for his future.'

'Good. I'm really pleased about that, because he grieved too much about our Molly. Aye, he deserves a fresh start, bless him. And think about what to do with your husband, love.'

The bride and groom left in Bill's van, their destination a hotel near the Mersey's banks, their immediate future tied up with Emily's daughter and the soon-to-be-delivered baby. When complicated travel arrangements had been completed, when all the other guests had left, Irene, Matthew, Mark and the Poveys climbed back into the Bentley.

'It got on me nerves,' declared Tilly, when they were half-way down the moor.

'What did?' asked Seth.

'Me hat,' replied Tilly smartly. 'I don't know why you made me buy it, Seth. Men have no taste at all. What do you think, Irene?'

Irene gripped the steering-wheel and kept her attention focused on the road. She knew that the purple feather would now go into the archives alongside Seth's shirt-flap, that the feather would increase in length with every telling of the tale, that the whole business would now become the fault of Seth Povey.

Matthew, too, had trouble containing his mirth, while Mark, still too young to have mastered completely the art of diplomacy, sounded like a victim of strangulation as he fought to control his glee.

'You want to watch that cough,' Tilly advised him, 'get yourself some Friar's Balsam.'

Seth stared innocently through the window and sighed. 'Well,' he declared after some consideration, 'I never in my life saw anything quite like that hat, Till. It suited you down to the ground, aye, it did.' He turned his head and looked at his wife. 'Can I have the feather? Only I could make a few fishing flies out of it . . .'

Seventeen

It was a large old house facing the main Liverpool road, set back among lawns, flower-beds and with a sizeable pond populated by tame mallards. These miscreants had learned to be brave, often quacking loudly beneath the windows of a captive audience, many of whom were on the maternity wing.

There were a dozen or so single rooms, then a couple of shared wards, each containing four beds. Stella Dyson, true to character, had opted for her own company. She had a high bed, a wash-basin, a chair and a huge crucifix above her head. It was sparse, no-nonsense and as quiet as a grave-yard, except for the ducks and the nuns.

Stella wondered what she had expected, but she found herself definitely unprepared for Sister Marie-Theresa. For a start, the tiny Irishwoman was possessed of an extraordinary beauty, the kind of physical perfection that screamed to be com-mitted to canvas. She moved quickly, spoke with the rapidity of a sub-machine gun and minced few words. 'Did you eat at all?' she asked.

'No, I didn't. I am a doctor.'

'Ah, did you think that ever made a difference? Sure, aren't doctors the daftest of the lot? We'd a brain surgeon here about six months ago, came in with a bellyful of triplets and chocolate ice-cream, said she couldn't resist it. I asked her what was it she couldn't resist, Wall's chocolate ice or the making of multiple babies, but there was no humour. Don't you find that with surgeons? Limp biscuits, the lot of them, not a smile to be had.'

Stella, who now had a thermometer lodged under her tongue, was at a disadvantage.

'So she had to lie here with a blood pressure that would have defeated the Richter scale until we cleared out the ice-cream. And the language out of her – Catholic, too, she was. You're not a Catholic, are you? Ah, well, never mind, nobody's perfect. Did you move your bowels?'

Stella nodded.

'We'll have you done and dusted in two shakes, a little sleep then, bingo, hello, new mother. Mr Barton's your man, I see. Now, there's one who proves the rule, for a finer medic you could never wish to meet. When he tells you he's a struck-off horse-doctor, just ignore him, he only does it to put you at your ease. I know for a fact he never operated on anything bigger than an Alsatian dog and the odd Siamese cat, so you'll be fine with him.'

Stella laughed, almost choked on her thermometer.

Marie-Theresa removed the cuff. 'Blood pressure's fine, there's many an expectant woman would give a hundred pounds for a reading like that.' She snatched the item from Stella's mouth and scrutinized it. 'And your temperature is normal, thank St Jude for that. So, Dr Dyson, will your family be along?'

'My mother and my doctor.'

'No baby's father?'

'No father.'

'Oh, I see, so you went straight for the bullseye before wandering around the dartboard? Good luck to you. I always thought fathers were an optional extra. My own was a sore trial, which is probably why I got me to a nunnery. Mind, I like the company here and the food's great, so I shan't complain. Though the clothes could do with a bit more style to them.'

Stella opened her mouth to reply, but the woman disappeared at lightning speed, just a whoosh of her long black skirt, a clattering of the giant rosary, then a closed door. The patient blinked. She felt as if she had gone five rounds with a verbal wrestler, no holds barred, two falls and counted out. Weren't nuns supposed to be holy?

No one could be pigeonholed, it seemed. She had not been judged by the good sister, had not been preached at, prayed over, converted to Catholicism. She remembered being called out to a convent in Bolton, recalled being treated with kindness as she had examined a sick sister, but there had been no levity among the flock there. Here, if Sister Marie-Theresa was typical, it would appear that life, like the ducks, had scaled the walls, that reality had soaked its way past statues with red or blue lights burning at their feet. It felt right, seemed a good place in which to give birth, no frills, just competence laced with humanity.

Simon came in. 'Hell's bells,' he declared irreverently, 'I've just been in the nursery. There's a guard dog there called Sister Vincentia and woe betide any intruder she doesn't like the look of. She almost had me fingerprinted. I wouldn't want to meet her on a dark night – she must be all of twenty stones and with the charm of a rampant crocodile. How are you?'

'Fat.'

'Soon be over.' He dropped into an armchair that had not been built for comfort. 'I spoke to Barton – he was struggling with seven down in his crossword, "criminal, air-condition, where all men fear to tread". I got it for him. It was convent – very apt. You get your pre-med in ten minutes.'

She closed her eyes. 'If I die, will you look after her? My mother will help you, I'm sure. Is she here yet?'

'No, but she phoned you last night from the hotel, didn't she?'

'Yes.'

'And you're not going to die. The anaesthetist is a top man.'

'Trained at Battersea Dogs' Home?'

'Of course,' he replied. 'Only the best for the Augustinian sisters. He's ninety-seven and he knows all about chloroform even if he can't spell it. Don't worry about his deafness, he's very good at sign language and he hasn't buried a patient yet—'

455

'Because they were all cremated – the old jokes are the best, Simon.' She looked directly at him. 'I keep thinking about Matthew. It's real now, you see. This is his baby. I think I'm frightened.'

Simon MacRae juggled his thoughts quickly. Stella was far too astute not to read something into a silence. 'Matthew is fine,' he said. 'He's in Bolton and he got a message to me via the surgery. I phoned him. He knows about the baby, Stella, and he sent you a message.'

'Oh, God.'

'He wishes you well and says that he's willing to take full paternal responsibility for the child. But he stressed that he's there for financial and moral support only. There will be no claim, Stella. He's going to marry Alice Povey. I had decided to tell you after the birth, but now seems a good time. You can go down to that theatre with no worries on that score.'

'Thank you,' she breathed.

The door opened and a balding man entered. 'Hello,' he said, 'I'm Ian Spencer, your anaesthetist. Just a quick examination, then your pre-med—' He stopped mid-sentence when the patient struggled into a sitting position and scrutinized him closely. 'Is something the matter?' he asked.

Stella studied his clothing. 'No, carry on,' she said. 'I was just checking for dog-hairs.'

'She's been let out of Whiston psychiatric department for the birth,' explained Simon. 'She goes back as soon as it's over.'

Ian Spencer, used to the gibes, listened to his

patient's heart, then checked her baby's. 'Ah, well,' he said, 'you're both ticking over nicely, no need for an oil change there.' He winked at Stella. 'See you in theatre. That terrible Marie-Theresa will be along to sort you out in a moment.' He took her hand and shook it, then left the room.

Stella swallowed nervously. 'The number of times I've explained to a patient that a Caesarian is nothing to worry about. Words are so easy.' She looked straight into Simon's eyes. 'Be there. Tell them to be quick. I don't want her getting too much anaesthetic. And tell them I'm not afraid of pain, that they must wake me as soon as possible.'

'I shall.' Simon, a seasoned practitioner with a reputation that pronounced him calm and sensible, was afraid. It was stupid, but he could not help himself. She was so frail, so thin: the only weight she carried was her baby and the fluids that cushioned it. He wanted to tell her yet again that he loved her, that he would always be there for her, but he dared not risk upsetting her.

'Go now,' she told him.

'Yes, I must scrub,' he replied.

'Joanna Margaret,' she whispered. 'That is to be her name. If I am . . . ill, make sure you remember her name.'

'Of course.' He rose, leaned over the bed and kissed her on the forehead. 'See you later.'

In the corridor, he dried his eyes and leaned against a wall. Opposite him, a serene-faced Immaculate Conception held out her hands as if offering comfort. He eyed her uneasily. Raised Catholic, Simon MacRae had dismissed his religion as a load of nonsense, bread to flesh, wine to blood, original sin, all cant and chant. Yet there lingered within him a slight suspicion that the learned clerics at his *alma mater* might have carried within their teachings a grain of truth. Like many before him and more still to come, he returned to his childhood. Stripped naked by fear, his soul spoke to the Blessed Virgin. 'Jesus, mercy, Mary, help.' Where had that come from?

Never mind, it was time to scrub.

'We must get up – Mam will be here in half an hour.' Alice looked at her proper watch, the one she wore on her left wrist. At the same time, she took the opportunity to examine her engagement ring, a sparkling solitaire set in yellow gold. 'Matthew?'

He turned his head on the pillow, smiled at her. 'It seems wrong,' he said. 'Poor Stella under the knife and here we are *in flagrante.*'

Alice agreed, though she kept the thought inside. 'Don't be silly,' she replied, 'we had to take our chance while Mark and your mother are out. Anyway, a man as starved as you were deserved a meal.'

He smiled. 'For a virgin, you're very knowledgeable.'

'I'm not a virgin any more, am I? Come on, darling, Stella will be fine. She's one of those people who could drive between cracks in an earthquake.'

'I should be there.'

'No, you shouldn't. All she wants is her mother

and her doctor. What the hell would you do, anyway? Walk up and down while she's in theatre, then smoke a big cigar once it's all over? We've got this sorted, love. That's Stella's baby. Stella doesn't want you and you don't want her. The little one will be your niece or nephew, so you'll still be related. Now, shape yourself, because my beloved mother doesn't believe in sex before marriage. And we've stuff to do – remember?'

'You have beautiful eyes.'

'You'll have a beautiful black eye if you don't get a move on.'

He sighed dramatically. 'You're going to be another Tilly, aren't you? God forbid that I should ever take up fishing. And no purple feathers, Alice, please. That article was enormous – we still don't know whether Bill Bright is married to Emily or to your mother's hat.'

'Did the hat have a licence?' she asked.

'It needed one,' laughed Matthew.

She leaped out of bed, naked as the day of her birth, but infinitely more desirable. He watched her while she dressed. A woman dressing was easily as beautiful as one who was shedding clothes. 'Talk to me,' he said.

'What? Why?'

'Then you won't need to say, "Look at me when I'm talking to you," because I'm looking anyway.'

She clouted him with her bra, then donned the lacy item.

Alice was nothing like Molly, and Matthew thanked God for that. Alice was a new country, an awakening, a fresh breeze that had gusted into his life like the clear air of the Pennines, invigorating, elemental. Like Molly, she was passionate; unlike Molly, she had more than enough to say for herself. She wanted children, demanded them; she wanted a proper house in Huddersfield, or the farmhouse if the Jenkinsons would kindly vacate it. For her wedding present, she had demanded some expensive books on psychiatric nursing and a yo-yo. He hadn't asked yet about the yo-yo, though he was prepared for some hilarious answers.

Fully dressed, she stood over him, a frown on her face, arms akimbo, grey-green eyes twinkling with devilment. 'Have you got a bucket and a long-handled mop?' she asked sweetly.

'I believe so, yes. Why?'

'Ever had a blanket bath?'

He shot out of the bed and chased her from the room. She was a clever one, oh, yes: she had stayed with him this morning because she knew that he would be tense, worried about Stella and the child.

Matthew dressed and sat at the dressing-table on the stool where Molly had used to sit. It didn't hurt. Looking at himself in the mirror was not painful either, until he thought about poor Stella Dyson. Simon MacRae was with her, as was her mother. According to Alice, Caesarian sections didn't take long – it would all be over within twenty minutes, and most of that was spent doing what Alice called the embroidery. It was half past ten: the section had been scheduled for ten o'clock and Dr MacRae had promised to phone as soon as there was news.

Half an hour. The phone might be a long way from the theatre; there might have been a delay; perhaps someone else was using the phone. No, Simon would be given access to just about any phone, because he was a doctor and he would not be forced to queue for the public telephone. It was a private hospital, too, so there would be phones everywhere. Thirty-two minutes past ten. No, thirty-three. Tilly was three minutes late.

He swallowed painfully. Although he owned no clear memory of his time with Stella, there had always been something there, an unease, a sense of having forgotten something important. It had been copulation, no more and no less; Stella had admitted – albeit through other people – her need for him, her own uncertainty about her motives. Yet the fact remained that he, Matthew Richards, had impregnated her. In twenty-five minutes it would be eleven o'clock.

She was dead. With a sudden but blinding sureness, he knew that he had killed Stella. He had been a factor in the death of her father, too . . . Oh, God, the phone was jangling and Alice was calling up the stairwell. 'I'll get it,' he shouted. But the instrument threw out three more raucous double rings before he staggered to the bedside table and lifted the receiver. 'Hello?'

'Matthew?'

Dear God, it was Emily and she was in tears. 'Emily,' he managed. The room was spinning slightly as he steadied himself, pressing the backs of his knees against the bed's edge. A part of him wanted to throw away the phone so that he would not hear what was coming. If he didn't hear the words, then none of it would be real. But no, he had been there before and had no intention of revisiting the dark zone.

'Emily? Talk to me. Please try to stop crying.'

'I'm sorry.'

'Just tell me, Emily.'

She blew her nose. 'Oh, Matthew, it's a little girl. Well, a big girl, really, over eight pounds. Are you there?'

'Yes.'

'She's called Joanna Margaret. Simon asked me to tell you about the birth, because he wanted to stay with Stella. Mr Barton said it went very well. The baby is beautiful. They say Caesars are lovely because they don't get squashed. Matthew?'

'I'm here. Give Stella my best wishes and . . . and kiss my niece for me, will you, Emily?'

'I will, love. Bless you.'

He replaced the receiver and sank on to the bed, his lower limbs refusing to support him through this moment. Stella had a little girl. Margaret, the second name, would be a tribute to Molly, whose full name had been Margaret. His body was racked with noisy sobs, then, suddenly, she was there, fragrant with the Chanel he had bought her, warm and holding him so tightly. 'A girl,' he managed, 'and both are well.'

Alice whispered into his ear all the silly things that pass between lovers in times of stress, then she dried his eyes with her long, brown hair and allowed that beautiful smile to light up her face.

'Never mind, love,' she said reassuringly, 'I've done geriatrics.'

'What?'

'Well, you're a good thirteen years older than me, sweetheart, so I shall have to keep an eye on you, shan't I? We don't want you slipping into your dotage. Come on, we've got to shock my mam, remember? This'll take the bend out of her feather.'

He was safe. Home would be where Alice was, here, there, in a Huddersfield semi, in a hut planted half-way between heaven and earth. Like Seth, he might appear henpecked to any untrained eye; like Seth, he would be wrapped in the happy warmth of a woman of humour, a woman who cared. And he wanted no more than that – no more, but certainly no less.

Stella Dyson drifted in and out of sleep, aware at each awakening that Simon was there, a constant presence. Aware also that there was something she must do, she fought to stay awake, but was defeated several times by the lingering effects of the anaesthetic. Nevertheless, she fought manfully and, after a ridiculously short time, she was able to examine herself. No drips, no drains, nothing fixed to her body. Christ, that bloody wound hurt – she would be needing analgesics soon.

She glanced to her right: Simon MacRae was asleep in his chair, a cup of coffee and a plate of biscuits ignored on a small table by his side. Now was the time. Knowing all about haematoma and the dangers of burst sutures, she slid noiselessly from her bed, teeth biting down into her lower lip to distract her mind from the other, more searing pain in her gut.

With her torso bent forward, she shuffled quietly to the door, opened it, stepped out into the corridor. She was lucky: her room was but two doors from the nursery. Every step was a trauma, every breath an effort, but she persevered, glad that the corridor was empty.

Sister 'Dragon' Vincentia was feeding a baby, a beautiful creature with a mass of black hair. It was Joanna. 'What are you doing out of bed?' asked the huge woman. 'You'll be falling over, for heaven's sake.'

Stella sat in a straight-backed chair. 'Give me my child,' she ordered breathlessly. 'Now. I want her now.'

'Let's see will she take this other half-ounce—'

'No. I shall feed her myself.'

Sister Vincentia had a wealth of experience behind her. 'Mother' to thousands of babies, she always knew best. Yet she owned a strong suspicion that this was her Waterloo, because Stella Dyson was a doctor, a no-nonsense type of person with a will hammered out in base metal. 'Will you breastfeed?'

Stella nodded.

'You'll have nothing yet.'

'Joanna will bring the milk in,' replied Stella, 'as long as she isn't exhausted first by chewing on a rubber teat.'

'You've had a Caesar.'

'I know. I was asleep at the time, but I'm aware

464

that I have undergone surgery. So, I want this child in my room. She's breathing well and knows how to suck, so I shall take her. Now. Immediately.' Her hands tingled in anticipation of touching the precious bundle in Sister Vincentia's arms. Still exhausted after surgery, she forced her eyes to do battle with the dragon's.

The undisputed mistress of the nursery placed Joanna in her mother's arms, then stood nearby to catch the bundle should Stella Dyson lose her strength. But determination was clearly winning the battle over weakness.

'Thank you,' said Stella. She opened her night-dress and guided the baby to her breast. It happened immediately, as soon as the child was hers. As if a floodgate had opened, all the grief, terror, happiness and bewilderment poured through a soul whose animation had been suspended for years. She wept quietly so as not to disturb the nursing infant, simply allowing the moisture from her eyes to drip into those new-born jet-black curls.

Sister Vincentia brought a chair and set it next to Stella's. She parked her corpulence in the seat and began to say her rosary. After an Our Father, ten Hail Marys and a Glory Be, she paused and spoke. 'I know this much, Dr Dyson, you will be an excellent mother. Whatever your grief, whatever your trouble, your bond with Joanna is wonderful. Look how she knows you.'

'Yes. She knows me, Sister.'

'I shall pray for you.'

'Thank you.'

'Now, give her to me and I shall dress her like a little queen, pink bonnet and a nice little matinée jacket. The young madam already looks a bit hefty for newborn – we shall have to put her in a size two with the sleeves rolled up.'

'She is a size,' Stella agreed.

Vincentia laughed. 'Away with your bother, woman, for she is gorgeous altogether. Howandever, we must get you back to your room and, after you've had a little rest, I shall bring Joanna Margaret to you. If she becomes a trouble, she can always have a little holiday here in the nursery with her auntie Vince.'

'It hurts,' whispered Stella.

'It will – you've had a great hole cut into your belly—'

'Not that,' Stella said. 'The love. It hurts.'

Vincentia the battleaxe wiped a tear from her own eye. 'I know that. I give birth to none, but they are all my children and my heart breaks every time one goes home.'

But that wasn't it, either. It was bigger than that, beyond all Stella's understanding. The love was Joanna, yet beyond Joanna. Whatever, it was certainly too much for a woman who still had anaesthetic in her veins. So she handed back her baby and allowed herself to be returned to her room.

At last, the van was working, though it produced a great deal of smoke and sounded a bit like a very old horse with a chest condition. Seth, who had taken advantage of Bolton Wakes, was still enjoying the odd extra holiday from work, so he had been coerced into helping Irene Richards in her garden. Mind, he was in his mufti, an old shirt, a flat cap and shoes that had seen better days, with the result that he was reasonably content. At least he wasn't done up like Bess's dinner with gravy on.

Tilly, hairnetted and sensible in cardigan and wrap-around floral apron, was preparing to do battle with the rest of Molly Richards' things. At last, Matthew seemed to be coming to his senses – and not before time. Molly's remaining possessions were to be cleared out and stored in the roof.

'You've not told me to be nice,' he commented, as he passed the fire station.

'Hmmph,' she breathed, 'sometimes even a sensible person gives up. I know you're going to show me up, so I just have to accept it. Try not to swear in front of Irene, and dig out the weeds, not flowers.'

'I do know the difference.'

'Well, they're all green, aren't they?'

'They might be, Till, but I'm not.'

Tilly's mind and heart were with Emily and her daughter, so near yet so far away in Liverpool. Would it all be over by now? Would Stella Dyson have the heart to be a mother? Still, Emily had a good husband to support her, so she wouldn't be on her own, no matter what happened. Tilly lurched forward as the traffic-lights changed.

'Sorry,' said Seth calmly, 'only me brakes still want adjustment.'

She 'hmmphed' again. 'Now, he tells me. Are

you driving me round in an unsafe vehicle, Seth Povey?'

He shrugged. 'You can always get out and walk.' He knew she wouldn't. He knew that she had to be there, no matter what, that she would sit by his side, that she would prefer to die with him. 'Well?'

'Oh, shut up and drive,' she snapped. 'Them bloody lights have been green for ages.'

He shut up and drove.

Everything was brighter, clearer. Stella wondered whether she had been looking at life through some kind of filter, a pair of sunglasses that had cut out the light, ear-muffs, too, which had dulled sound – even her sense of smell had improved. She wished that the latter had remained muted, because she was allowed no food. 'Let your innards settle,' Marie-Theresa had advised, 'or you'll get some mortallious wind. And you should be fast asleep, madam. I never saw anybody recover so quickly – it isn't normal. You shouldn't be eating even this little bit – you could start vomiting and burst your stitches.'

Stella would have risked the mortallious wind, but she was offered no choice in the matter. While Simon went out for a snack, she was offered two slices of buttered bread and a microscopic amount of jam. This she demolished in a matter of seconds and wondered what all the fuss was about. Still sleepy, still waiting for her baby to be fetched from the nursery, she felt hungry enough to tackle a carthorse.

Simon returned.

'What did you have?' she asked.

'A scone with strawberry jam and cream,' he answered mischievously.

'I hate you.'

'I know.'

She didn't hate him, didn't hate anyone. It was as if everything negative had been eliminated with the afterbirth, as if she, too, was newborn. She picked up her anthology, found the page she had marked. 'Tennyson,' she announced, her voice not as clear as normal.

'Sleep,' he ordered.

She looked straight at him. 'A long time dead, Simon. Today I'm alive.'

'All right, let's have it.' In recent days, she had taken to reading aloud any poem that seemed pertinent. As most poets tended to concentrate on the transient nature of life, Simon had listened to some miserable verse of late.

'Tennyson,' she announced again.

God. Wasn't Tennyson another miserable and very dead soul?

She cleared her tired throat. 'This one means something.'

They all meant something. Simon sighed and waited for the meaning to be forced upon him. He had listened to enough bloody misery to last anyone a lifetime.

'A shadow flits before me –
Not thou, but like to thee,
O God! that it were possible
For one short hour to see

The souls we loved, that they might tell us
What and where they be.'

He looked at her. 'Is that it?'

'Yes. Don't you see? That's Molly and she's gone, so she has to stay gone. Much as I should like to see my sister again, I cannot. When I said that Joanna would be mine and Molly's, well, she can't be. She can't be Molly's shadow, either.'

'Right.'

'You think I've gone daft, don't you? But there are so many ways of looking at life, Simon. If we use only our own eyes, we will be half blind. There is more than science – there is spirit, *ego*, *id*, me, you, them.' She waved a hand towards the window.

'Do you mean those flaming ducks?'

Exasperated, she sighed. 'No. Yes. Everything, everyone, all of it. We're all searching. It's just that some of us haven't realized that. We look for truth. Every writer seeks truth, every painter looks to interpret his vision, every musician wants purity in his expressed . . . Oh, what a Philistine.'

'Sorry.'

She moved to the next bookmark. 'Right, now listen to this, because it tells you something. It's Robert Bridges. This is for you: this is what I want to say to you. All right?'

He nodded. Why couldn't she just say what she had to say without reference to a load of dead people's work? Stella had always been good at saying what she meant; she had never needed tools. Oh, well, best to humour her, he supposed . . .

470

'Love can tell, and love alone,
Whence the million stars were strewn,
Why each atom knows its own,
How, in spite of woe and death,
Gay is life, and sweet is breath:
This he taught us, this we knew,
Happy in his science true,
Hand in hand as we stood
'Neath the shadows of the wood.
Heart to heart as we lay
In the dawning of the day.'

'Right,' he said, when the book had been snapped shut.

'Art is science and science is art,' she declared. 'There is no division. Simon, I am alive, so alive. Drunk with anaesthesia, tired after surgery, but it has all fallen away – don't you see that? My silence is over. I want to run and sing and shout. I want to go back to university and learn all the stuff I never read. Life is there to be found.'

He pushed a closed fist to his mouth, lowered his head and pondered, read between the lines of Tennyson and Bridges, heard what she had been saying. 'So, the dawn of the day is Molly laid to rest and Joanna born.'

'Yes. And?'

He scarcely dared to say it, yet he must. Anaesthesia had some strange side-effects, yet no. Stella had been drifting in this new direction long before the birth of her daughter. He lifted his head. 'I am the dawning, too. Is that it?'

She nodded.

'You love me?'

'Yes, I do. I'm not using you now. I found my truth without the poets, Simon. I love you very much.'

He closed his eyes and thanked God for Tennyson and Bridges, for delivering this beloved woman to him, for those bloody ducks beneath the window. It was over and it was just beginning. He, Stella and little Joanna Margaret were on their way home.

Mark and Irene were waiting at the front gate of The Briars. Mark nudged his grandmother. 'This is going to be fun. He's dressed for gardening and Tilly's in her usual suit of armour.'

'Smile,' said Irene.

Mark smiled at the two approaching figures. He and Irene had returned from town just seconds earlier and both were slightly breathless. 'Are Dad and Alice inside?' he asked, the words forced from the corner of his mouth.

'In Coniston,' whispered Irene. 'Try to look casual.'

'I can't smile and look casual,' he replied.

'Just do your best.'

Tilly arrived a few strides ahead of her husband. 'We've no brakes,' she announced. 'It took him ten minutes to stop. I'll have to make a hole in the floor, then I can drag me feet along like I used to do on our Alice's bike.'

Seth looked up at the sky. 'She's exaggerating,' he declared. 'We just need a few adjustments, that's all.' He noticed Mark's expression, which was so casual as to be almost inane. 'Are you all right?' he asked.

'Yes.'

Tilly could smell a rat, but she ploughed on in her usual manner. 'Well, I've got work to do. I can't stand here like cheese at fourpence.' She addressed Irene. 'Seth's ready to do your garden.'

Irene licked her lips nervously. 'Matthew wants to see you both,' she said. 'I don't know what it's about, but he asked us to send you in the minute you arrived. Didn't he, Mark?'

'What? Oh, yes, yes, he did.'

Tilly scrutinized the Richardses, then looked at her husband. 'He shouldn't be inside a house in that state. He's dressed for outside work. If I'd known he'd be wanted inside, I'd have dressed him a bit better.'

Seth winked at Irene. 'She'd have put me in a purple hat,' he said.

Tilly was in no mood for repartee: she took her husband's arm and dragged him through Coniston's gateway. Why did folk change the rules all the while? She couldn't be doing with people who kept moving the goalposts – they should be sent off with a good hiding.

They reached the back door. 'Don't touch anything,' she advised him. 'Don't lean on anything, don't breathe on anything. I've been shown up enough today with that bloody van, smoke everywhere and exploding like a gun in a cowboy film. Yes, yes, I know it's the exhaust. Well, it's me what's flaming exhausted and I've a bathroom to see to.'

Seth was quite happy to be going inside; he wasn't keen on gardening and had been praying for rain all through the journey. He followed his wife into the deserted kitchen. The aroma of bacon hung in the air, so breakfast must have been taken quite late.

'Hello?' shouted Tilly. 'Anybody there?'

The front door opened and closed. Tilly heard someone walking through the hallway, then thought she caught the edge of a few whispered words. 'There's summat fishy going on,' she advised her husband. 'Dining room. Now. Come on.' She picked up the kitchen poker and handed it to Seth. 'Here. If it's burglars, hit them with that.'

'Get away with your bother,' he replied, but his words died when he saw the expression on Tilly's face. Any self-respecting burglar would run a mile from a physog like that – even Attila the Hun would have quaked in his wellies. Sighing resignedly, Seth led his wife into the dining room.

Matthew and Alice were standing in front of the fireplace; Mark and Irene hovered nervously near the window. 'Oh, it was you,' said Tilly, to the latter pair. 'You must have come in at the front when we came in at the back, so . . .' Her eyes strayed to the table. There was a great big silver bucket with ice in it and a champagne bottle sticking out of its top.

'We only just got back with the cake,' said Irene.

Tilly strode to the dining table. In its centre and surrounded by plates of snacks sat a large item of confectionery. 'Whose birthday is it?' she asked.

'Read it,' said Alice.

' "Alice and Matthew",' whispered Tilly. ' "Alice and Matthew"? What's going on? Is it . . .? Have you . . .? Oh, Alice.' She sat down in the nearest chair and burst into tears.

Alice held Matthew back. 'Leave her,' she ordered. 'Two minutes and she'll be back to normal.'

Seth grinned broadly and handed the poker to the master of the house. 'Well,' he began, his voice rather unsteady, 'congratulations. You've got a good girl there.' He turned to his wife. Who but Seth could possibly know how to deal with this little woman whose happiness was too big to contain? He listened for a moment, made sure that these were, indeed, tears of joy, then he spoke to her. 'Till?'

She lifted her head. 'What?'

'There's going to be another wedding. Now, I'm not saying anything about that . . . you know . . . that hat, but you wouldn't want to be seen twice in the same one, would you? I mean, you'd feel right shown up if you had to wear it again. Wouldn't she, Irene?'

'Er . . . perhaps she would, yes.'

Mark turned away and looked through the window. He could not bear to see Tilly crying, yet he had to fight a horrible urge to laugh. The purple feather, which was, in reality, no more than a few inches long, grew with each telling of the tale and was now roughly the size of Bolton town hall.

Tilly dried her eyes. 'I shall have a new hat,' she

declared, 'and this time, I'll choose it meself. Men!' she spat. 'They don't know the first thing about fashion, do they, Irene?'

It was over. There followed hugs, kisses, the cutting of the cake, the cracking open of champagne. Tilly giggled when the bubbles went up her nose, Seth wished he could have a pint of bitter instead.

Bess barked and Mark took her out into the garden. He stood under the apple tree, looked at the swing in which his mother had often sat, jumped when a hand touched his shoulder. 'Oh, hello, Dad.'

'Thinking about your mother, son?'

'Yes. I often do.'

'So do I.' Matthew picked up a stick and threw it, watched Bess as she caught and worried it. 'I'm glad you like Alice. She's not a replacement, but I love her very much.'

'I know you do.'

'And Mark, you have a new cousin. She was born this morning.'

The younger man looked at the dog, called her name. 'Not a sister, then? Is she not my sister?'

Bess brought the stick, dropped it, sat and panted until it was airborne again.

'She will be whatever Stella wants her to be,' said Matthew. 'Stella is a woman of such devastating honesty that I'm sure she will tell the child about her true parentage – when the time is right, of course. But you are my son, my one hundred per cent firstborn. I wish . . . I wish I'd done it all differently, Mark.'

'I know you do.' Mark looked his father full in

the face. 'It was a time of great misery, Dad. When Mother got cancer, you suffered it, too. You couldn't have let a kid in to that. I was lonely, but what could I have done? There was nothing to be done. If I had sat with her like you did, who knows? I might have been as ill as you were.'

Matthew bit down on his lip until he tasted blood. 'You have your mother's forgiving nature.'

Mark shook his head. 'No. I'm just like you. You make mistakes and so do I. We're human. I'm no more forgiving than anyone – I just grew up quickly. Be happy, please. I just want you to be happy.'

They sat on the old bench where Molly had sat, watched her swing as it drifted back and forth, just as it had when she had recently vacated it. Bess, bored with her stick, settled down at their feet, head resting on her paws, ears cocked in case one of these beloved humans found something to say to her.

'Can I be your best man?' Mark asked.

The father swallowed a lump in his throat. 'Always,' he answered. 'You will always be my best man.' He slid an arm about his son's shoulders and held him tightly. Now, they could start again.

THE END

A Tribute to Lillian Helm

I cannot close this chapter in my life without saying something about Lillian Helm, though words to describe her are difficult to find, as she was a one-off, an individual of great character.

For eight years, she looked after the half of me that is Ruthie; yet she also cared for Linda, the real me. She did my hair and nails, my make-up, made sure I was wearing the right clothes on those days when I had to go out and be Ruthie on TV, Ruthie signing books, Ruthie attending some function looking halfway decent.

When my son was ill, she was here; when my sister died, she was here; when I was afraid, she was here; when a huge amount of money was stolen from me, she was here and ready to kill the perpetrator. She took no nonsense, always spoke her feelings exactly, made sure that her opinions were known.

Describe Lillian? How? Yet that is my job, so I must attempt it. She owned the courage of Churchill, the gentleness of a saint, the mouth of a fully-fledged Scouser, intelligent, witty and humorous. She loved the colour purple, wore a great deal of jewellery, was stylish, organized and industrious.

An individual to her untimely end, she was taken to the crematorium by a pair of black geldings brought up specially from London. At the funeral, a very ill lady begged to be let out of hospital just so that she could say farewell to this fine woman. A light had gone out and we shall never meet Lillian's like again.

To Tommy, Ronnie and Jenny, I say God bless, she suffers no more. To Lilly May, the longed-for grandchild she did not survive to see, I say these words are about your grandmother. When you are old enough, read them and know that you must be proud of Grandma Lillian. She was truly remarkable and I know that Almighty God will be enjoying her company, of which pleasure we mere mortals are now deprived.

Lillian, I treasured you; so many valued you.

Sleep now in the arms of angels.

Love, Linda-Ruthie.

A SELECTED LIST OF FINE NOVELS
AVAILABLE FROM CORGI BOOKS

THE PRICES SHOWN BELOW WERE CORRECT AT THE TIME OF GOING TO PRESS. HOWEVER
TRANSWORLD PUBLISHERS RESERVE THE RIGHT TO SHOW NEW RETAIL PRICES ON COVERS
WHICH MAY DIFFER FROM THOSE PREVIOUSLY ADVERTISED IN THE TEXT OR ELSEWHERE.

All Transworld titles are available by post from:
Bookpost, PO Box 29, Douglas, Isle of Man, IM99 1BQ
Credit cards accepted. Please telephone 01624 836000,
fax 01624 837033, Internet http://www.bookpost.co.uk
or e-mail: bookshop@enterprise.net for details.
Free postage and packing in the UK. Overseas customers: allow
£1 per book (paperbacks) and £3 per book (hardbacks).